SUPER DINOSAUR™

CREATED BY
ROBERT KIRKMAN & JASON HOWARD

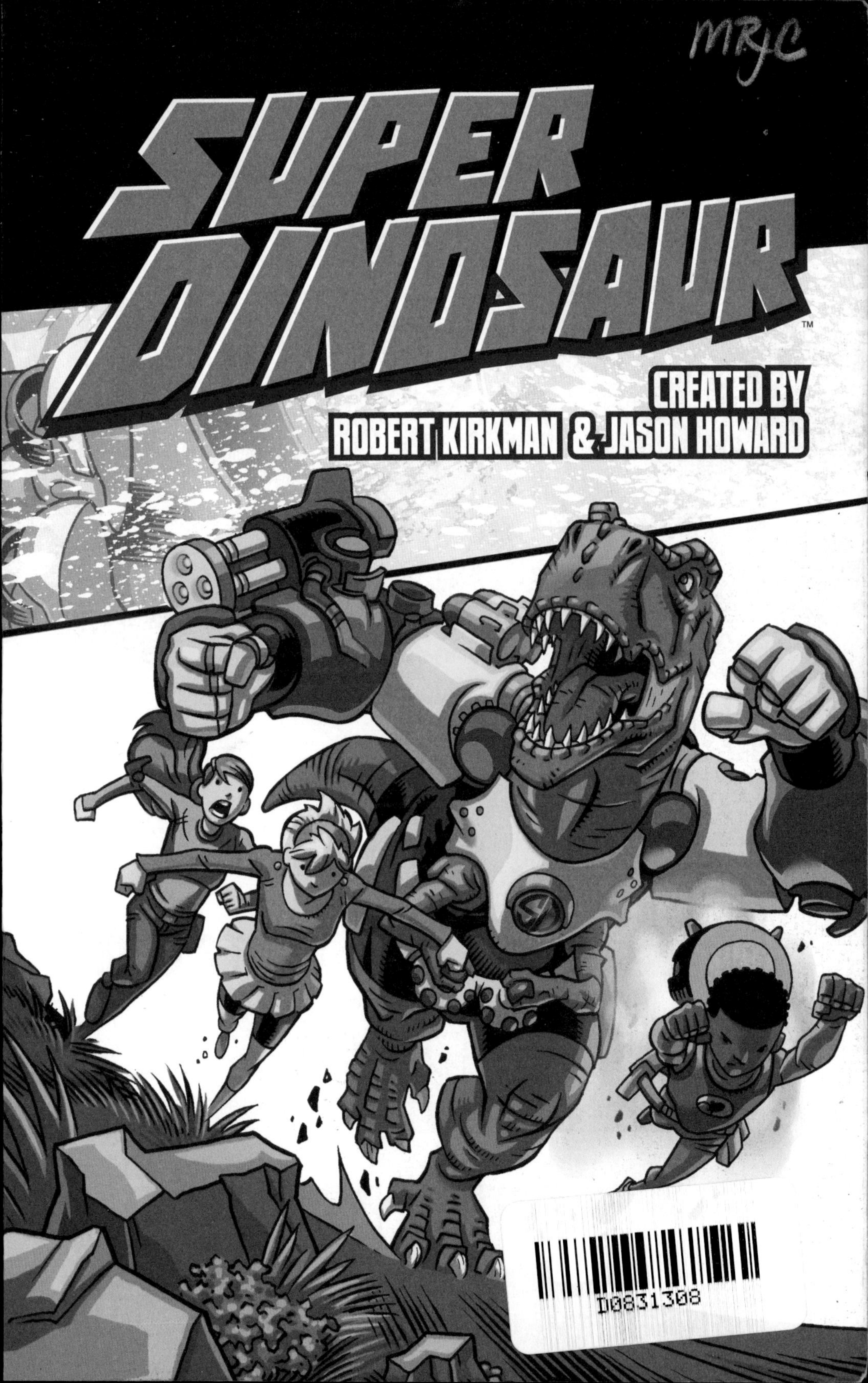

ROBERT KIRKMAN
WRITER

JASON HOWARD
ART & COLORS

CLIFF RATHBURN
INKER

RUS WOOTON
LETTERER

SEAN MACKIEWICZ
EDITOR

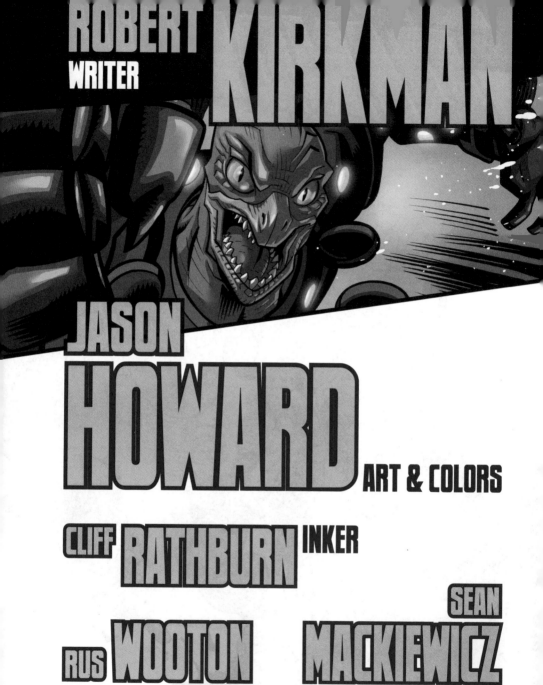

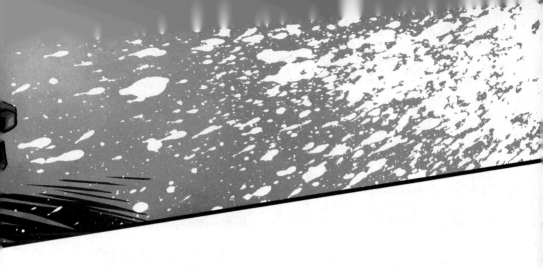

SUPER DINOSAUR, VOLUME 3
ISBN: 978-1-60706-667-5
First Printing

Published by Image Comics, Inc. Office of publication: 2001 Center St., Sixth Floor, Berkeley, California 94704. Copyright © 2013 Robert Kirkman, LLC & Jason Howard. All rights reserved. Originally published in single magazine format as SUPER DINOSAUR #12-17. SUPER DINOSAUR™ (including all prominent characters featured in this issue), its logo and all character likenesses are trademarks of Robert Kirkman, LLC & Jason Howard, unless otherwise noted. Image Comics® and its logos are registered trademarks of Image Comics, Inc. No part of this publication may be reproduced or transmitted, in any form or by any means (except for short excerpts for review purposes) without the express written permission of Image Comics, Inc. All names, characters, events and locales in this publication are entirely fictional. Any resemblance to actual persons (living and/or dead), events or places, without satiric intent, is coincidental. For information regarding the CPSIA on this printed material call: 203-595-3636 and provide reference # RICH – 472221.

PRINTED IN THE USA

IMAGE COMICS, INC.
Robert Kirkman - chief operating officer
Erik Larsen - chief financial officer
Todd McFarlane - president
Marc Silvestri - chief executive officer
Jim Valentino - vice-president
Eric Stephenson - publisher
Ron Richards - director of business development
Jennifer de Guzman - pr & marketing director
Branwyn Bigglestone - accounts manager
Emily Miller - accounting assistant
Jamie Parreno - marketing assistant
Jenna Savage - administrative assistant
Kevin Yuen - digital rights coordinator
Jonathan Chan - production manager
Drew Gill - art director
Monica Garcia - production artist
Vincent Kukua - production artist
Jana Cook - production artist
www.imagecomics.com

SKYBOUND™

For SKYBOUND ENTERTAINMENT

Robert Kirkman - CEO
J.J. Didde - President
Sean Mackiewicz - Editorial Director
Shawn Kirkham - Director of Business Development
Helen Leigh - Office Manager
Brandon West - Inventory Control
Feldman Public Relations LA - Public Relations

For international rights inquiries, please contact: foreign@skybound.com

WWW.SKYBOUND.COM

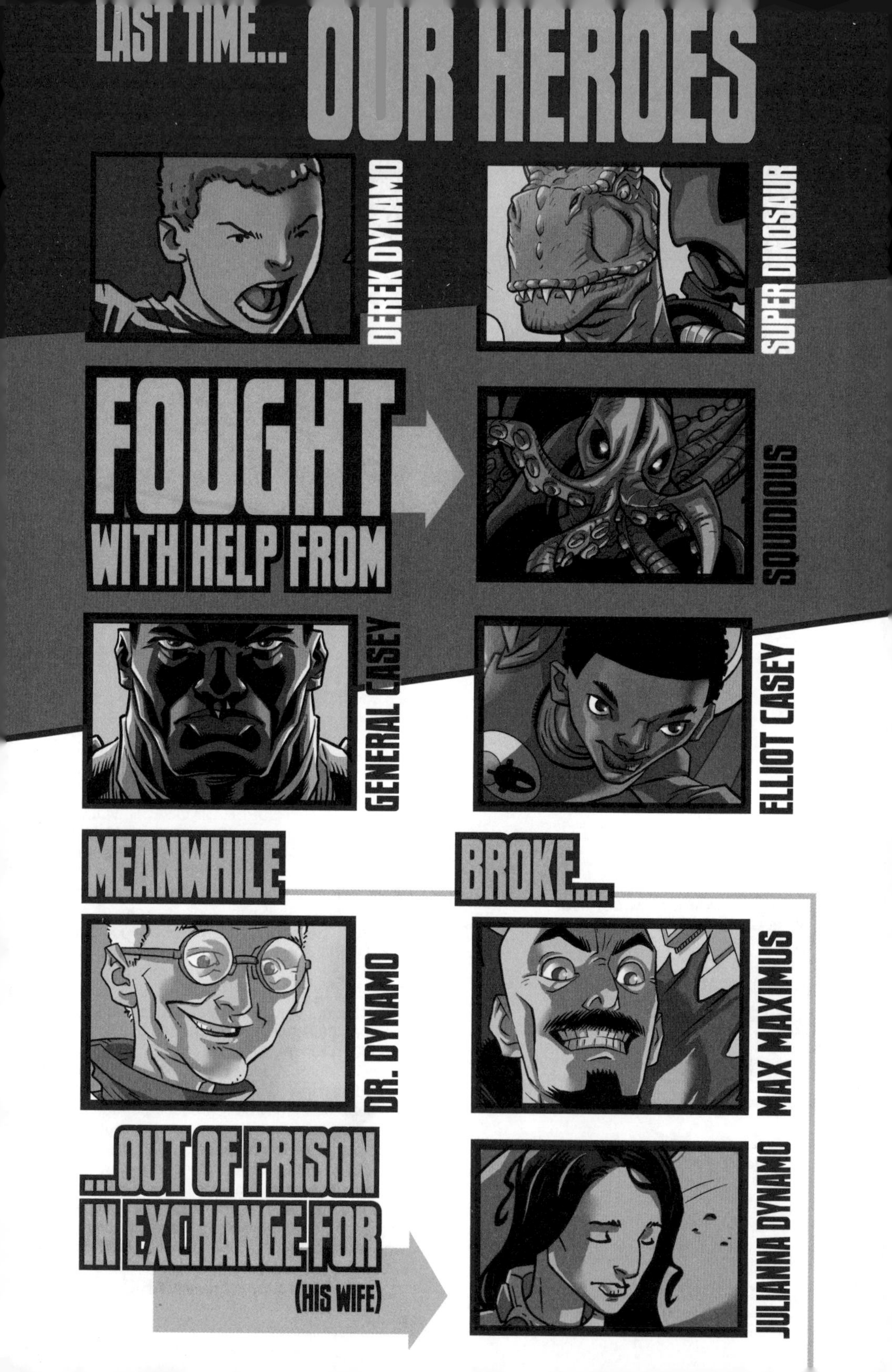

LAST TIME... OUR HEROES
DEREK DYNAMO
SUPER DINOSAUR
FOUGHT
SQUIDIOUS
WITH HELP FROM
GENERAL CASEY
ELLIOT CASEY
MEANWHILE
DR. DYNAMO
BROKE...
MAX MAXIMUS
...OUT OF PRISON
IN EXCHANGE FOR
(HIS WIFE)
JULIANNA DYNAMO

IT WAS A TRICK!

DR. DYNAMO WAS INJURED AND MAXIMUS REUNITED WITH HIS CLONE

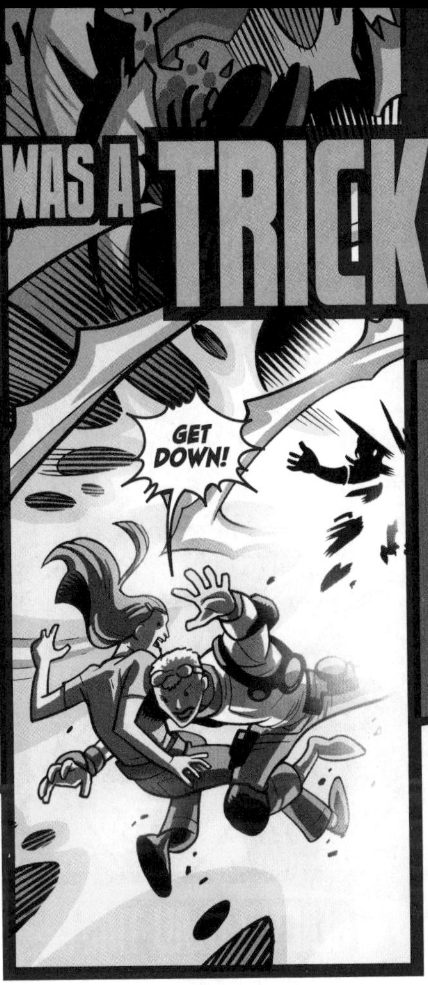
GET DOWN!

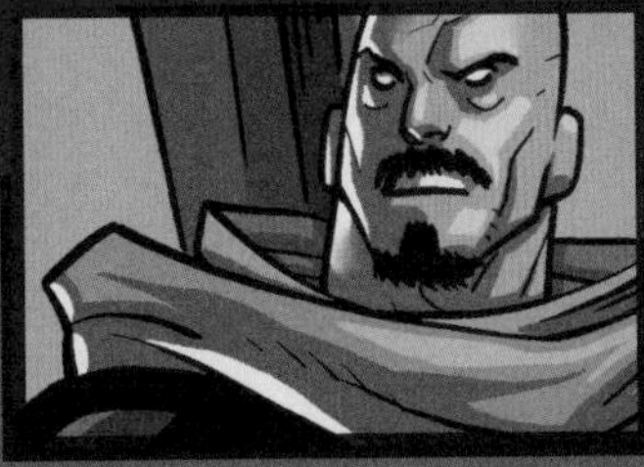

MINIMUS

ON A LIGHTER NOTE

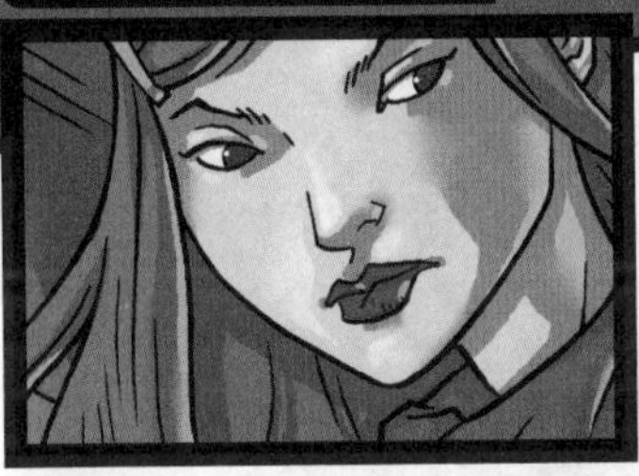

ERICA KINGSTON

LEARNED TO PLAY BASKETBALL

EARTHCORE (GENERAL CASEY'S OUTFIT)

CAPTURED... ...WHO TURNED OUT TO BE A

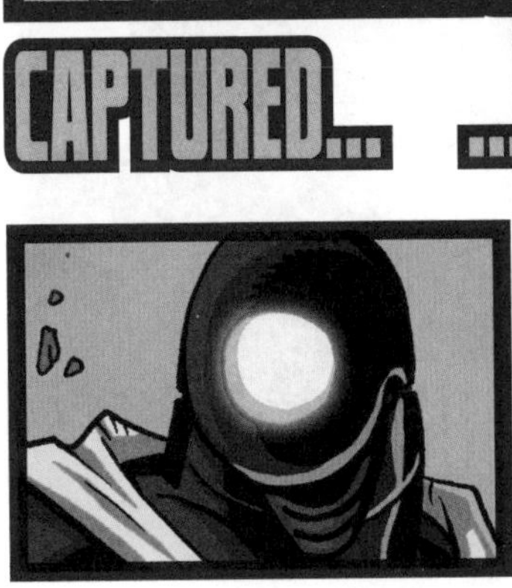

THE EXILE

=

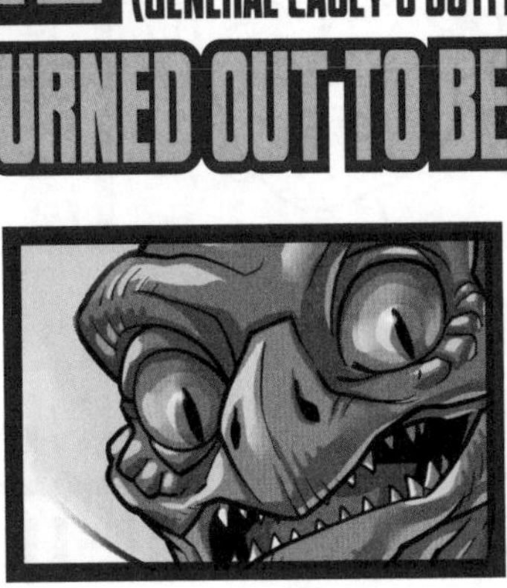

REPTILIOD

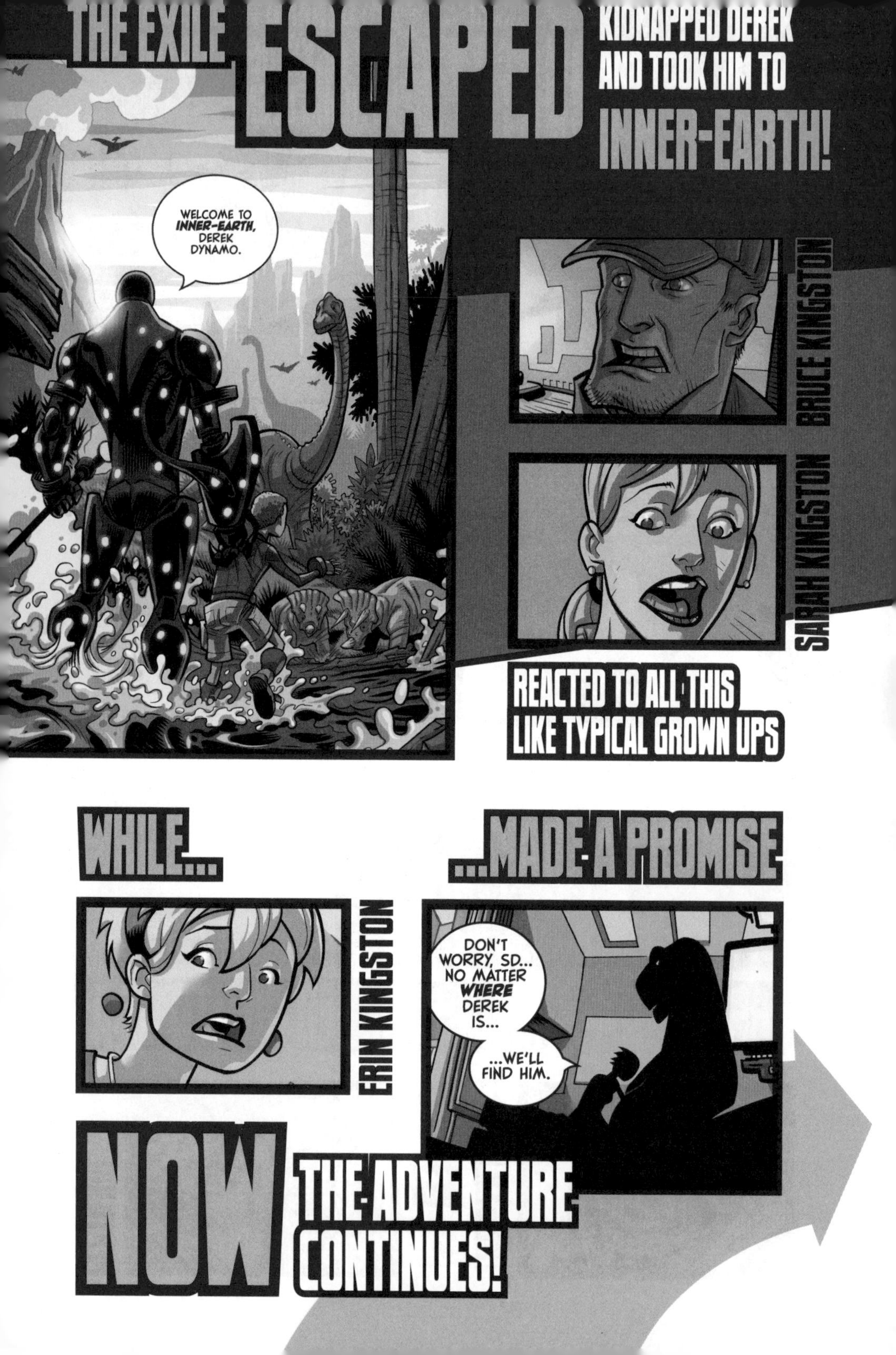
THE EXILE
ESCAPED
KIDNAPPED DEREK AND TOOK HIM TO
INNER-EARTH!
WELCOME TO INNER-EARTH, DEREK DYNAMO.
BRUCE KINGSTON
SARAH KINGSTON
REACTED TO ALL THIS LIKE TYPICAL GROWN UPS
WHILE...
ERIN KINGSTON
...MADE A PROMISE
DON'T WORRY, SD... NO MATTER WHERE DEREK IS...
...WE'LL FIND HIM.
NOW
THE ADVENTURE CONTINUES!

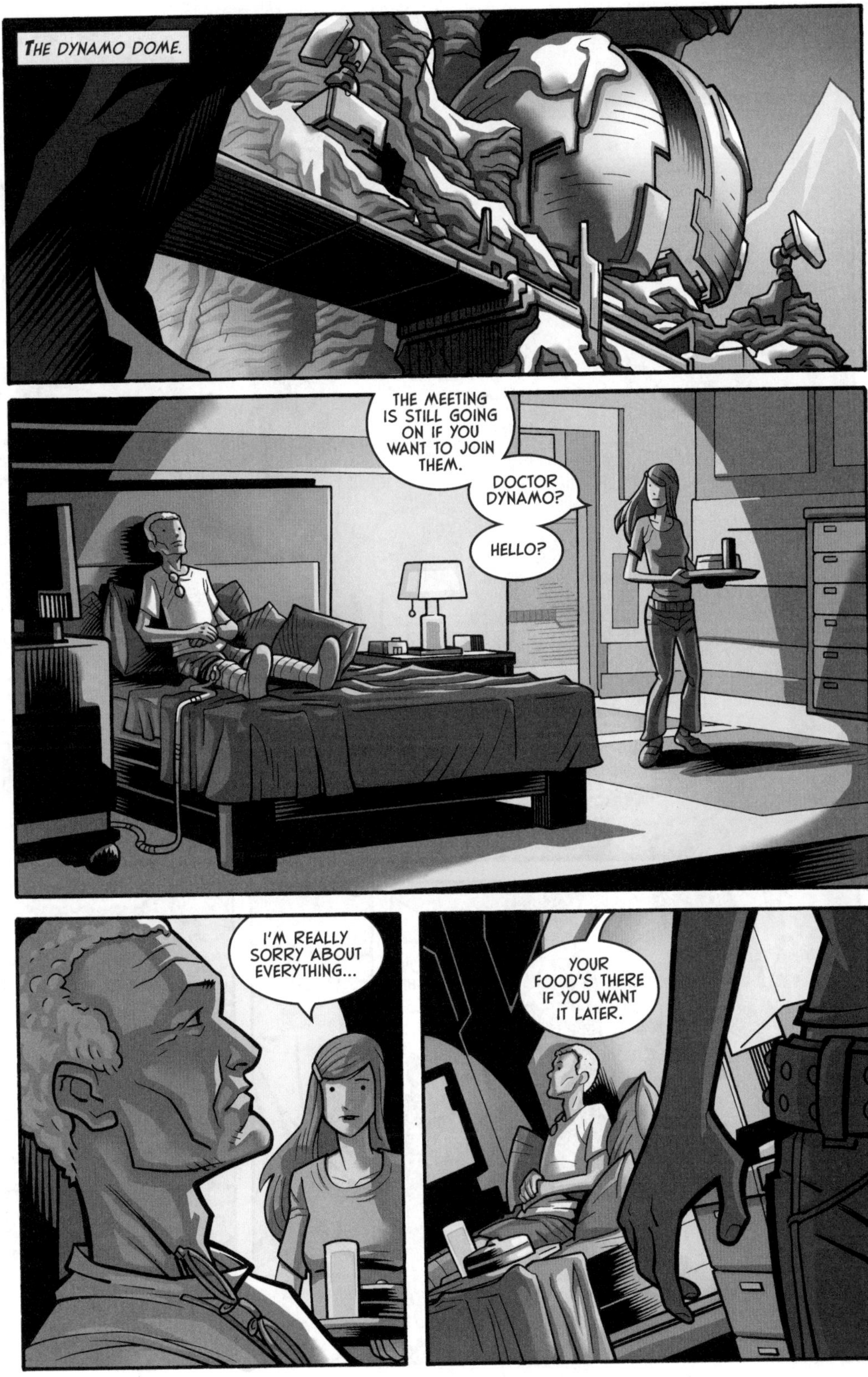
THE DYNAMO DOME.
THE MEETING IS STILL GOING ON IF YOU WANT TO JOIN THEM.
DOCTOR DYNAMO?
HELLO?
I'M REALLY SORRY ABOUT EVERYTHING...
YOUR FOOD'S THERE IF YOU WANT IT LATER.

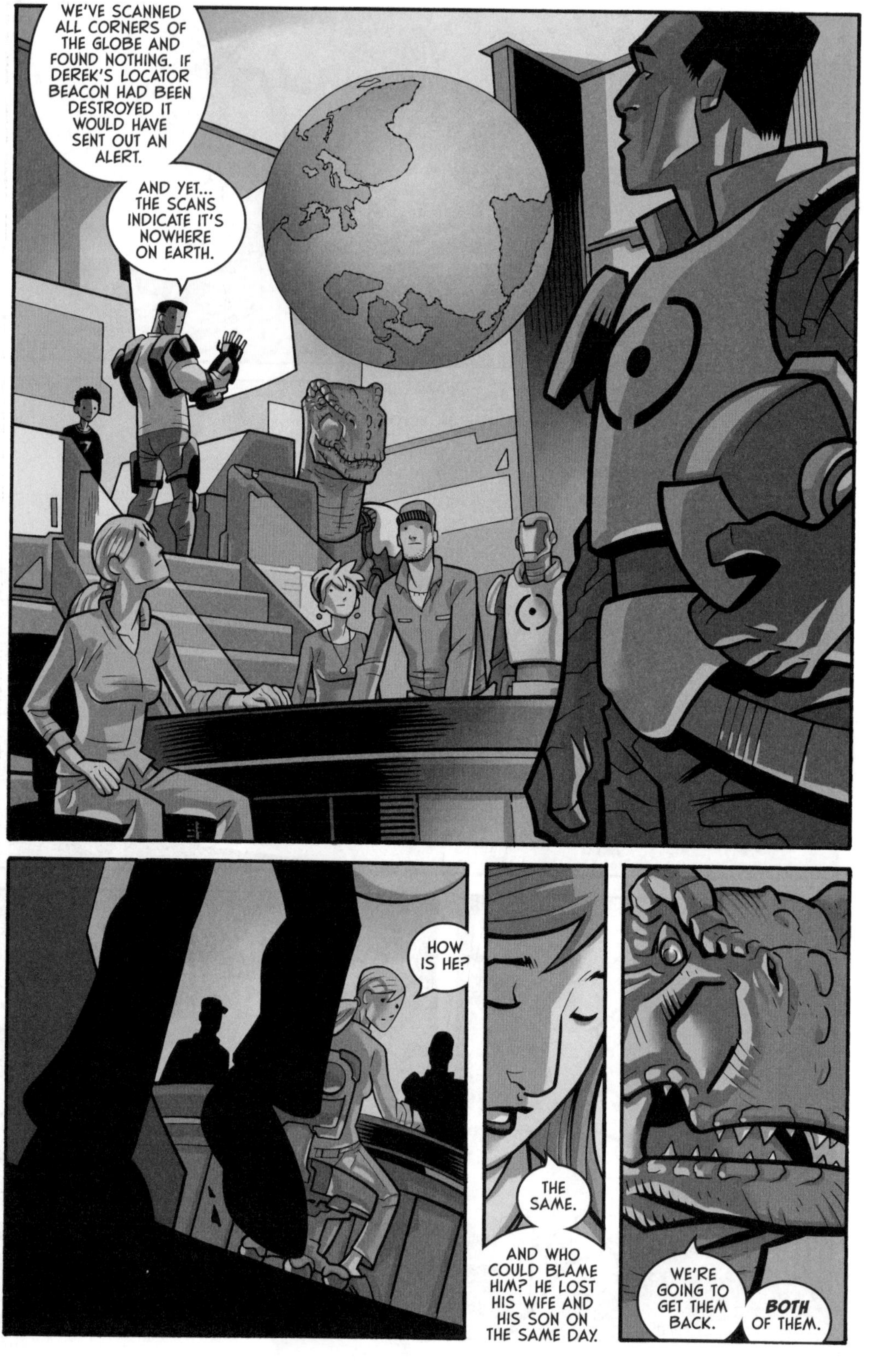
WE'VE SCANNED ALL CORNERS OF THE GLOBE AND FOUND NOTHING. IF DEREK'S LOCATOR BEACON HAD BEEN DESTROYED IT WOULD HAVE SENT OUT AN ALERT.
AND YET... THE SCANS INDICATE IT'S NOWHERE ON EARTH.
HOW IS HE?
THE SAME.
AND WHO COULD BLAME HIM? HE LOST HIS WIFE AND HIS SON ON THE SAME DAY.
WE'RE GOING TO GET THEM BACK.
BOTH OF THEM.

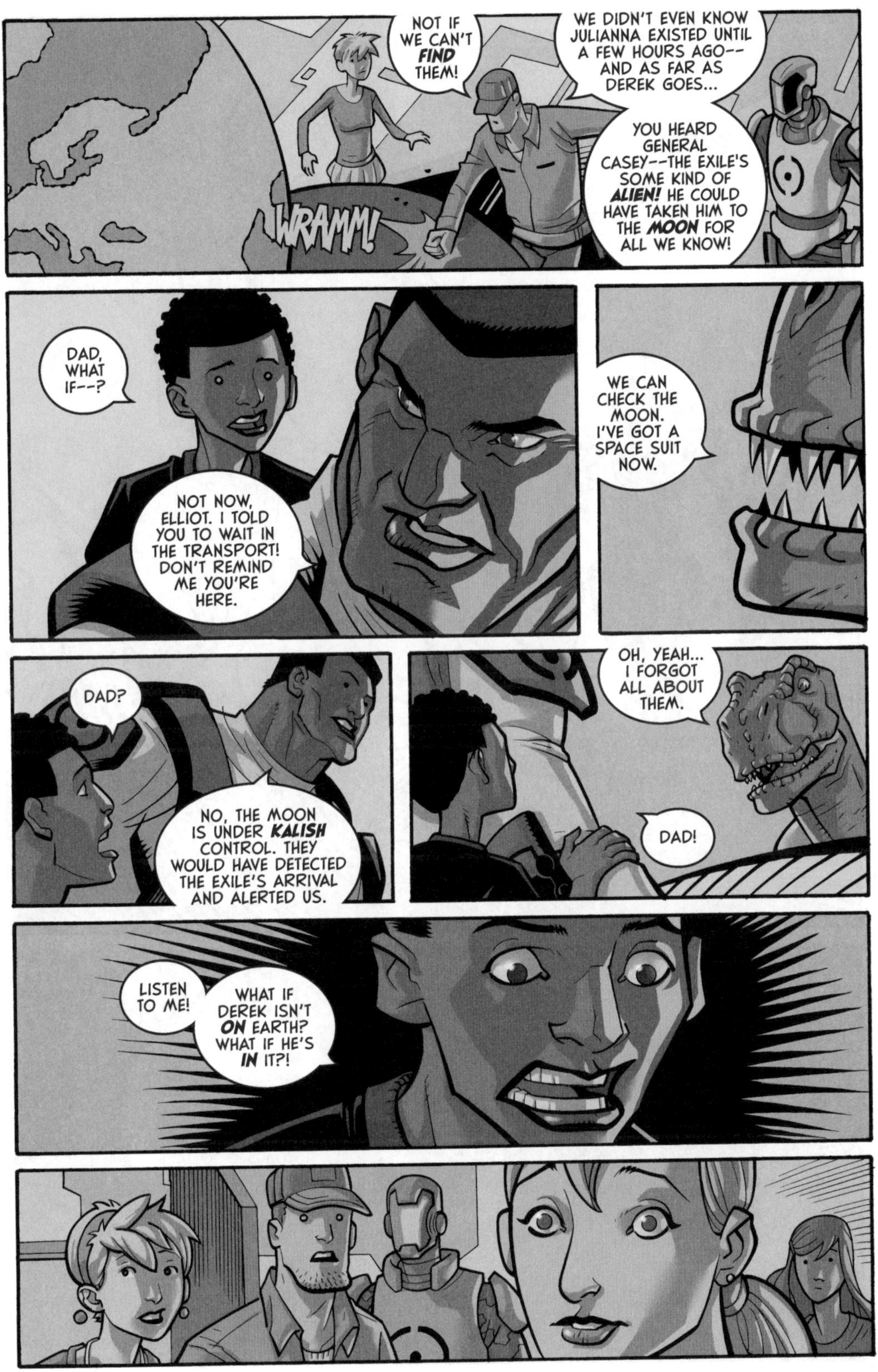
NOT IF WE CAN'T FIND THEM!
WE DIDN'T EVEN KNOW JULIANNA EXISTED UNTIL A FEW HOURS AGO-- AND AS FAR AS DEREK GOES...
WRAMM!
YOU HEARD GENERAL CASEY--THE EXILE'S SOME KIND OF ALIEN! HE COULD HAVE TAKEN HIM TO THE MOON FOR ALL WE KNOW!
DAD, WHAT IF--?
NOT NOW, ELLIOT. I TOLD YOU TO WAIT IN THE TRANSPORT! DON'T REMIND ME YOU'RE HERE.
WE CAN CHECK THE MOON. I'VE GOT A SPACE SUIT NOW.
DAD?
NO, THE MOON IS UNDER KALISH CONTROL. THEY WOULD HAVE DETECTED THE EXILE'S ARRIVAL AND ALERTED US.
OH, YEAH... I FORGOT ALL ABOUT THEM.
DAD!
LISTEN TO ME!
WHAT IF DEREK ISN'T ON EARTH? WHAT IF HE'S IN IT?!

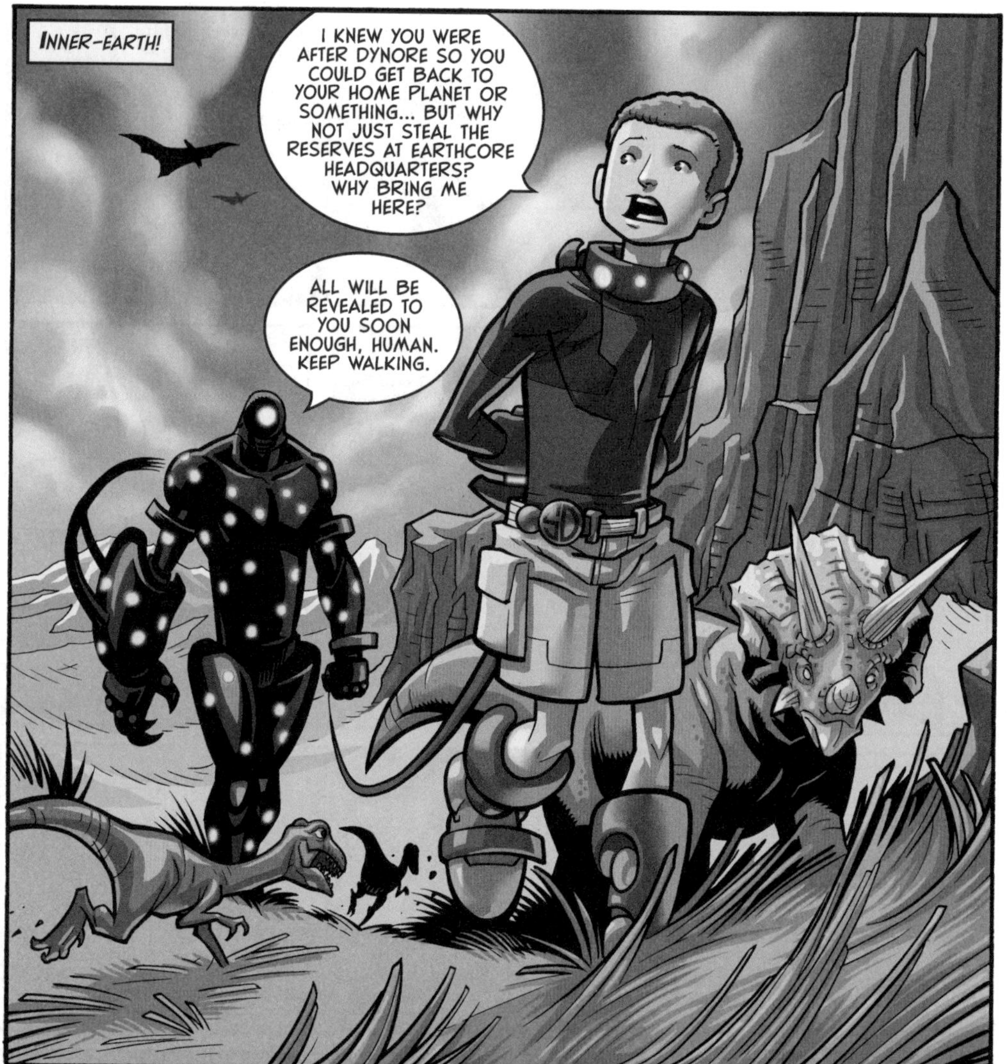
INNER-EARTH!
I KNEW YOU WERE AFTER DYNORE SO YOU COULD GET BACK TO YOUR HOME PLANET OR SOMETHING... BUT WHY NOT JUST STEAL THE RESERVES AT EARTHCORE HEADQUARTERS? WHY BRING ME HERE?
ALL WILL BE REVEALED TO YOU SOON ENOUGH, HUMAN. KEEP WALKING.

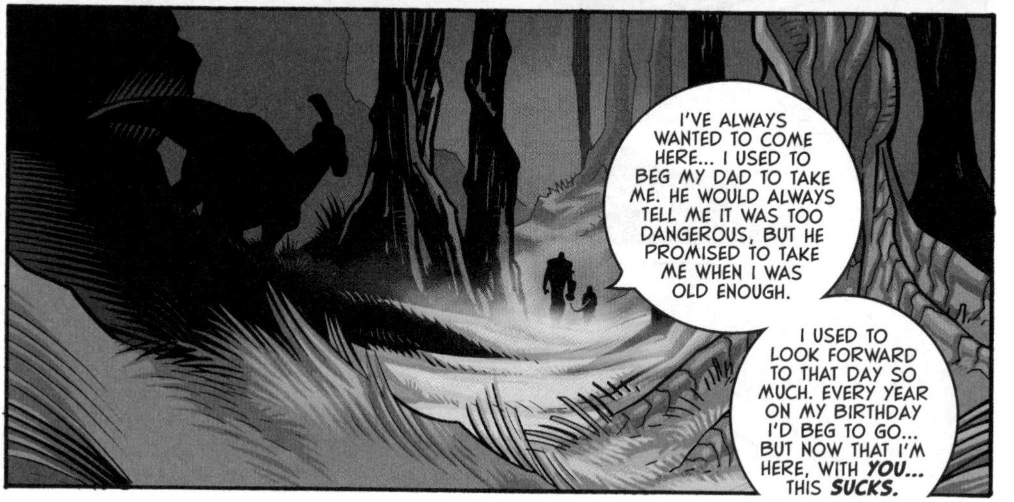
I'VE ALWAYS WANTED TO COME HERE... I USED TO BEG MY DAD TO TAKE ME. HE WOULD ALWAYS TELL ME IT WAS TOO DANGEROUS, BUT HE PROMISED TO TAKE ME WHEN I WAS OLD ENOUGH.
I USED TO LOOK FORWARD TO THAT DAY SO MUCH. EVERY YEAR ON MY BIRTHDAY I'D BEG TO GO... BUT NOW THAT I'M HERE, WITH *YOU*... THIS ***SUCKS.***

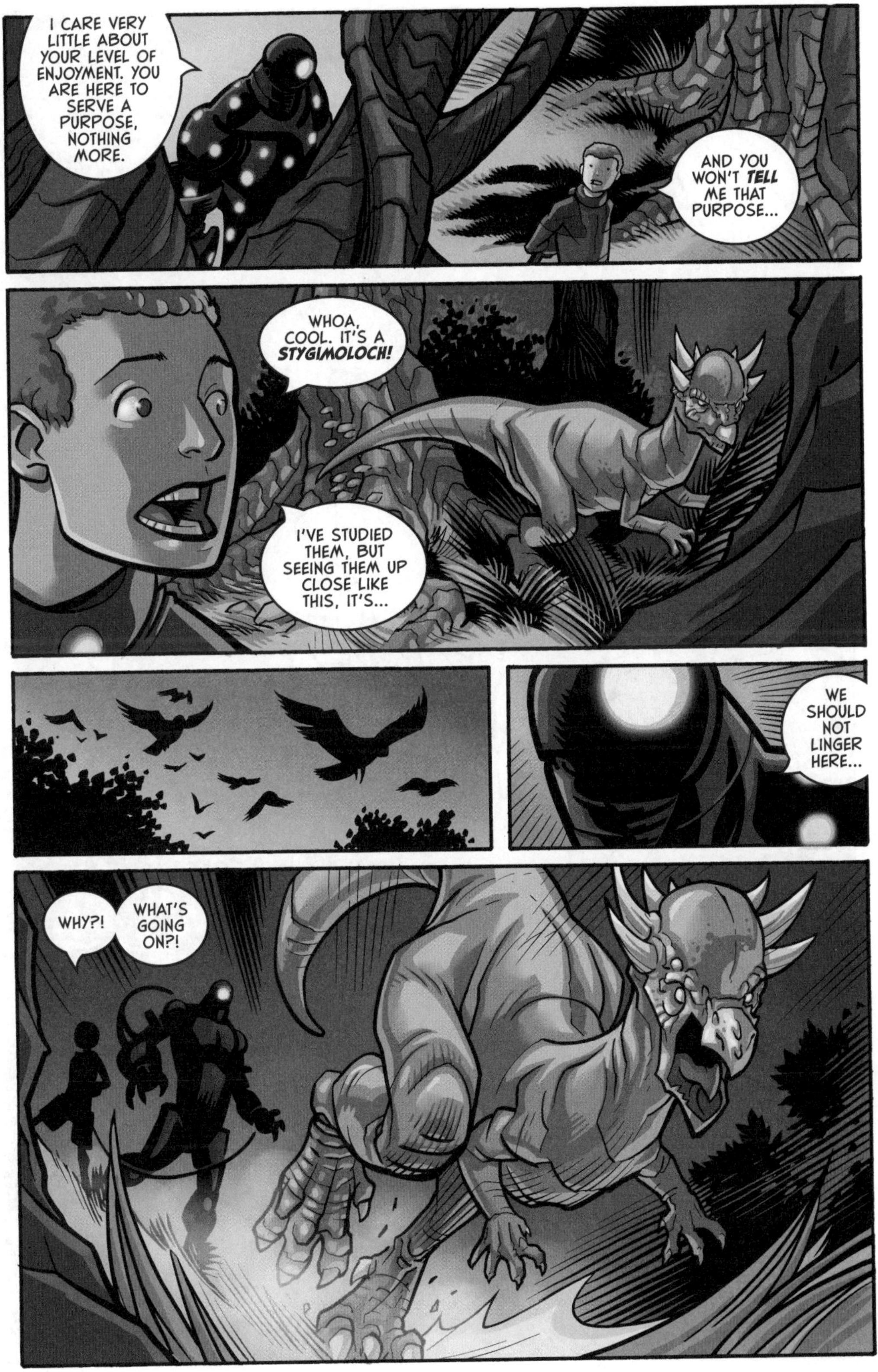
I CARE VERY LITTLE ABOUT YOUR LEVEL OF ENJOYMENT. YOU ARE HERE TO SERVE A PURPOSE, NOTHING MORE.
AND YOU WON'T TELL ME THAT PURPOSE...
WHOA, COOL. IT'S A STYGIMOLOCH!
I'VE STUDIED THEM, BUT SEEING THEM UP CLOSE LIKE THIS, IT'S...
WE SHOULD NOT LINGER HERE...
WHY?!
WHAT'S GOING ON?!

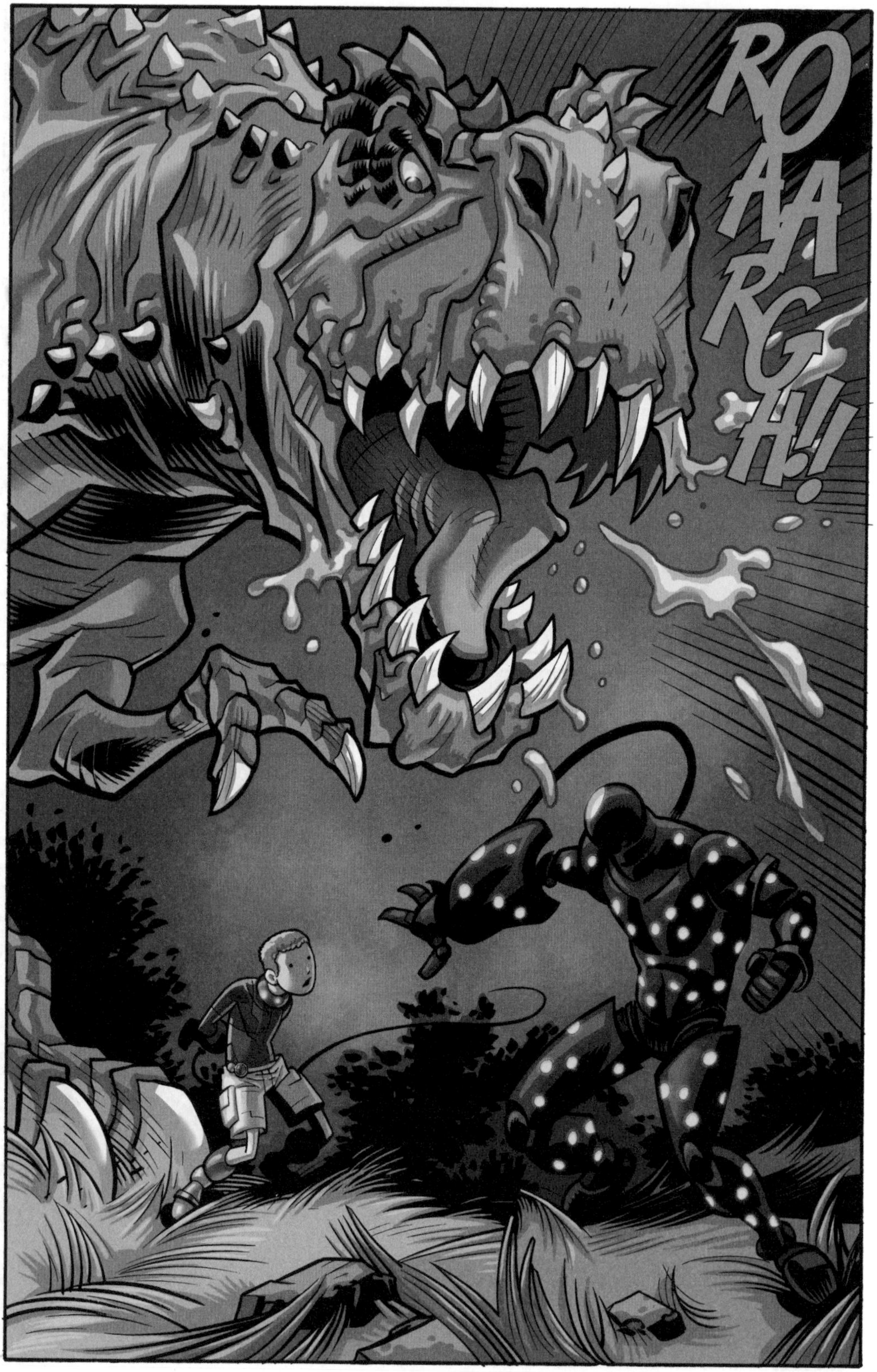
ROAARGH!!

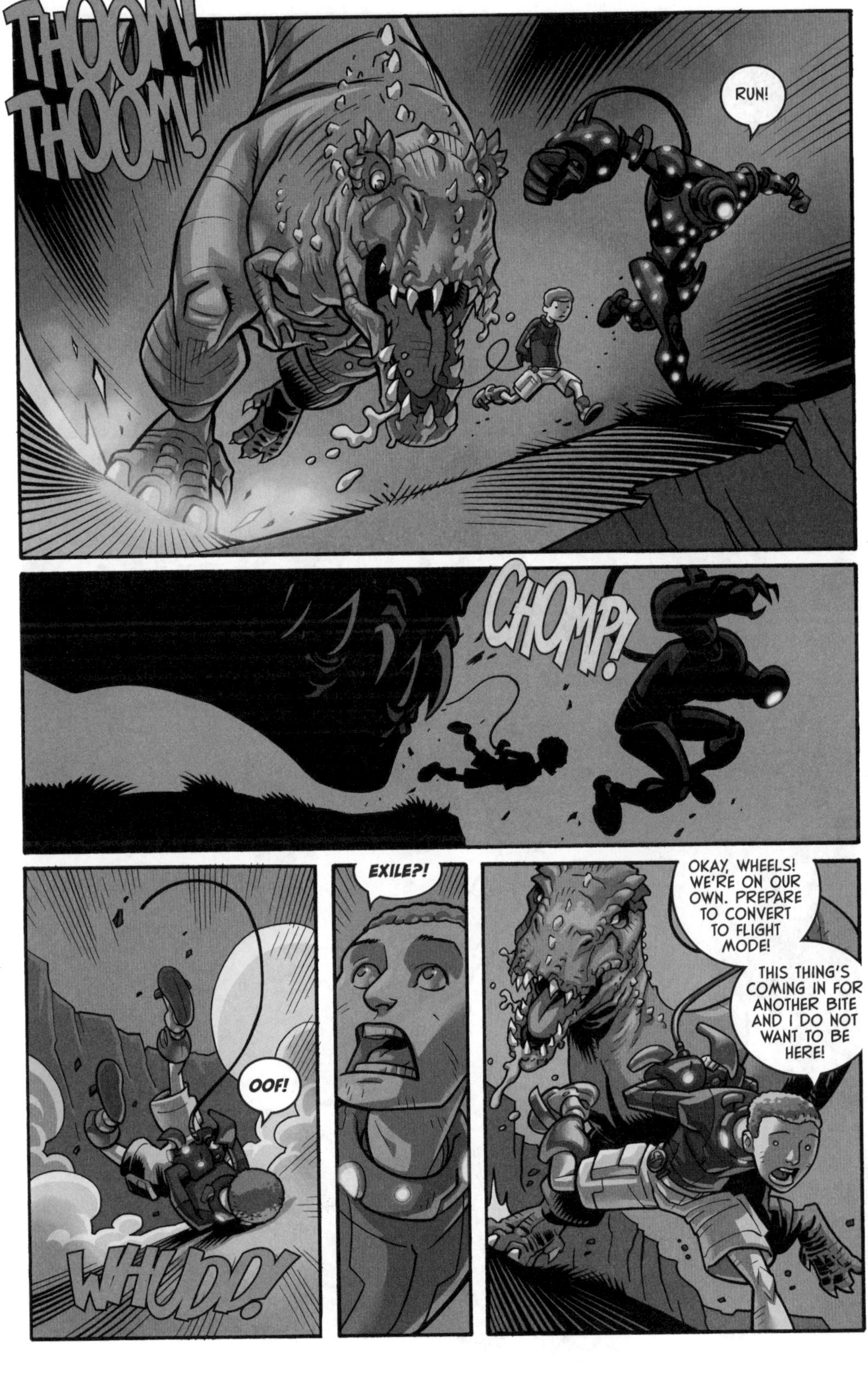
THOOM! THOOM!
RUN!
CHOMP!
OOF!
WHUDD!
EXILE?!
OKAY, WHEELS! WE'RE ON OUR OWN. PREPARE TO CONVERT TO FLIGHT MODE!
THIS THING'S COMING IN FOR ANOTHER BITE AND I DO NOT WANT TO BE HERE!

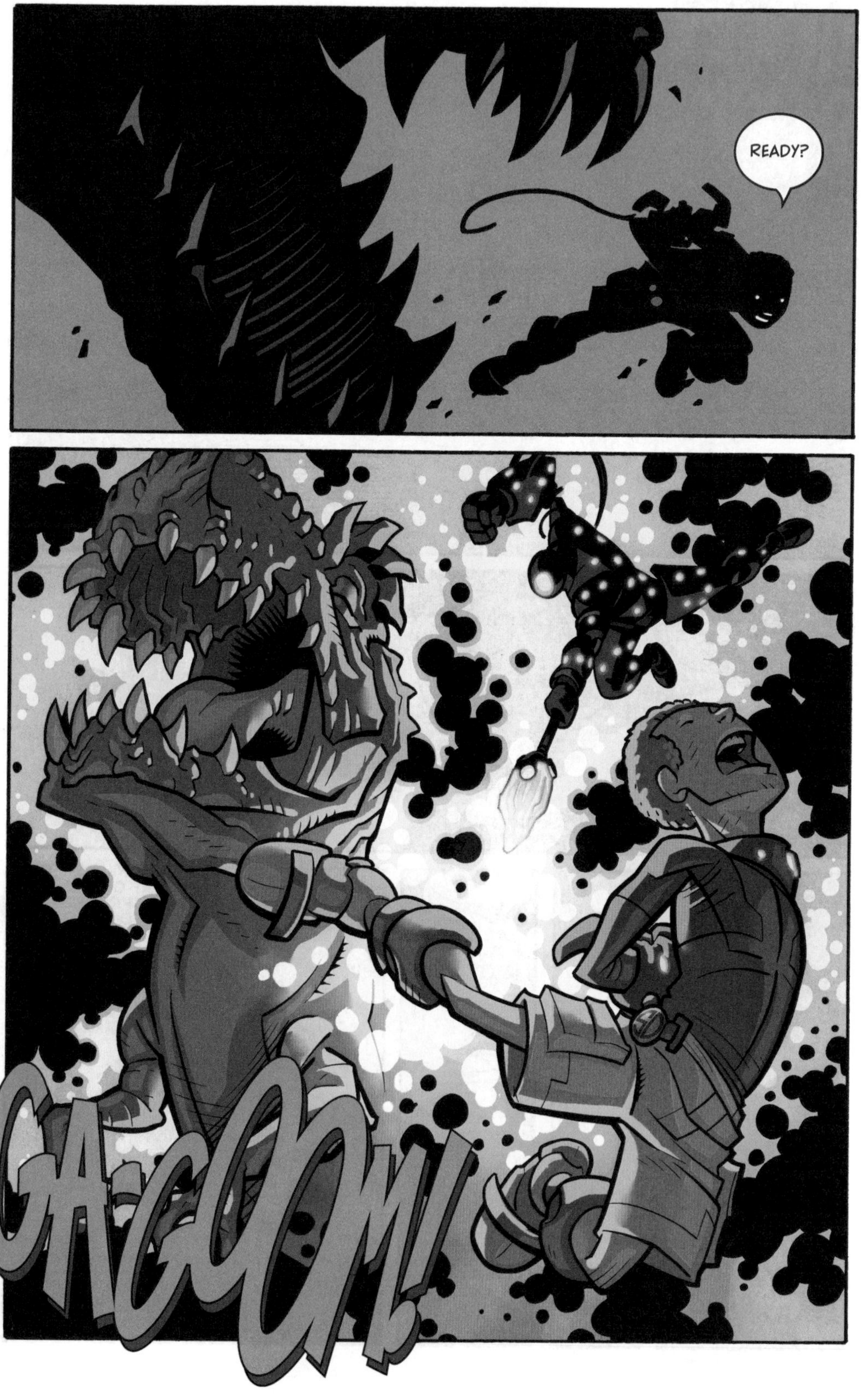
READY?

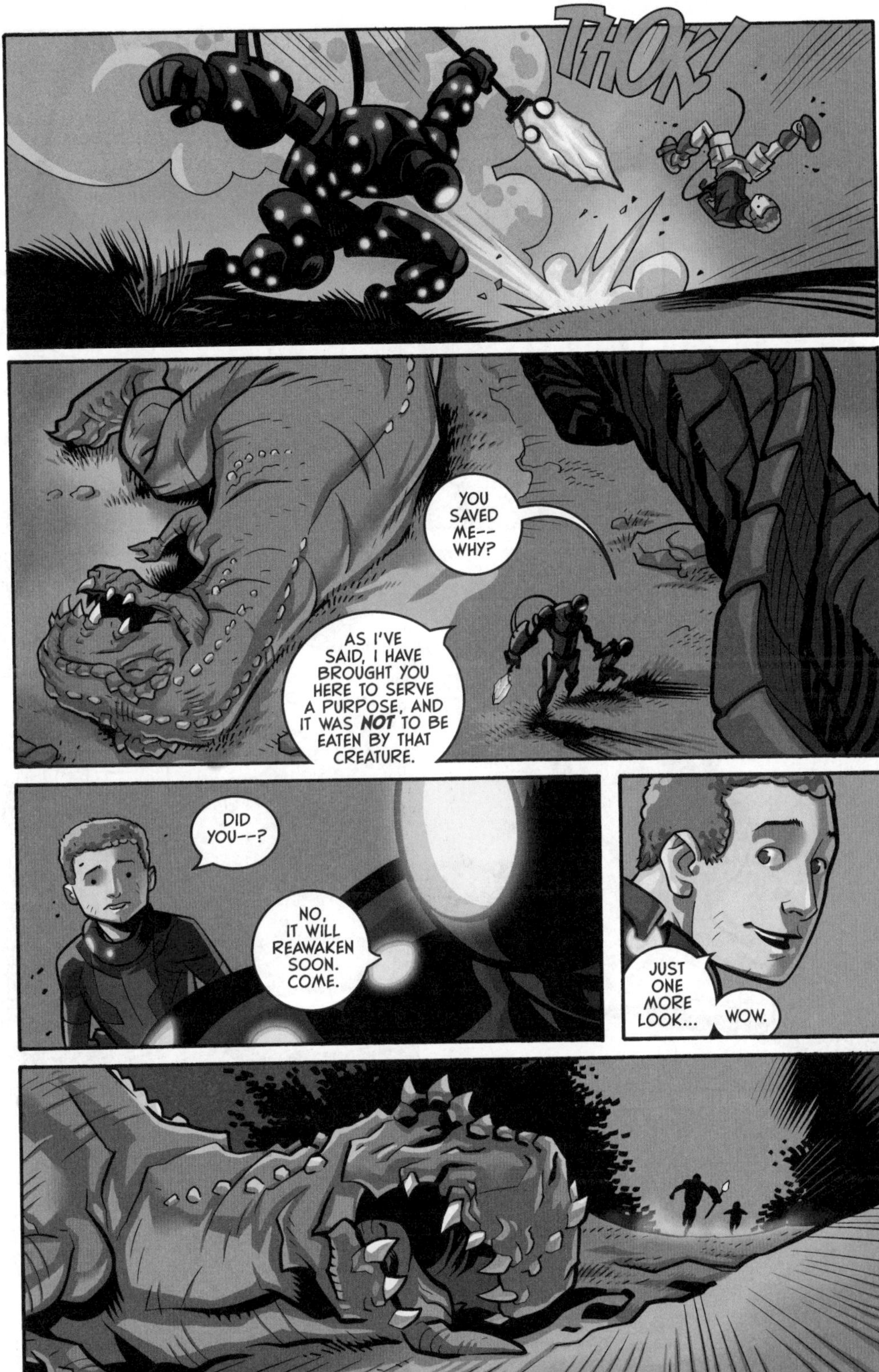
THOK!
YOU SAVED ME--WHY?
AS I'VE SAID, I HAVE BROUGHT YOU HERE TO SERVE A PURPOSE, AND IT WAS **NOT** TO BE EATEN BY THAT CREATURE.
DID YOU--?
NO, IT WILL REAWAKEN SOON. COME.
JUST ONE MORE LOOK...
WOW.

THE DYNAMO DOME.
YOUR DAD IS LOOKING INTO IT. I WANT TO FIND DEREK AS MUCH AS EVERYONE ELSE-- HE'S MY BEST FRIEND. BUT WE CAN'T JUST RUN OFF ON OUR OWN.
WE CAN'T EVEN GET TO INNER-EARTH ON OUR OWN, ELLIOT.
DUDE, WE'RE ON A MISSION NOW, USE MY CODE NAME.
SORRY, BULLET BLAST.
IT'S ROCKET SHOCK, NOW.
ANYONE OUTSIDE?
NO.
OKAY. LISTEN UP, WE CAN TOTALLY GET INTO INNER-EARTH ON OUR OWN. THE REASON THE DYNAMO DOME WAS BUILT HERE IS BECAUSE OF THE TUNNEL TO INNER-EARTH BELOW IT.
WE KNOW WHERE DEREK IS. IT'S NOT A GUESS. WHERE ELSE WOULD THE EXILE TAKE HIM? HASN'T HE BEEN TRYING TO FIND A WAY INTO INNER-EARTH THIS WHOLE TIME?
AND ONCE WE GET TO INNER-EARTH, WE'LL TOTALLY BE ABLE TO TRACK DEREK. HIS LOCATION BEACON WILL BE IN RANGE.

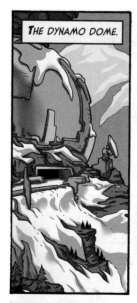

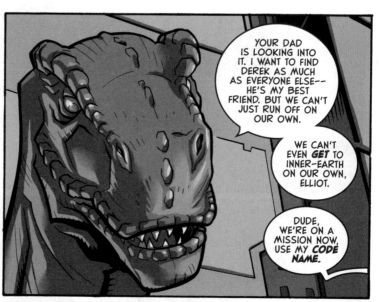

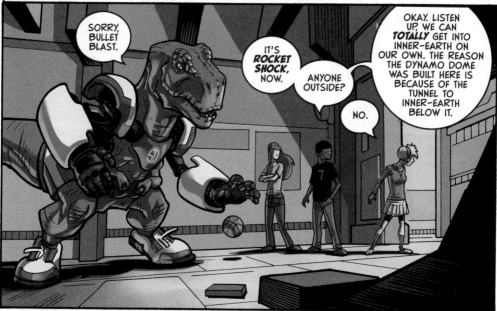

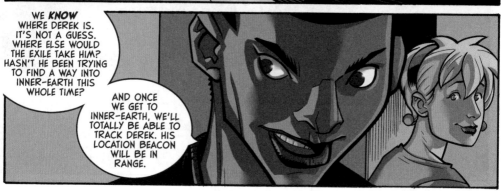

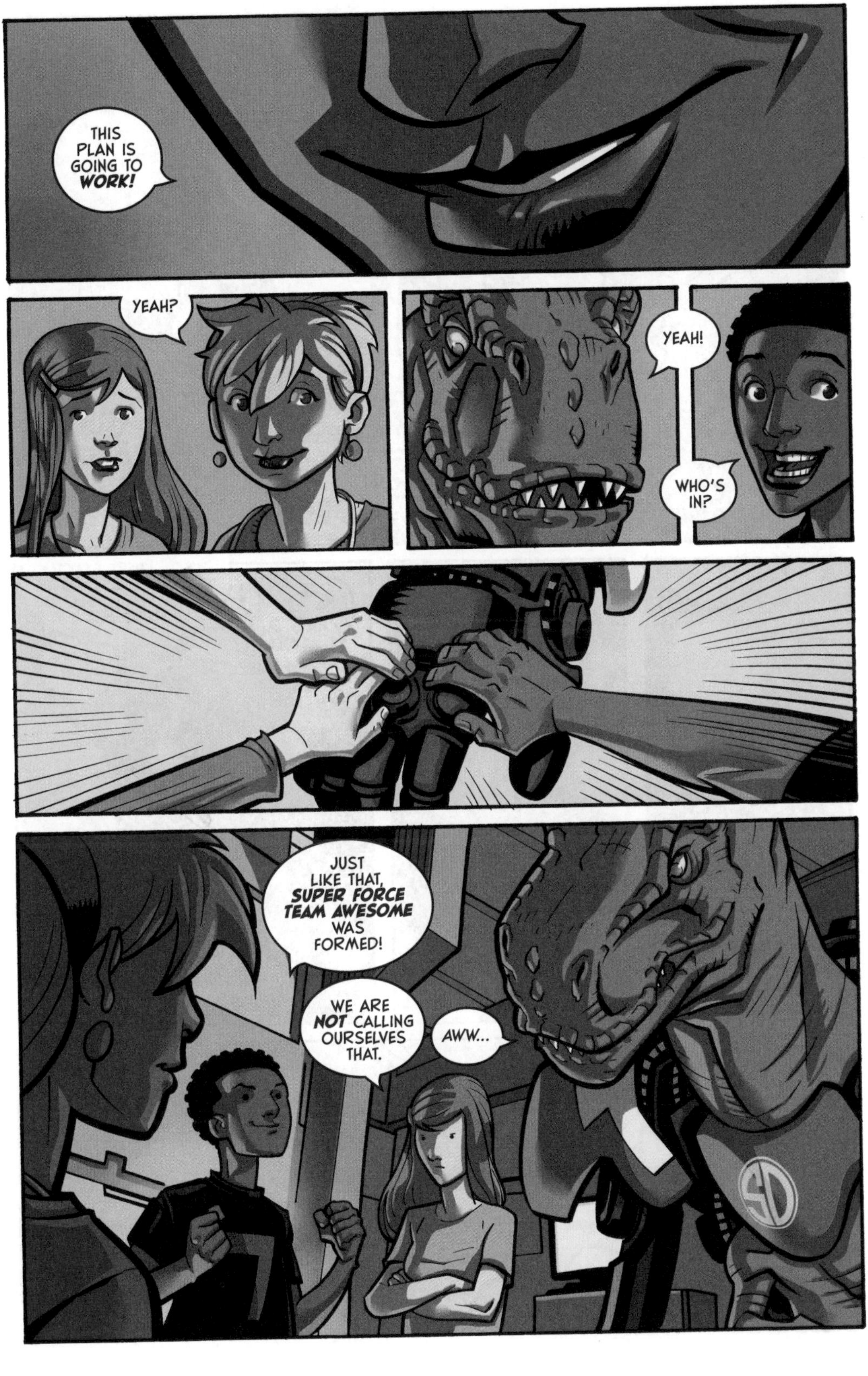
THIS PLAN IS GOING TO **WORK!**
YEAH?
YEAH!
WHO'S IN?
JUST LIKE THAT, ***SUPER FORCE TEAM AWESOME*** WAS FORMED!
WE ARE ***NOT*** CALLING OURSELVES THAT.
AWW...

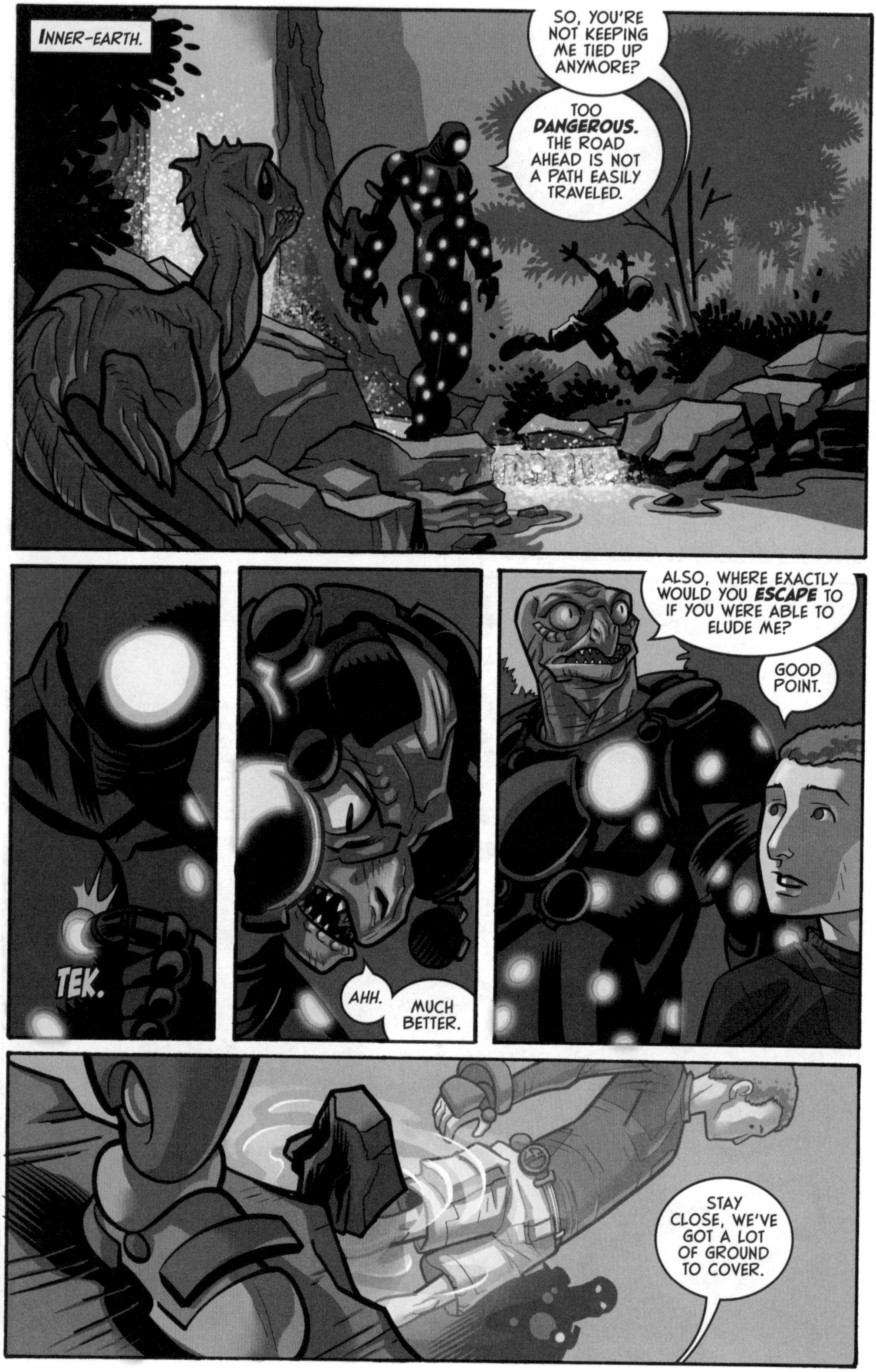
INNER-EARTH.
SO, YOU'RE NOT KEEPING ME TIED UP ANYMORE?
TOO DANGEROUS. THE ROAD AHEAD IS NOT A PATH EASILY TRAVELED.
TEK.
AHH.
MUCH BETTER.
ALSO, WHERE EXACTLY WOULD YOU ESCAPE TO IF YOU WERE ABLE TO ELUDE ME?
GOOD POINT.
STAY CLOSE, WE'VE GOT A LOT OF GROUND TO COVER.

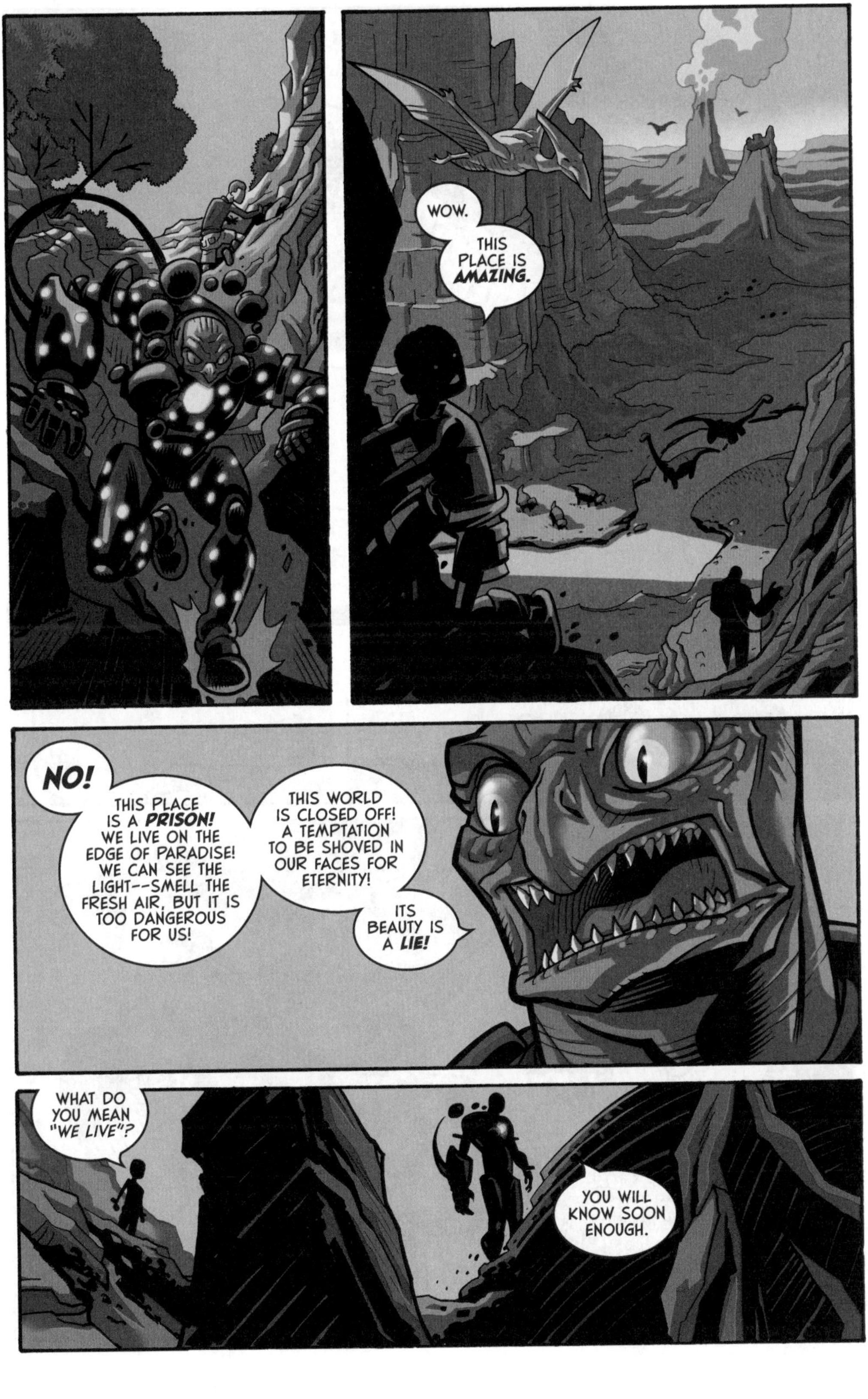
WOW.
THIS PLACE IS AMAZING.
NO!
THIS PLACE IS A PRISON! WE LIVE ON THE EDGE OF PARADISE! WE CAN SEE THE LIGHT--SMELL THE FRESH AIR, BUT IT IS TOO DANGEROUS FOR US!
THIS WORLD IS CLOSED OFF! A TEMPTATION TO BE SHOVED IN OUR FACES FOR ETERNITY!
ITS BEAUTY IS A LIE!
WHAT DO YOU MEAN "WE LIVE"?
YOU WILL KNOW SOON ENOUGH.

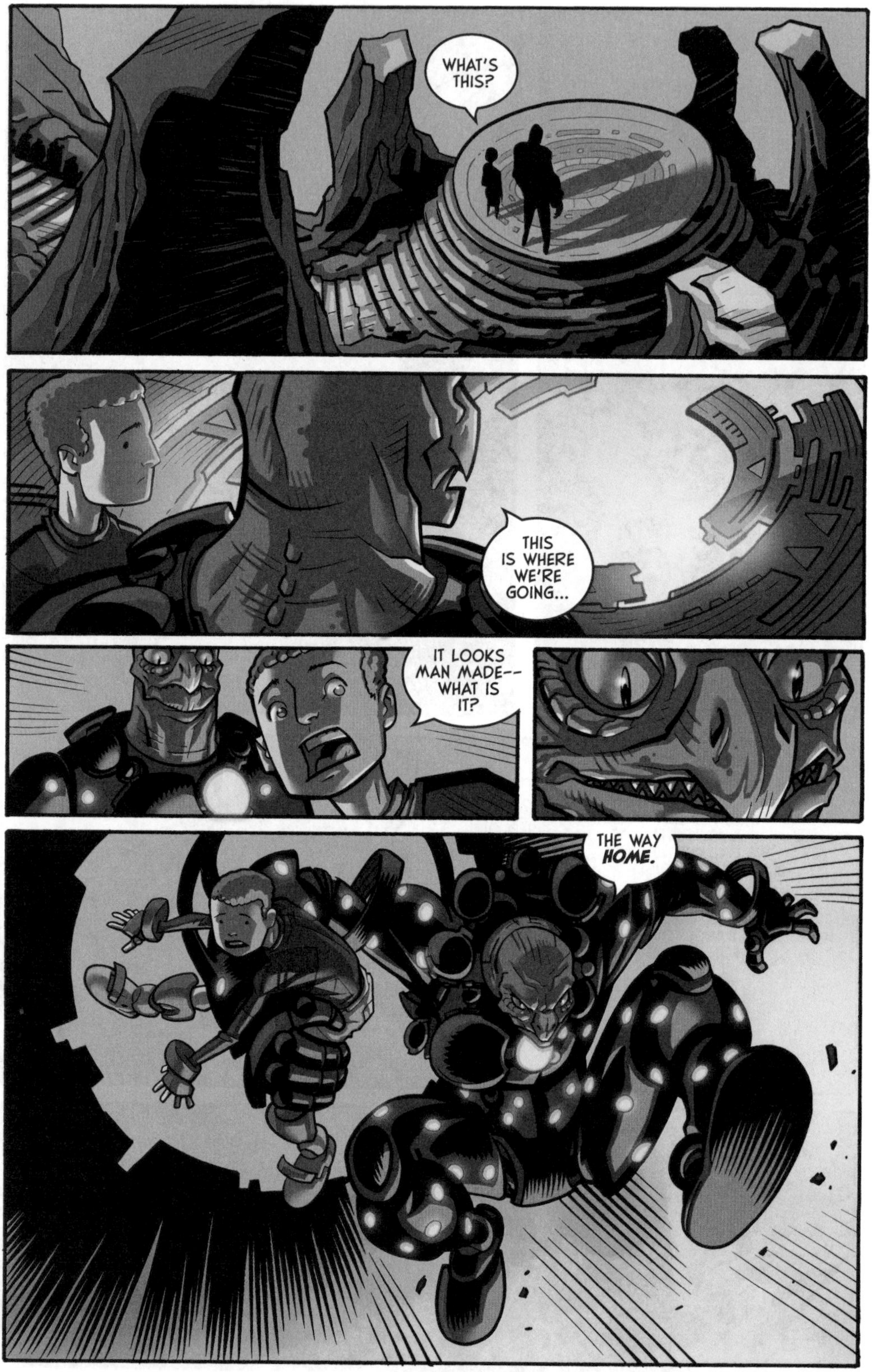
WHAT'S THIS?
THIS IS WHERE WE'RE GOING...
IT LOOKS MAN MADE-- WHAT IS IT?
THE WAY **HOME.**

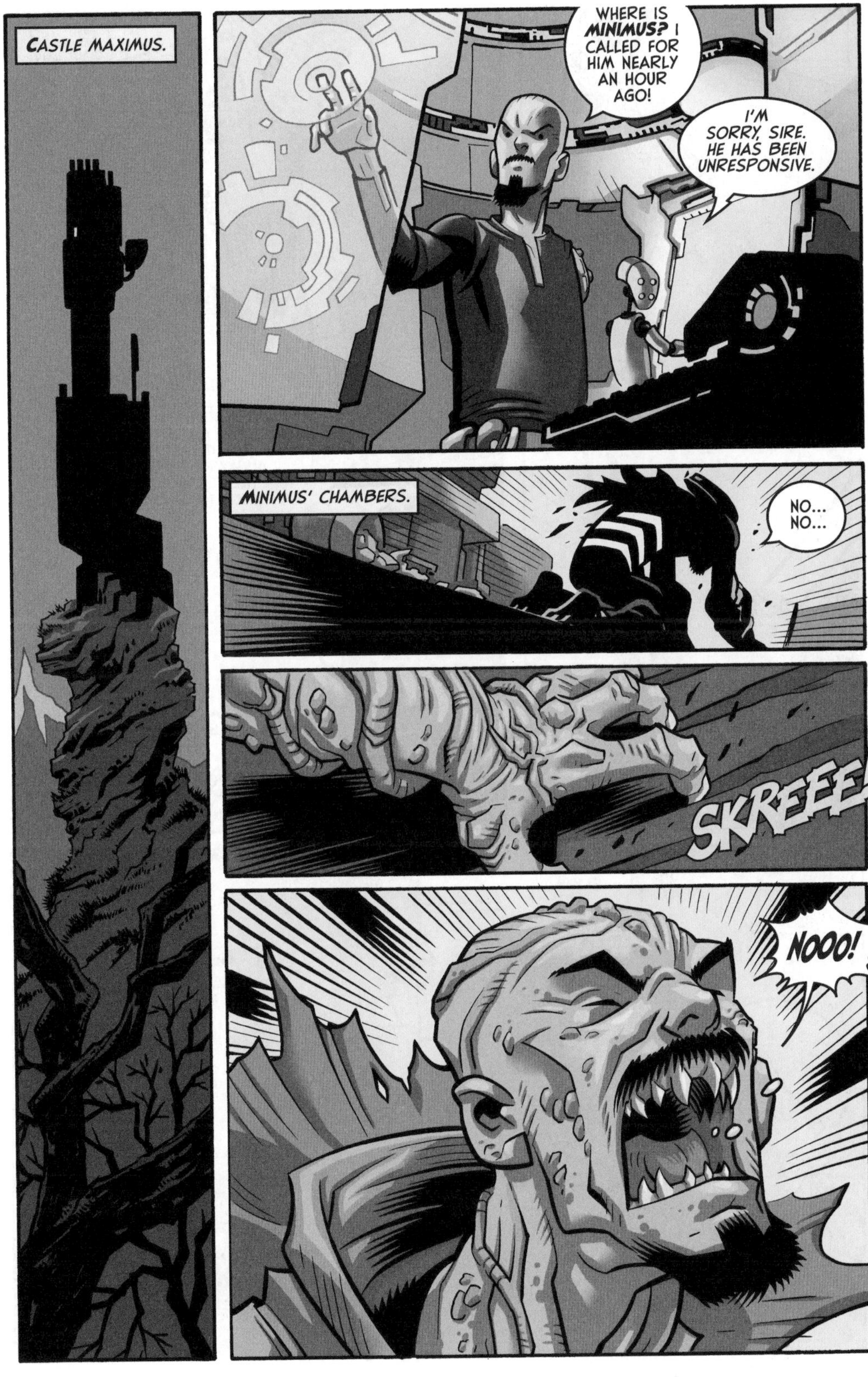
CASTLE MAXIMUS.
WHERE IS MINIMUS? I CALLED FOR HIM NEARLY AN HOUR AGO!
I'M SORRY, SIRE. HE HAS BEEN UNRESPONSIVE.
MINIMUS' CHAMBERS.
NO... NO...
SKREEE!
NOOO!

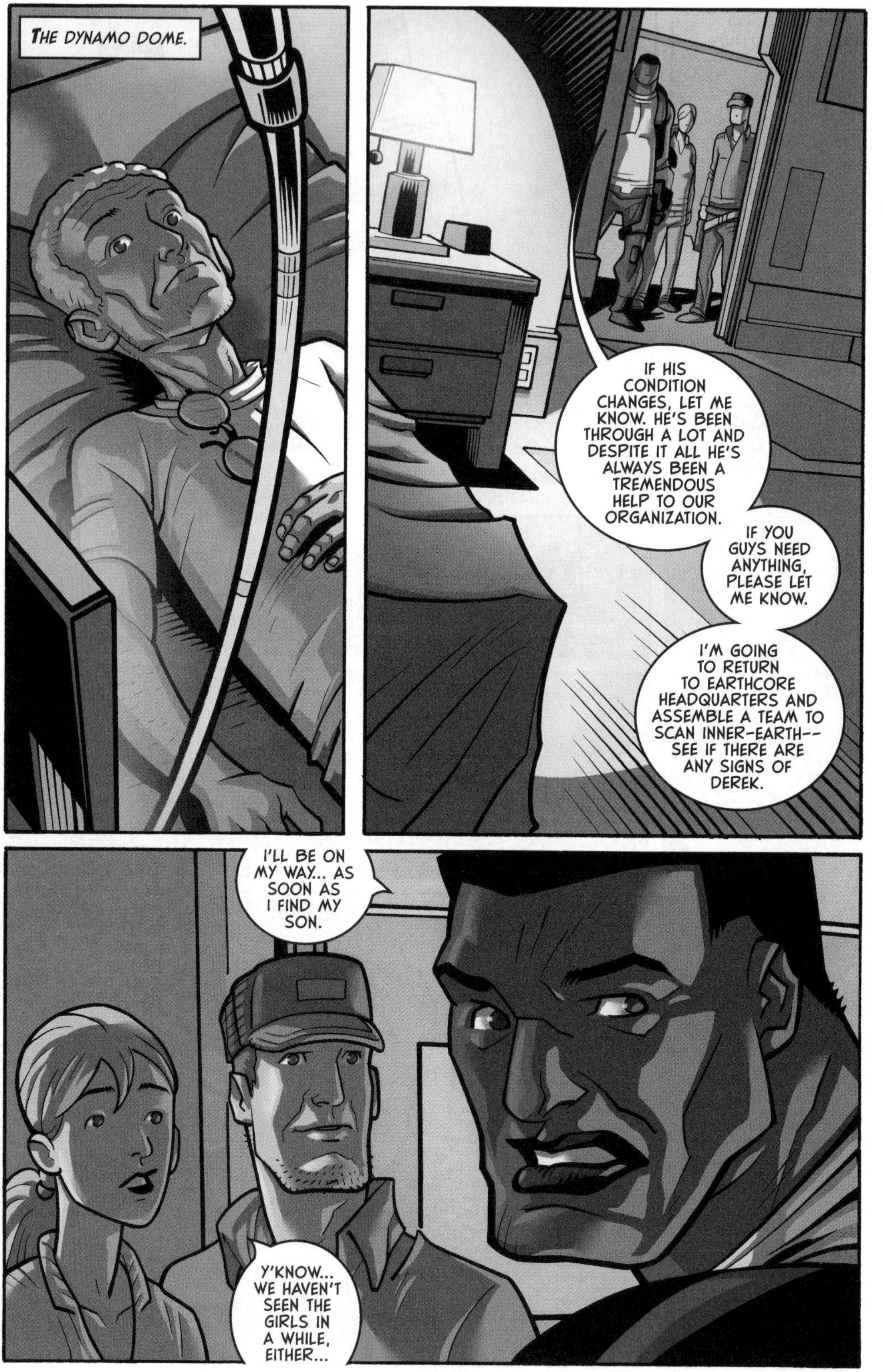

THE DYNAMO DOME.
IF HIS CONDITION CHANGES, LET ME KNOW. HE'S BEEN THROUGH A LOT AND DESPITE IT ALL HE'S ALWAYS BEEN A TREMENDOUS HELP TO OUR ORGANIZATION.
IF YOU GUYS NEED ANYTHING, PLEASE LET ME KNOW.
I'M GOING TO RETURN TO EARTHCORE HEADQUARTERS AND ASSEMBLE A TEAM TO SCAN INNER-EARTH-- SEE IF THERE ARE ANY SIGNS OF DEREK.
I'LL BE ON MY WAY... AS SOON AS I FIND MY SON.
Y'KNOW... WE HAVEN'T SEEN THE GIRLS IN A WHILE, EITHER...

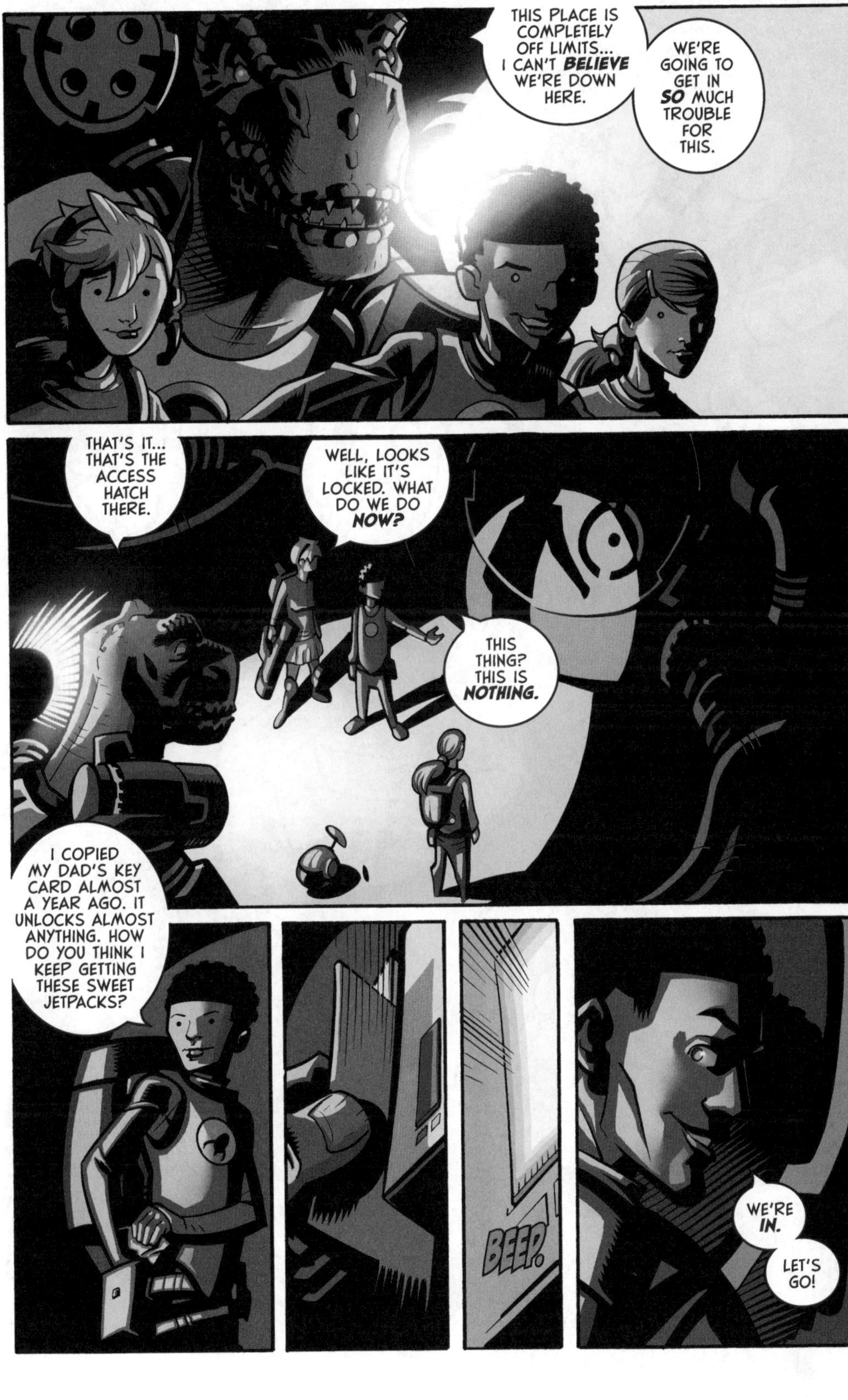

THIS PLACE IS COMPLETELY OFF LIMITS... I CAN'T **BELIEVE** WE'RE DOWN HERE.
WE'RE GOING TO GET IN **SO** MUCH TROUBLE FOR THIS.
THAT'S IT... THAT'S THE ACCESS HATCH THERE.
WELL, LOOKS LIKE IT'S LOCKED. WHAT DO WE DO **NOW?**
THIS THING? THIS IS **NOTHING.**
I COPIED MY DAD'S KEY CARD ALMOST A YEAR AGO. IT UNLOCKS ALMOST ANYTHING. HOW DO YOU THINK I KEEP GETTING THESE SWEET JETPACKS?
BEEP.
WE'RE **IN.**
LET'S GO!

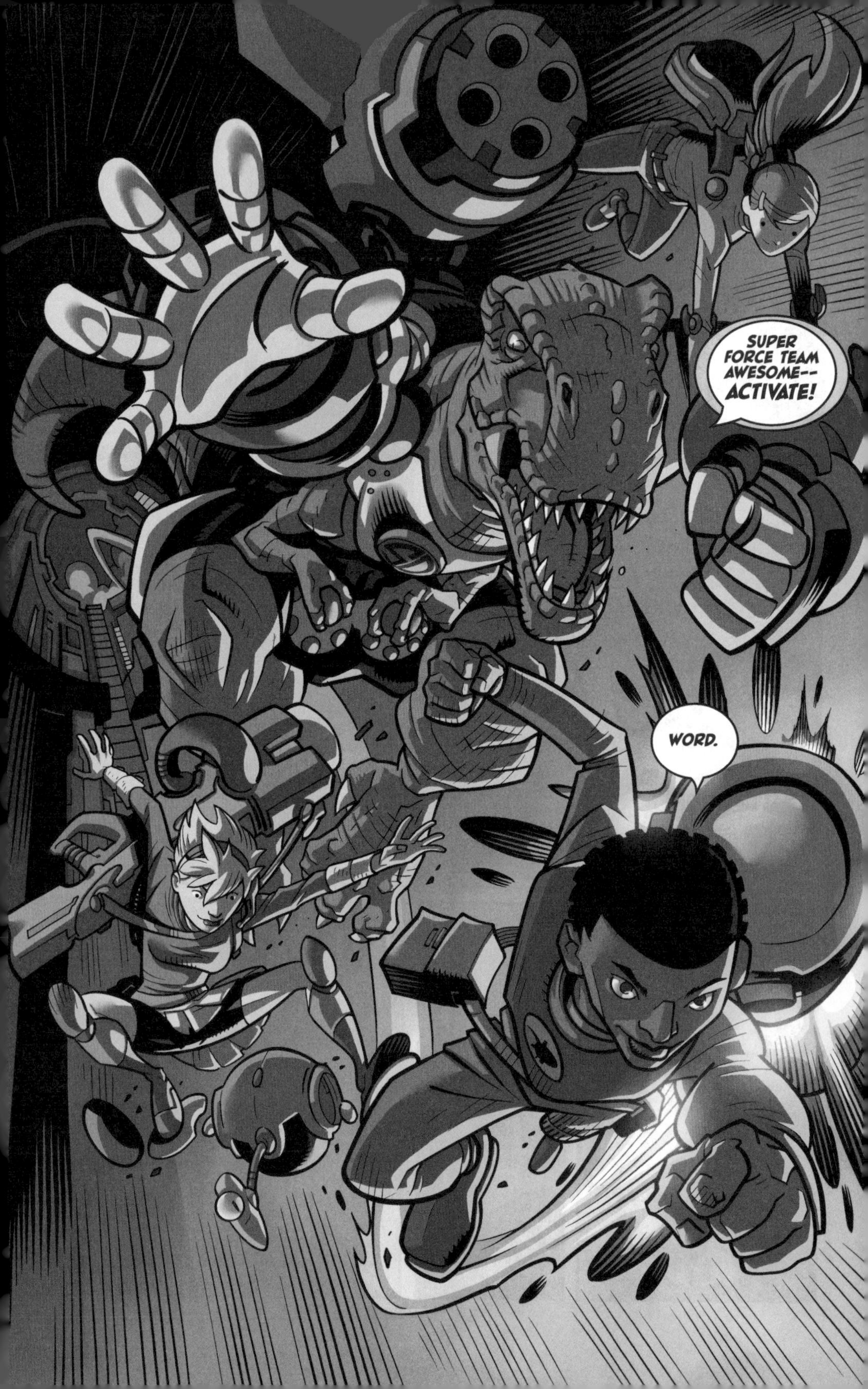
SUPER FORCE TEAM AWESOME--ACTIVATE!
WORD.

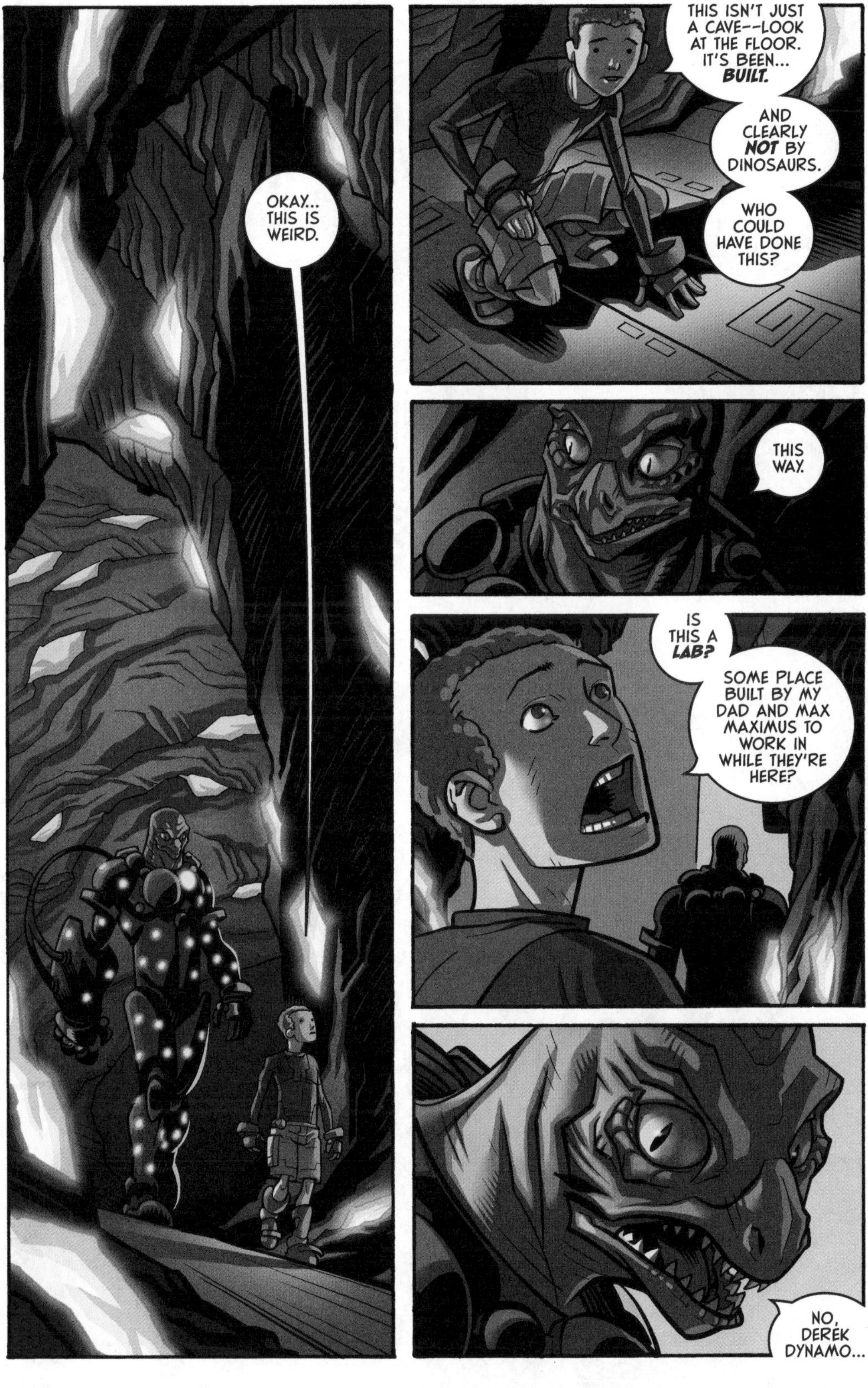

OKAY... THIS IS WEIRD.
THIS ISN'T JUST A CAVE--LOOK AT THE FLOOR. IT'S BEEN... ***BUILT.***
AND CLEARLY ***NOT*** BY DINOSAURS.
WHO COULD HAVE DONE THIS?
THIS WAY.
IS THIS A ***LAB?***
SOME PLACE BUILT BY MY DAD AND MAX MAXIMUS TO WORK IN WHILE THEY'RE HERE?
NO, DEREK DYNAMO...

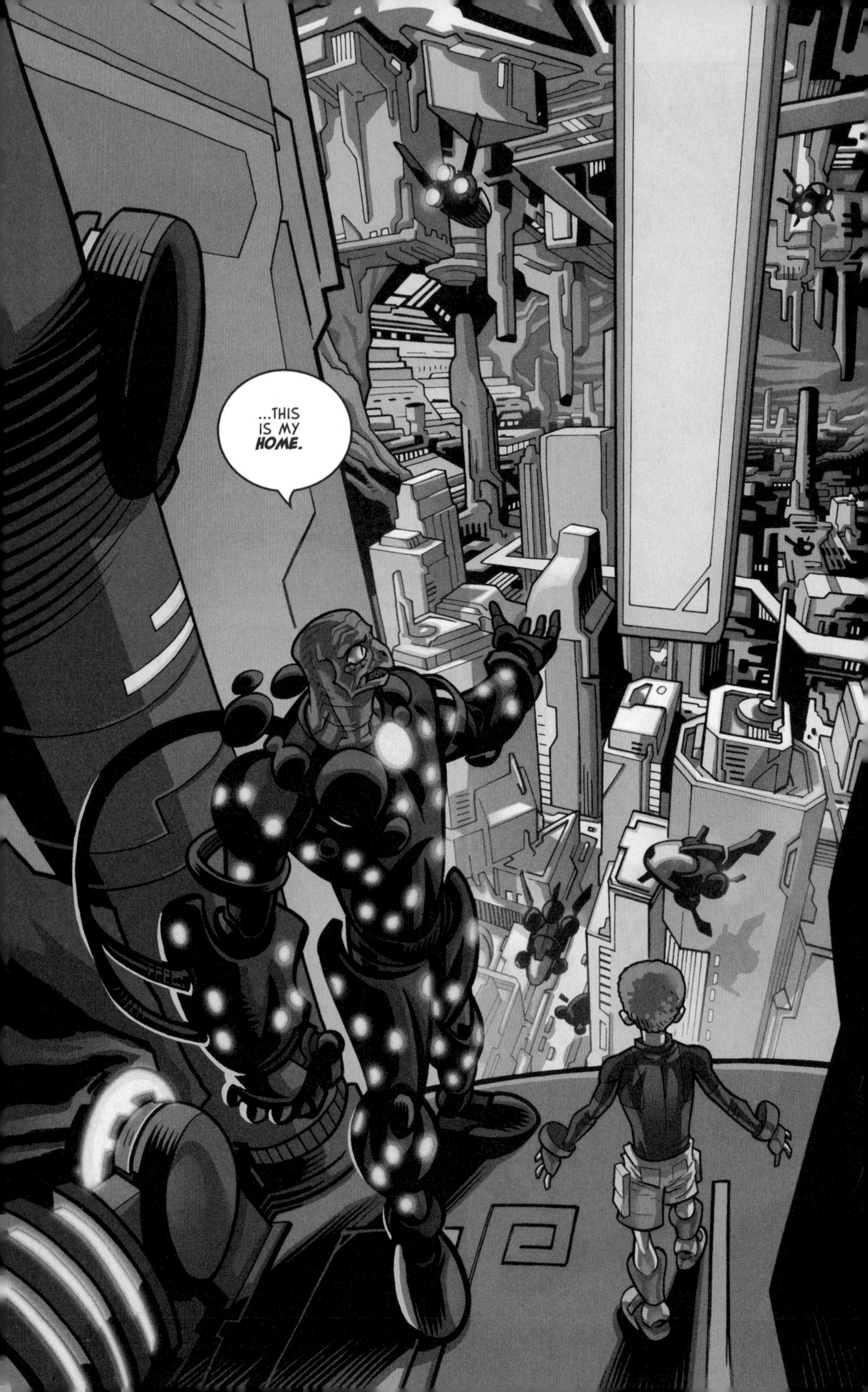
...THIS IS MY *HOME.*

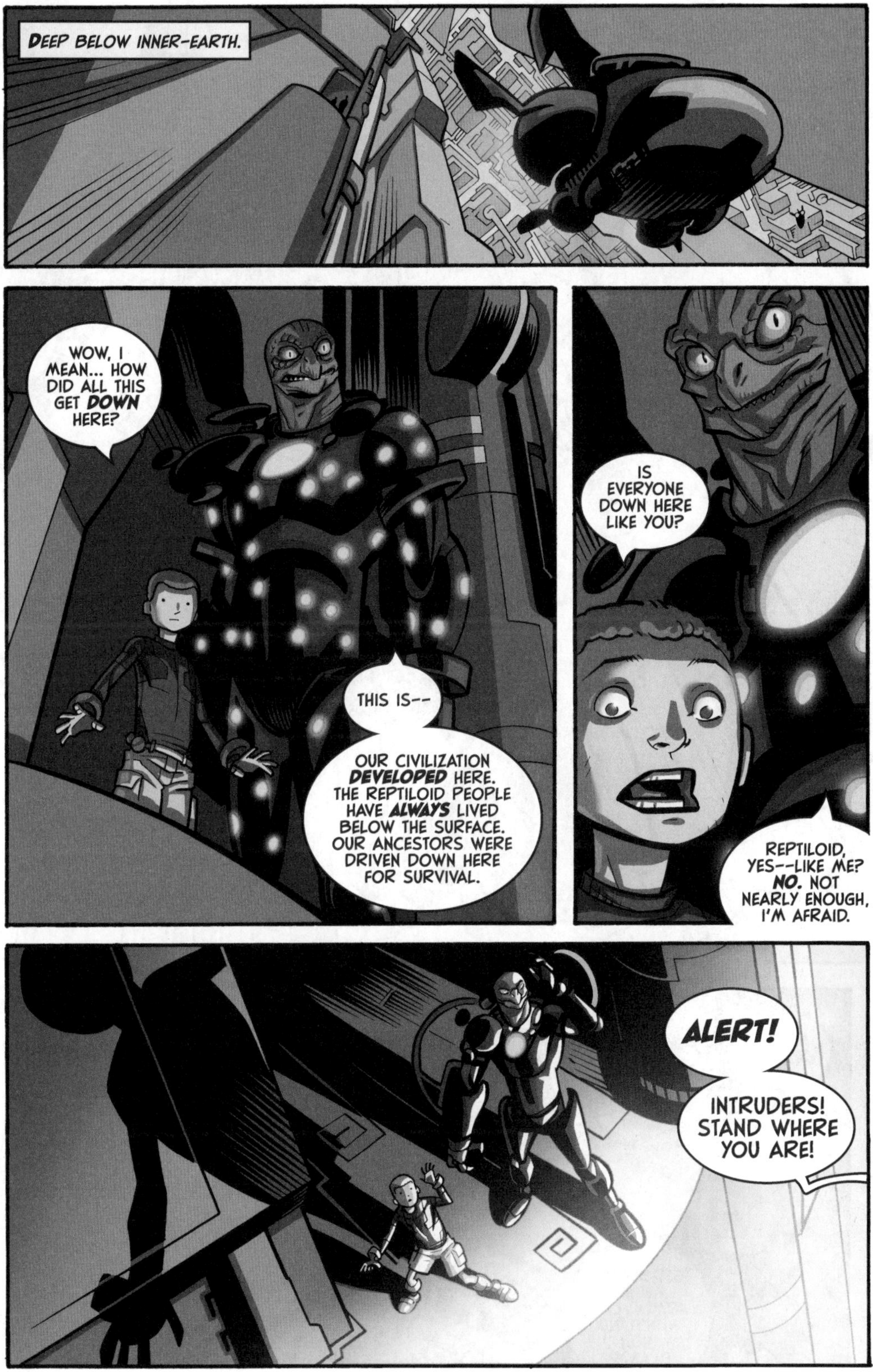
DEEP BELOW INNER-EARTH.
WOW, I MEAN... HOW DID ALL THIS GET DOWN HERE?
THIS IS--
OUR CIVILIZATION DEVELOPED HERE. THE REPTILOID PEOPLE HAVE ALWAYS LIVED BELOW THE SURFACE. OUR ANCESTORS WERE DRIVEN DOWN HERE FOR SURVIVAL.
IS EVERYONE DOWN HERE LIKE YOU?
REPTILOID, YES--LIKE ME? NO. NOT NEARLY ENOUGH, I'M AFRAID.
ALERT!
INTRUDERS! STAND WHERE YOU ARE!

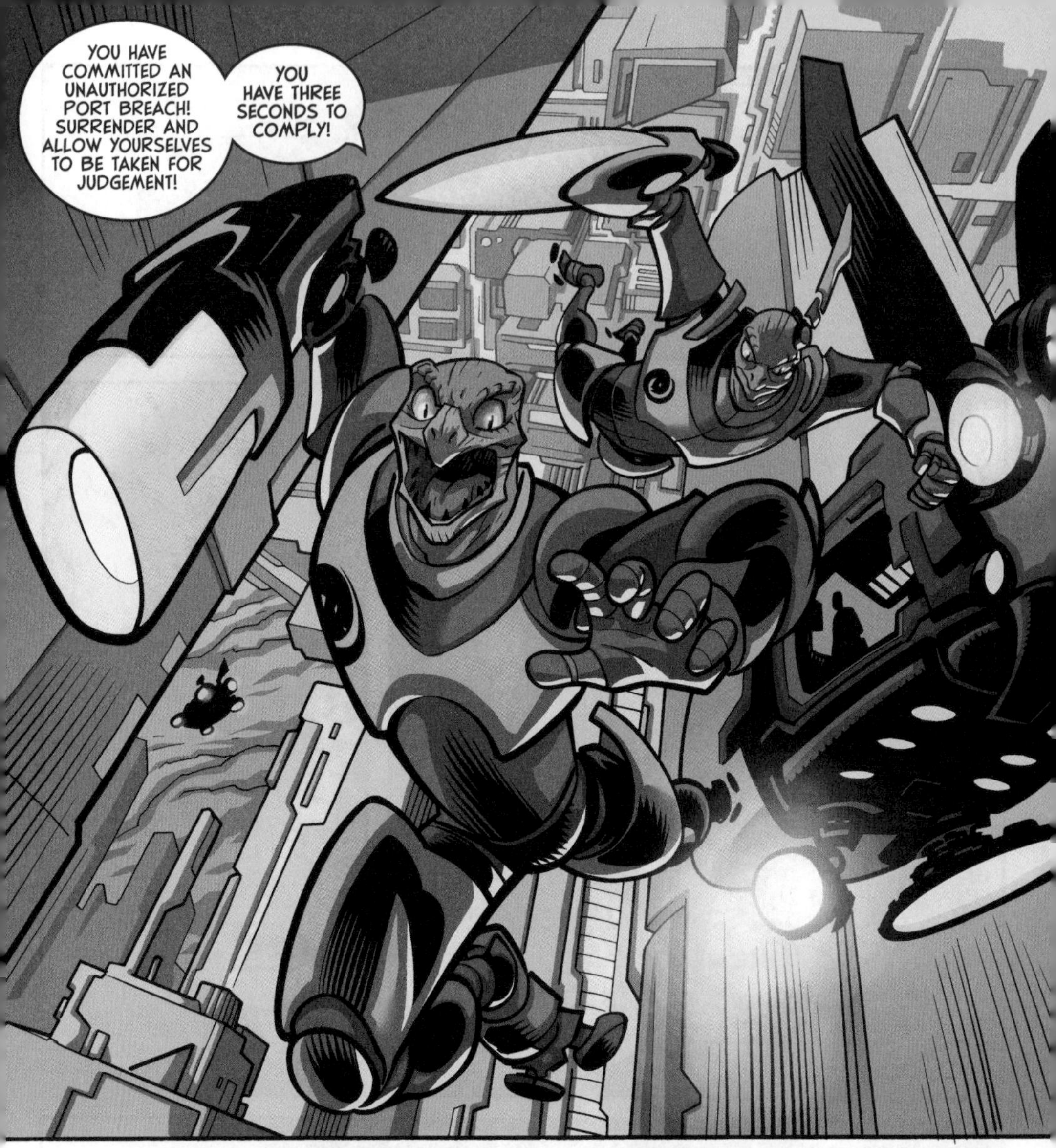
YOU HAVE COMMITTED AN UNAUTHORIZED PORT BREACH! SURRENDER AND ALLOW YOURSELVES TO BE TAKEN FOR JUDGEMENT!
YOU HAVE THREE SECONDS TO COMPLY!

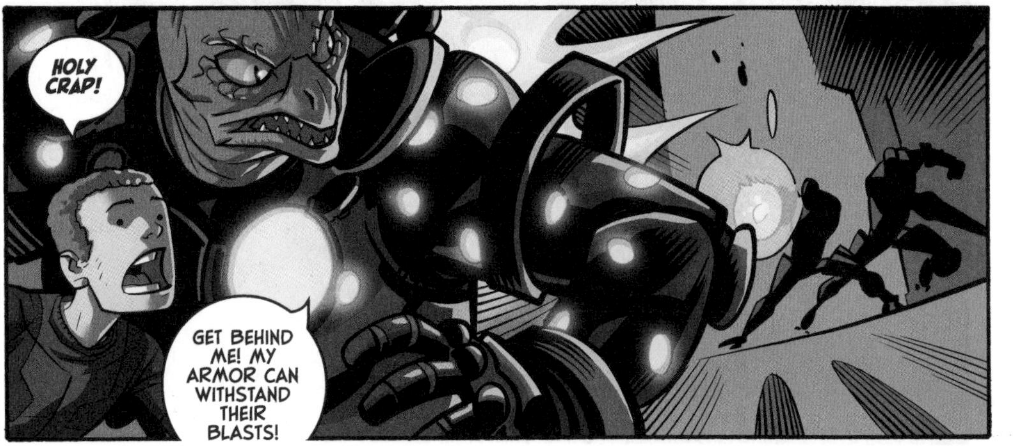
HOLY CRAP!
GET BEHIND ME! MY ARMOR CAN WITHSTAND THEIR BLASTS!

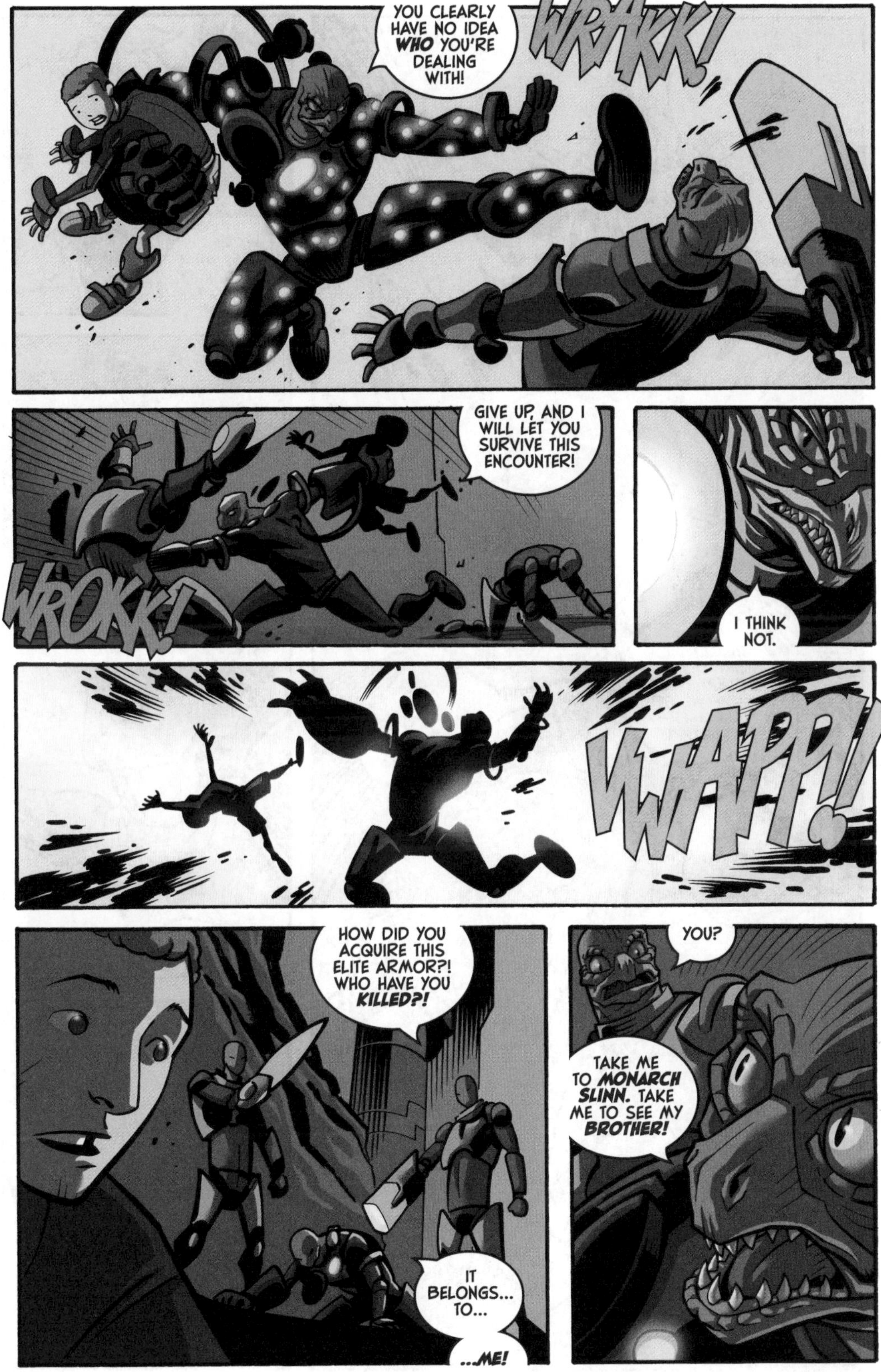
YOU CLEARLY HAVE NO IDEA WHO YOU'RE DEALING WITH!
WRAKK!
GIVE UP, AND I WILL LET YOU SURVIVE THIS ENCOUNTER!
WROKK!
I THINK NOT.
WAPP!!
HOW DID YOU ACQUIRE THIS ELITE ARMOR?! WHO HAVE YOU KILLED?!
IT BELONGS... TO...
...ME!
YOU?
TAKE ME TO MONARCH SLINN. TAKE ME TO SEE MY BROTHER!

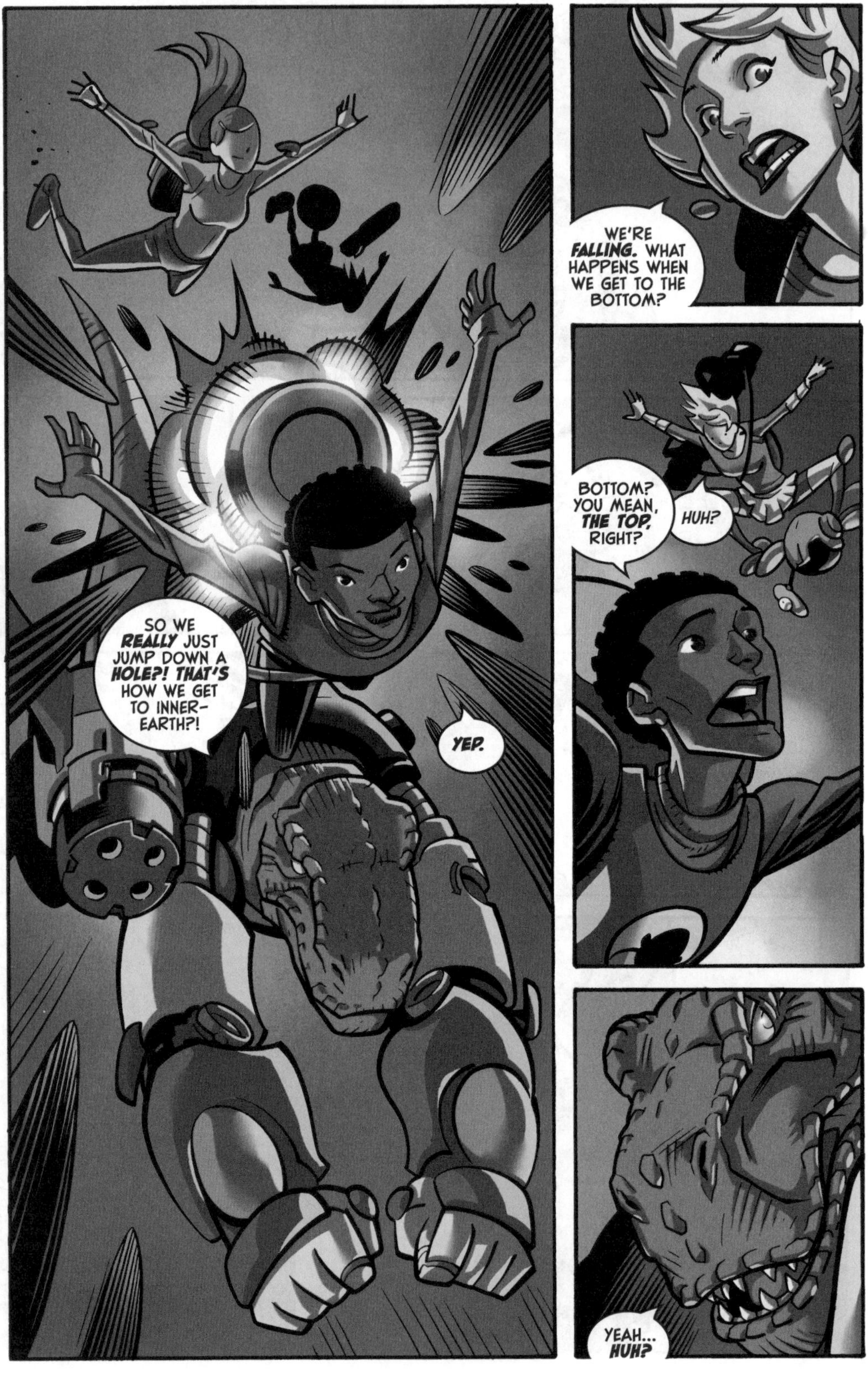

SO WE REALLY JUST JUMP DOWN A HOLE?! THAT'S HOW WE GET TO INNER-EARTH?!
YEP.
WE'RE FALLING. WHAT HAPPENS WHEN WE GET TO THE BOTTOM?
BOTTOM? YOU MEAN, THE TOP, RIGHT?
HUH?
YEAH... HUH?

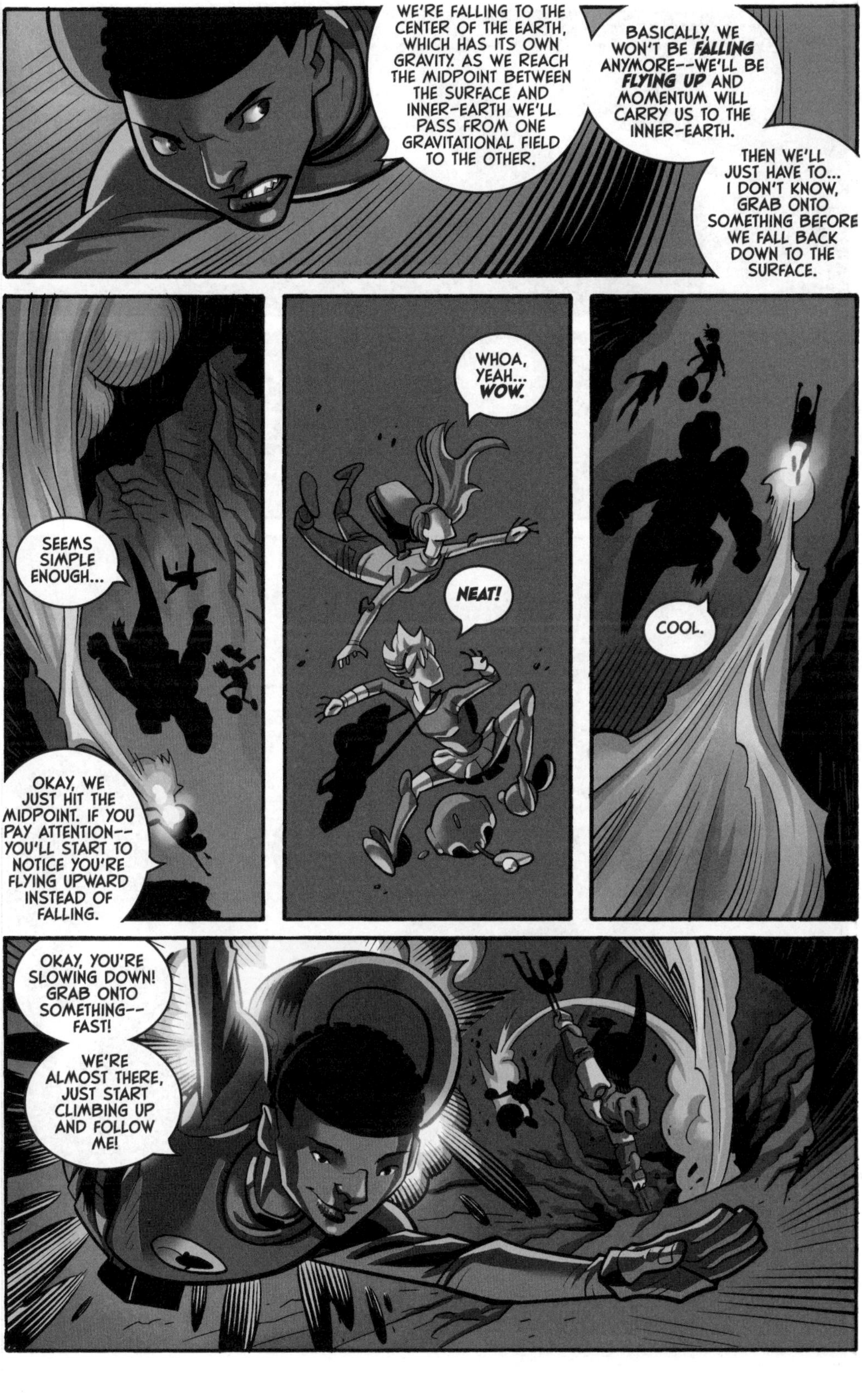
WE'RE FALLING TO THE CENTER OF THE EARTH, WHICH HAS ITS OWN GRAVITY. AS WE REACH THE MIDPOINT BETWEEN THE SURFACE AND INNER-EARTH WE'LL PASS FROM ONE GRAVITATIONAL FIELD TO THE OTHER.
BASICALLY, WE WON'T BE FALLING ANYMORE--WE'LL BE FLYING UP AND MOMENTUM WILL CARRY US TO THE INNER-EARTH.
THEN WE'LL JUST HAVE TO... I DON'T KNOW, GRAB ONTO SOMETHING BEFORE WE FALL BACK DOWN TO THE SURFACE.
SEEMS SIMPLE ENOUGH...
OKAY, WE JUST HIT THE MIDPOINT. IF YOU PAY ATTENTION--YOU'LL START TO NOTICE YOU'RE FLYING UPWARD INSTEAD OF FALLING.
WHOA, YEAH... WOW.
NEAT!
COOL.
OKAY, YOU'RE SLOWING DOWN! GRAB ONTO SOMETHING--FAST!
WE'RE ALMOST THERE, JUST START CLIMBING UP AND FOLLOW ME!

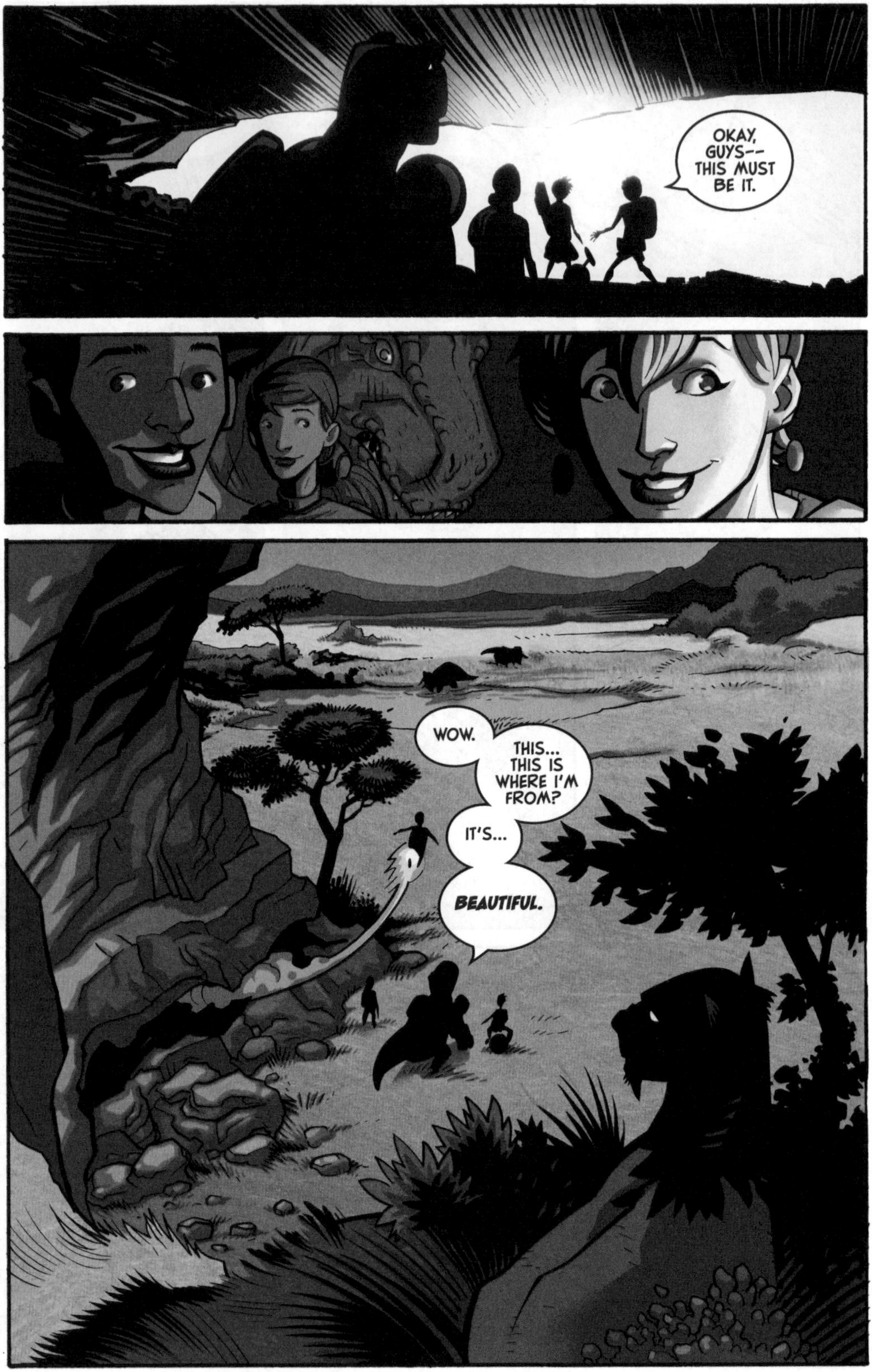
OKAY, GUYS-- THIS MUST BE IT.
WOW.
THIS... THIS IS WHERE I'M FROM?
IT'S...
BEAUTIFUL.

ARE YOU PICKING UP DEREK'S SIGNAL?

THERE'S A LOT OF INTERFERENCE. I NEED TO ADJUST TO COMPENSATE.

MIGHT TAKE A FEW MINUTES.

SD? WHAT'S THE MATTER?

ISN'T THIS *COOL?*

I WAS LONELY *BEFORE* DEREK LEFT... FEELING LIKE I DIDN'T *BELONG.*

I NEVER REALLY FIT IN TO BEGIN WITH... AND WITH DEREK GONE-- IT'S BEEN *WORSE.*

I THOUGHT COMING HERE, SEEING MY OWN KIND WOULD HELP, BUT NOW...

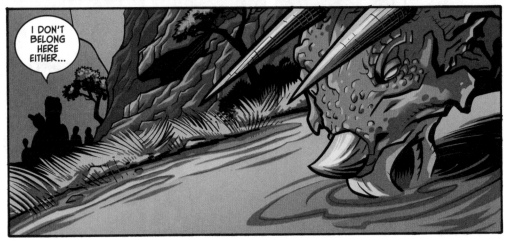

I DON'T BELONG HERE EITHER...

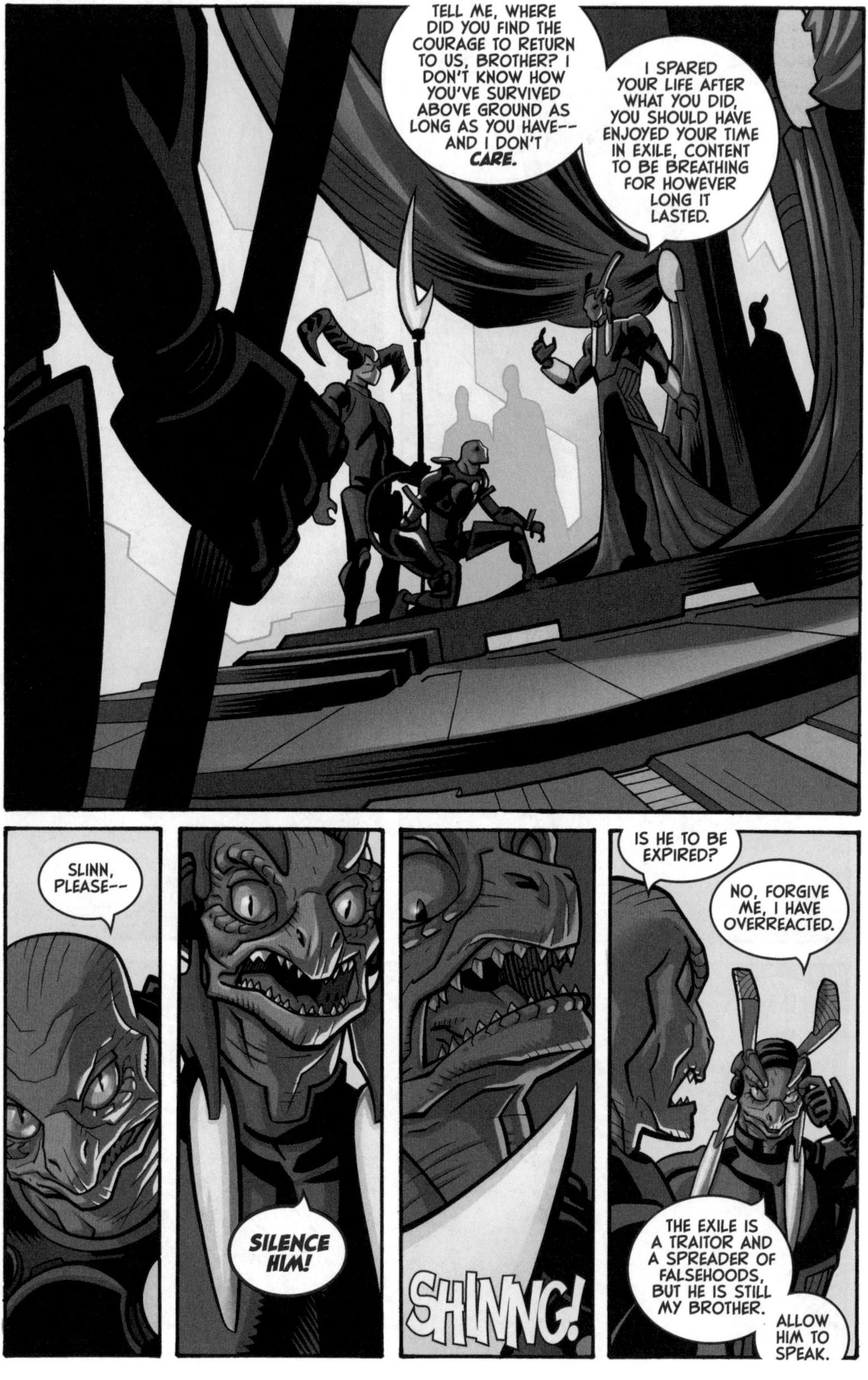
TELL ME, WHERE DID YOU FIND THE COURAGE TO RETURN TO US, BROTHER? I DON'T KNOW HOW YOU'VE SURVIVED ABOVE GROUND AS LONG AS YOU HAVE-- AND I DON'T *CARE.*
I SPARED YOUR LIFE AFTER WHAT YOU DID, YOU SHOULD HAVE ENJOYED YOUR TIME IN EXILE, CONTENT TO BE BREATHING FOR HOWEVER LONG IT LASTED.
SLINN, PLEASE--
SILENCE HIM!
SHINNG!
IS HE TO BE EXPIRED?
NO, FORGIVE ME, I HAVE OVERREACTED.
THE EXILE IS A TRAITOR AND A SPREADER OF FALSEHOODS, BUT HE IS STILL MY BROTHER.
ALLOW HIM TO SPEAK.

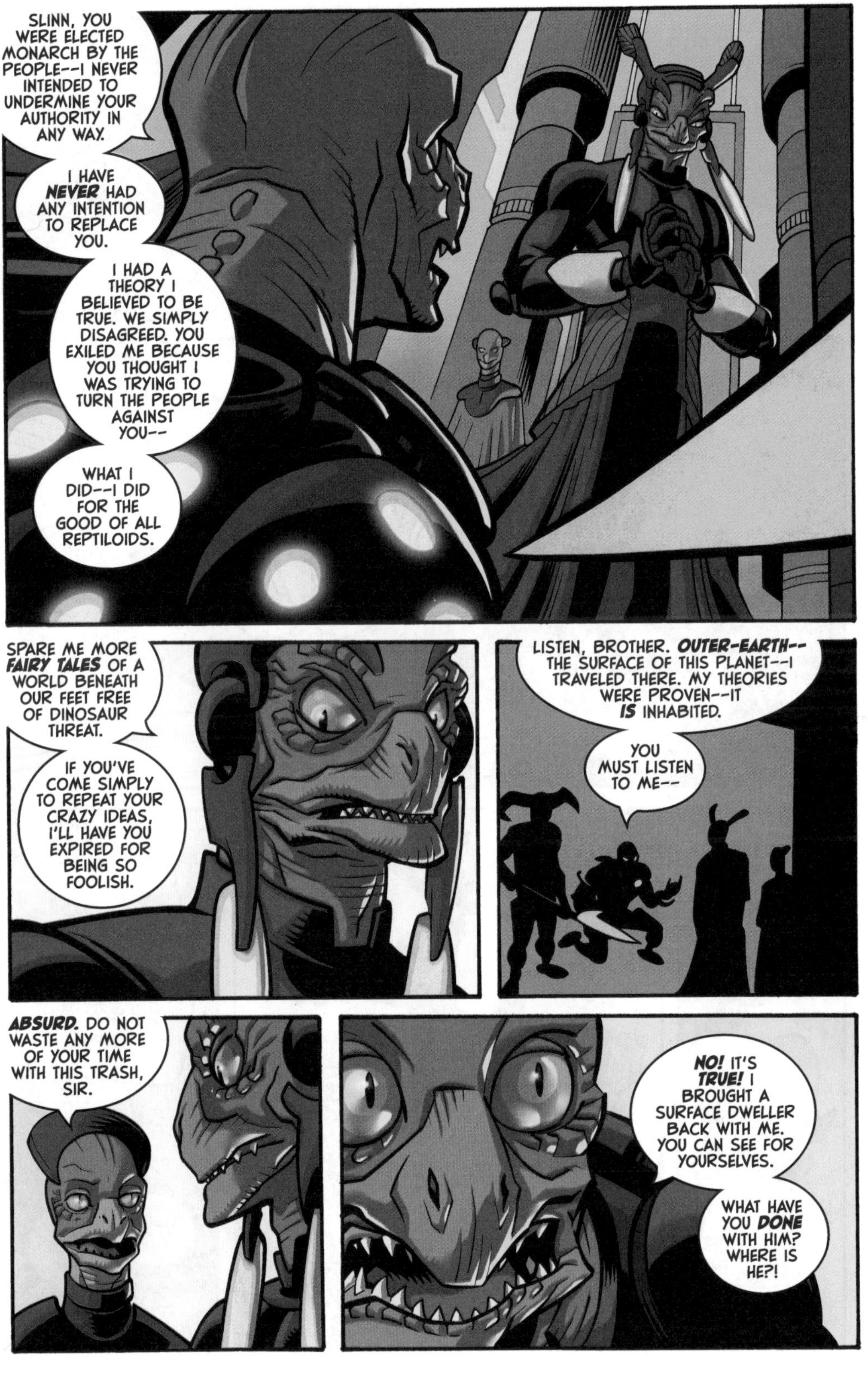
SLINN, YOU WERE ELECTED MONARCH BY THE PEOPLE--I NEVER INTENDED TO UNDERMINE YOUR AUTHORITY IN ANY WAY.
I HAVE **NEVER** HAD ANY INTENTION TO REPLACE YOU.
I HAD A THEORY I BELIEVED TO BE TRUE. WE SIMPLY DISAGREED. YOU EXILED ME BECAUSE YOU THOUGHT I WAS TRYING TO TURN THE PEOPLE AGAINST YOU--
WHAT I DID--I DID FOR THE GOOD OF ALL REPTILOIDS.
SPARE ME MORE **FAIRY TALES** OF A WORLD BENEATH OUR FEET FREE OF DINOSAUR THREAT.
IF YOU'VE COME SIMPLY TO REPEAT YOUR CRAZY IDEAS, I'LL HAVE YOU EXPIRED FOR BEING SO FOOLISH.
LISTEN, BROTHER. **OUTER-EARTH--** THE SURFACE OF THIS PLANET--I TRAVELED THERE. MY THEORIES WERE PROVEN--IT **IS** INHABITED.
YOU MUST LISTEN TO ME--
ABSURD. DO NOT WASTE ANY MORE OF YOUR TIME WITH THIS TRASH, SIR.
NO! IT'S **TRUE!** I BROUGHT A SURFACE DWELLER BACK WITH ME. YOU CAN SEE FOR YOURSELVES.
WHAT HAVE YOU **DONE** WITH HIM? WHERE IS HE?!

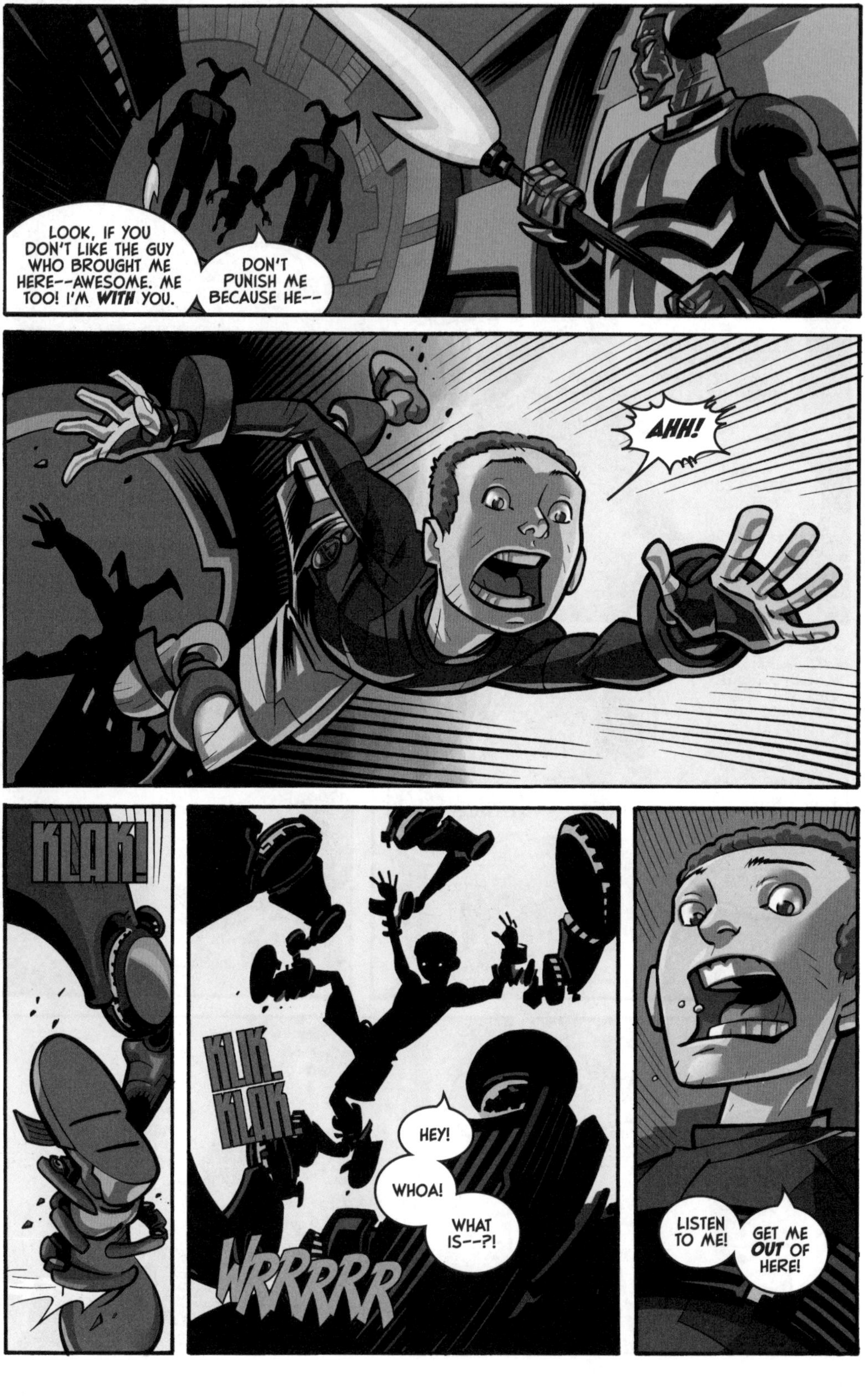
LOOK, IF YOU DON'T LIKE THE GUY WHO BROUGHT ME HERE--AWESOME. ME TOO! I'M WITH YOU.
DON'T PUNISH ME BECAUSE HE--
AHH!
KLAK!
KLIK. KLAK.
HEY!
WHOA!
WHAT IS--?!
WRRRRR
LISTEN TO ME!
GET ME OUT OF HERE!

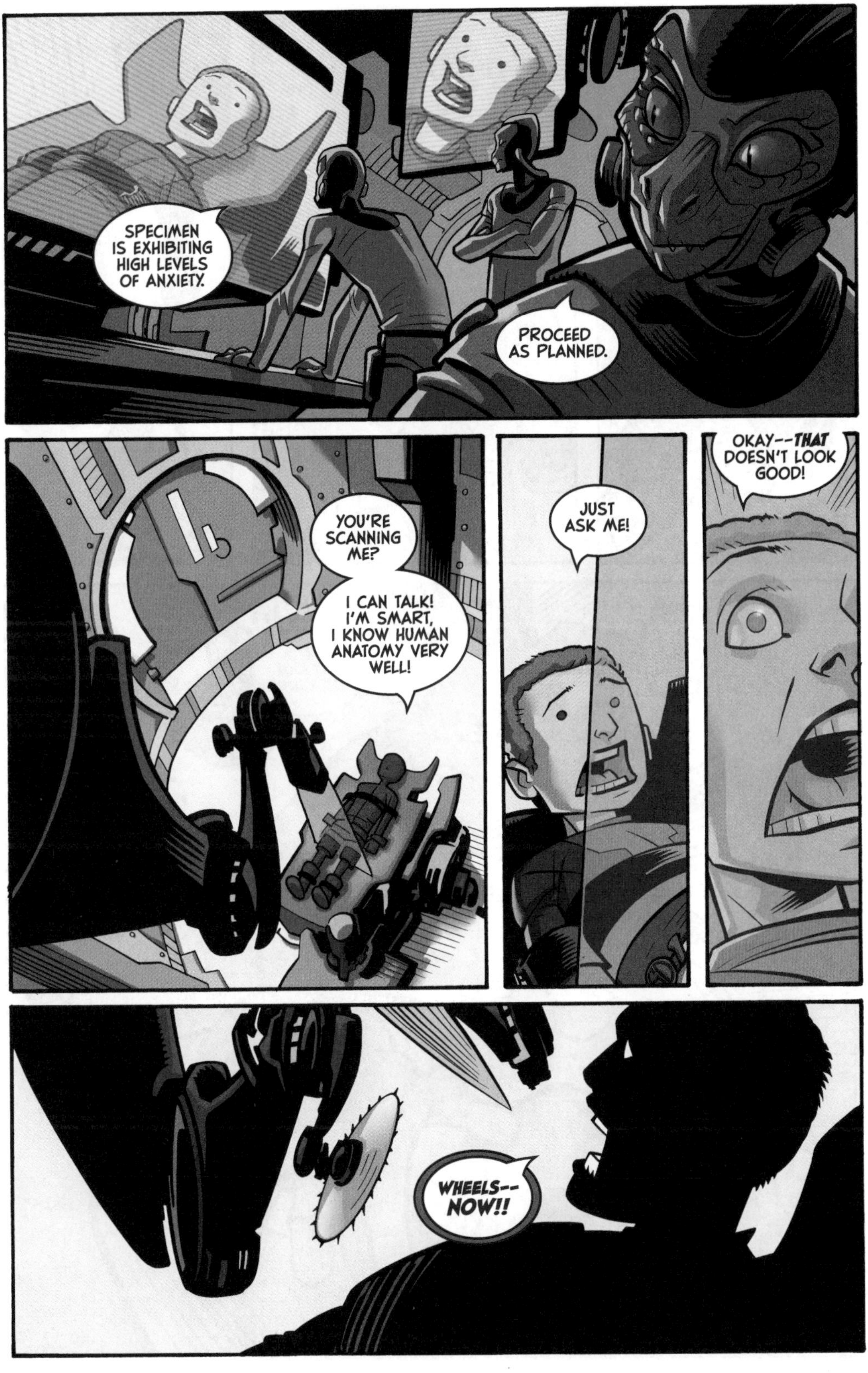
SPECIMEN IS EXHIBITING HIGH LEVELS OF ANXIETY.
PROCEED AS PLANNED.
YOU'RE SCANNING ME?
I CAN TALK! I'M SMART, I KNOW HUMAN ANATOMY VERY WELL!
JUST ASK ME!
OKAY--THAT DOESN'T LOOK GOOD!
WHEELS--NOW!!

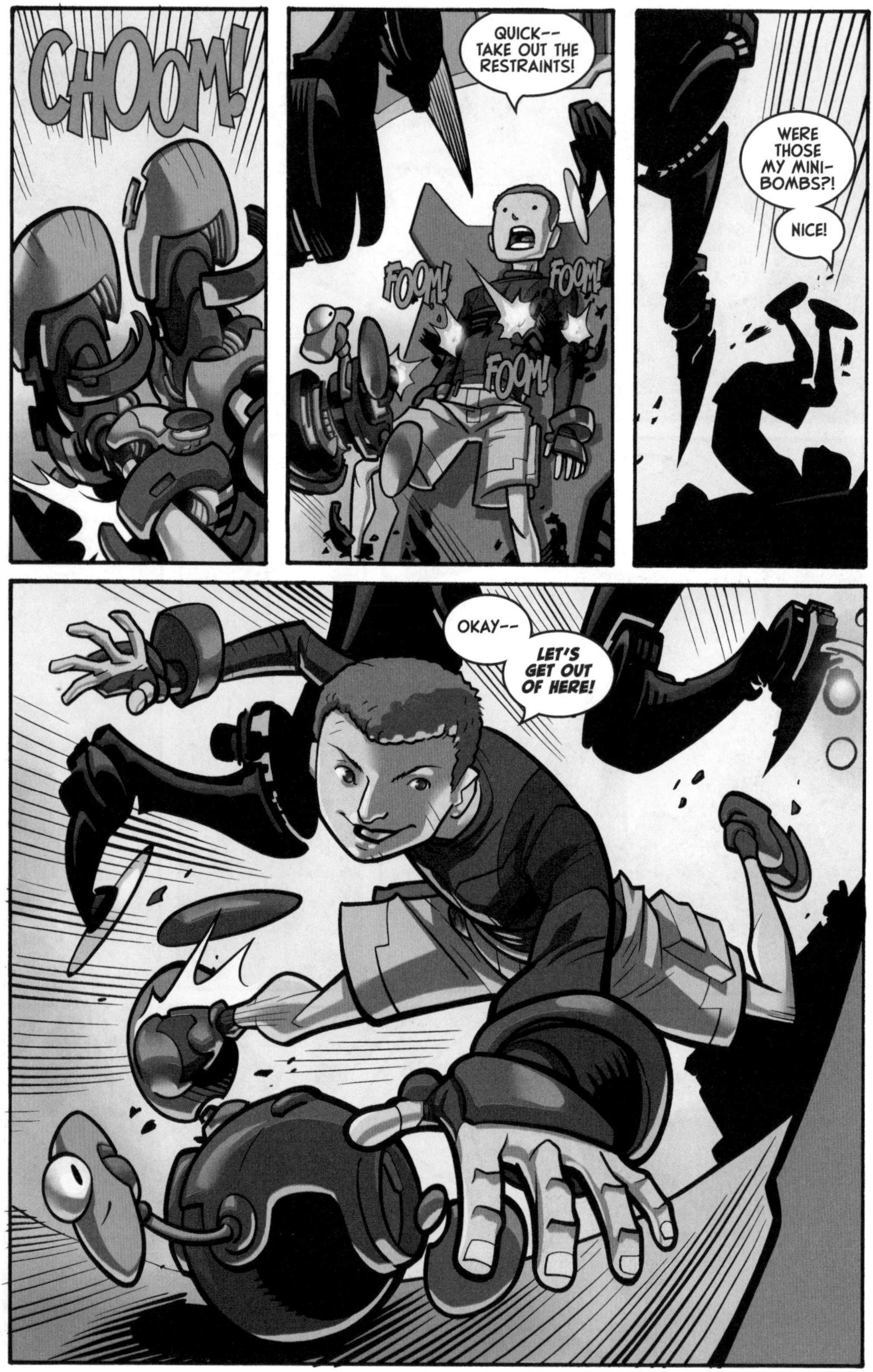
CHOOM!
QUICK-- TAKE OUT THE RESTRAINTS!
FOOM!
FOOM!
FOOM!
WERE THOSE MY MINI-BOMBS?!
NICE!
OKAY--
LET'S GET OUT OF HERE!

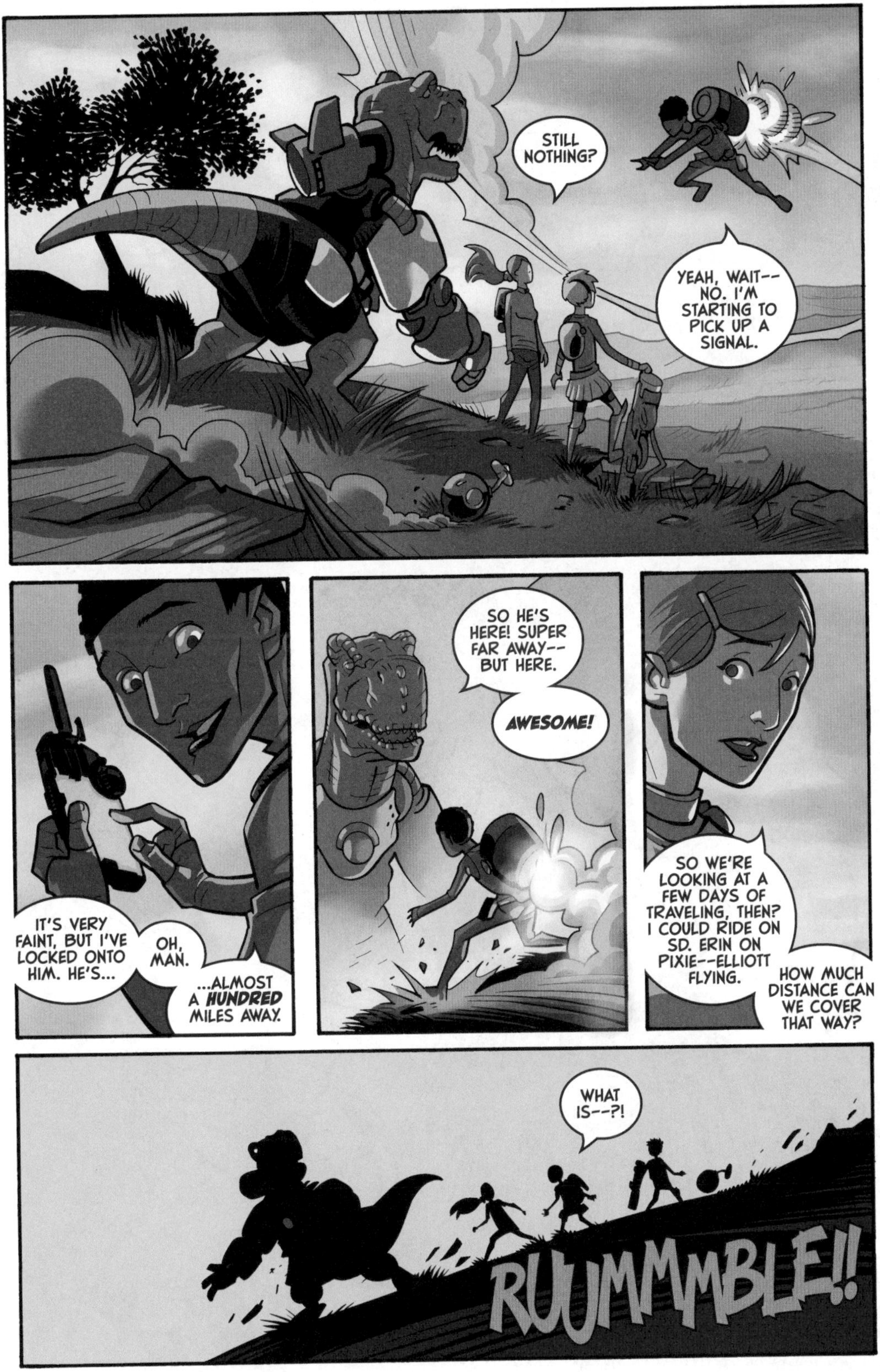
STILL NOTHING?
YEAH, WAIT-- NO. I'M STARTING TO PICK UP A SIGNAL.
IT'S VERY FAINT, BUT I'VE LOCKED ONTO HIM. HE'S...
OH, MAN.
...ALMOST A HUNDRED MILES AWAY.
SO HE'S HERE! SUPER FAR AWAY-- BUT HERE.
AWESOME!
SO WE'RE LOOKING AT A FEW DAYS OF TRAVELING, THEN? I COULD RIDE ON SD. ERIN ON PIXIE--ELLIOTT FLYING.
HOW MUCH DISTANCE CAN WE COVER THAT WAY?
WHAT IS--?!
RUUMMMBLE!!

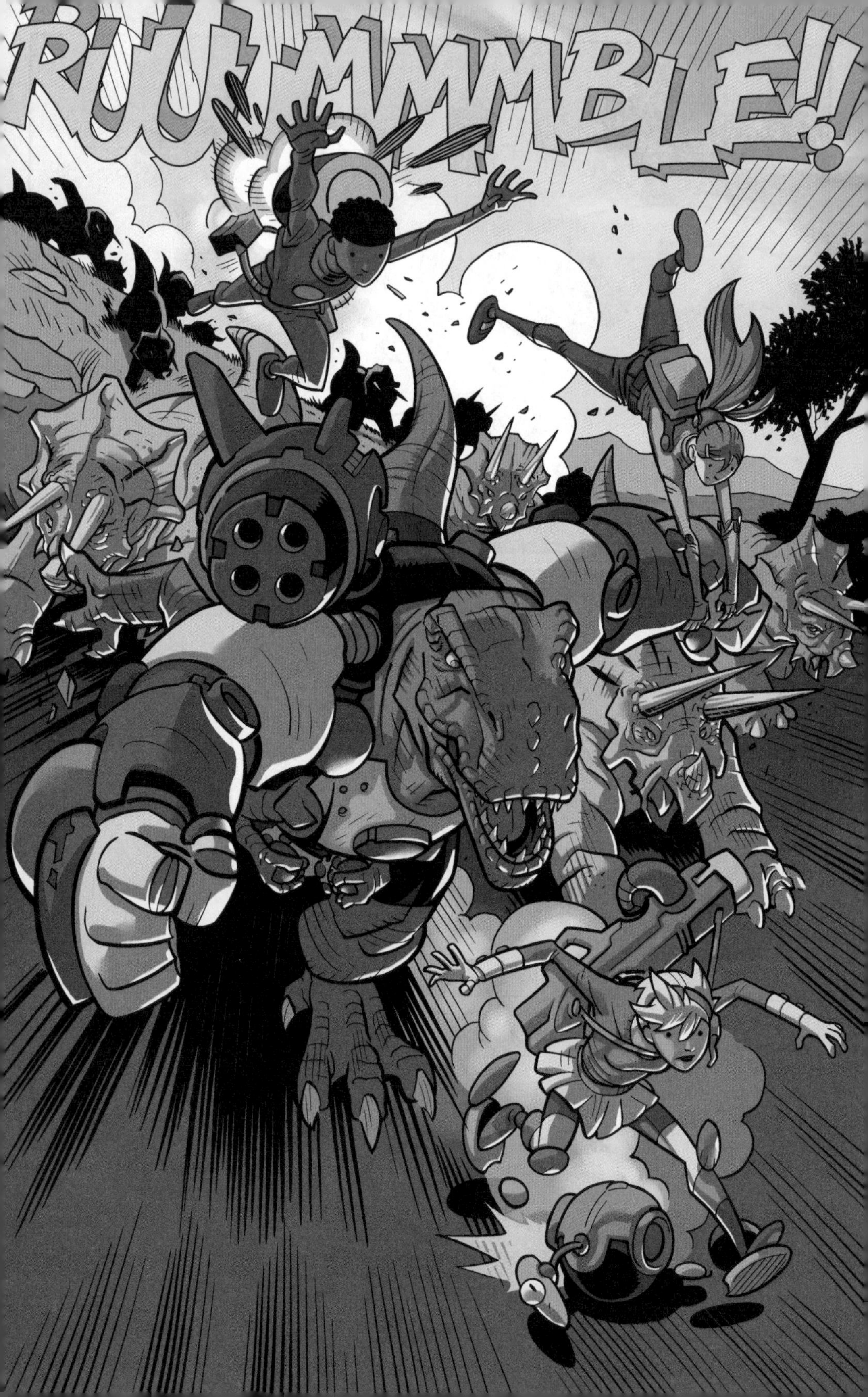
RUUMMMMBLE!!

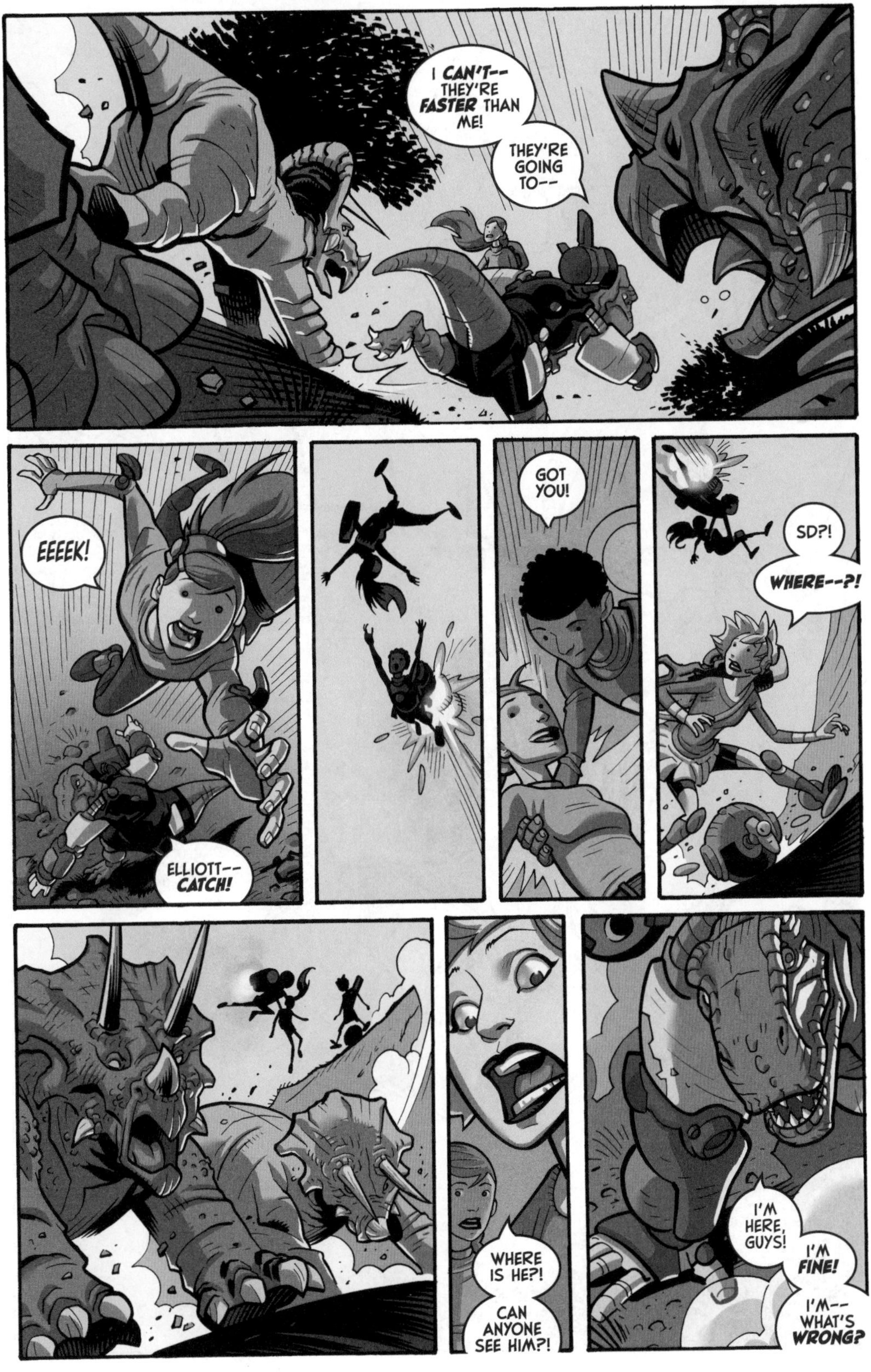
I CAN'T-- THEY'RE FASTER THAN ME!
THEY'RE GOING TO--
EEEEK!
ELLIOTT-- CATCH!
GOT YOU!
SD?!
WHERE--?!
WHERE IS HE?!
CAN ANYONE SEE HIM?!
I'M HERE, GUYS!
I'M FINE!
I'M-- WHAT'S WRONG?

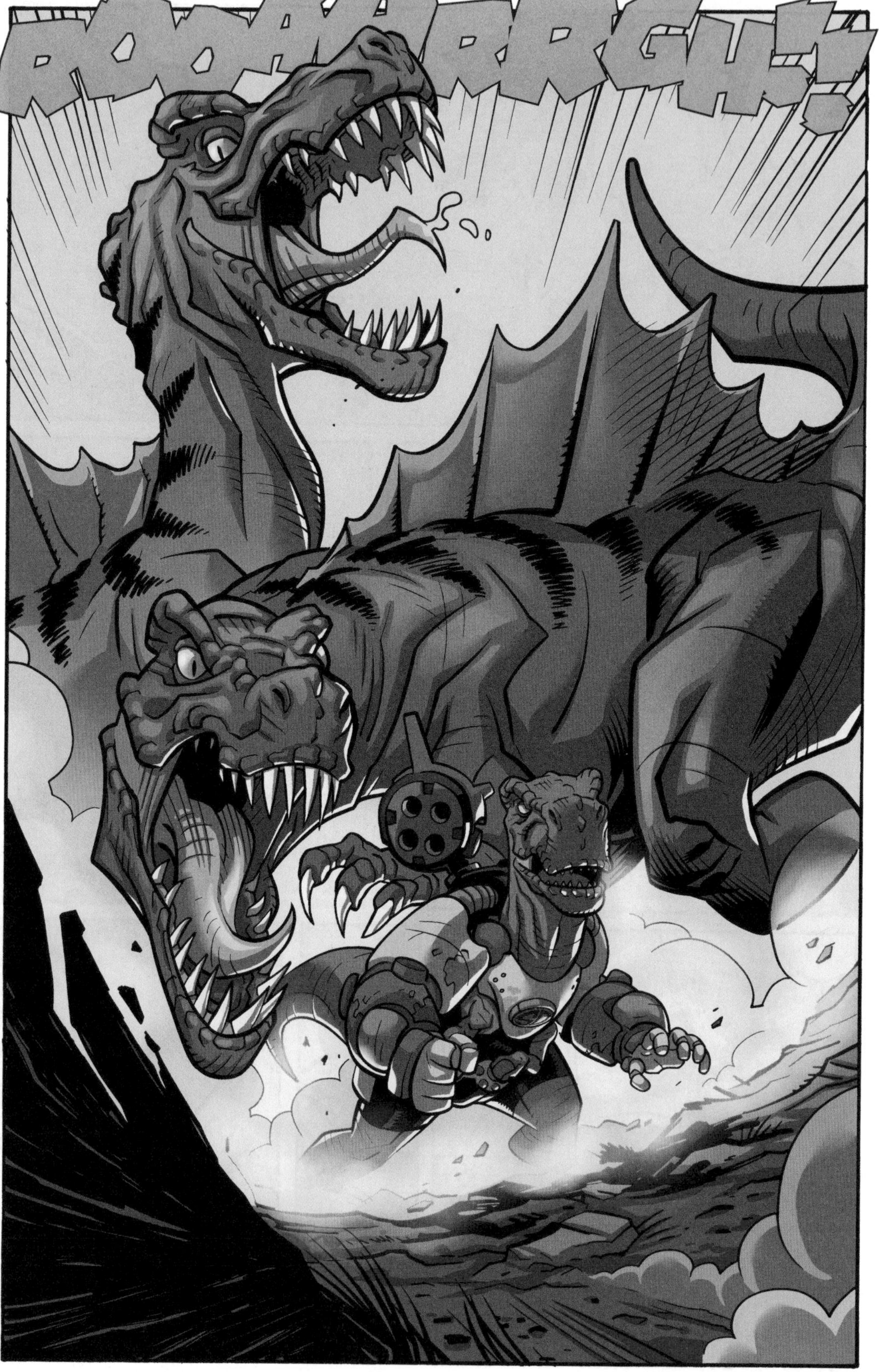
ROOAARRGH!!

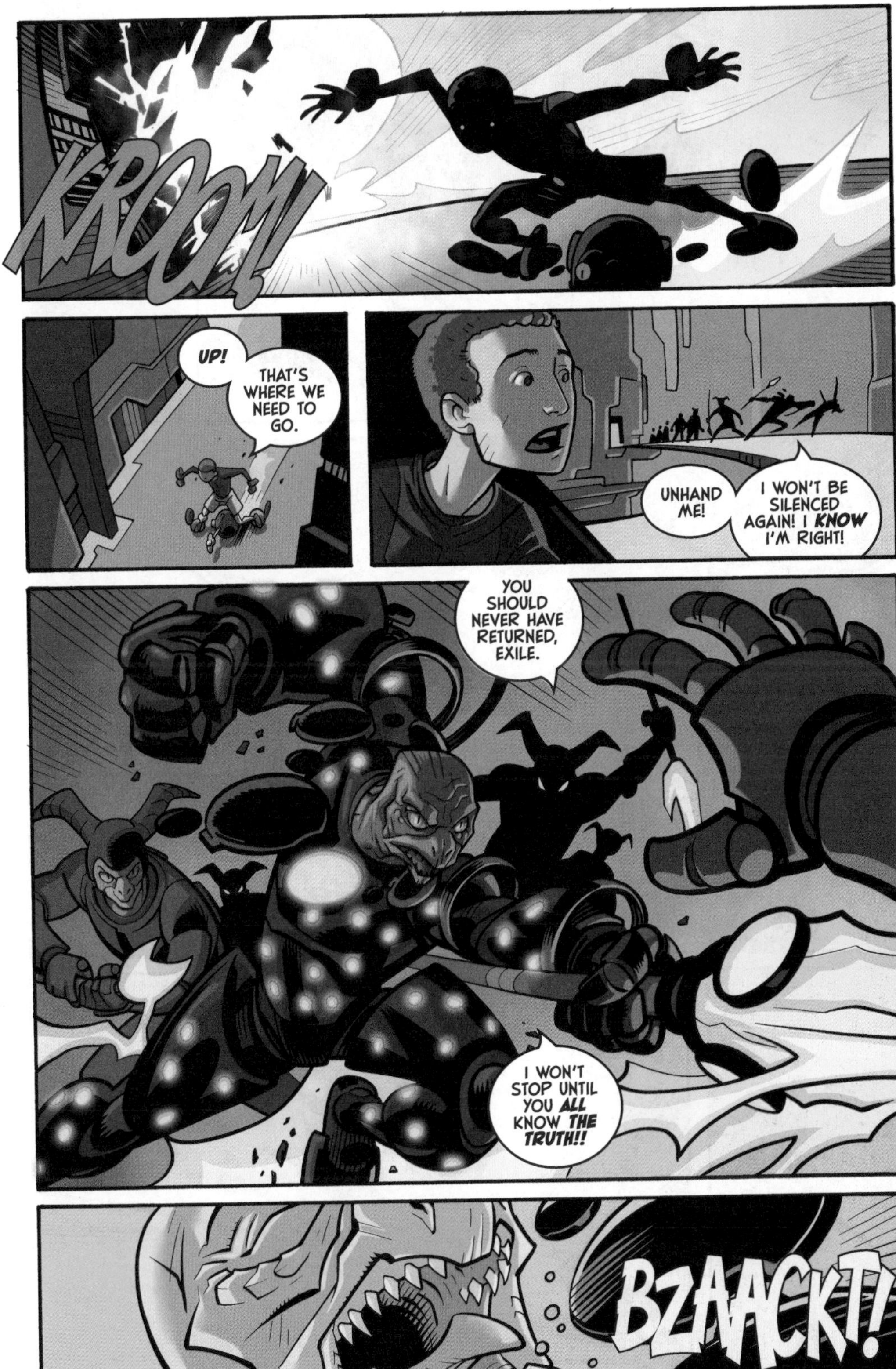
KROOM!
UP!
THAT'S WHERE WE NEED TO GO.
UNHAND ME!
I WON'T BE SILENCED AGAIN! I KNOW I'M RIGHT!
YOU SHOULD NEVER HAVE RETURNED, EXILE.
I WON'T STOP UNTIL YOU ALL KNOW THE TRUTH!!
BZAACKT!

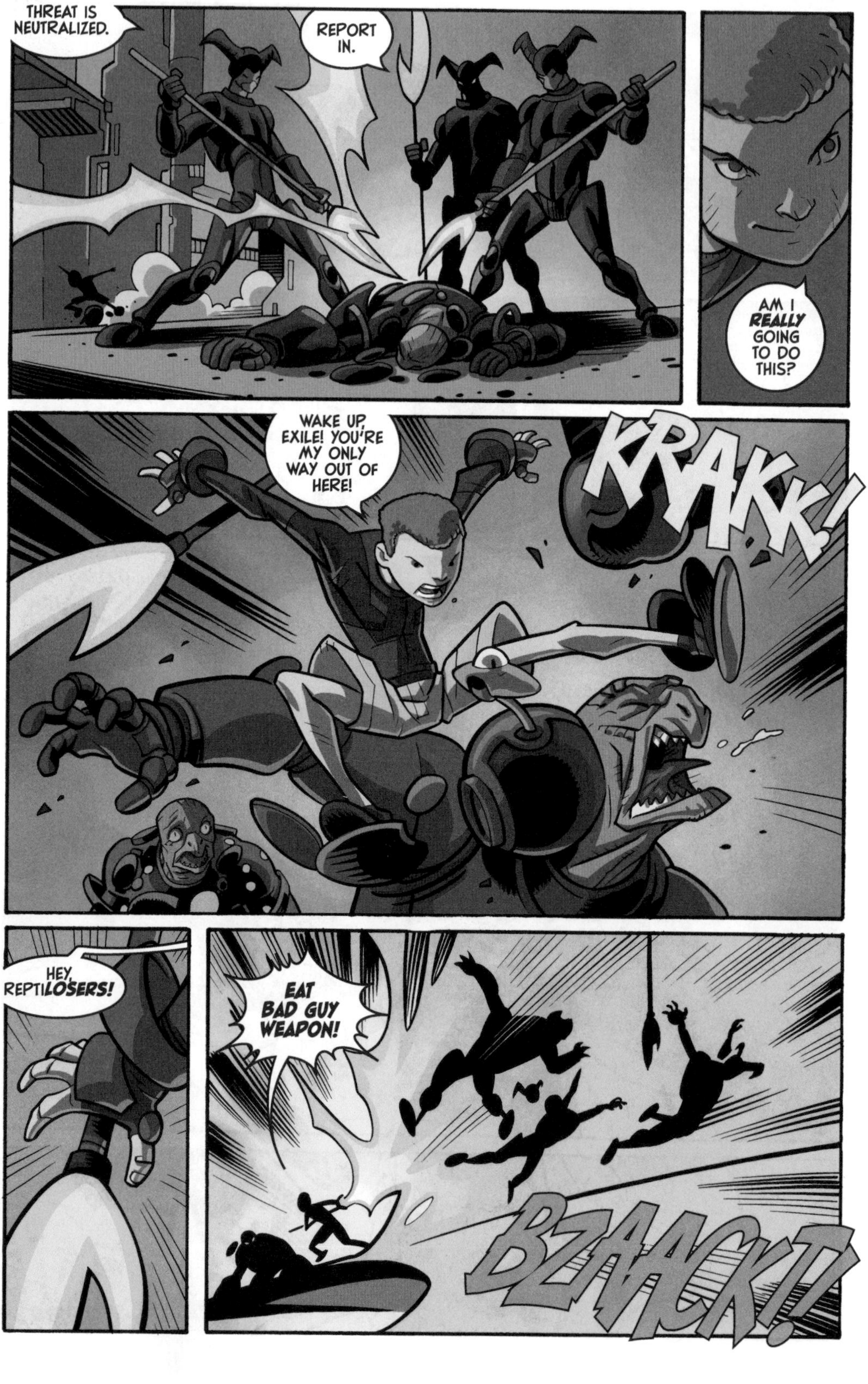
THREAT IS NEUTRALIZED.
REPORT IN.
AM I *REALLY* GOING TO DO THIS?
WAKE UP, EXILE! YOU'RE MY ONLY WAY OUT OF HERE!
KRAKK!
HEY, REPTI*LOSERS!*
EAT BAD GUY WEAPON!
BZAACK!!

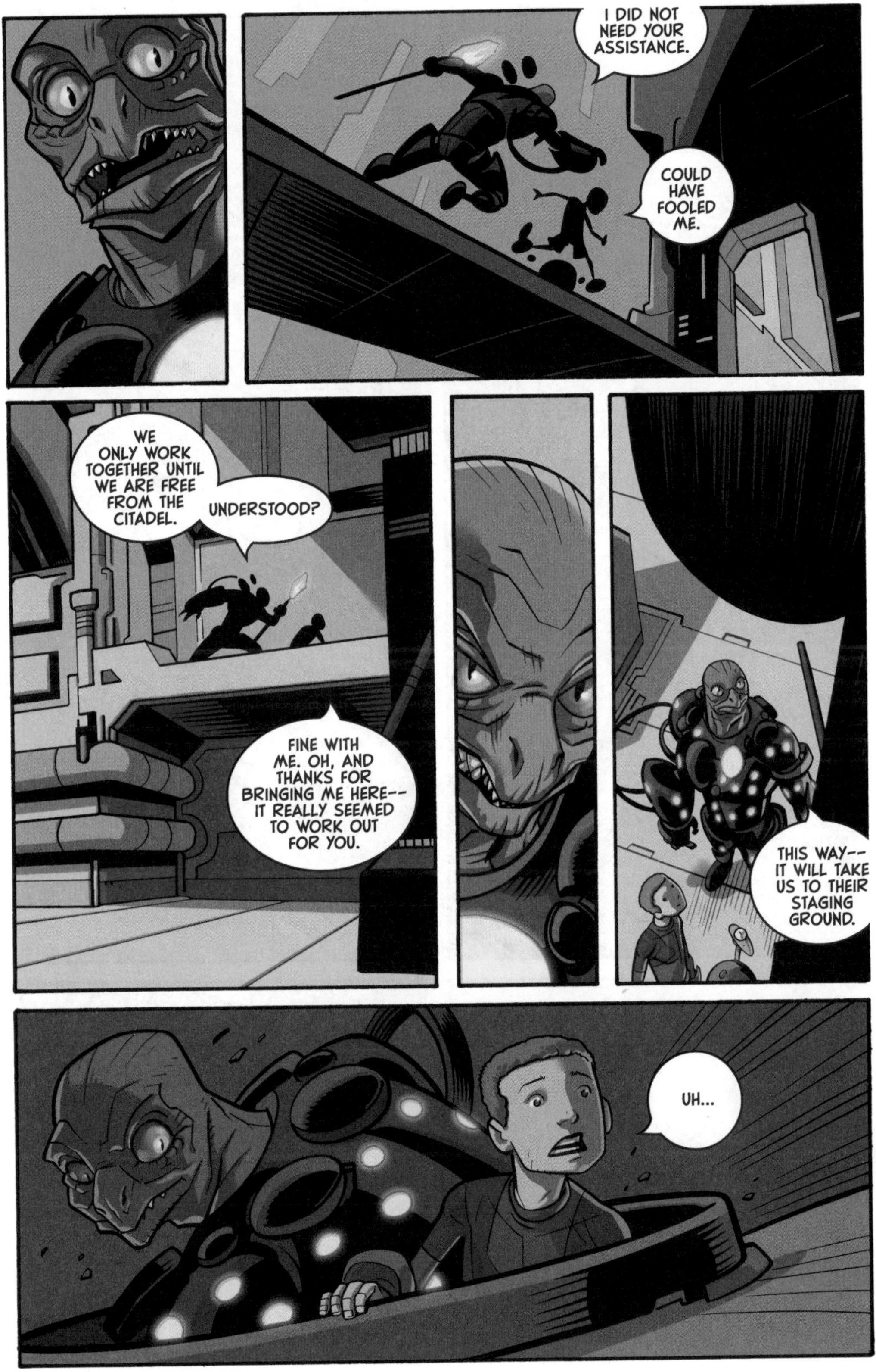
I DID NOT NEED YOUR ASSISTANCE.
COULD HAVE FOOLED ME.
WE ONLY WORK TOGETHER UNTIL WE ARE FREE FROM THE CITADEL.
UNDERSTOOD?
FINE WITH ME. OH, AND THANKS FOR BRINGING ME HERE--IT REALLY SEEMED TO WORK OUT FOR YOU.
THIS WAY--IT WILL TAKE US TO THEIR STAGING GROUND.
UH...

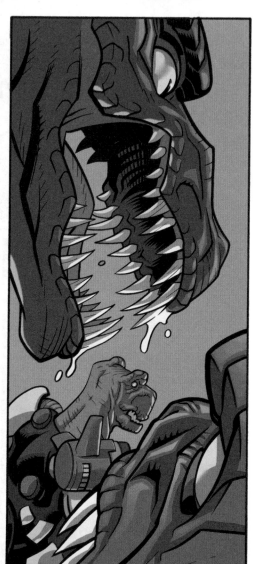

OH, CRAP.

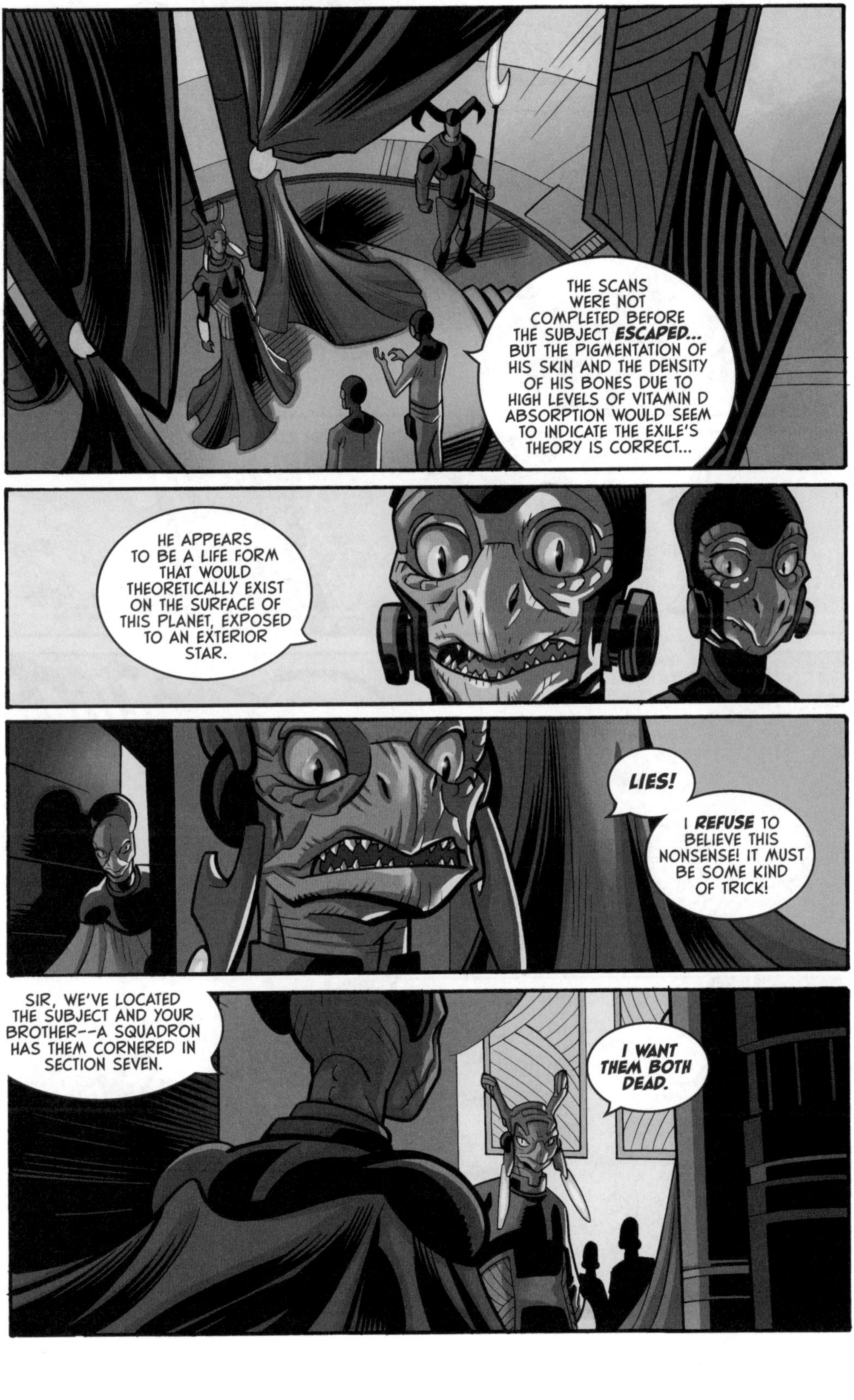
THE SCANS WERE NOT COMPLETED BEFORE THE SUBJECT ***ESCAPED...*** BUT THE PIGMENTATION OF HIS SKIN AND THE DENSITY OF HIS BONES DUE TO HIGH LEVELS OF VITAMIN D ABSORPTION WOULD SEEM TO INDICATE THE EXILE'S THEORY IS CORRECT...
HE APPEARS TO BE A LIFE FORM THAT WOULD THEORETICALLY EXIST ON THE SURFACE OF THIS PLANET, EXPOSED TO AN EXTERIOR STAR.
LIES!
I ***REFUSE*** TO BELIEVE THIS NONSENSE! IT MUST BE SOME KIND OF TRICK!
SIR, WE'VE LOCATED THE SUBJECT AND YOUR BROTHER--A SQUADRON HAS THEM CORNERED IN SECTION SEVEN.
I WANT THEM BOTH DEAD.

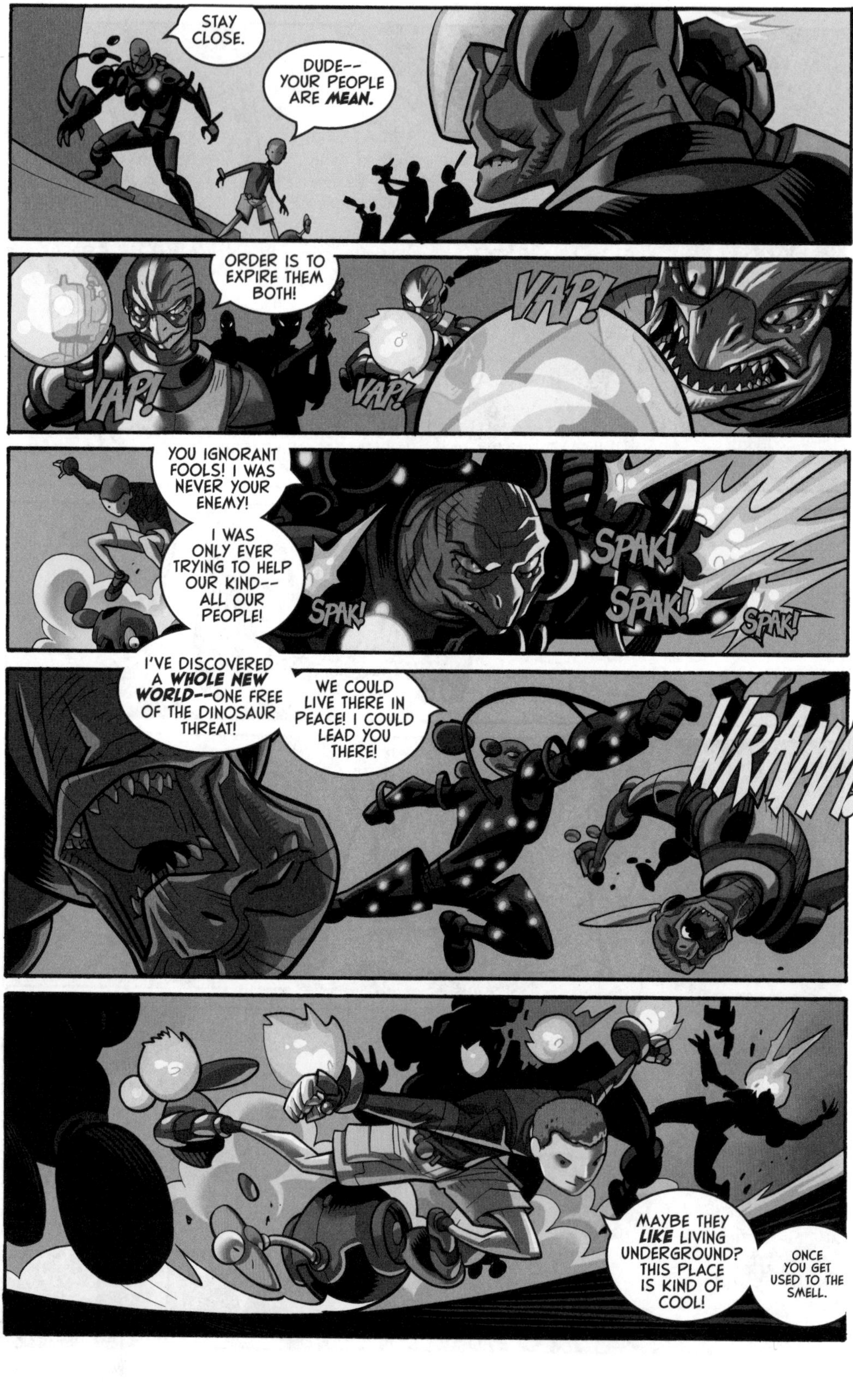
STAY CLOSE.
DUDE-- YOUR PEOPLE ARE MEAN.
ORDER IS TO EXPIRE THEM BOTH!
VAP!
VAP!
VAP!
YOU IGNORANT FOOLS! I WAS NEVER YOUR ENEMY!
I WAS ONLY EVER TRYING TO HELP OUR KIND-- ALL OUR PEOPLE!
SPAK!
SPAK!
SPAK!
SPAK!
I'VE DISCOVERED A WHOLE NEW WORLD--ONE FREE OF THE DINOSAUR THREAT!
WE COULD LIVE THERE IN PEACE! I COULD LEAD YOU THERE!
WRAMM!
MAYBE THEY LIKE LIVING UNDERGROUND? THIS PLACE IS KIND OF COOL!
ONCE YOU GET USED TO THE SMELL.

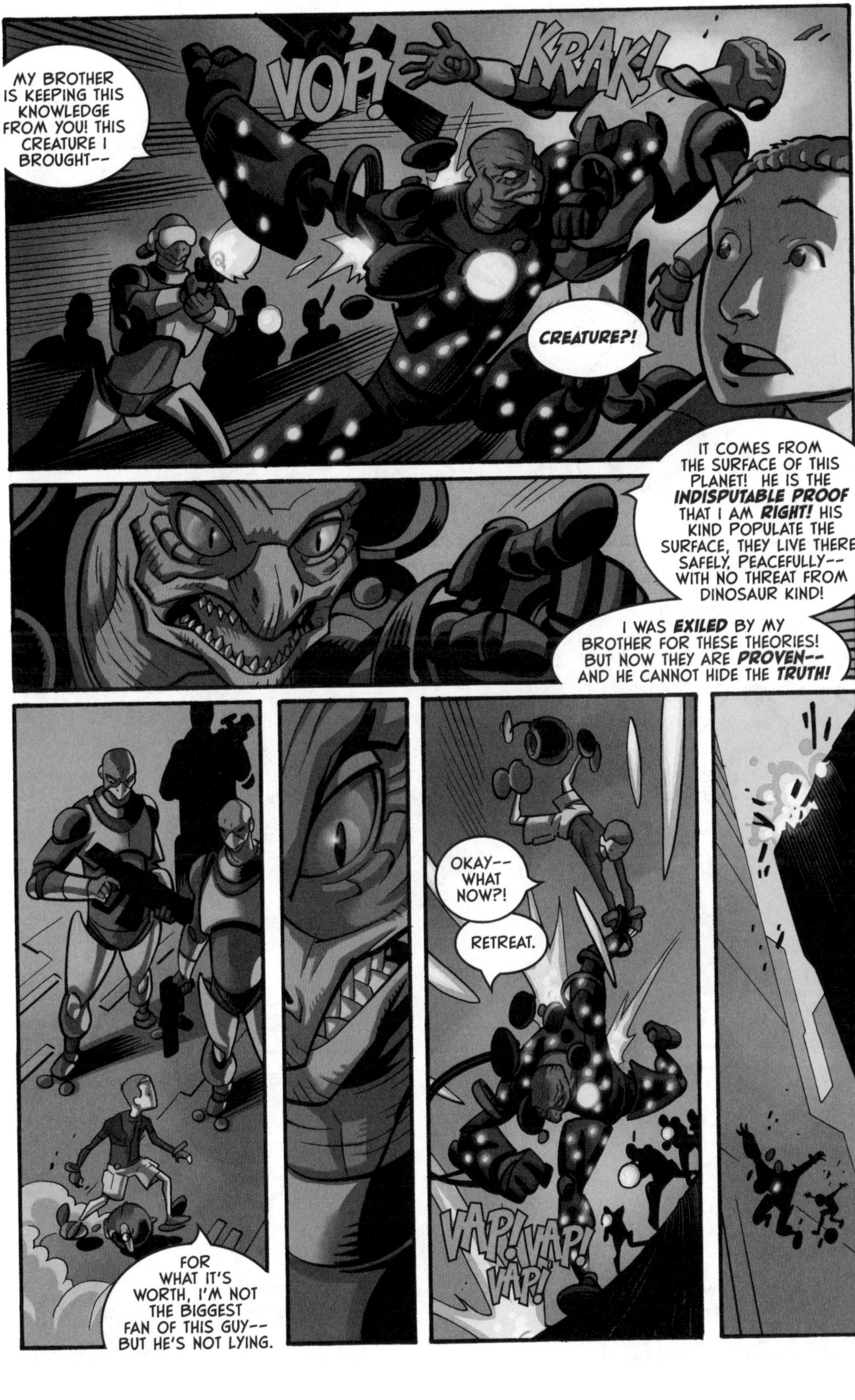
MY BROTHER IS KEEPING THIS KNOWLEDGE FROM YOU! THIS CREATURE I BROUGHT--
VOP!
KRAK!
CREATURE?!
IT COMES FROM THE SURFACE OF THIS PLANET! HE IS THE **INDISPUTABLE PROOF** THAT I AM **RIGHT!** HIS KIND POPULATE THE SURFACE, THEY LIVE THERE, SAFELY, PEACEFULLY-- WITH NO THREAT FROM DINOSAUR KIND!
I WAS **EXILED** BY MY BROTHER FOR THESE THEORIES! BUT NOW THEY ARE **PROVEN--** AND HE CANNOT HIDE THE **TRUTH!**
FOR WHAT IT'S WORTH, I'M NOT THE BIGGEST FAN OF THIS GUY-- BUT HE'S NOT LYING.
OKAY-- WHAT NOW?!
RETREAT.
VAP! VAP! VAP!

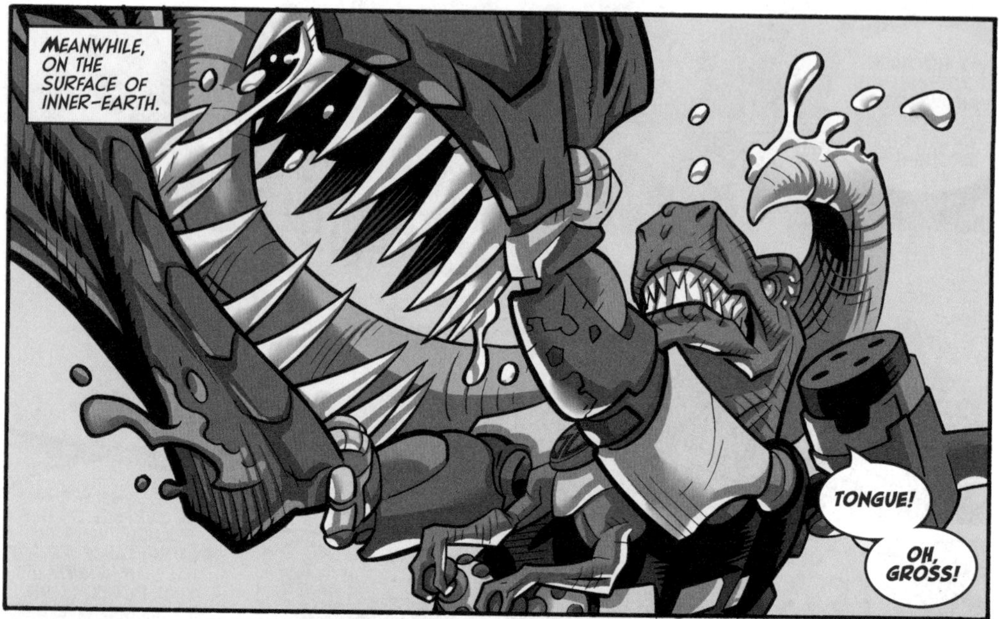
MEANWHILE, ON THE SURFACE OF INNER-EARTH.
TONGUE!
OH, GROSS!

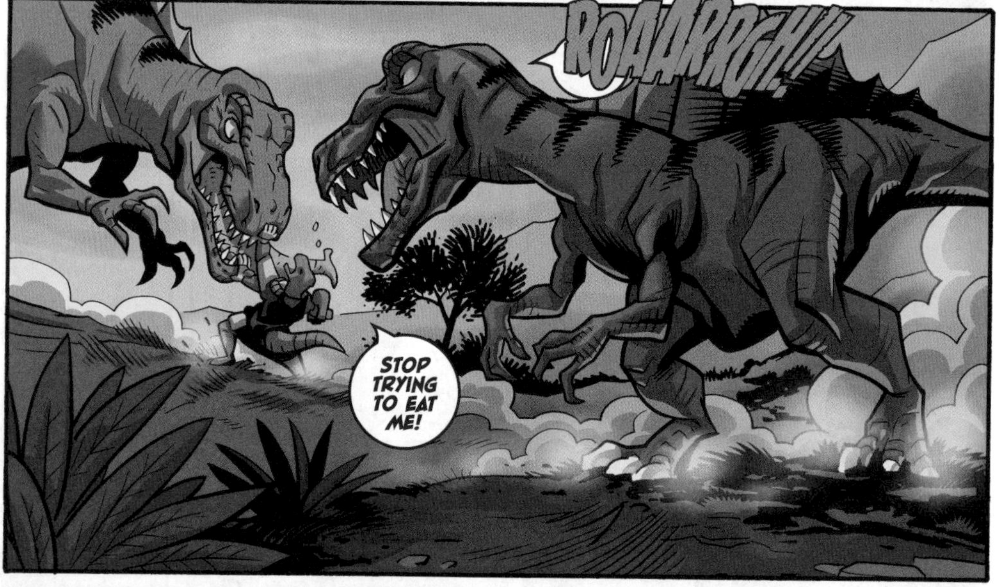
ROAAARRGH!!
STOP TRYING TO EAT ME!

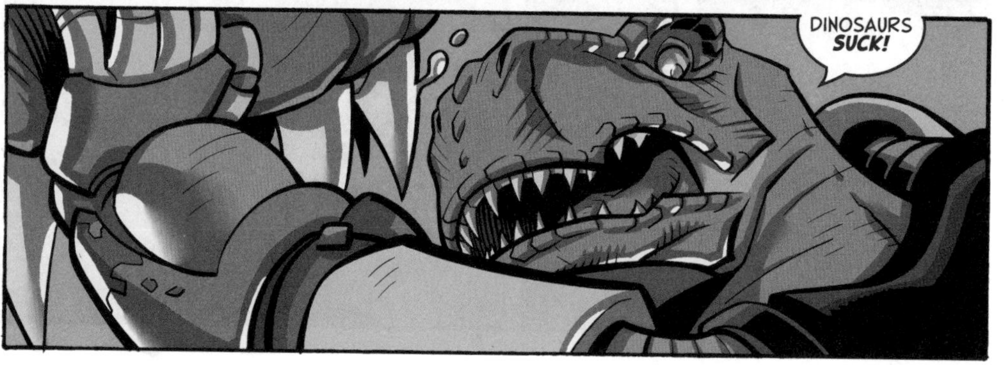
DINOSAURS SUCK!

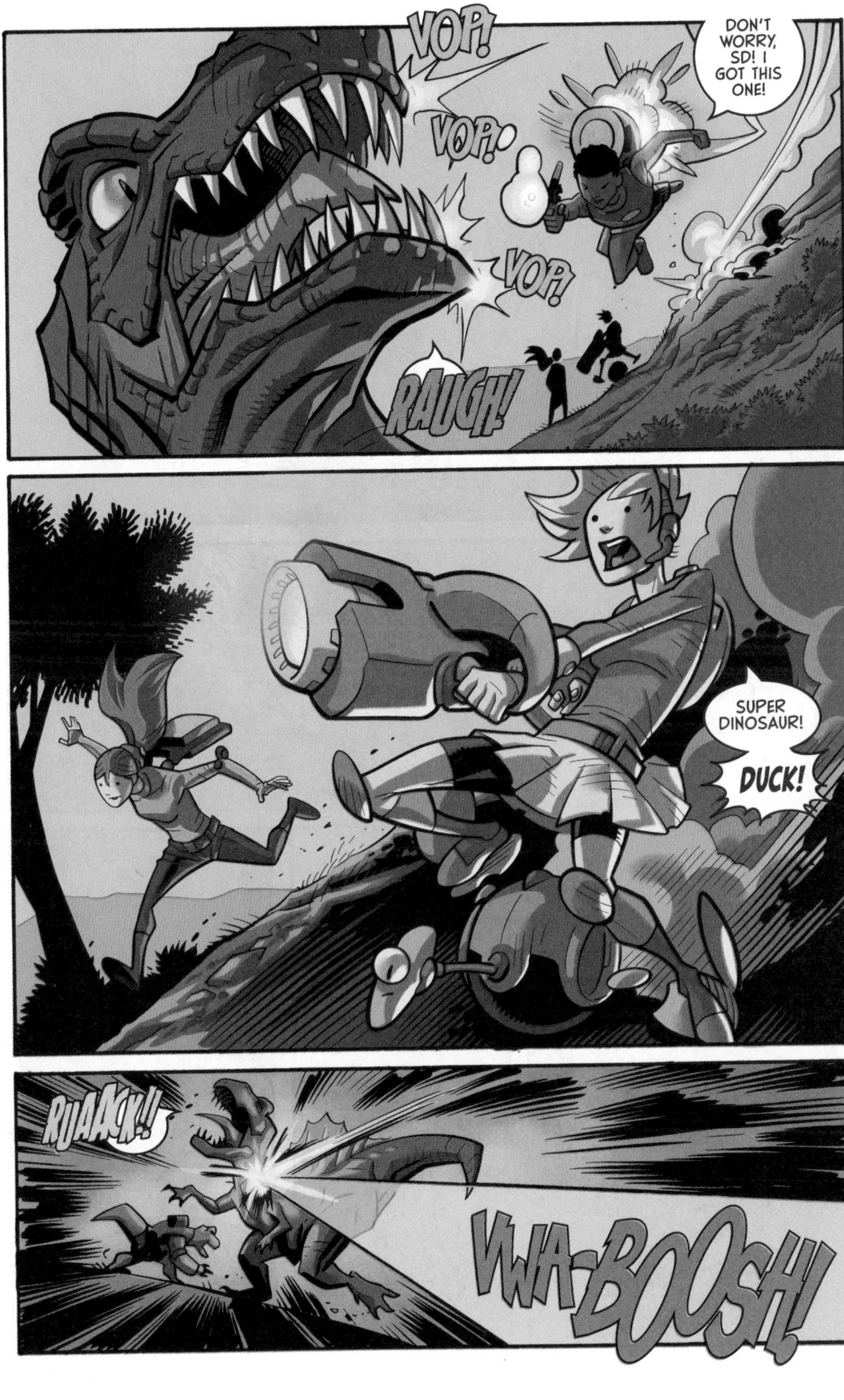
VOP!
VOP!
VOP!
DON'T WORRY, SD! I GOT THIS ONE!
RAUGH!
SUPER DINOSAUR!
DUCK!
RUAAACK!!
VWA-BOOSH!

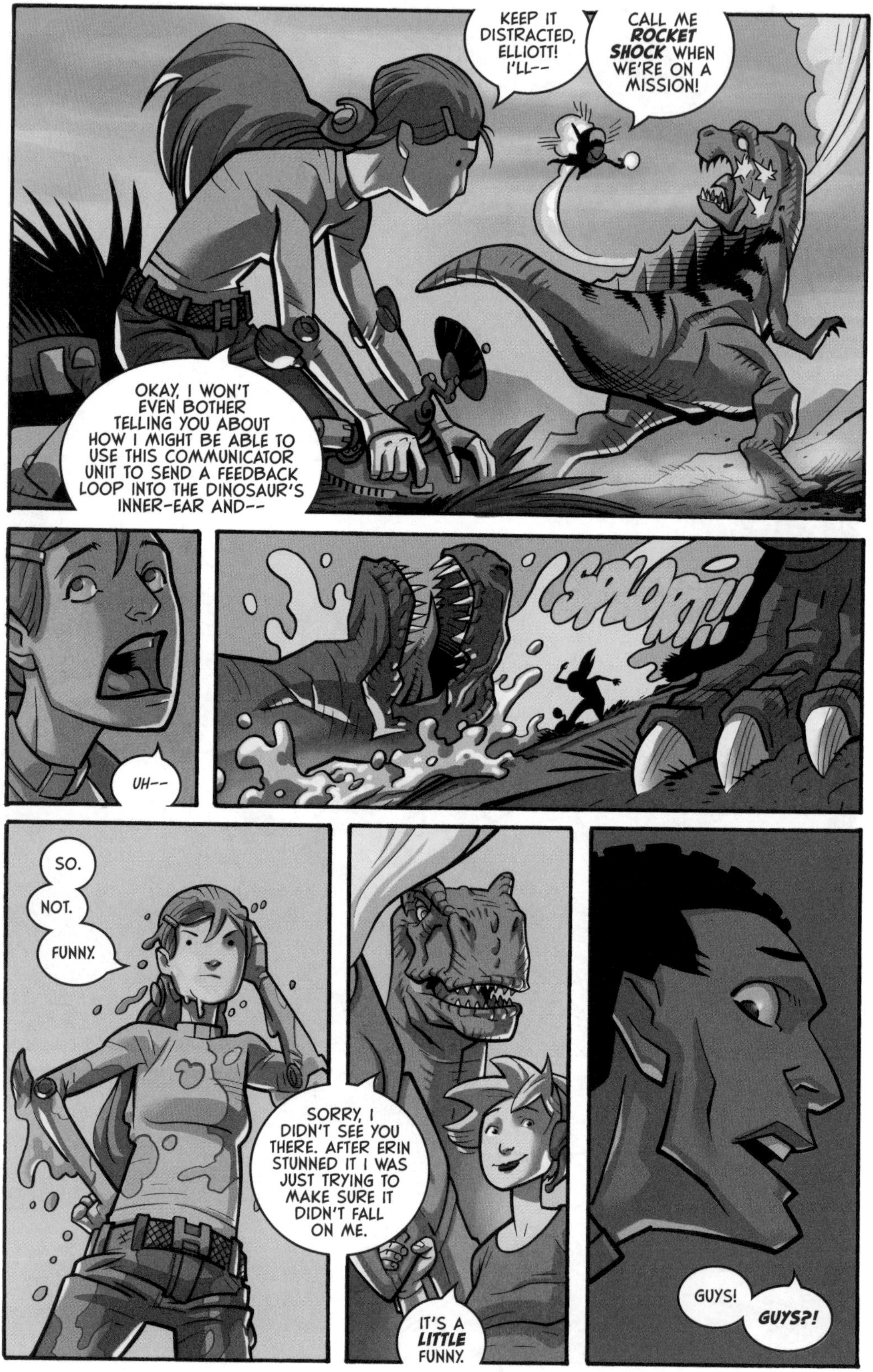
KEEP IT DISTRACTED, ELLIOTT! I'LL--
CALL ME ROCKET SHOCK WHEN WE'RE ON A MISSION!
OKAY, I WON'T EVEN BOTHER TELLING YOU ABOUT HOW I MIGHT BE ABLE TO USE THIS COMMUNICATOR UNIT TO SEND A FEEDBACK LOOP INTO THE DINOSAUR'S INNER-EAR AND--
UH--
SPLORT!!
SO.
NOT.
FUNNY.
SORRY, I DIDN'T SEE YOU THERE. AFTER ERIN STUNNED IT I WAS JUST TRYING TO MAKE SURE IT DIDN'T FALL ON ME.
IT'S A LITTLE FUNNY.
GUYS!
GUYS?!

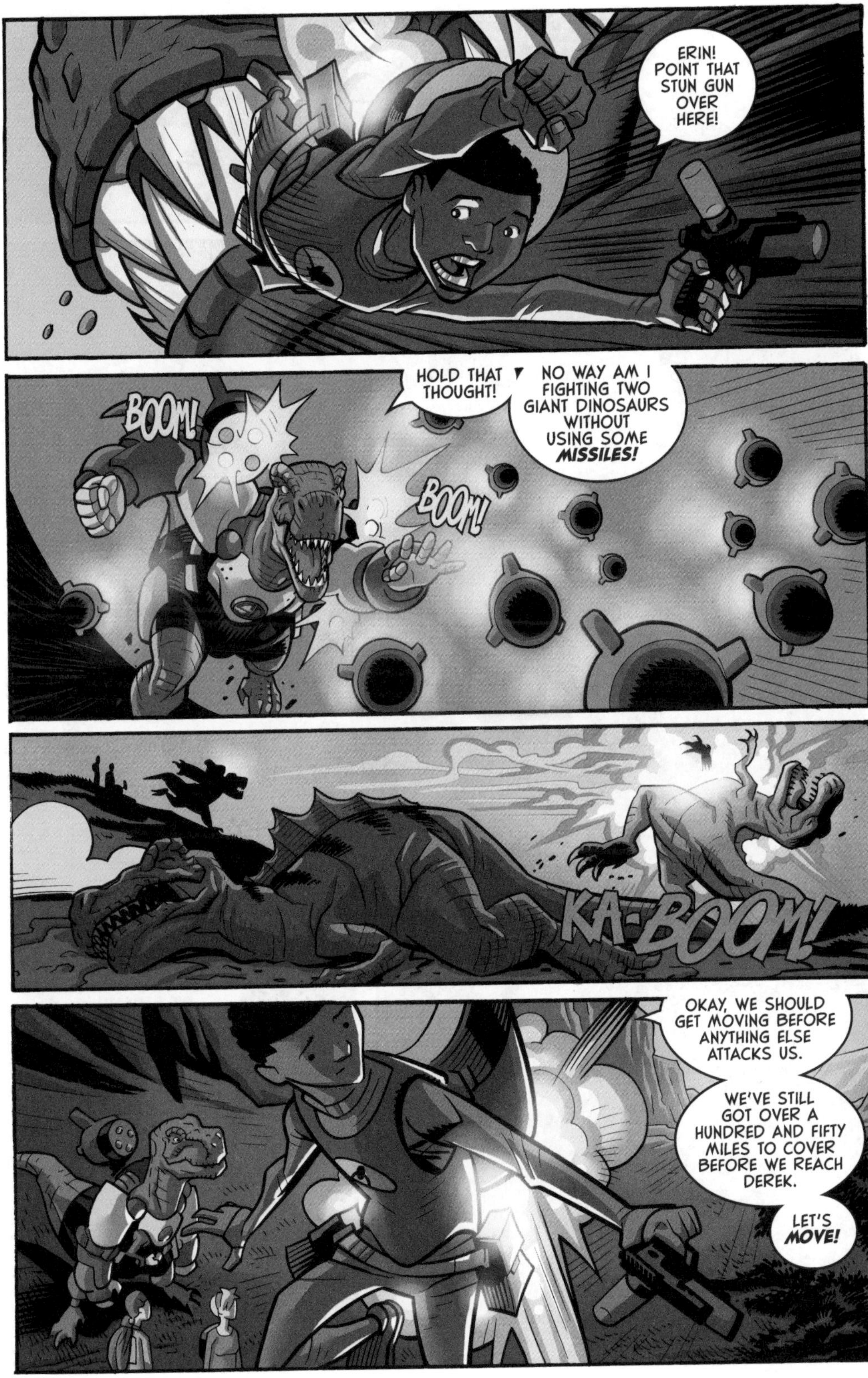
ERIN! POINT THAT STUN GUN OVER HERE!
BOOM!
HOLD THAT THOUGHT!
NO WAY AM I FIGHTING TWO GIANT DINOSAURS WITHOUT USING SOME MISSILES!
BOOM!
KA-BOOM!
OKAY, WE SHOULD GET MOVING BEFORE ANYTHING ELSE ATTACKS US.
WE'VE STILL GOT OVER A HUNDRED AND FIFTY MILES TO COVER BEFORE WE REACH DEREK.
LET'S MOVE!

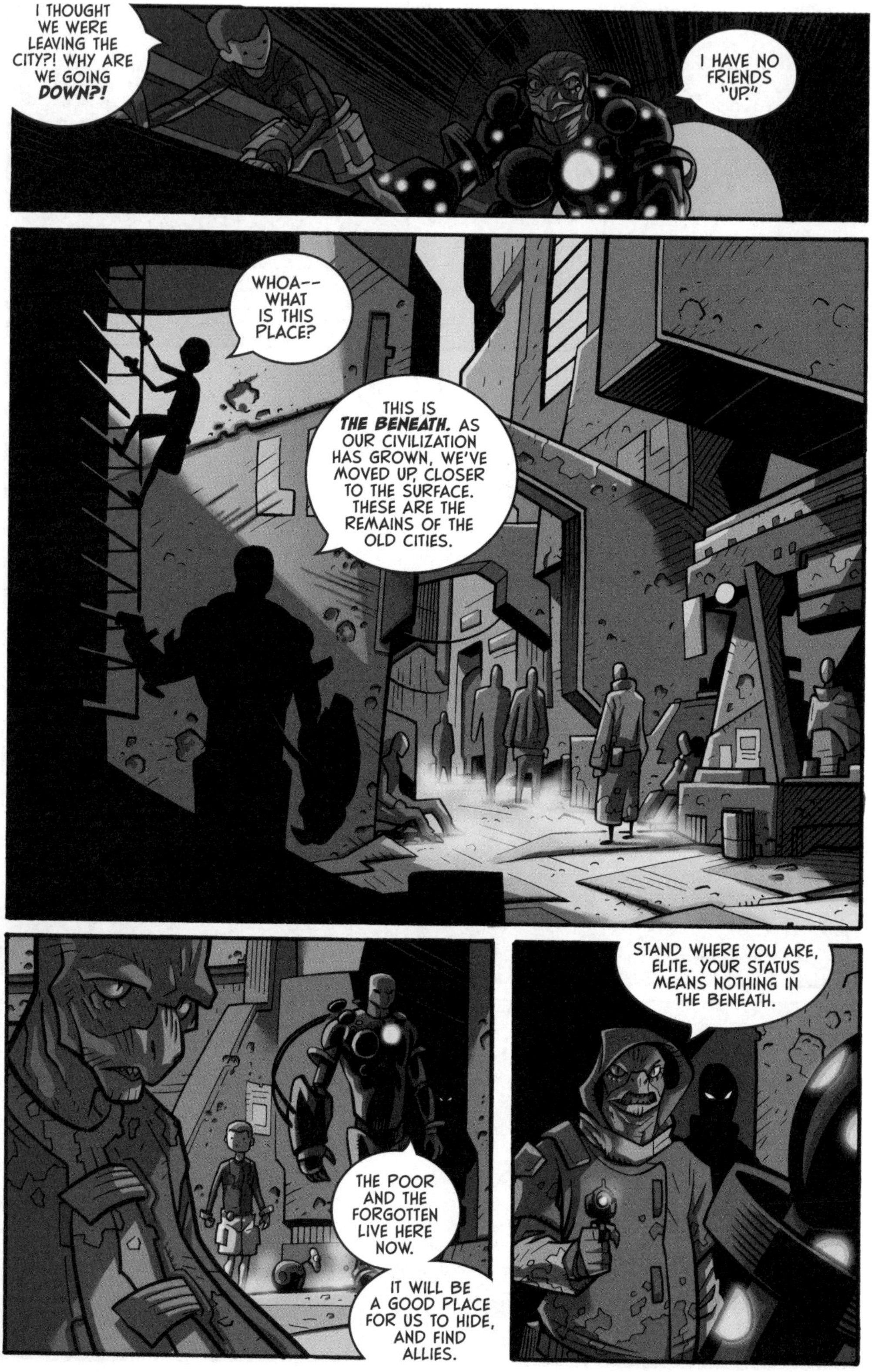
I THOUGHT WE WERE LEAVING THE CITY?! WHY ARE WE GOING **DOWN?!**
I HAVE NO FRIENDS "UP."
WHOA-- WHAT IS THIS PLACE?
THIS IS **THE BENEATH.** AS OUR CIVILIZATION HAS GROWN, WE'VE MOVED UP, CLOSER TO THE SURFACE. THESE ARE THE REMAINS OF THE OLD CITIES.
THE POOR AND THE FORGOTTEN LIVE HERE NOW.
IT WILL BE A GOOD PLACE FOR US TO HIDE, AND FIND ALLIES.
STAND WHERE YOU ARE, ELITE. YOUR STATUS MEANS NOTHING IN THE BENEATH.

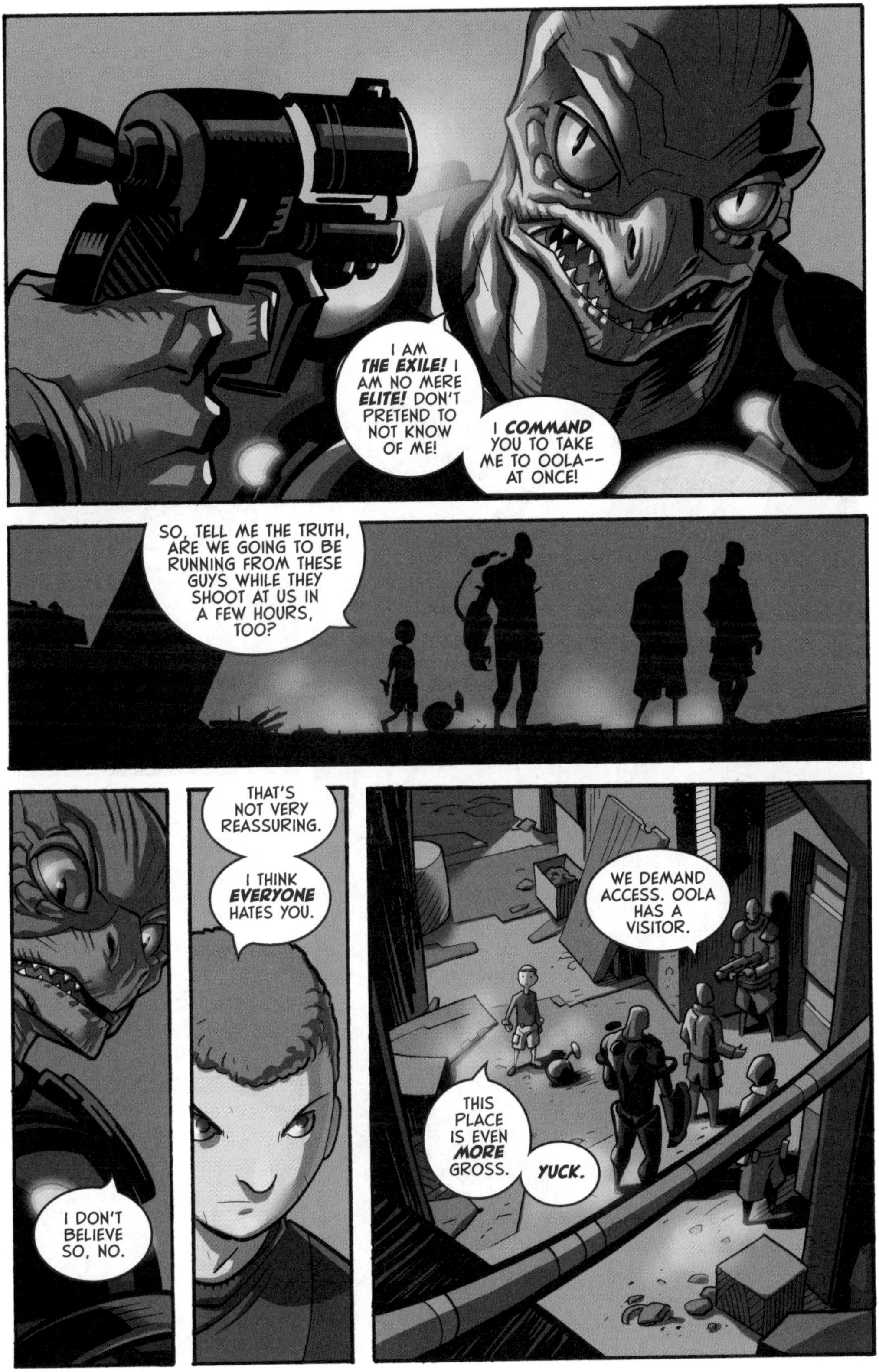
I AM THE EXILE! I AM NO MERE ELITE! DON'T PRETEND TO NOT KNOW OF ME!
I COMMAND YOU TO TAKE ME TO OOLA-- AT ONCE!
SO, TELL ME THE TRUTH, ARE WE GOING TO BE RUNNING FROM THESE GUYS WHILE THEY SHOOT AT US IN A FEW HOURS, TOO?
I DON'T BELIEVE SO, NO.
THAT'S NOT VERY REASSURING.
I THINK EVERYONE HATES YOU.
WE DEMAND ACCESS. OOLA HAS A VISITOR.
THIS PLACE IS EVEN MORE GROSS.
YUCK.

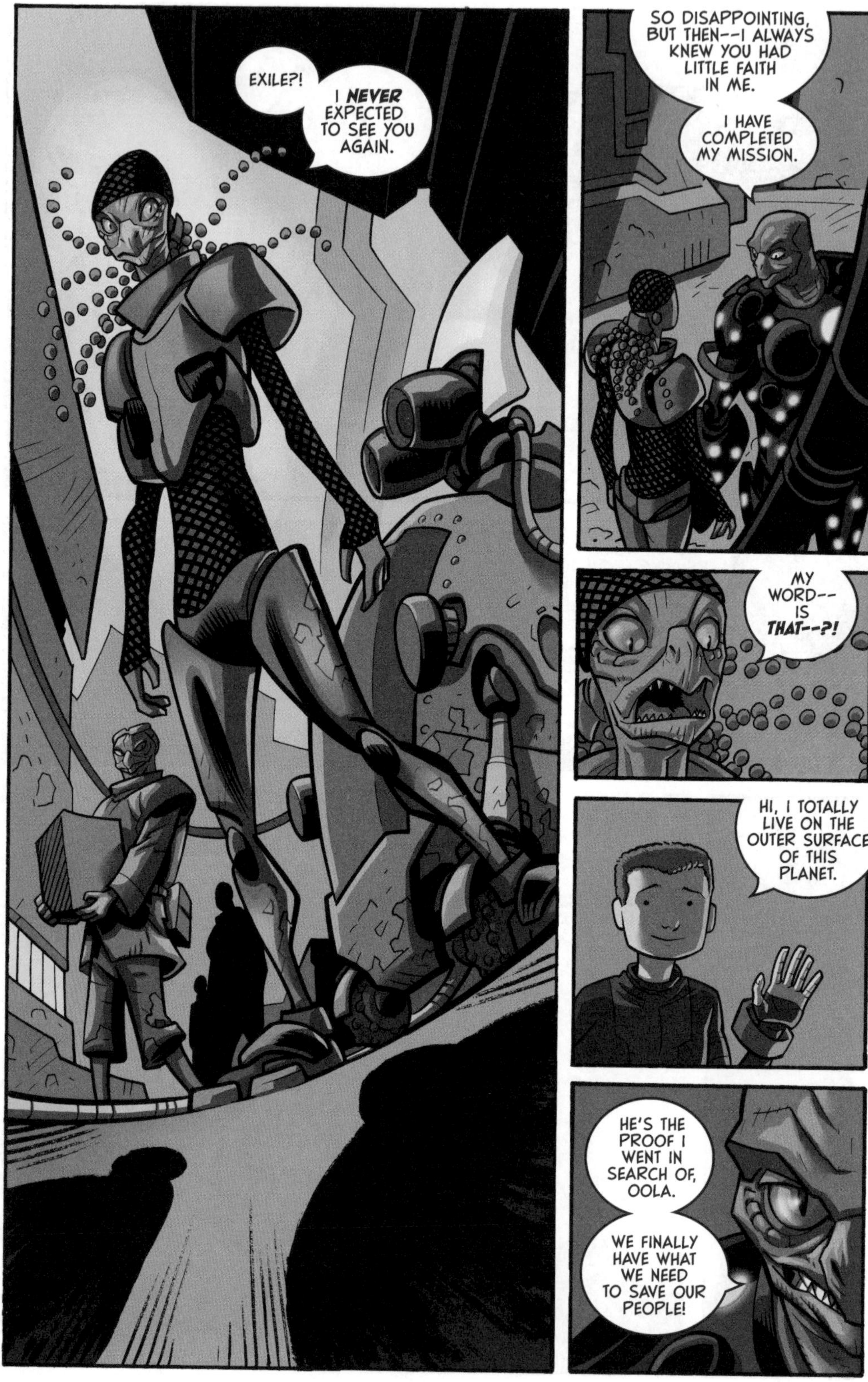
EXILE?!
I **NEVER** EXPECTED TO SEE YOU AGAIN.
SO DISAPPOINTING, BUT THEN--I ALWAYS KNEW YOU HAD LITTLE FAITH IN ME.
I HAVE COMPLETED MY MISSION.
MY WORD--IS ***THAT--?!***
HI, I TOTALLY LIVE ON THE OUTER SURFACE OF THIS PLANET.
HE'S THE PROOF I WENT IN SEARCH OF, OOLA.
WE FINALLY HAVE WHAT WE NEED TO SAVE OUR PEOPLE!

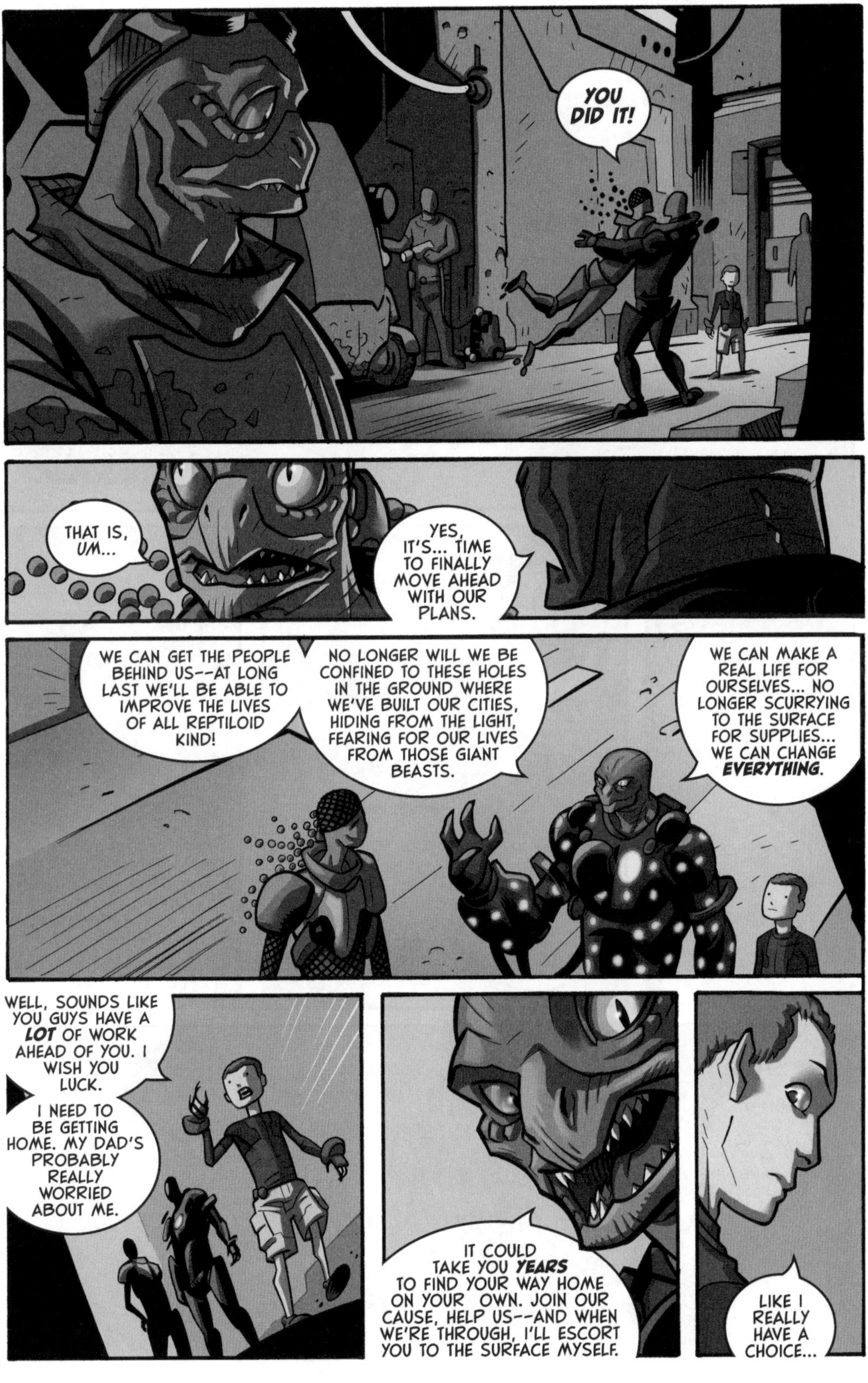
YOU DID IT!
THAT IS, UM...
YES, IT'S... TIME TO FINALLY MOVE AHEAD WITH OUR PLANS.
WE CAN GET THE PEOPLE BEHIND US--AT LONG LAST WE'LL BE ABLE TO IMPROVE THE LIVES OF ALL REPTILOID KIND!
NO LONGER WILL WE BE CONFINED TO THESE HOLES IN THE GROUND WHERE WE'VE BUILT OUR CITIES, HIDING FROM THE LIGHT, FEARING FOR OUR LIVES FROM THOSE GIANT BEASTS.
WE CAN MAKE A REAL LIFE FOR OURSELVES... NO LONGER SCURRYING TO THE SURFACE FOR SUPPLIES... WE CAN CHANGE EVERYTHING.
WELL, SOUNDS LIKE YOU GUYS HAVE A LOT OF WORK AHEAD OF YOU. I WISH YOU LUCK.
I NEED TO BE GETTING HOME. MY DAD'S PROBABLY REALLY WORRIED ABOUT ME.
IT COULD TAKE YOU YEARS TO FIND YOUR WAY HOME ON YOUR OWN. JOIN OUR CAUSE, HELP US--AND WHEN WE'RE THROUGH, I'LL ESCORT YOU TO THE SURFACE MYSELF.
LIKE I REALLY HAVE A CHOICE...

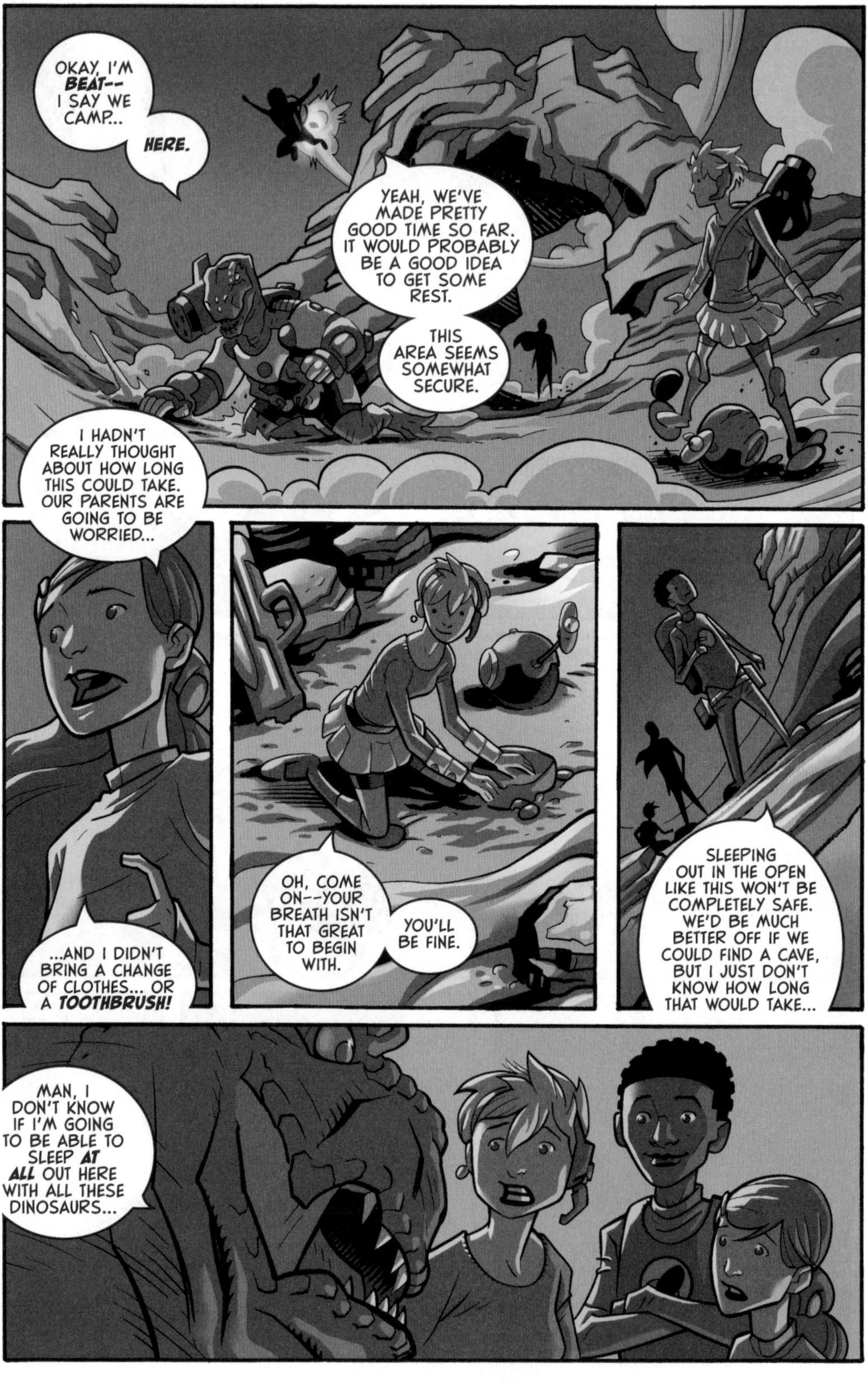
OKAY, I'M **BEAT--** I SAY WE CAMP...
HERE.
YEAH, WE'VE MADE PRETTY GOOD TIME SO FAR. IT WOULD PROBABLY BE A GOOD IDEA TO GET SOME REST.
THIS AREA SEEMS SOMEWHAT SECURE.
I HADN'T REALLY THOUGHT ABOUT HOW LONG THIS COULD TAKE. OUR PARENTS ARE GOING TO BE WORRIED...
...AND I DIDN'T BRING A CHANGE OF CLOTHES... OR A **TOOTHBRUSH!**
OH, COME ON--YOUR BREATH ISN'T THAT GREAT TO BEGIN WITH.
YOU'LL BE FINE.
SLEEPING OUT IN THE OPEN LIKE THIS WON'T BE COMPLETELY SAFE. WE'D BE MUCH BETTER OFF IF WE COULD FIND A CAVE, BUT I JUST DON'T KNOW HOW LONG THAT WOULD TAKE...
MAN, I DON'T KNOW IF I'M GOING TO BE ABLE TO SLEEP **AT ALL** OUT HERE WITH ALL THESE DINOSAURS...

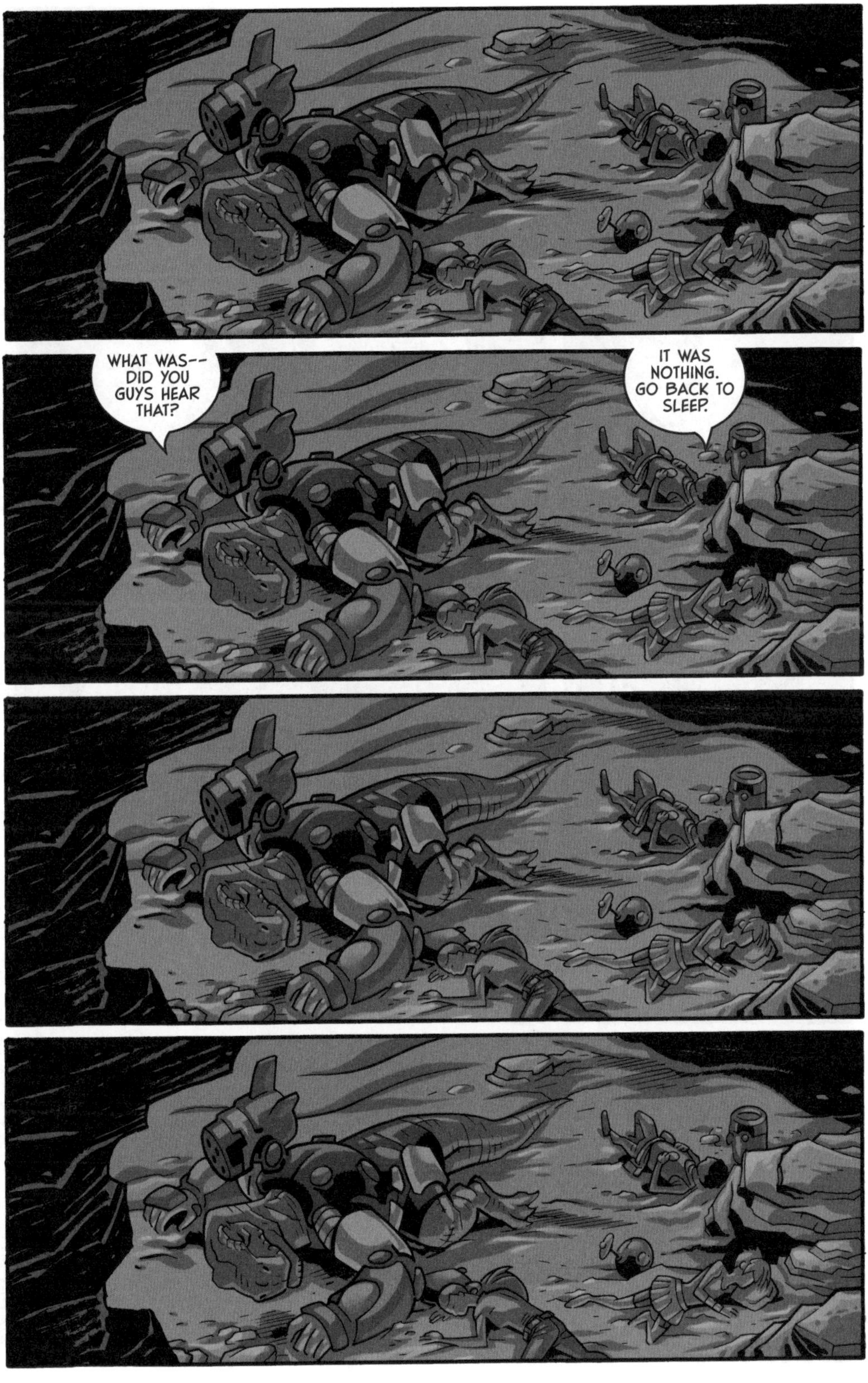
WHAT WAS--DID YOU GUYS HEAR THAT?
IT WAS NOTHING. GO BACK TO SLEEP.

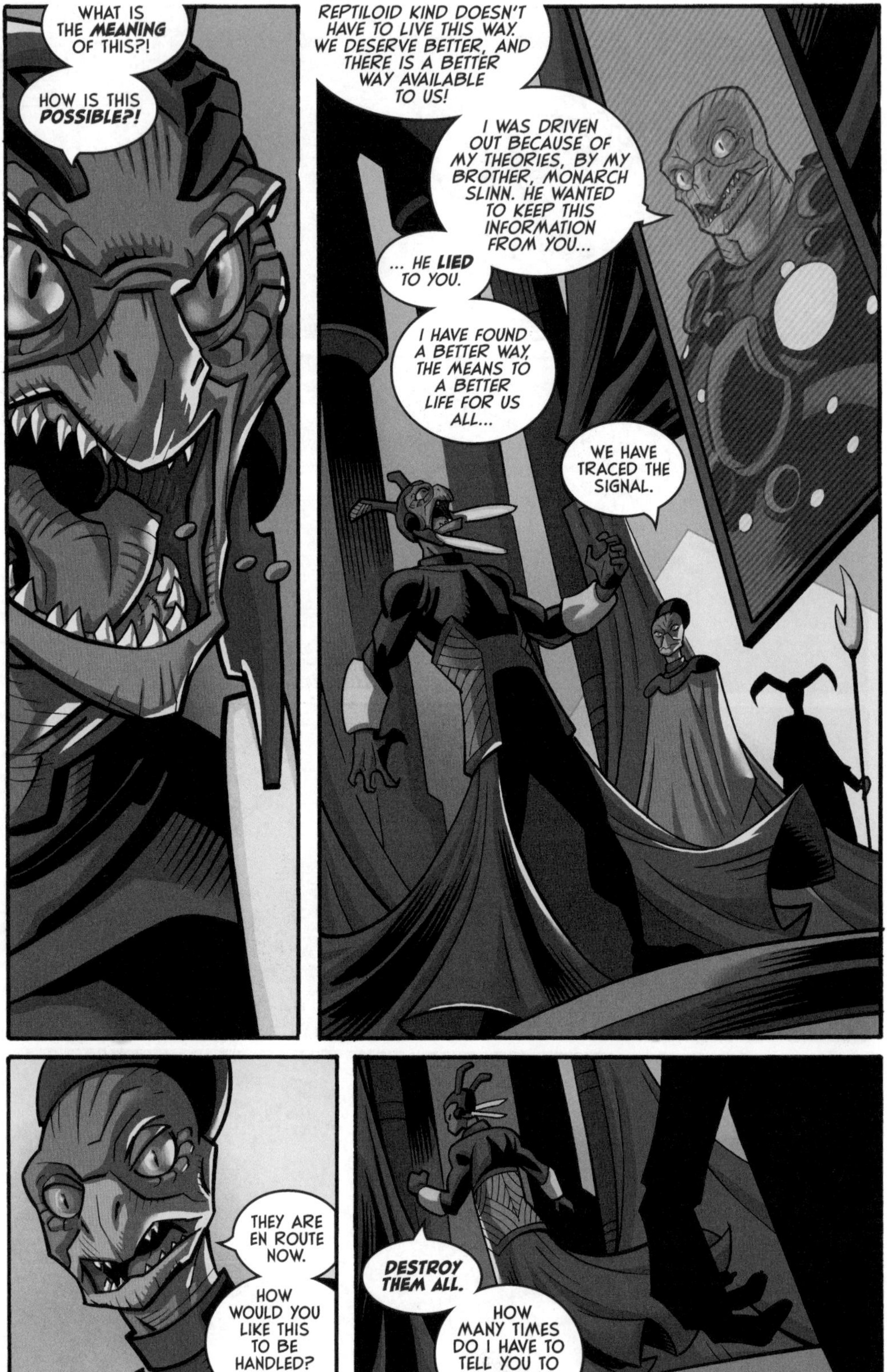
WHAT IS THE MEANING OF THIS?!
HOW IS THIS POSSIBLE?!
REPTILOID KIND DOESN'T HAVE TO LIVE THIS WAY. WE DESERVE BETTER, AND THERE IS A BETTER WAY AVAILABLE TO US!
I WAS DRIVEN OUT BECAUSE OF MY THEORIES, BY MY BROTHER, MONARCH SLINN. HE WANTED TO KEEP THIS INFORMATION FROM YOU...
... HE LIED TO YOU.
I HAVE FOUND A BETTER WAY, THE MEANS TO A BETTER LIFE FOR US ALL...
WE HAVE TRACED THE SIGNAL.
THEY ARE EN ROUTE NOW.
HOW WOULD YOU LIKE THIS TO BE HANDLED?
DESTROY THEM ALL.
HOW MANY TIMES DO I HAVE TO TELL YOU TO KILL THEM?

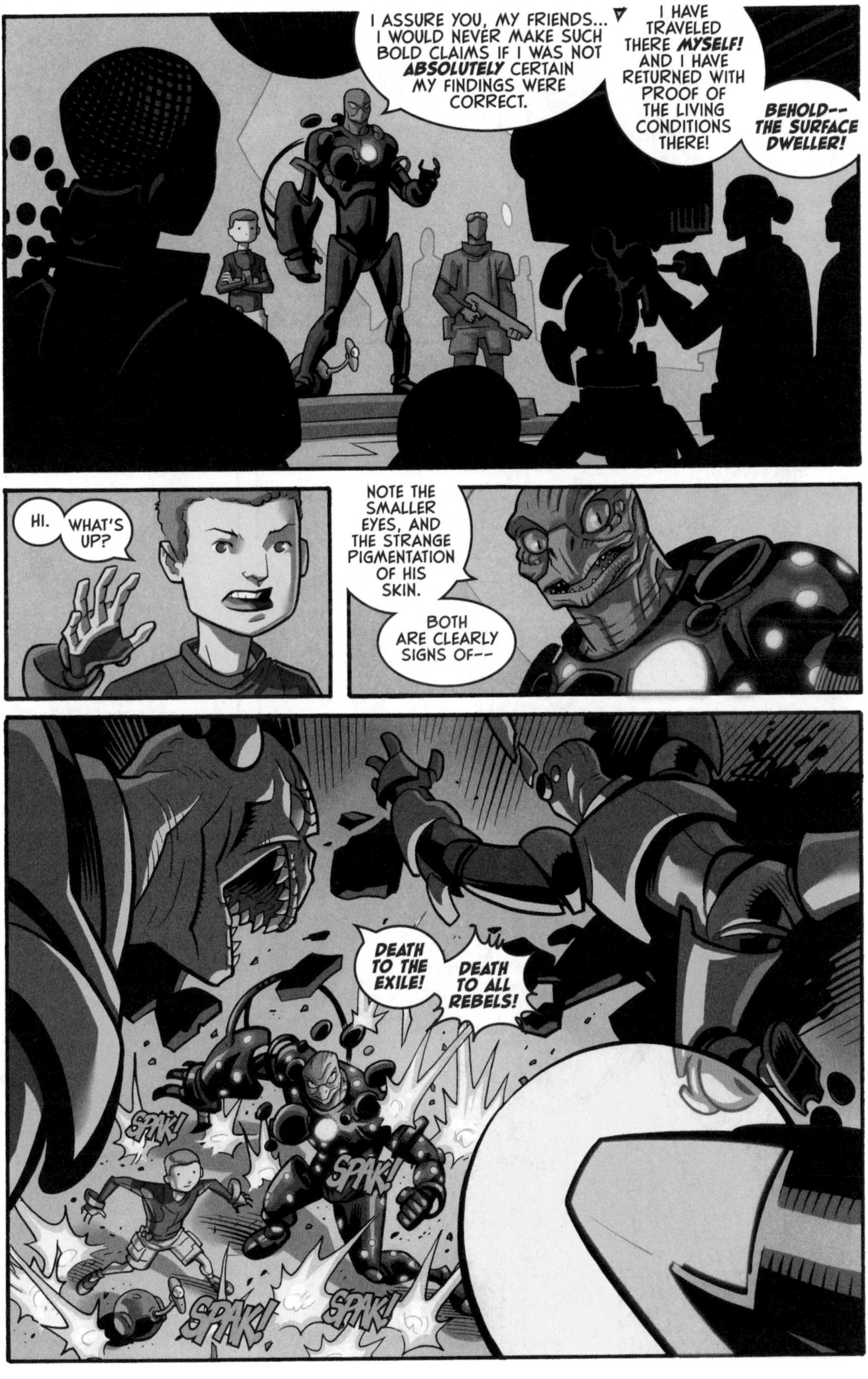
I ASSURE YOU, MY FRIENDS... I WOULD NEVER MAKE SUCH BOLD CLAIMS IF I WAS NOT *ABSOLUTELY* CERTAIN MY FINDINGS WERE CORRECT.
I HAVE TRAVELED THERE *MYSELF!* AND I HAVE RETURNED WITH PROOF OF THE LIVING CONDITIONS THERE!
BEHOLD-- THE SURFACE DWELLER!
HI.
WHAT'S UP?
NOTE THE SMALLER EYES, AND THE STRANGE PIGMENTATION OF HIS SKIN.
BOTH ARE CLEARLY SIGNS OF--
DEATH TO THE EXILE!
DEATH TO ALL REBELS!
SPAK!
SPAK!
SPAK!
SPAK!

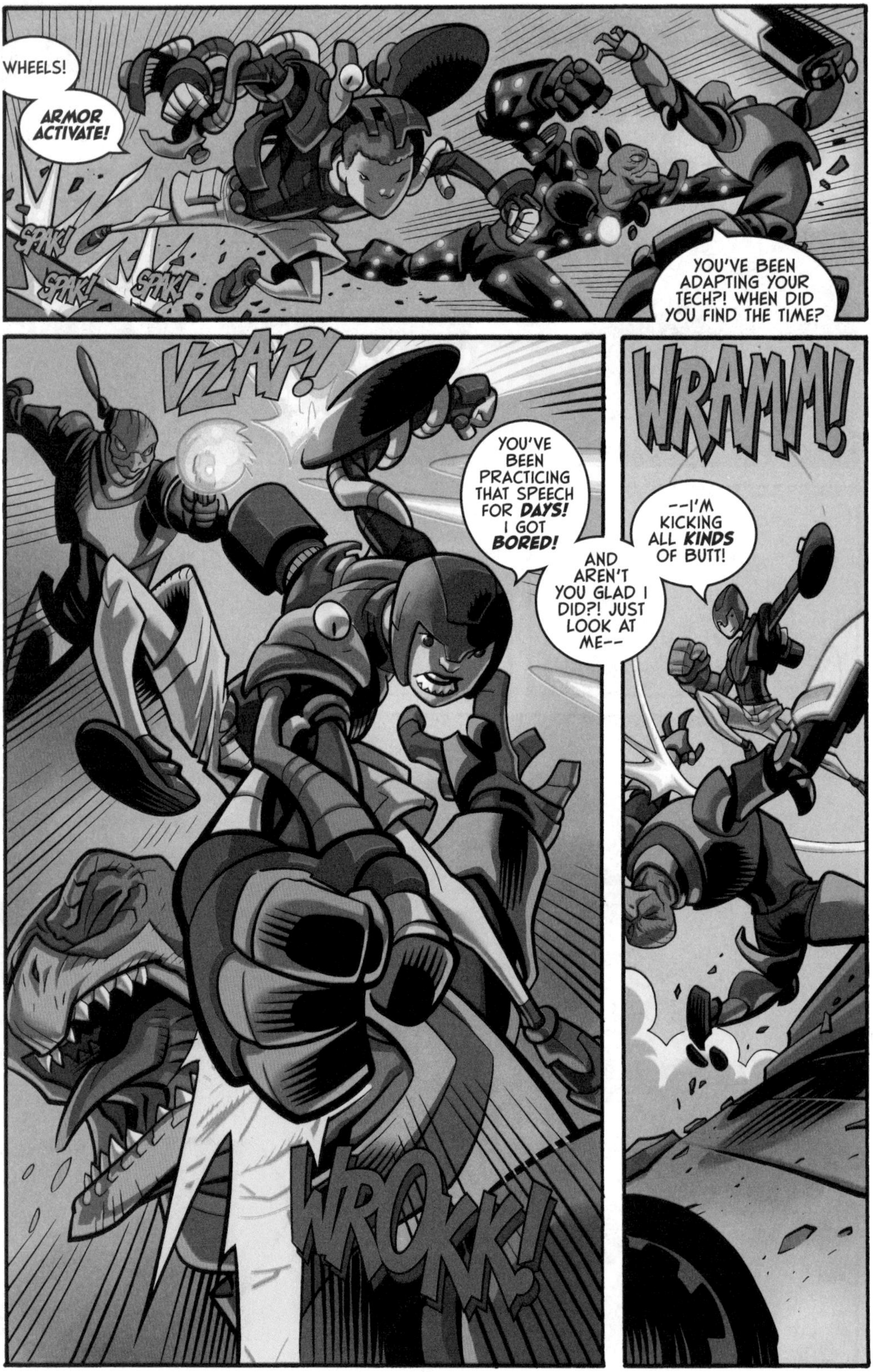
WHEELS!
ARMOR ACTIVATE!
SPAK!
SPAK!
SPAK!
YOU'VE BEEN ADAPTING YOUR TECH?! WHEN DID YOU FIND THE TIME?
VZAP!
YOU'VE BEEN PRACTICING THAT SPEECH FOR DAYS! I GOT BORED!
AND AREN'T YOU GLAD I DID?! JUST LOOK AT ME--
WROKK!
WRAMM!
--I'M KICKING ALL KINDS OF BUTT!

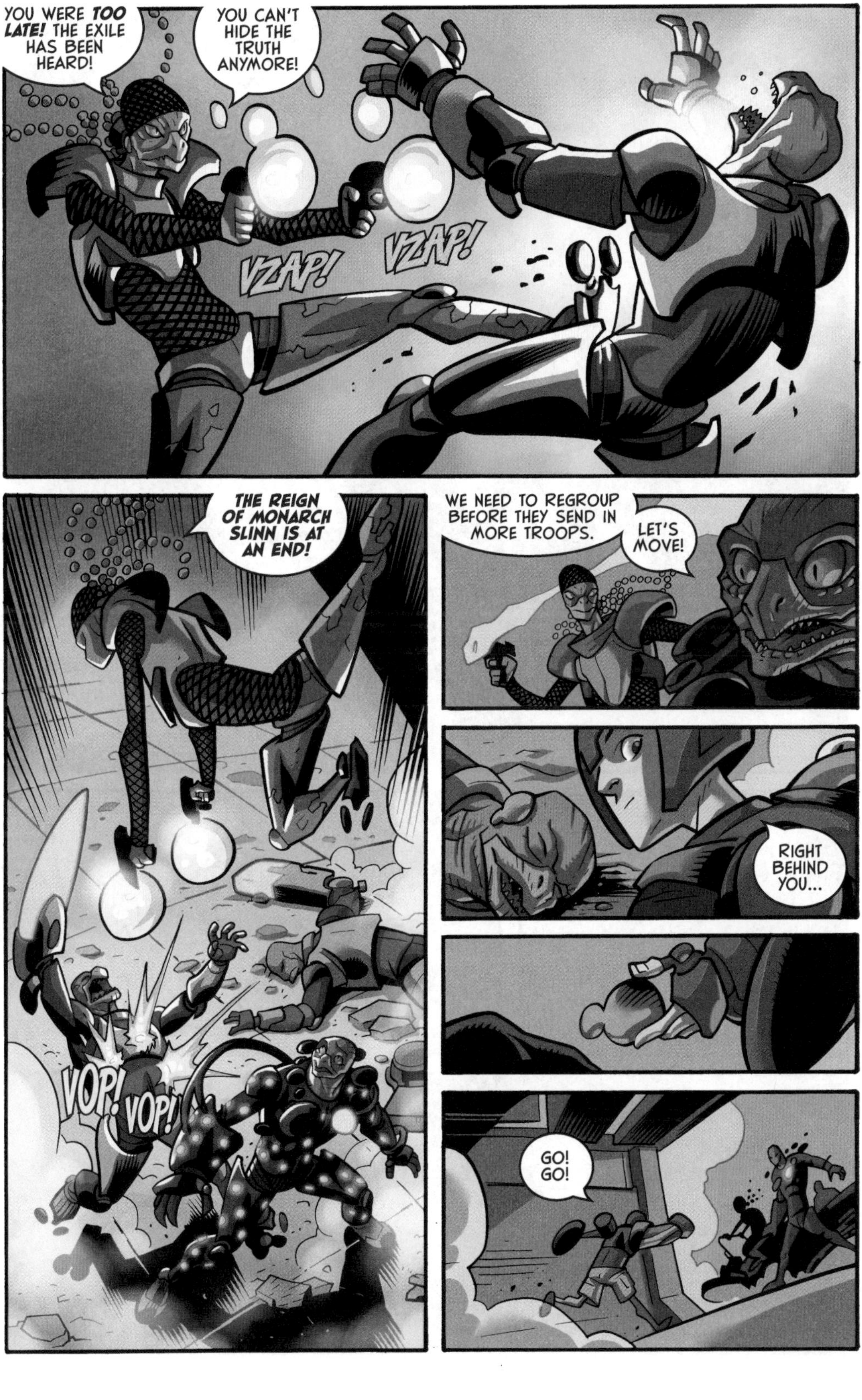
YOU WERE TOO LATE! THE EXILE HAS BEEN HEARD!
YOU CAN'T HIDE THE TRUTH ANYMORE!
VZAP!
VZAP!
THE REIGN OF MONARCH SLINN IS AT AN END!
VOP!
VOP!
WE NEED TO REGROUP BEFORE THEY SEND IN MORE TROOPS.
LET'S MOVE!
RIGHT BEHIND YOU...
GO! GO!

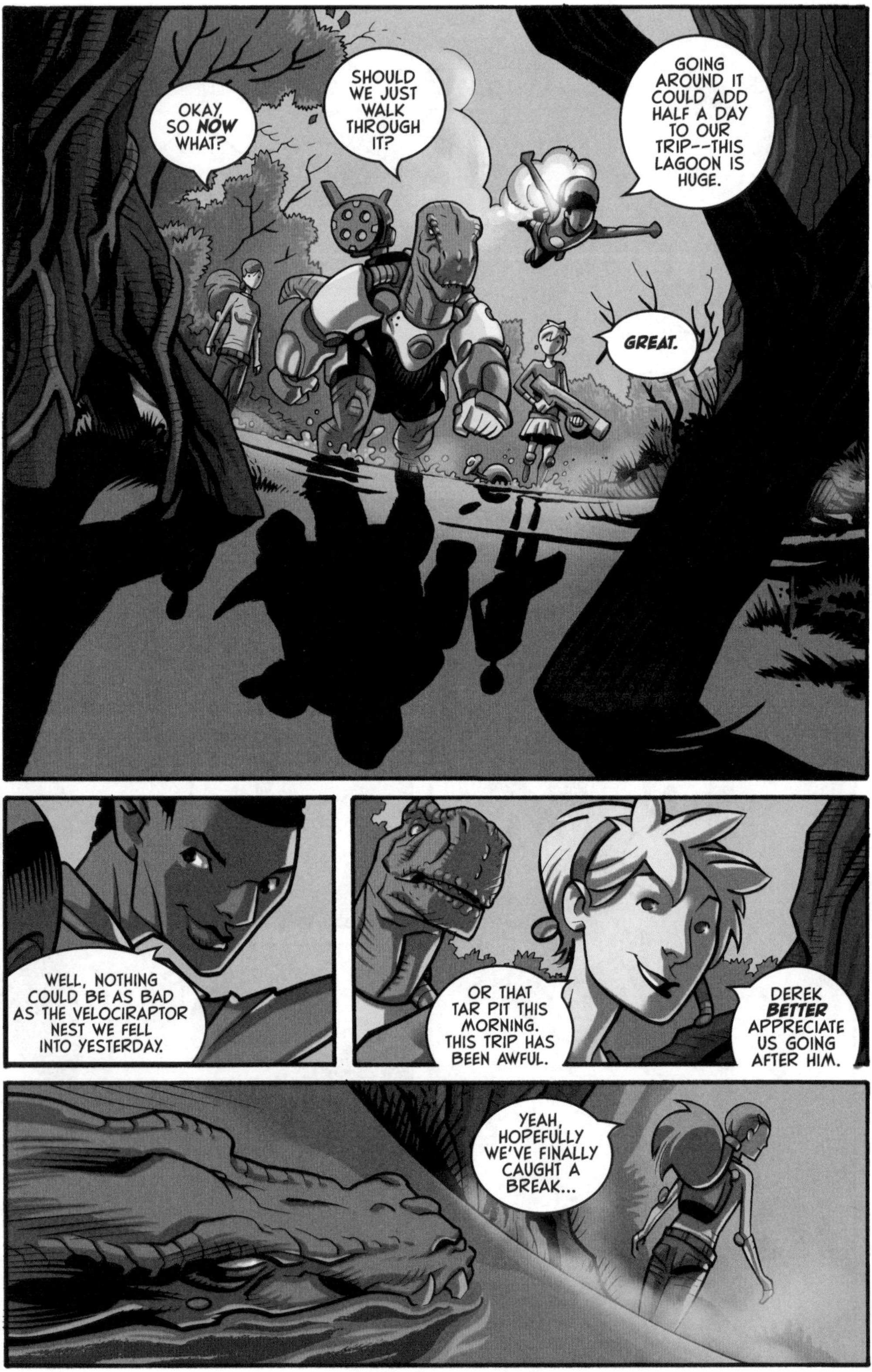
OKAY, SO **NOW** WHAT?
SHOULD WE JUST WALK THROUGH IT?
GOING AROUND IT COULD ADD HALF A DAY TO OUR TRIP--THIS LAGOON IS HUGE.
GREAT.
WELL, NOTHING COULD BE AS BAD AS THE VELOCIRAPTOR NEST WE FELL INTO YESTERDAY.
OR THAT TAR PIT THIS MORNING. THIS TRIP HAS BEEN AWFUL.
DEREK **BETTER** APPRECIATE US GOING AFTER HIM.
YEAH, HOPEFULLY WE'VE FINALLY CAUGHT A BREAK...

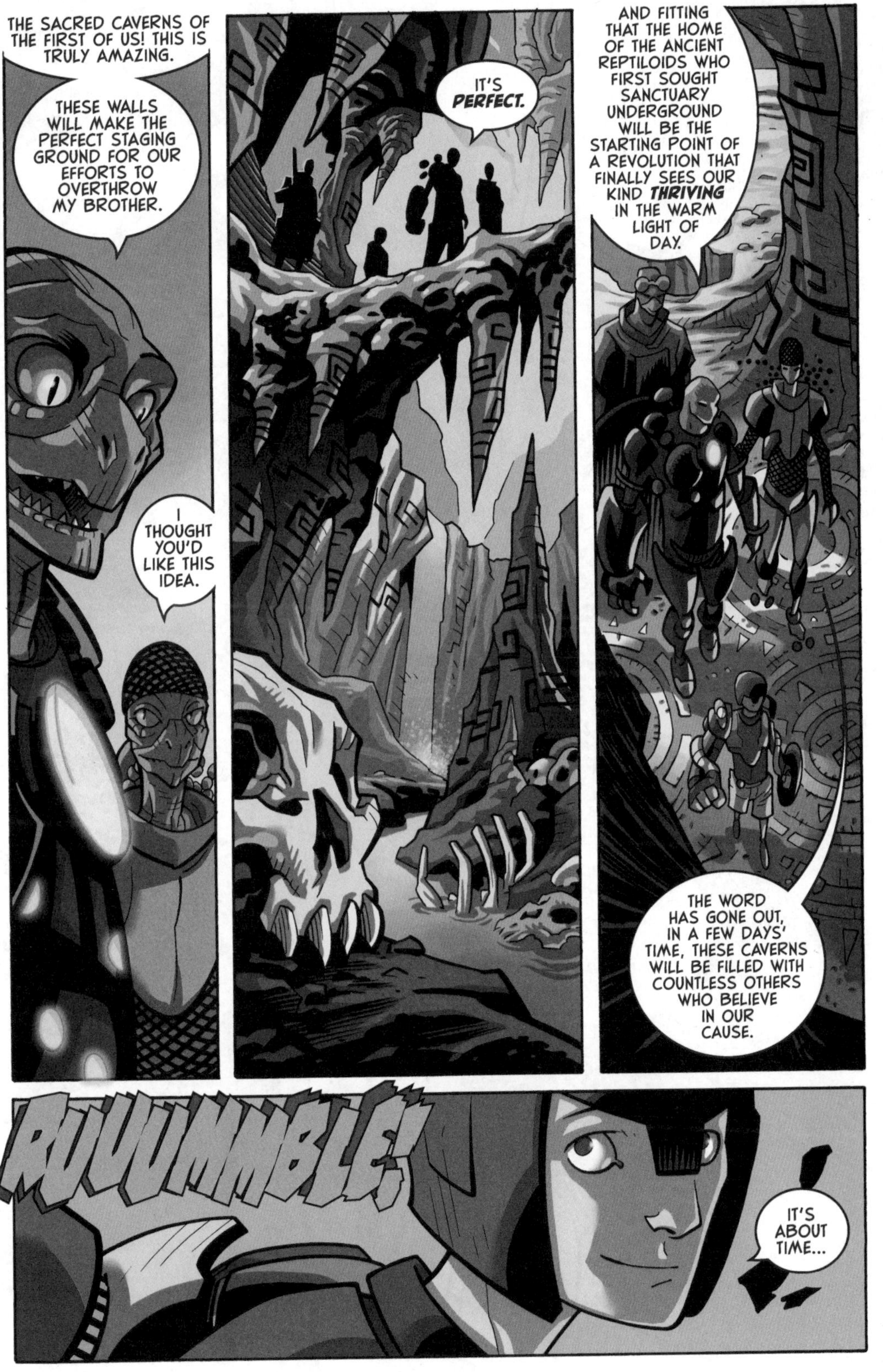
THE SACRED CAVERNS OF THE FIRST OF US! THIS IS TRULY AMAZING.
THESE WALLS WILL MAKE THE PERFECT STAGING GROUND FOR OUR EFFORTS TO OVERTHROW MY BROTHER.
I THOUGHT YOU'D LIKE THIS IDEA.
IT'S PERFECT.
AND FITTING THAT THE HOME OF THE ANCIENT REPTILOIDS WHO FIRST SOUGHT SANCTUARY UNDERGROUND WILL BE THE STARTING POINT OF A REVOLUTION THAT FINALLY SEES OUR KIND THRIVING IN THE WARM LIGHT OF DAY.
THE WORD HAS GONE OUT, IN A FEW DAYS' TIME, THESE CAVERNS WILL BE FILLED WITH COUNTLESS OTHERS WHO BELIEVE IN OUR CAUSE.
RUUUMMBLE!
IT'S ABOUT TIME...

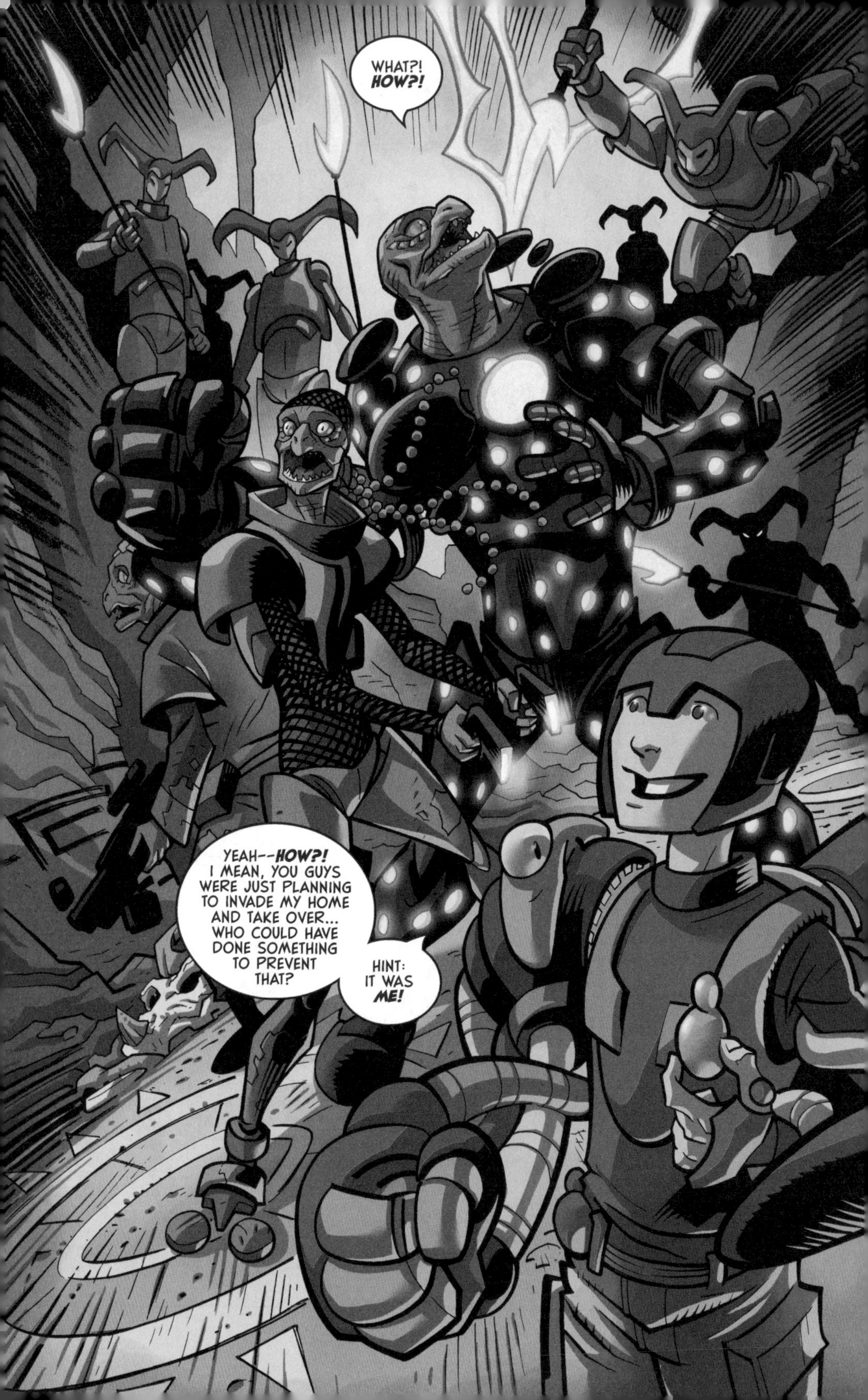
WHAT?! HOW?!
YEAH--HOW?! I MEAN, YOU GUYS WERE JUST PLANNING TO INVADE MY HOME AND TAKE OVER... WHO COULD HAVE DONE SOMETHING TO PREVENT THAT?
HINT: IT WAS ME!

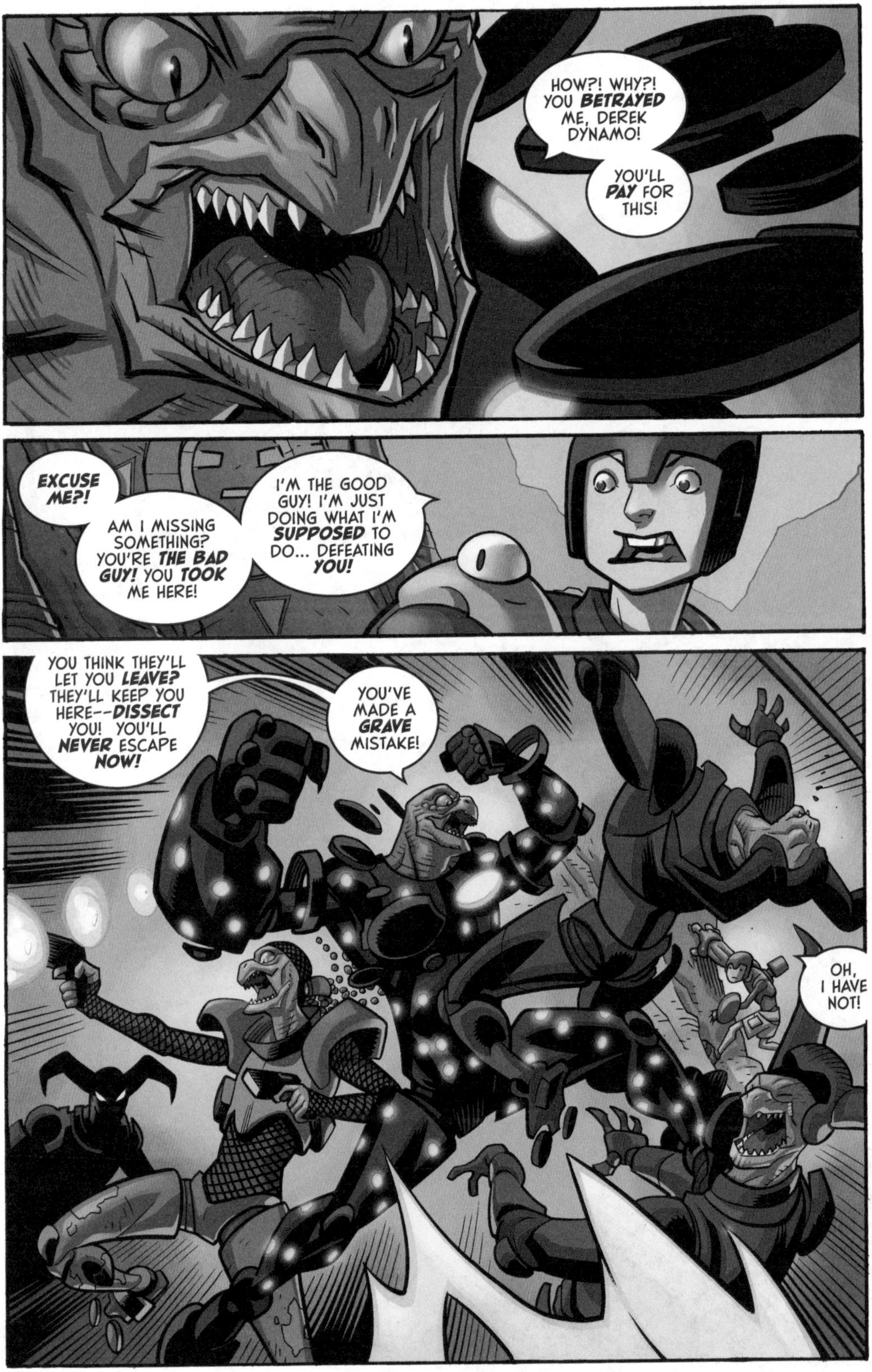
HOW?! WHY?! YOU BETRAYED ME, DEREK DYNAMO!
YOU'LL PAY FOR THIS!
EXCUSE ME?!
AM I MISSING SOMETHING? YOU'RE THE BAD GUY! YOU TOOK ME HERE!
I'M THE GOOD GUY! I'M JUST DOING WHAT I'M SUPPOSED TO DO... DEFEATING YOU!
YOU THINK THEY'LL LET YOU LEAVE? THEY'LL KEEP YOU HERE--DISSECT YOU! YOU'LL NEVER ESCAPE NOW!
YOU'VE MADE A GRAVE MISTAKE!
OH, I HAVE NOT!

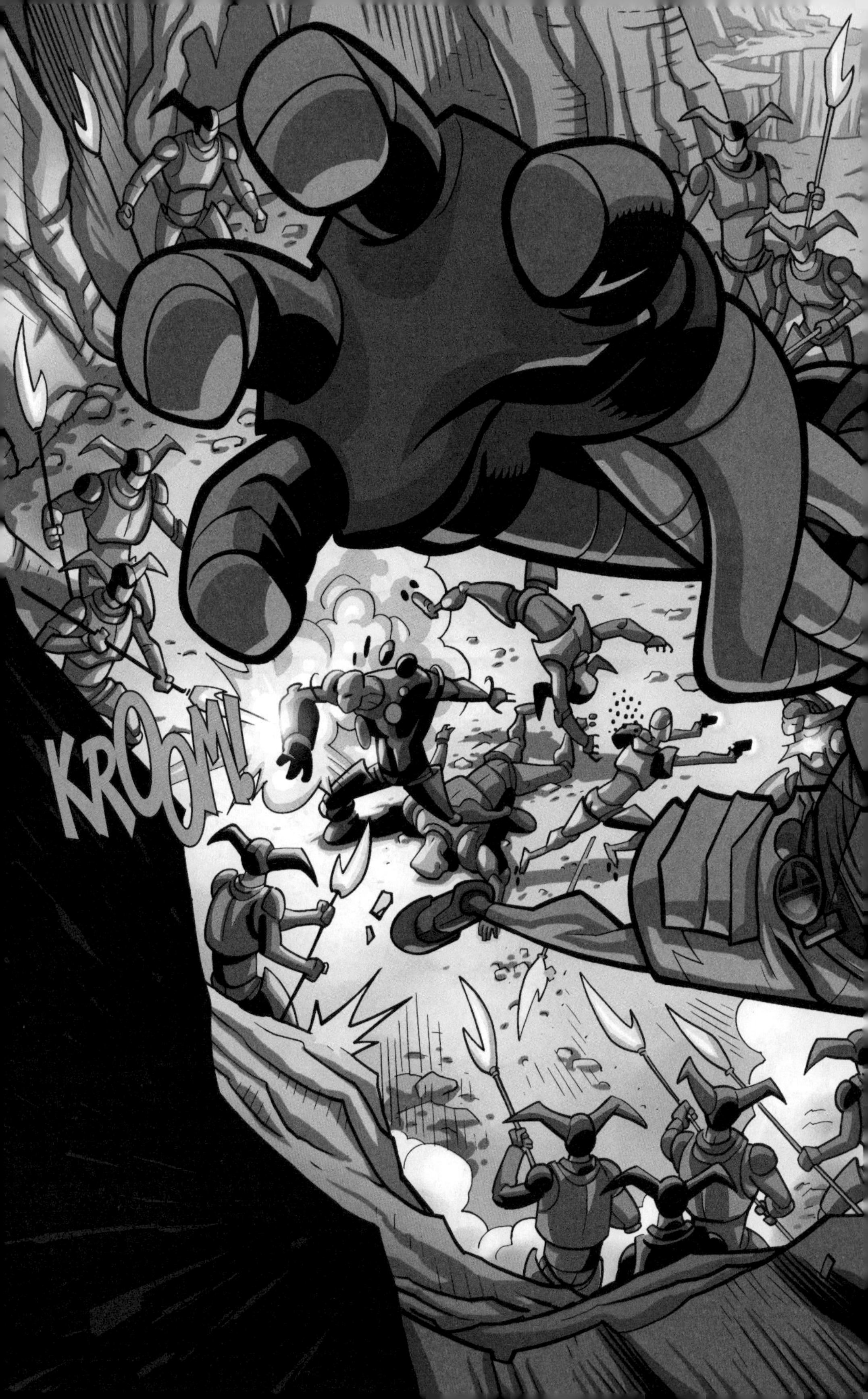
KROOM!

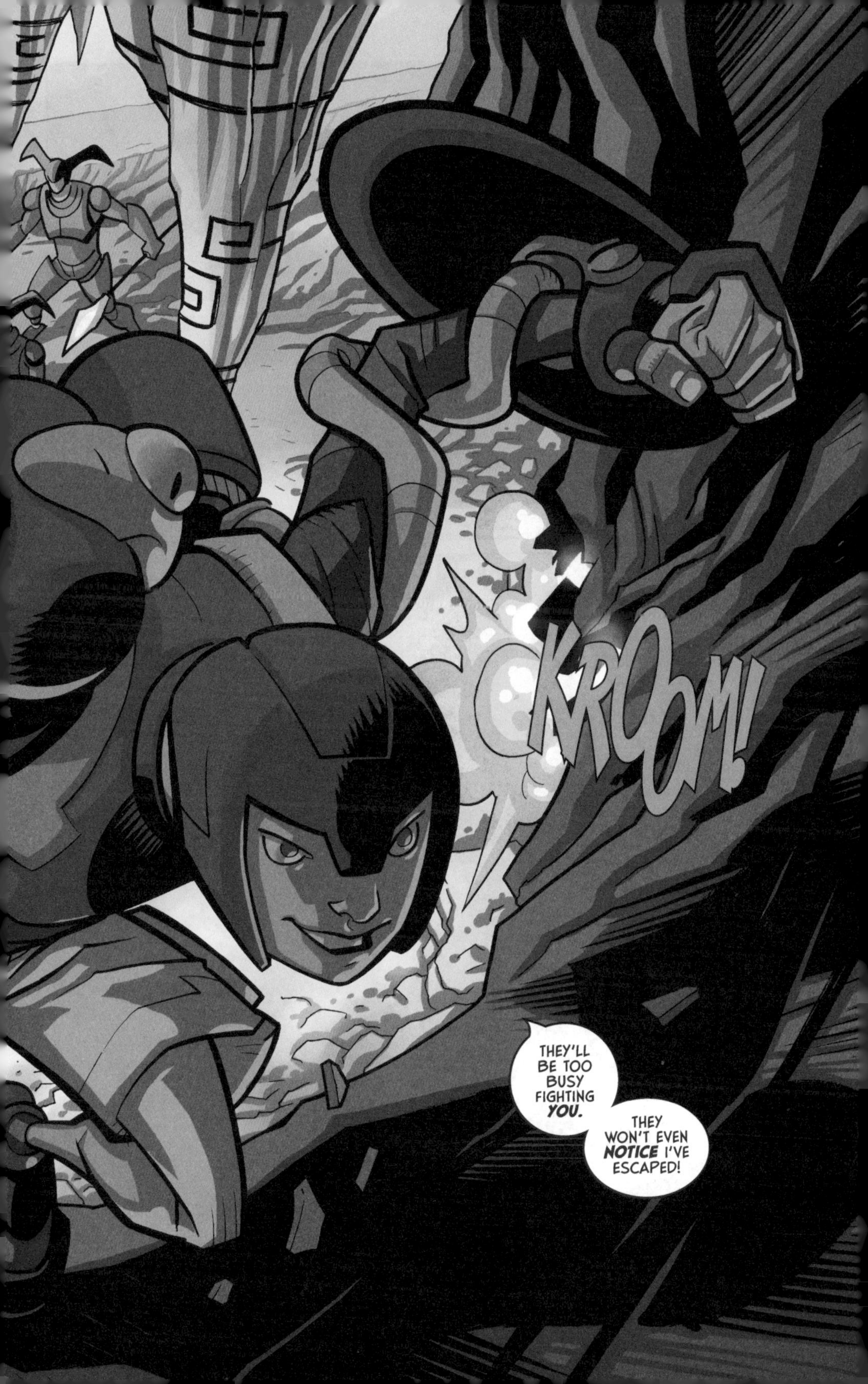
KROOM!
THEY'LL BE TOO BUSY FIGHTING *YOU.*
THEY WON'T EVEN *NOTICE* I'VE ESCAPED!

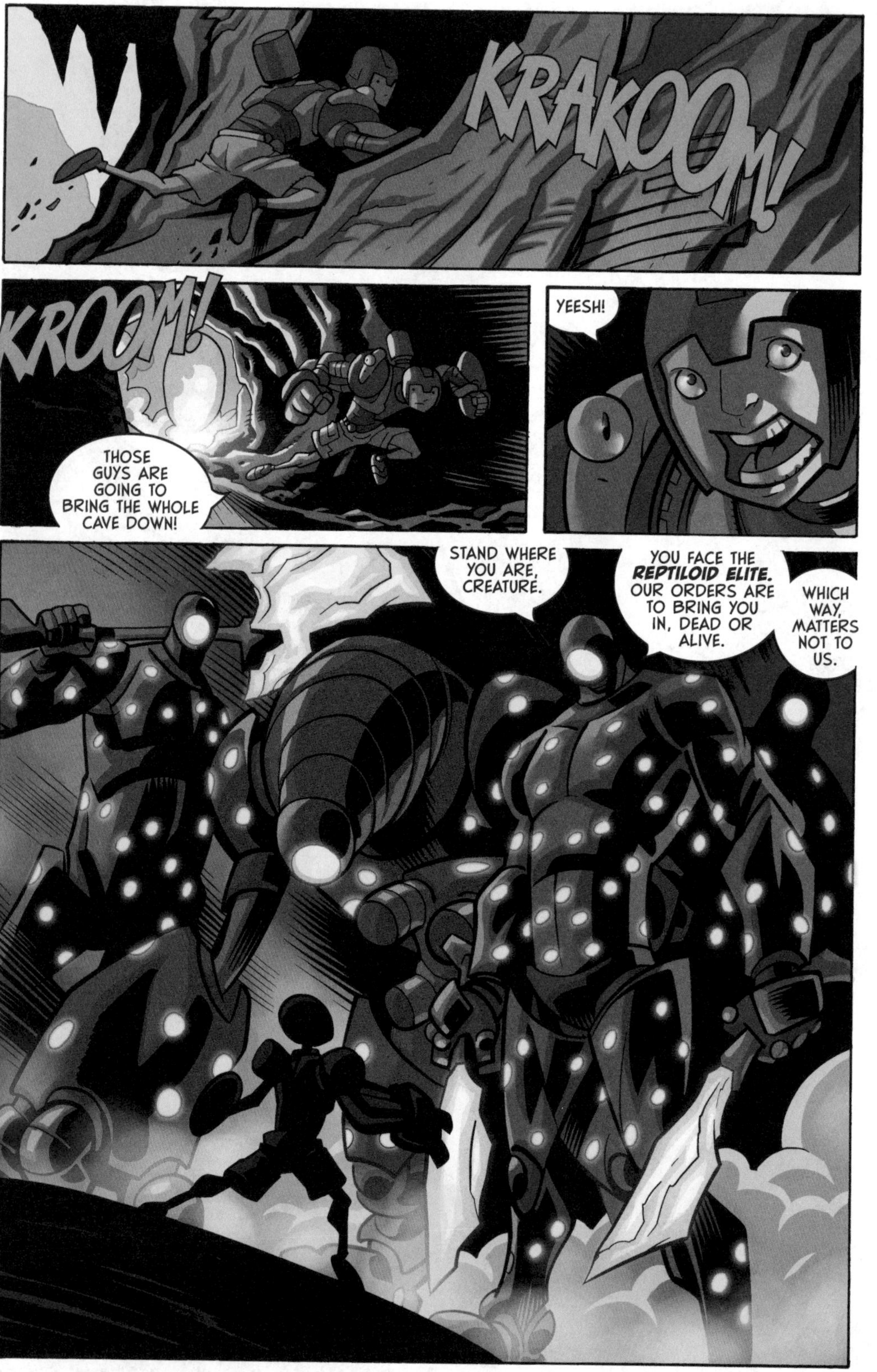
KRAKOOM!
KROOM!
THOSE GUYS ARE GOING TO BRING THE WHOLE CAVE DOWN!
YEESH!
STAND WHERE YOU ARE, CREATURE.
YOU FACE THE **REPTILOID ELITE.** OUR ORDERS ARE TO BRING YOU IN, DEAD OR ALIVE.
WHICH WAY, MATTERS NOT TO US.

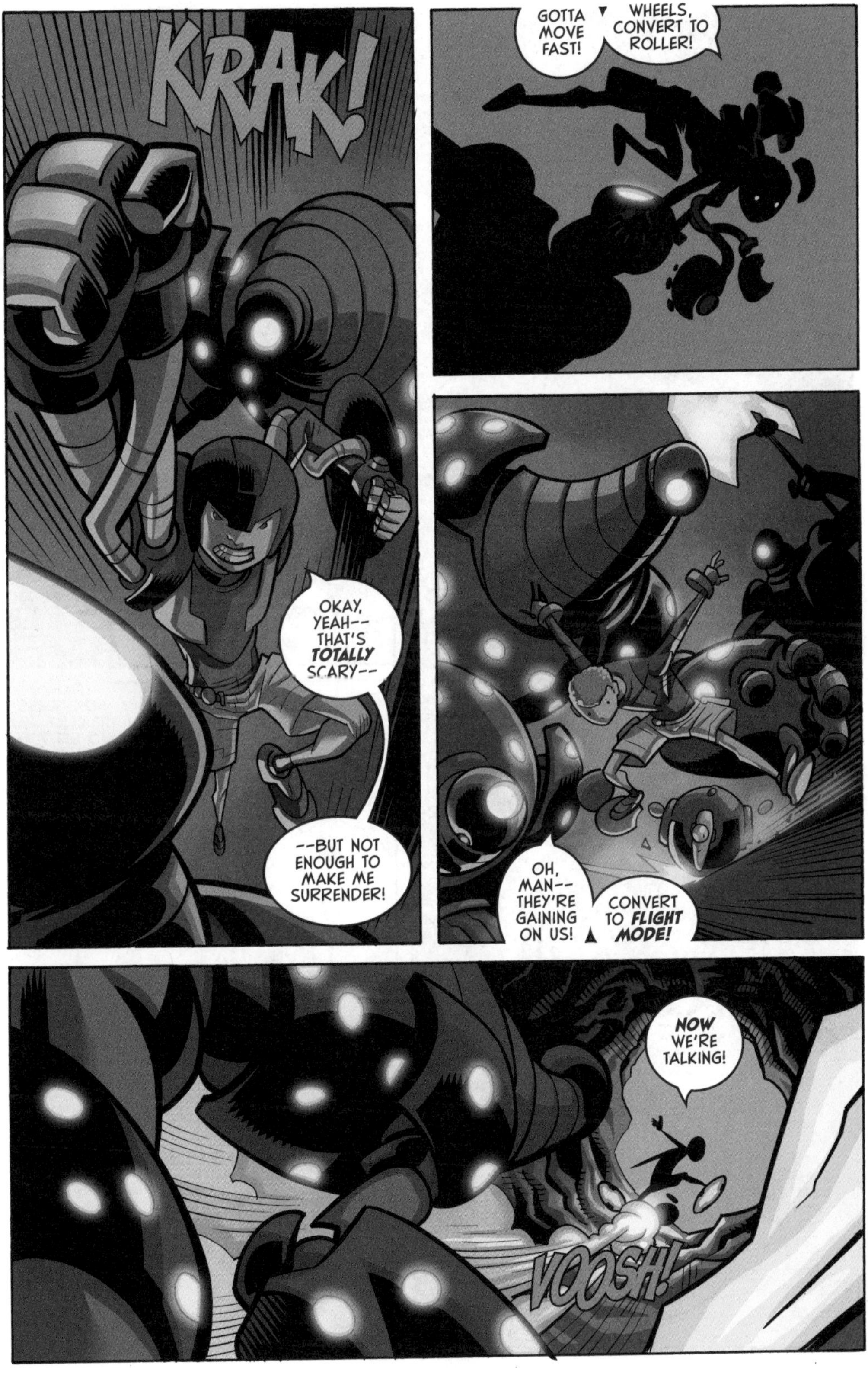
KRAK!
OKAY, YEAH-- THAT'S TOTALLY SCARY--
--BUT NOT ENOUGH TO MAKE ME SURRENDER!
GOTTA MOVE FAST!
WHEELS, CONVERT TO ROLLER!
OH, MAN-- THEY'RE GAINING ON US!
CONVERT TO FLIGHT MODE!
NOW WE'RE TALKING!
VOOSH!

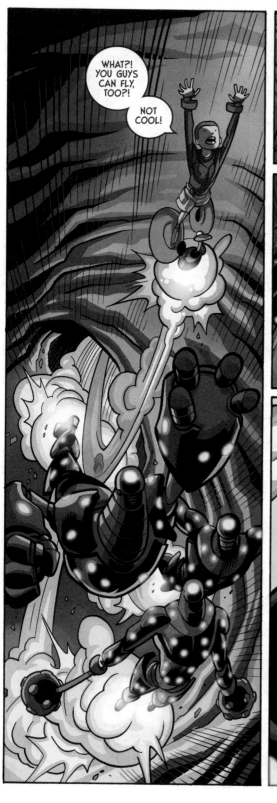

WHAT?! YOU GUYS CAN FLY, TOO?!

NOT COOL!

SHOOM!

PICK UP THE PACE, ELITES! WE CAN'T LET HIM ESCAPE!

OKAY, SO I GUESS THE ONLY WAY TO GET YOU TO STOP CHASING ME--

--IS TO STOP RUNNING!

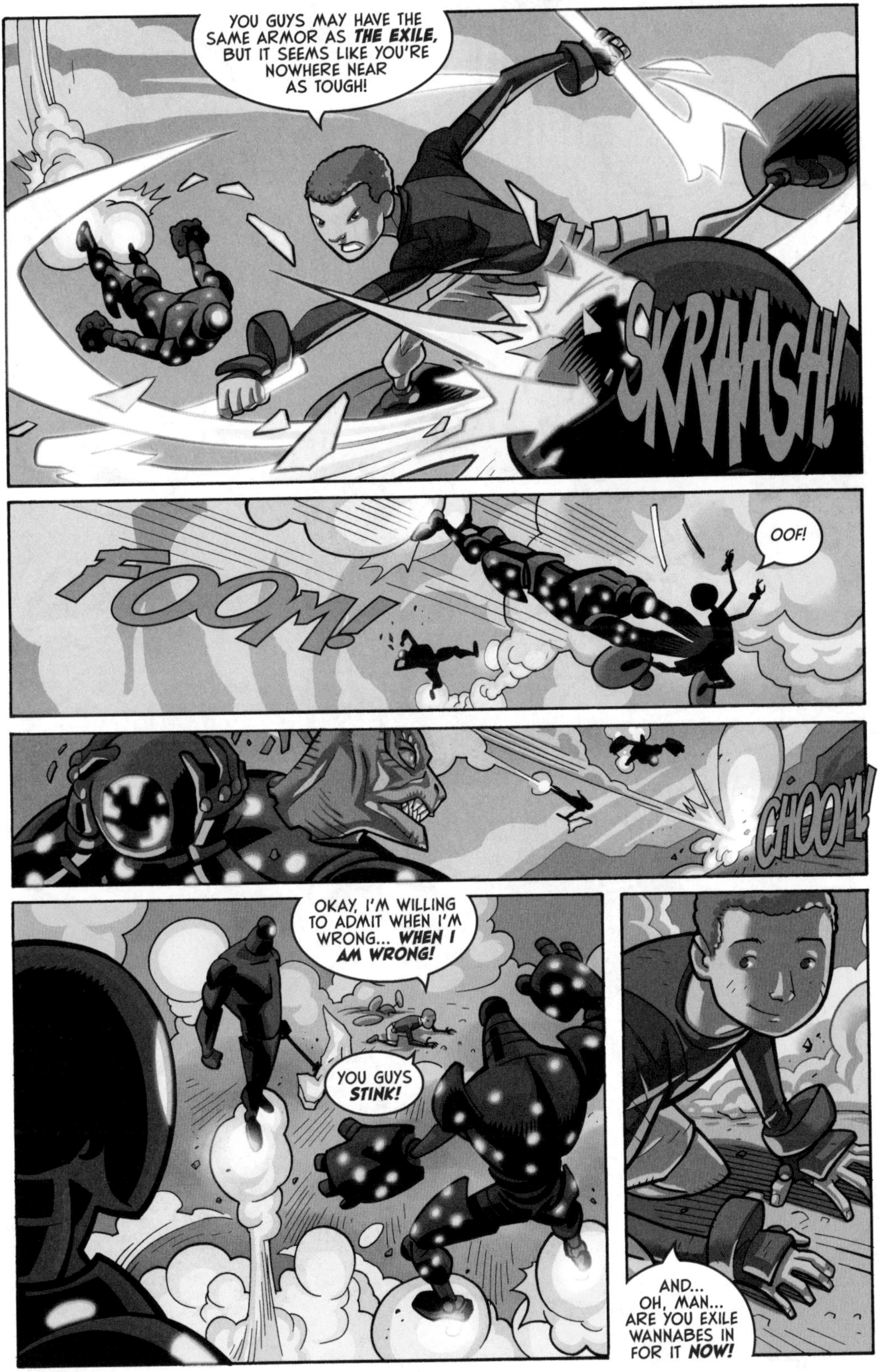
YOU GUYS MAY HAVE THE SAME ARMOR AS **THE EXILE,** BUT IT SEEMS LIKE YOU'RE NOWHERE NEAR AS TOUGH!
SKRAASH!
FOOM!
OOF!
CHOOM!
OKAY, I'M WILLING TO ADMIT WHEN I'M WRONG... **WHEN I AM WRONG!**
YOU GUYS **STINK!**
AND... OH, MAN... ARE YOU EXILE WANNABES IN FOR IT **NOW!**

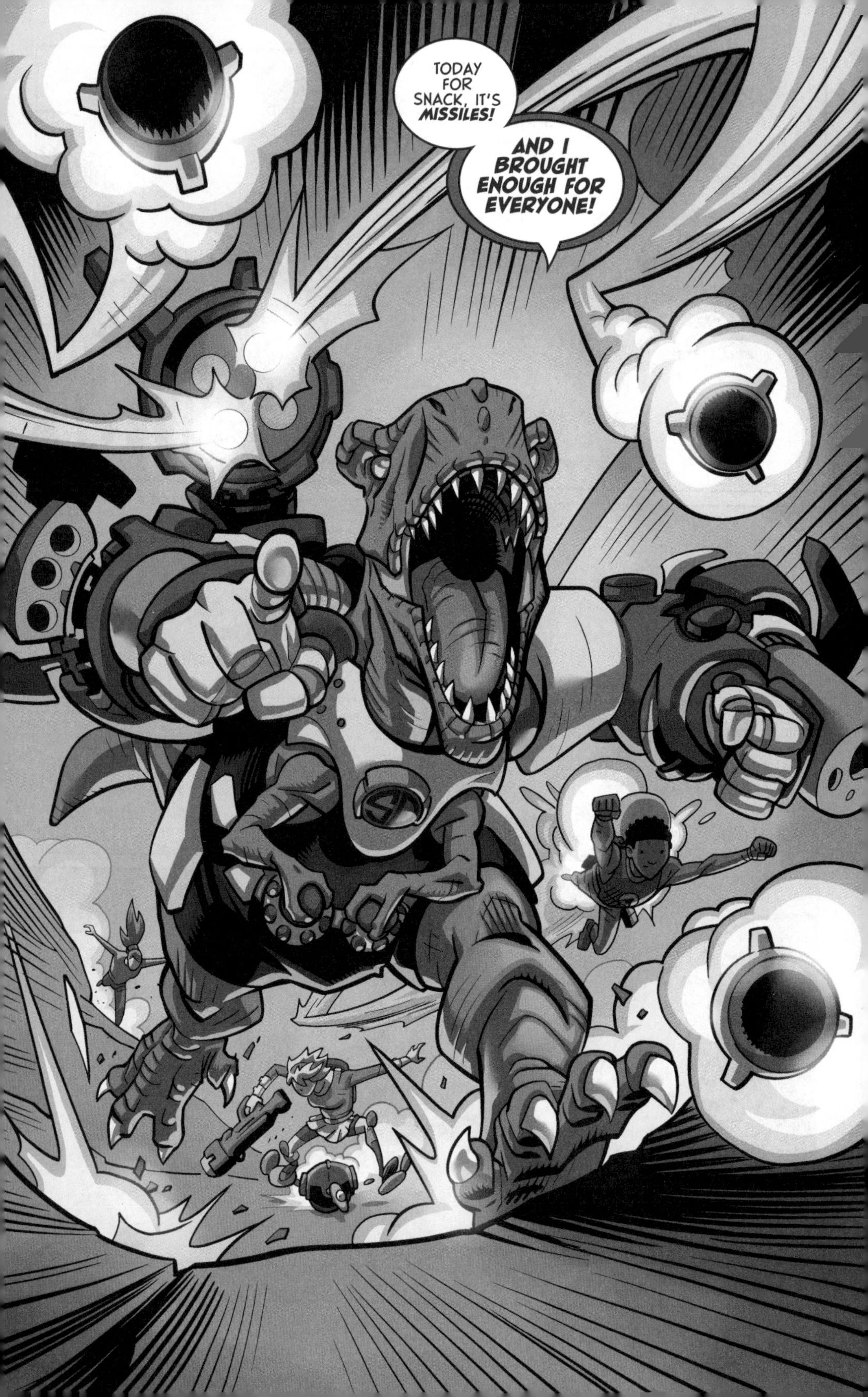
TODAY FOR SNACK, IT'S *MISSILES!*
AND I BROUGHT ENOUGH FOR EVERYONE!

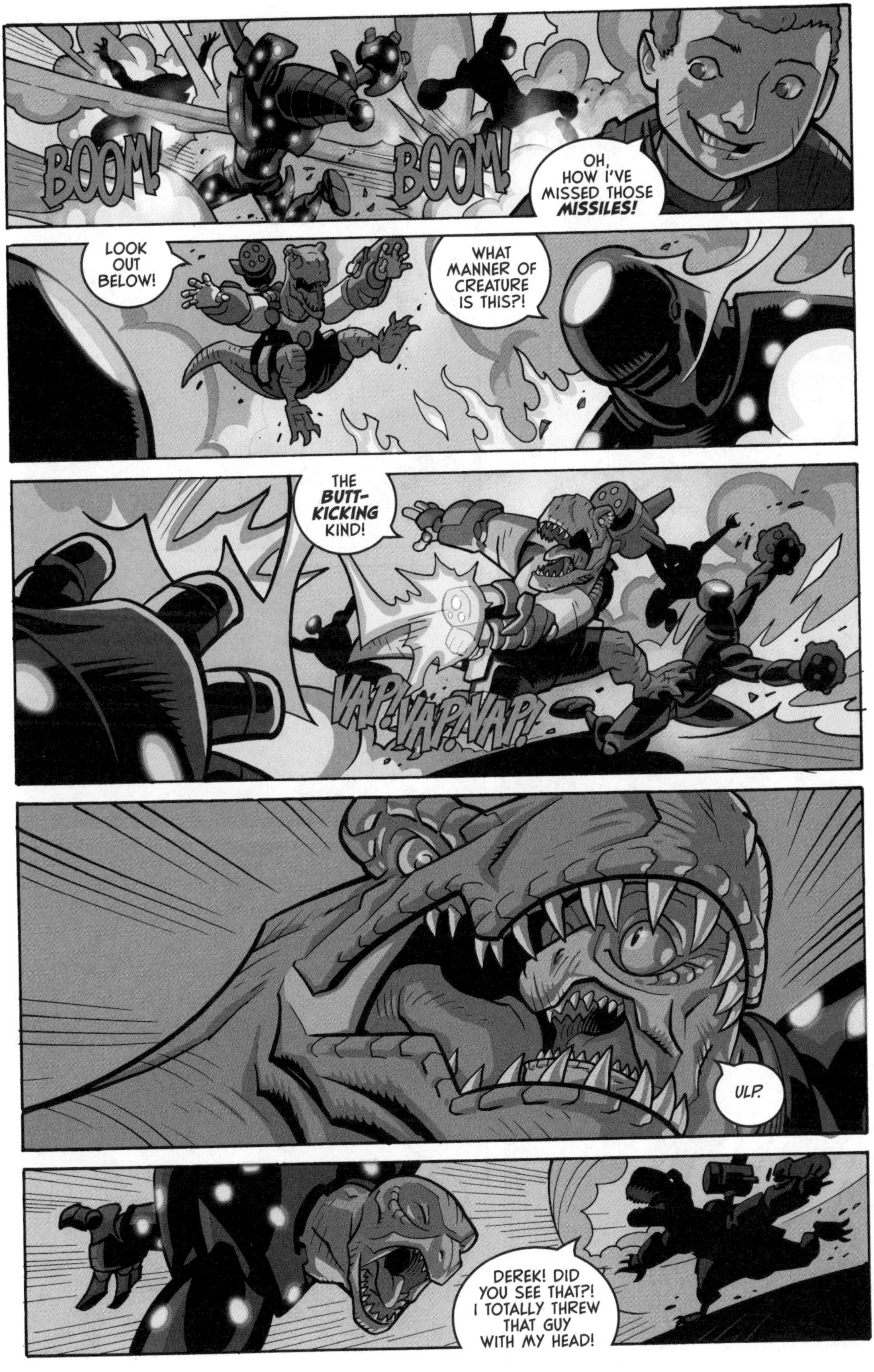
BOOM!
BOOM!
OH, HOW I'VE MISSED THOSE MISSILES!
LOOK OUT BELOW!
WHAT MANNER OF CREATURE IS THIS?!
THE BUTT-KICKING KIND!
VAP! VAP! VAP!
ULP.
DEREK! DID YOU SEE THAT?! I TOTALLY THREW THAT GUY WITH MY HEAD!

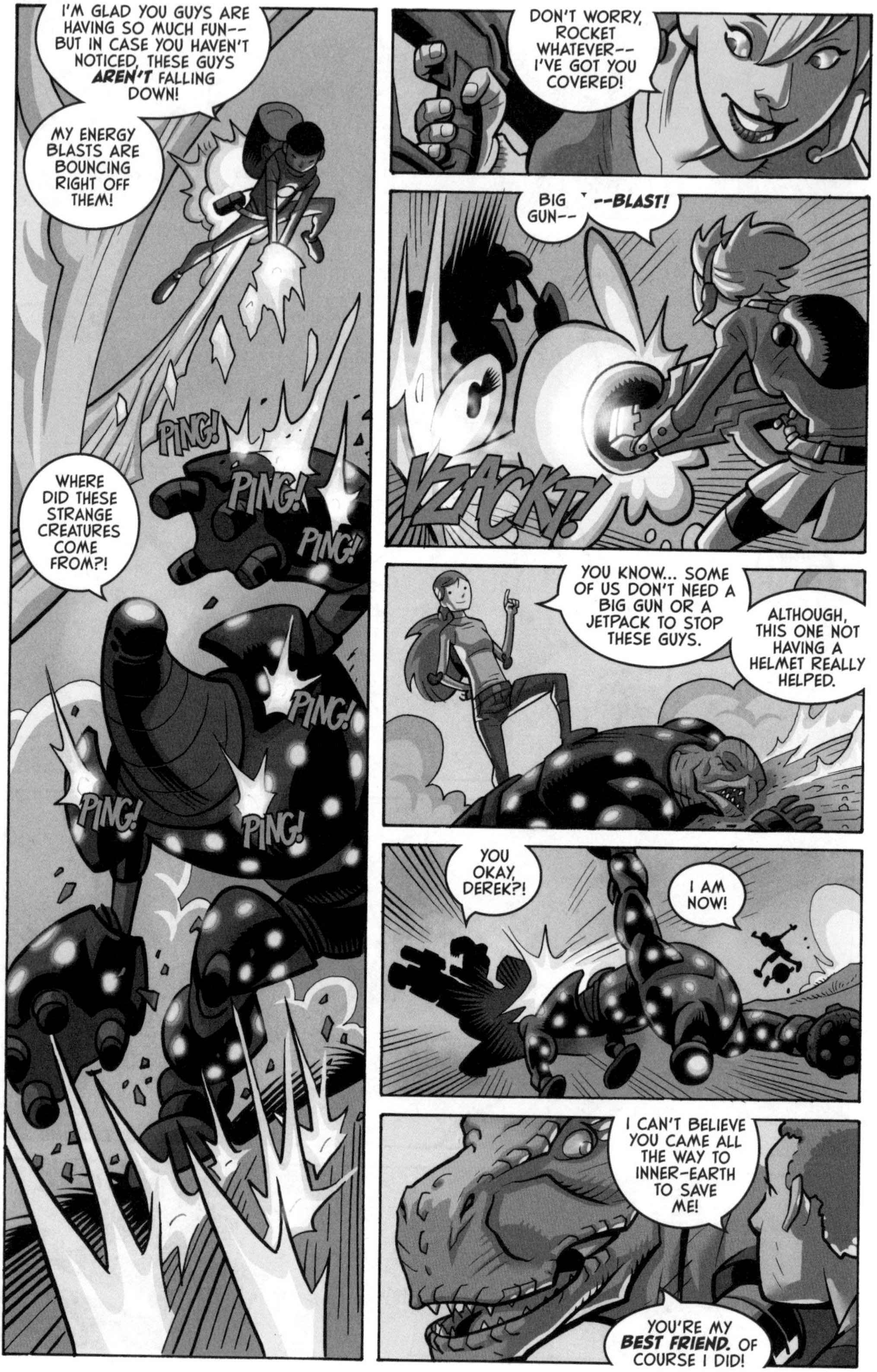

I'M GLAD YOU GUYS ARE HAVING SO MUCH FUN-- BUT IN CASE YOU HAVEN'T NOTICED, THESE GUYS **AREN'T** FALLING DOWN!
MY ENERGY BLASTS ARE BOUNCING RIGHT OFF THEM!
PING!
PING!
PING!
WHERE DID THESE STRANGE CREATURES COME FROM?!
PING!
PING!
PING!
DON'T WORRY, ROCKET WHATEVER-- I'VE GOT YOU COVERED!
BIG GUN--
--**BLAST!**
VZACKT!
YOU KNOW... SOME OF US DON'T NEED A BIG GUN OR A JETPACK TO STOP THESE GUYS.
ALTHOUGH, THIS ONE NOT HAVING A HELMET REALLY HELPED.
YOU OKAY, DEREK?!
I AM NOW!
I CAN'T BELIEVE YOU CAME ALL THE WAY TO INNER-EARTH TO SAVE ME!
YOU'RE MY **BEST FRIEND.** OF COURSE I DID!

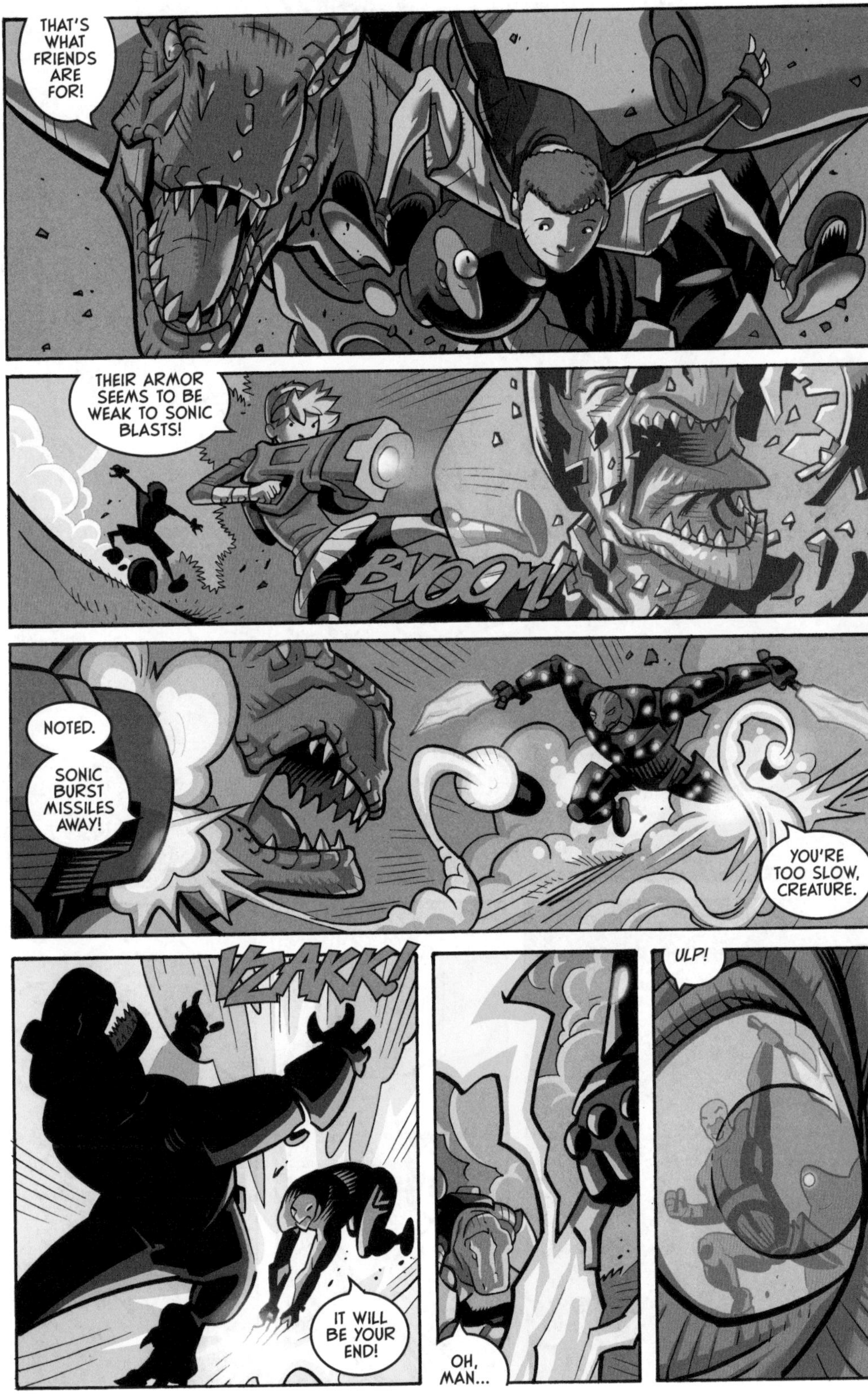
THAT'S WHAT FRIENDS ARE FOR!
THEIR ARMOR SEEMS TO BE WEAK TO SONIC BLASTS!
BVOOM!
NOTED.
SONIC BURST MISSILES AWAY!
YOU'RE TOO SLOW, CREATURE.
VZAKK!
IT WILL BE YOUR END!
OH, MAN...
ULP!

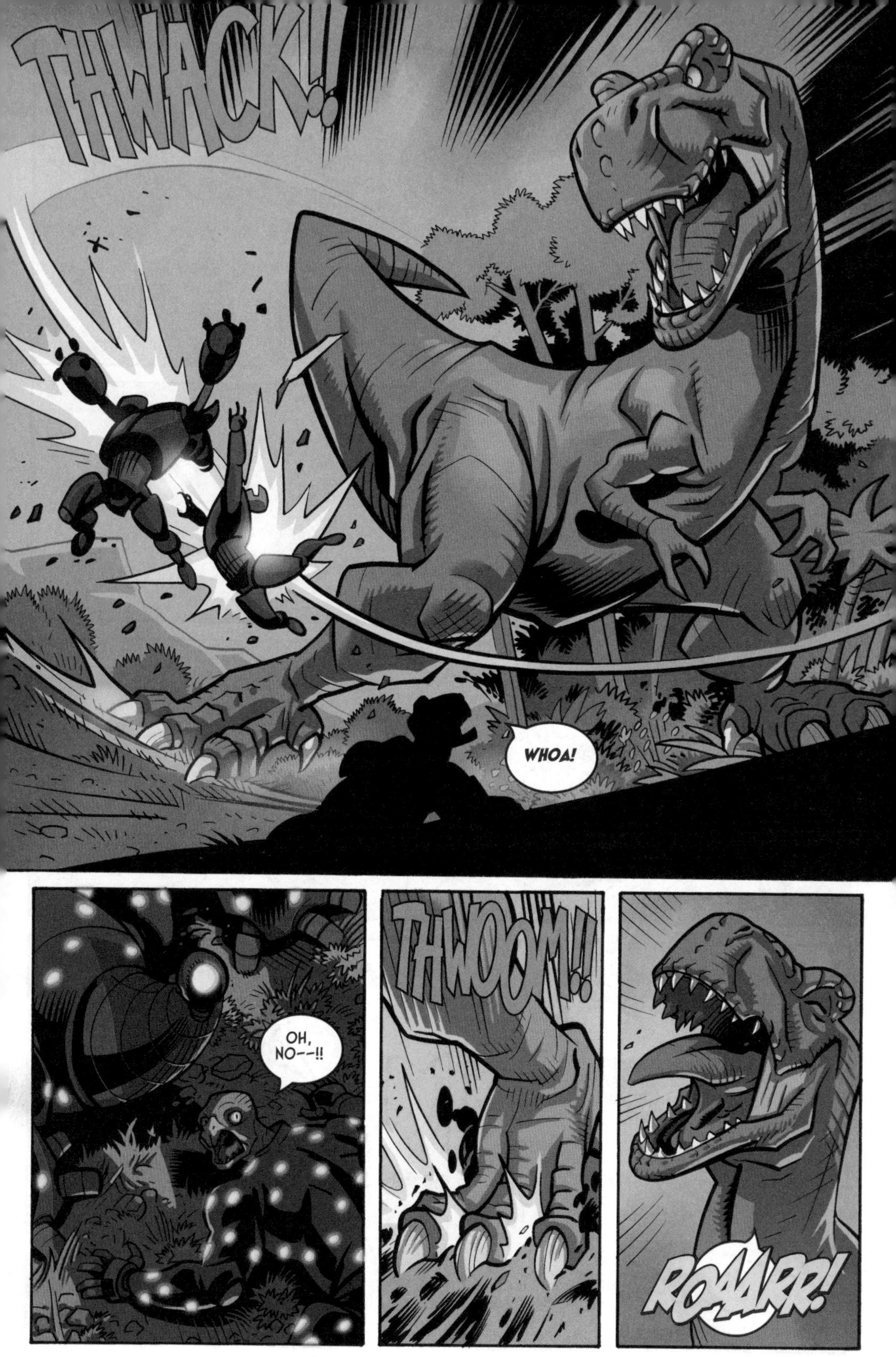
THWACK!!
WHOA!
OH, NO--!!
THWOOM!!
ROAARR!

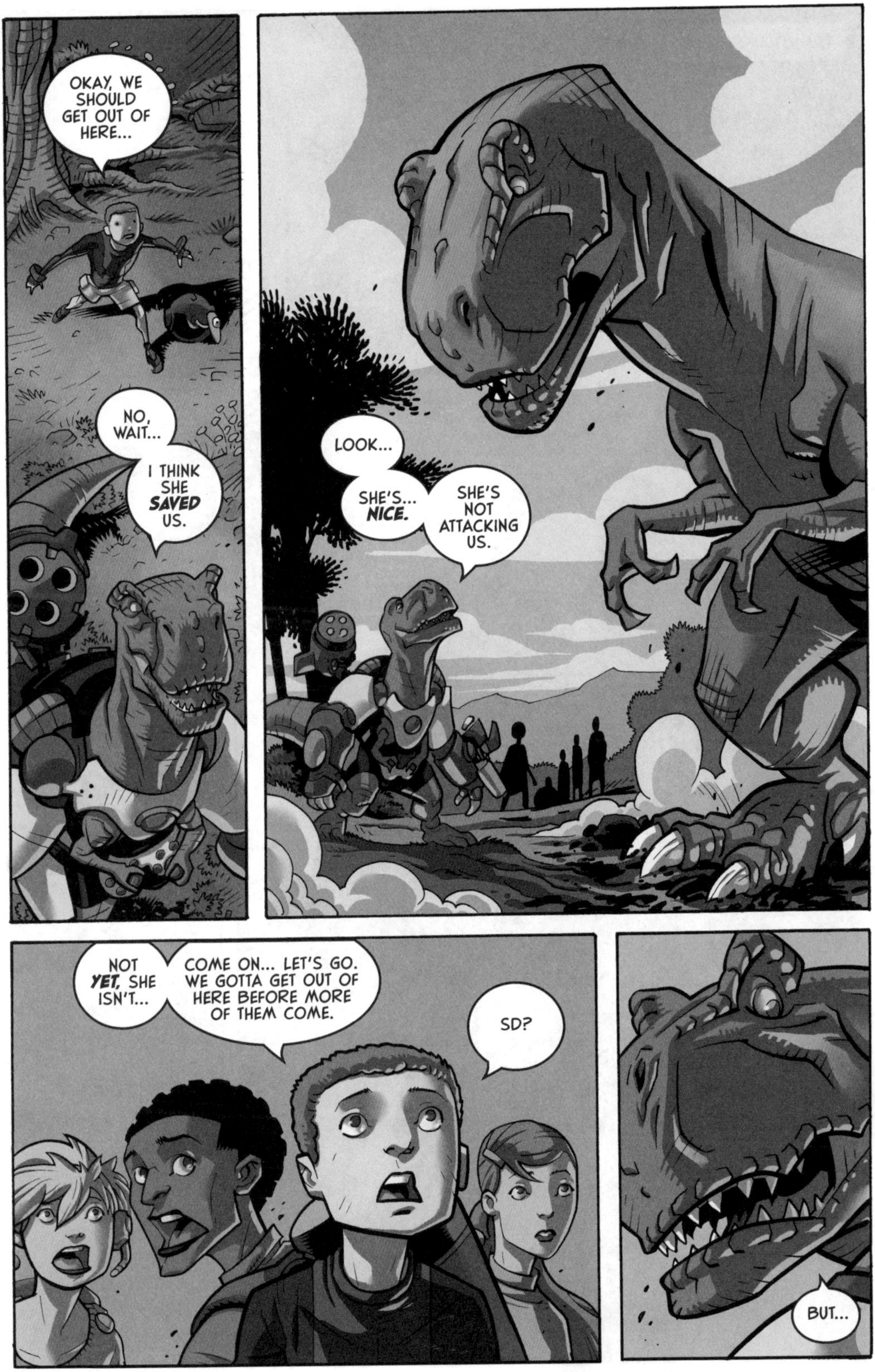
OKAY, WE SHOULD GET OUT OF HERE...
NO, WAIT...
I THINK SHE SAVED US.
LOOK...
SHE'S... NICE.
SHE'S NOT ATTACKING US.
NOT YET, SHE ISN'T...
COME ON... LET'S GO. WE GOTTA GET OUT OF HERE BEFORE MORE OF THEM COME.
SD?
BUT...

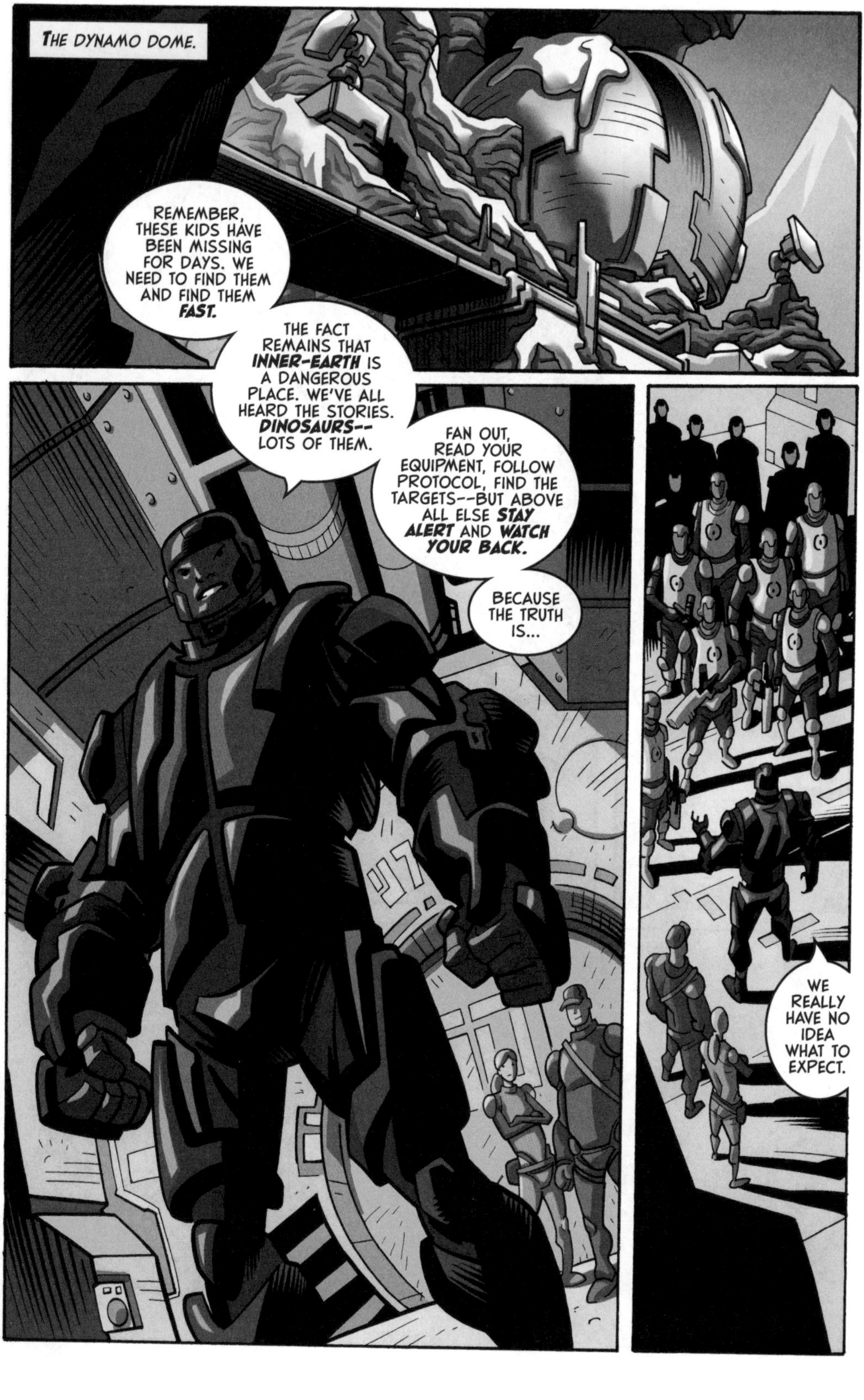
THE DYNAMO DOME.
REMEMBER, THESE KIDS HAVE BEEN MISSING FOR DAYS. WE NEED TO FIND THEM AND FIND THEM FAST.
THE FACT REMAINS THAT INNER-EARTH IS A DANGEROUS PLACE. WE'VE ALL HEARD THE STORIES. DINOSAURS--LOTS OF THEM.
FAN OUT, READ YOUR EQUIPMENT, FOLLOW PROTOCOL, FIND THE TARGETS--BUT ABOVE ALL ELSE STAY ALERT AND WATCH YOUR BACK.
BECAUSE THE TRUTH IS...
WE REALLY HAVE NO IDEA WHAT TO EXPECT.

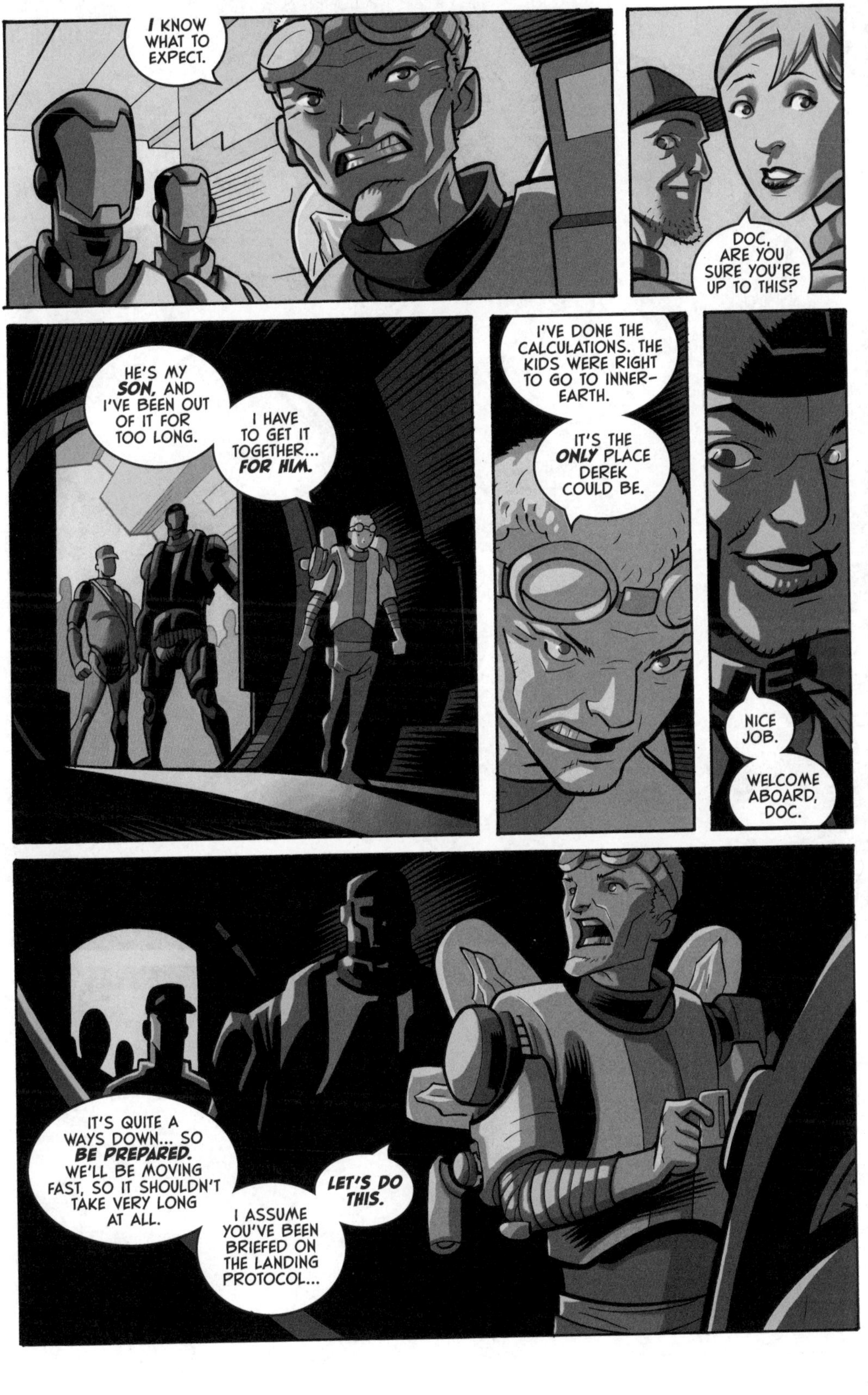
I KNOW WHAT TO EXPECT.
DOC, ARE YOU SURE YOU'RE UP TO THIS?
HE'S MY SON, AND I'VE BEEN OUT OF IT FOR TOO LONG.
I HAVE TO GET IT TOGETHER... FOR HIM.
I'VE DONE THE CALCULATIONS. THE KIDS WERE RIGHT TO GO TO INNER-EARTH.
IT'S THE ONLY PLACE DEREK COULD BE.
NICE JOB.
WELCOME ABOARD, DOC.
IT'S QUITE A WAYS DOWN... SO BE PREPARED. WE'LL BE MOVING FAST, SO IT SHOULDN'T TAKE VERY LONG AT ALL.
I ASSUME YOU'VE BEEN BRIEFED ON THE LANDING PROTOCOL...
LET'S DO THIS.

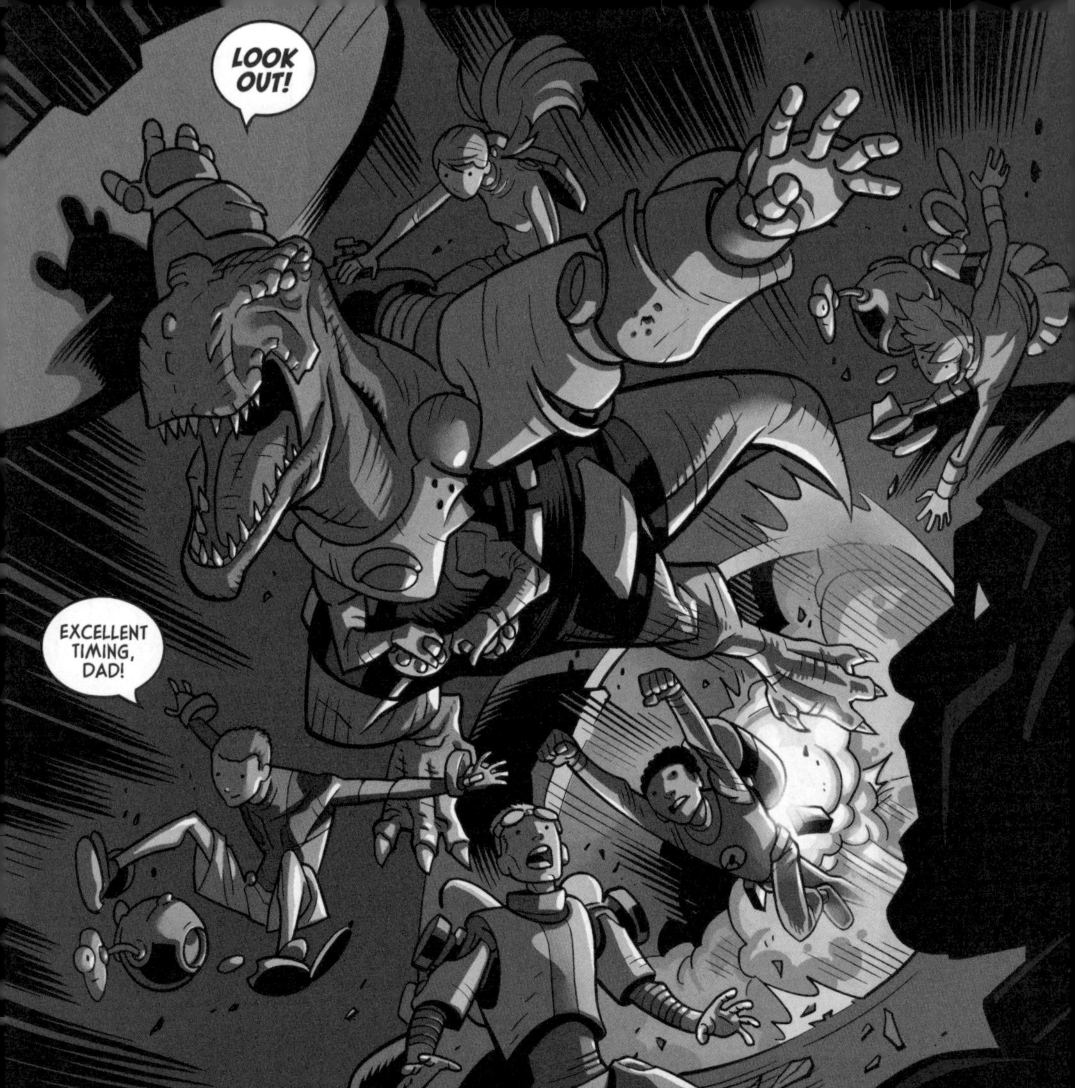
LOOK OUT!
EXCELLENT TIMING, DAD!

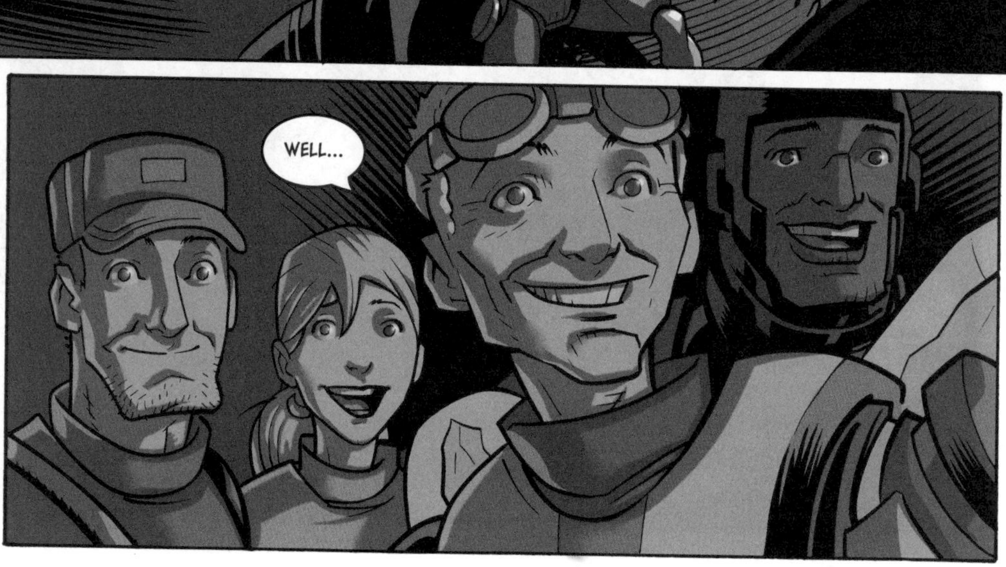
WELL...

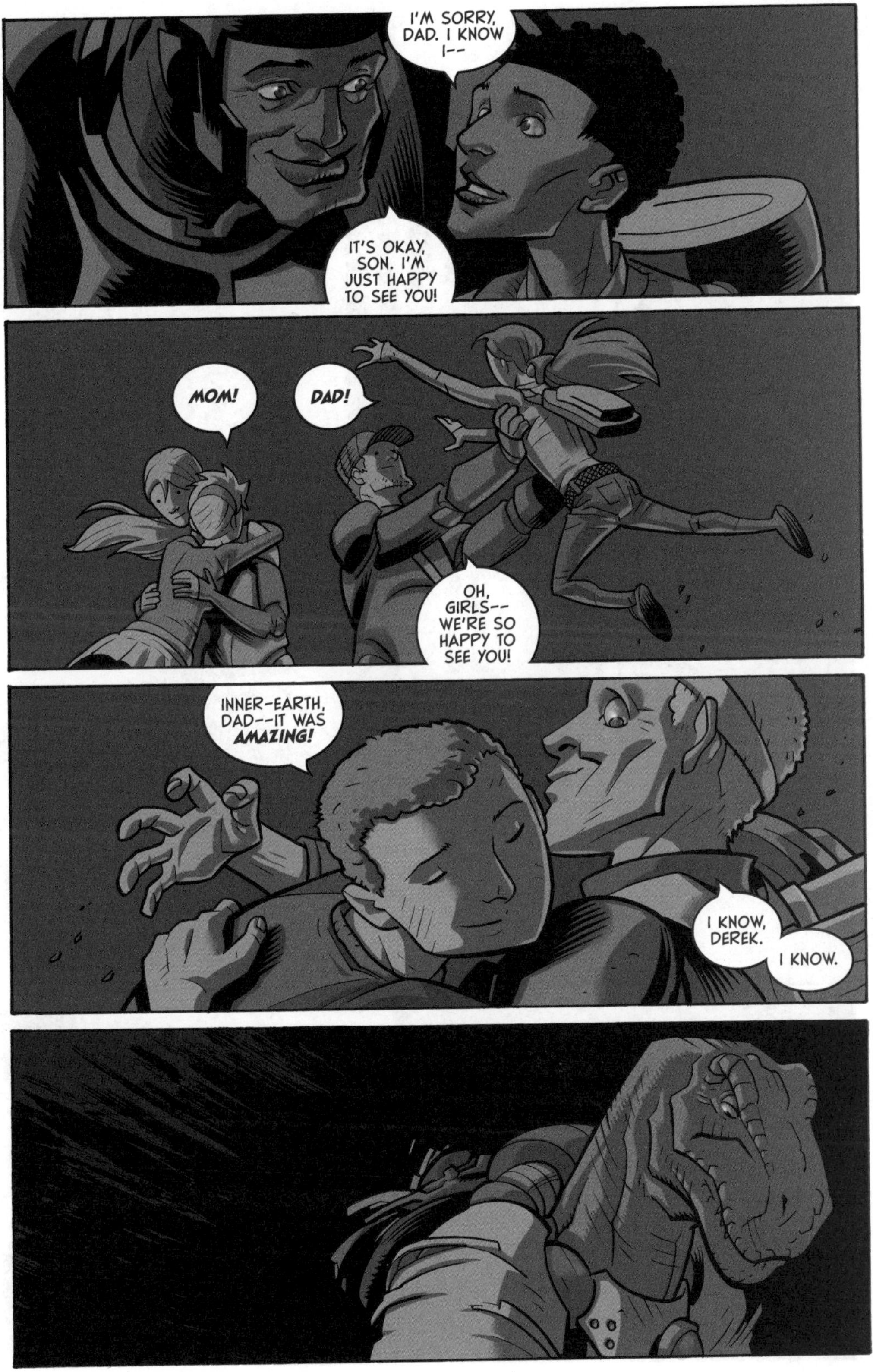
I'M SORRY, DAD. I KNOW I--
IT'S OKAY, SON. I'M JUST HAPPY TO SEE YOU!
MOM!
DAD!
OH, GIRLS-- WE'RE SO HAPPY TO SEE YOU!
INNER-EARTH, DAD--IT WAS AMAZING!
I KNOW, DEREK.
I KNOW.

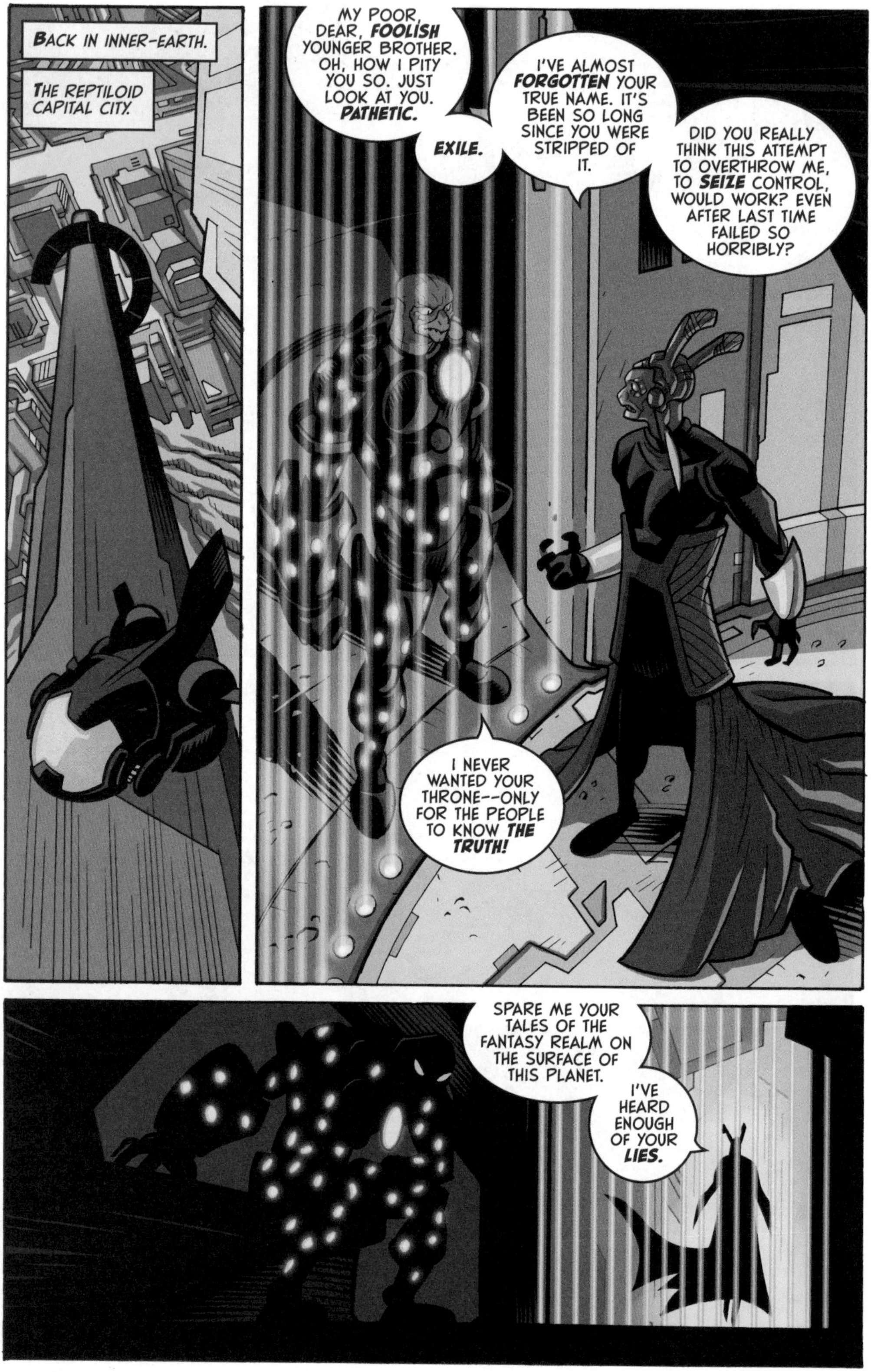
BACK IN INNER-EARTH.
THE REPTILOID CAPITAL CITY.
MY POOR, DEAR, FOOLISH YOUNGER BROTHER. OH, HOW I PITY YOU SO. JUST LOOK AT YOU. PATHETIC.
EXILE.
I'VE ALMOST FORGOTTEN YOUR TRUE NAME. IT'S BEEN SO LONG SINCE YOU WERE STRIPPED OF IT.
DID YOU REALLY THINK THIS ATTEMPT TO OVERTHROW ME, TO SEIZE CONTROL, WOULD WORK? EVEN AFTER LAST TIME FAILED SO HORRIBLY?
I NEVER WANTED YOUR THRONE--ONLY FOR THE PEOPLE TO KNOW THE TRUTH!
SPARE ME YOUR TALES OF THE FANTASY REALM ON THE SURFACE OF THIS PLANET.
I'VE HEARD ENOUGH OF YOUR LIES.

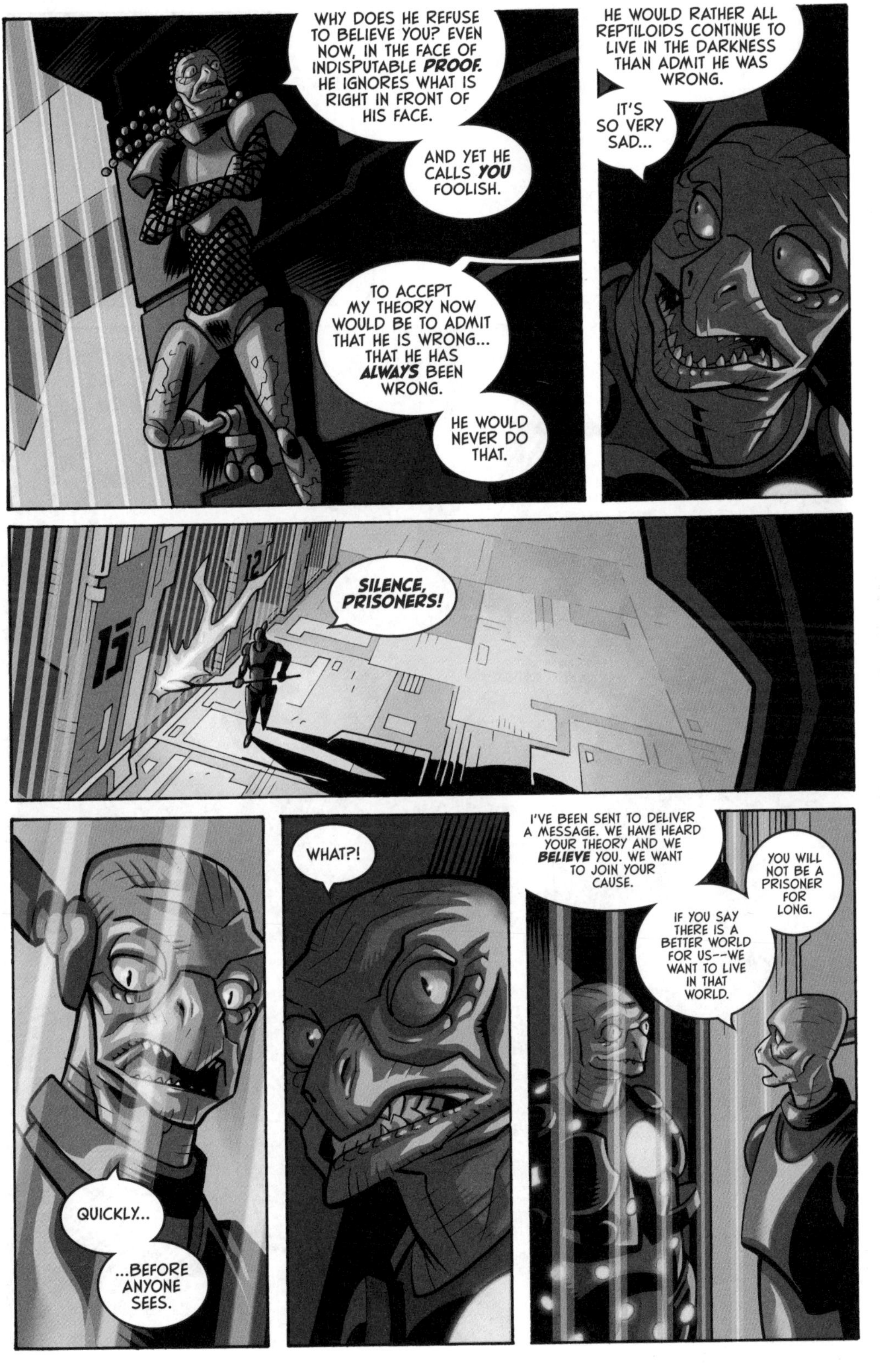
WHY DOES HE REFUSE TO BELIEVE YOU? EVEN NOW, IN THE FACE OF INDISPUTABLE **PROOF.** HE IGNORES WHAT IS RIGHT IN FRONT OF HIS FACE.
AND YET HE CALLS **YOU** FOOLISH.
TO ACCEPT MY THEORY NOW WOULD BE TO ADMIT THAT HE IS WRONG... THAT HE HAS **ALWAYS** BEEN WRONG.
HE WOULD NEVER DO THAT.
HE WOULD RATHER ALL REPTILOIDS CONTINUE TO LIVE IN THE DARKNESS THAN ADMIT HE WAS WRONG.
IT'S SO VERY SAD...
15
12
SILENCE, PRISONERS!
QUICKLY...
...BEFORE ANYONE SEES.
WHAT?!
I'VE BEEN SENT TO DELIVER A MESSAGE. WE HAVE HEARD YOUR THEORY AND WE **BELIEVE** YOU. WE WANT TO JOIN YOUR CAUSE.
IF YOU SAY THERE IS A BETTER WORLD FOR US--WE WANT TO LIVE IN THAT WORLD.
YOU WILL NOT BE A PRISONER FOR LONG.

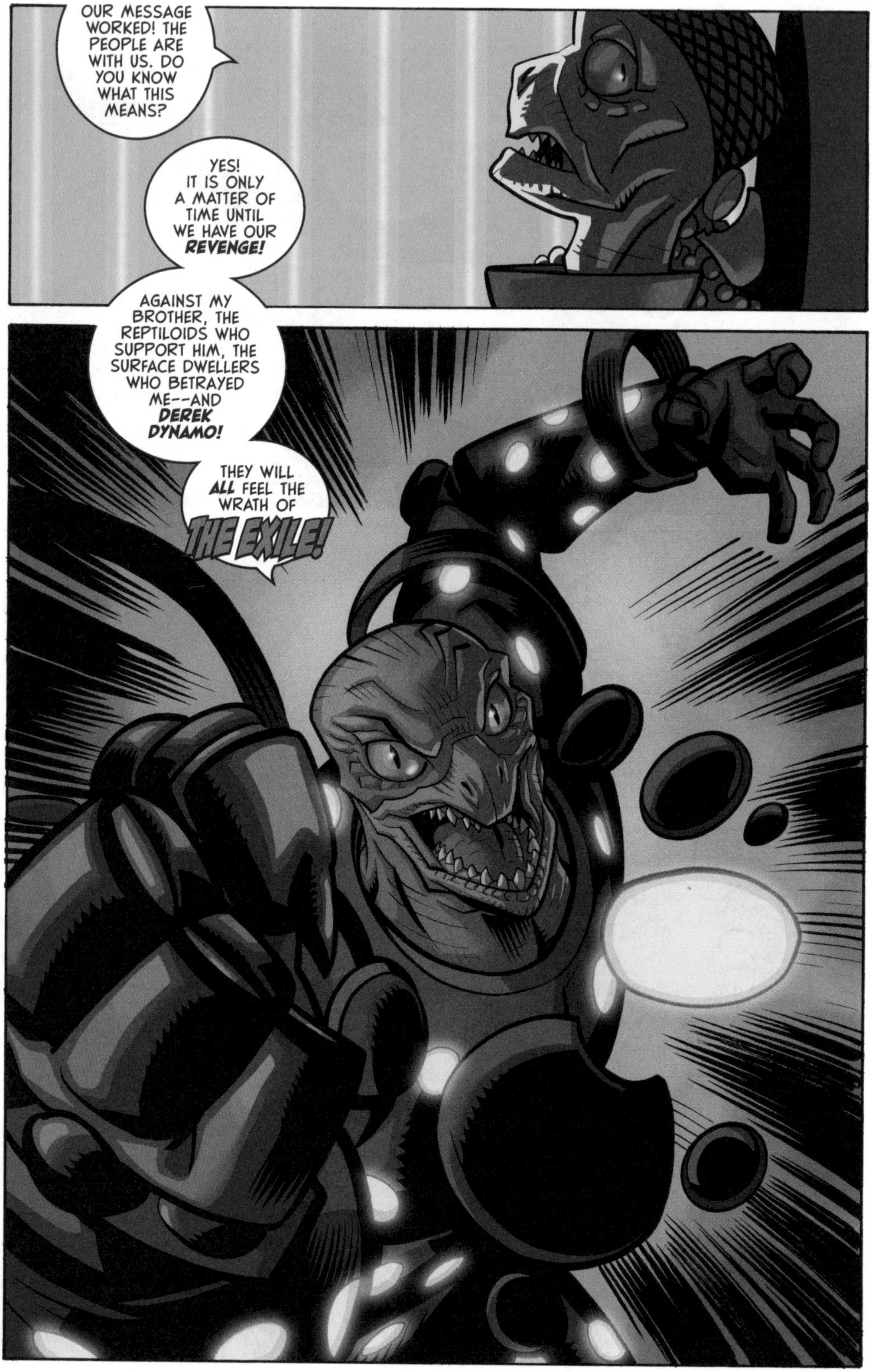
OUR MESSAGE WORKED! THE PEOPLE ARE WITH US. DO YOU KNOW WHAT THIS MEANS?
YES! IT IS ONLY A MATTER OF TIME UNTIL WE HAVE OUR REVENGE!
AGAINST MY BROTHER, THE REPTILOIDS WHO SUPPORT HIM, THE SURFACE DWELLERS WHO BETRAYED ME--AND DEREK DYNAMO!
THEY WILL ALL FEEL THE WRATH OF THE EXILE!

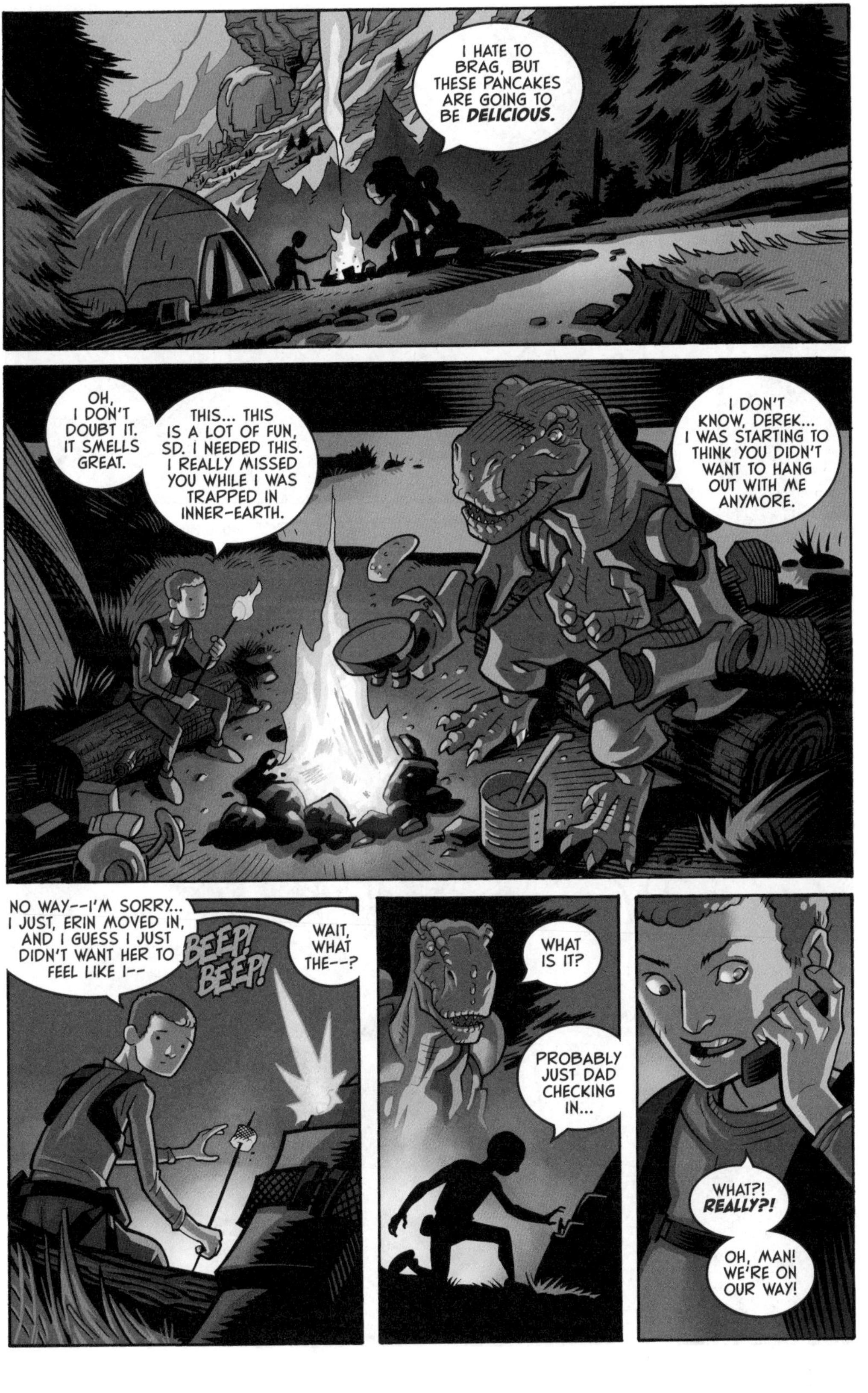
I HATE TO BRAG, BUT THESE PANCAKES ARE GOING TO BE *DELICIOUS.*
OH, I DON'T DOUBT IT. IT SMELLS GREAT.
THIS... THIS IS A LOT OF FUN, SD. I NEEDED THIS. I REALLY MISSED YOU WHILE I WAS TRAPPED IN INNER-EARTH.
I DON'T KNOW, DEREK... I WAS STARTING TO THINK YOU DIDN'T WANT TO HANG OUT WITH ME ANYMORE.
NO WAY--I'M SORRY... I JUST, ERIN MOVED IN, AND I GUESS I JUST DIDN'T WANT HER TO FEEL LIKE I--
BEEP! BEEP!
WAIT, WHAT THE--?
WHAT IS IT?
PROBABLY JUST DAD CHECKING IN...
WHAT?! ***REALLY?!***
OH, MAN! WE'RE ON OUR WAY!

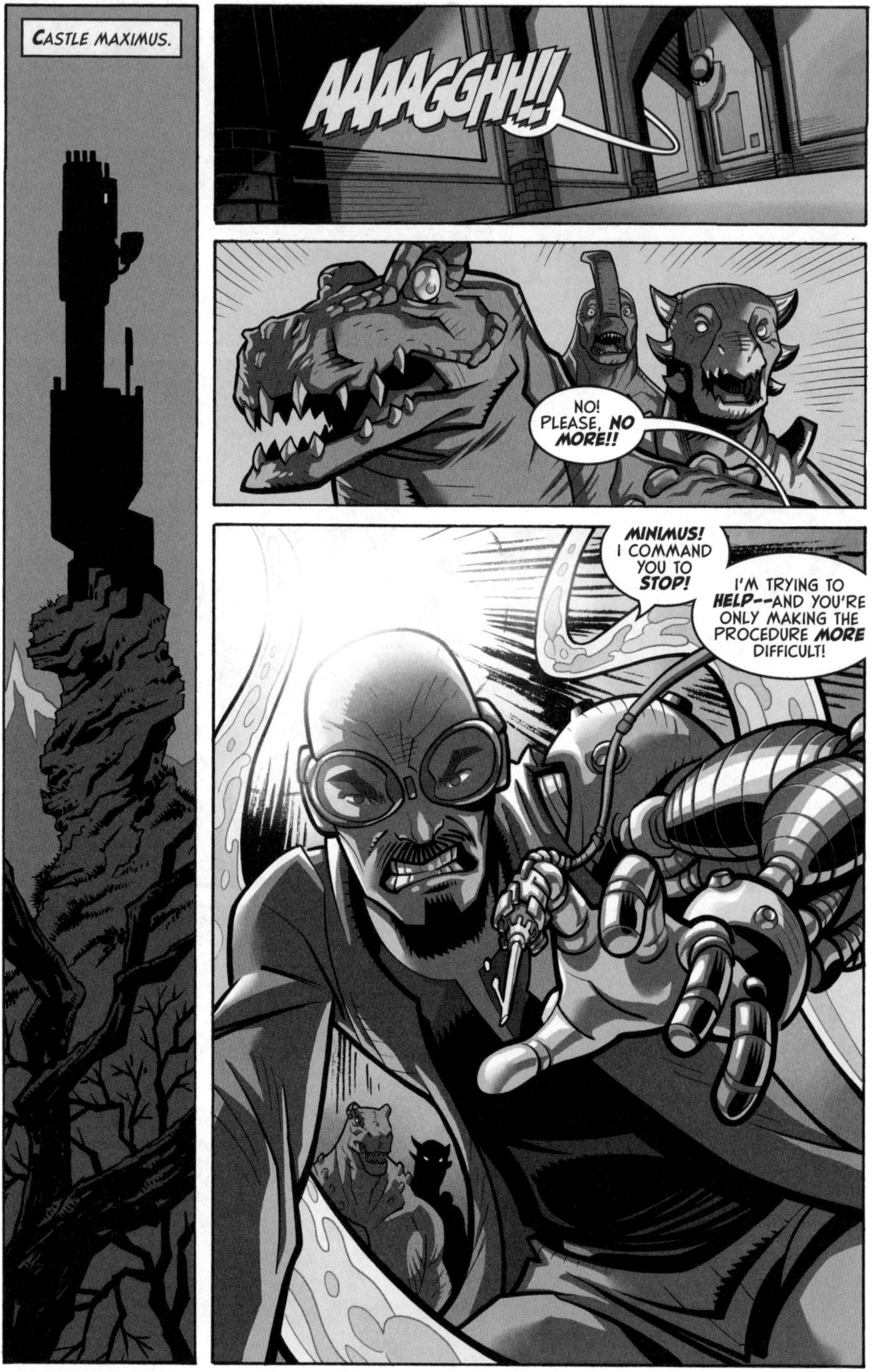
CASTLE MAXIMUS.
AAAAGGHH!!
NO! PLEASE, NO MORE!!
MINIMUS! I COMMAND YOU TO STOP!
I'M TRYING TO HELP--AND YOU'RE ONLY MAKING THE PROCEDURE MORE DIFFICULT!

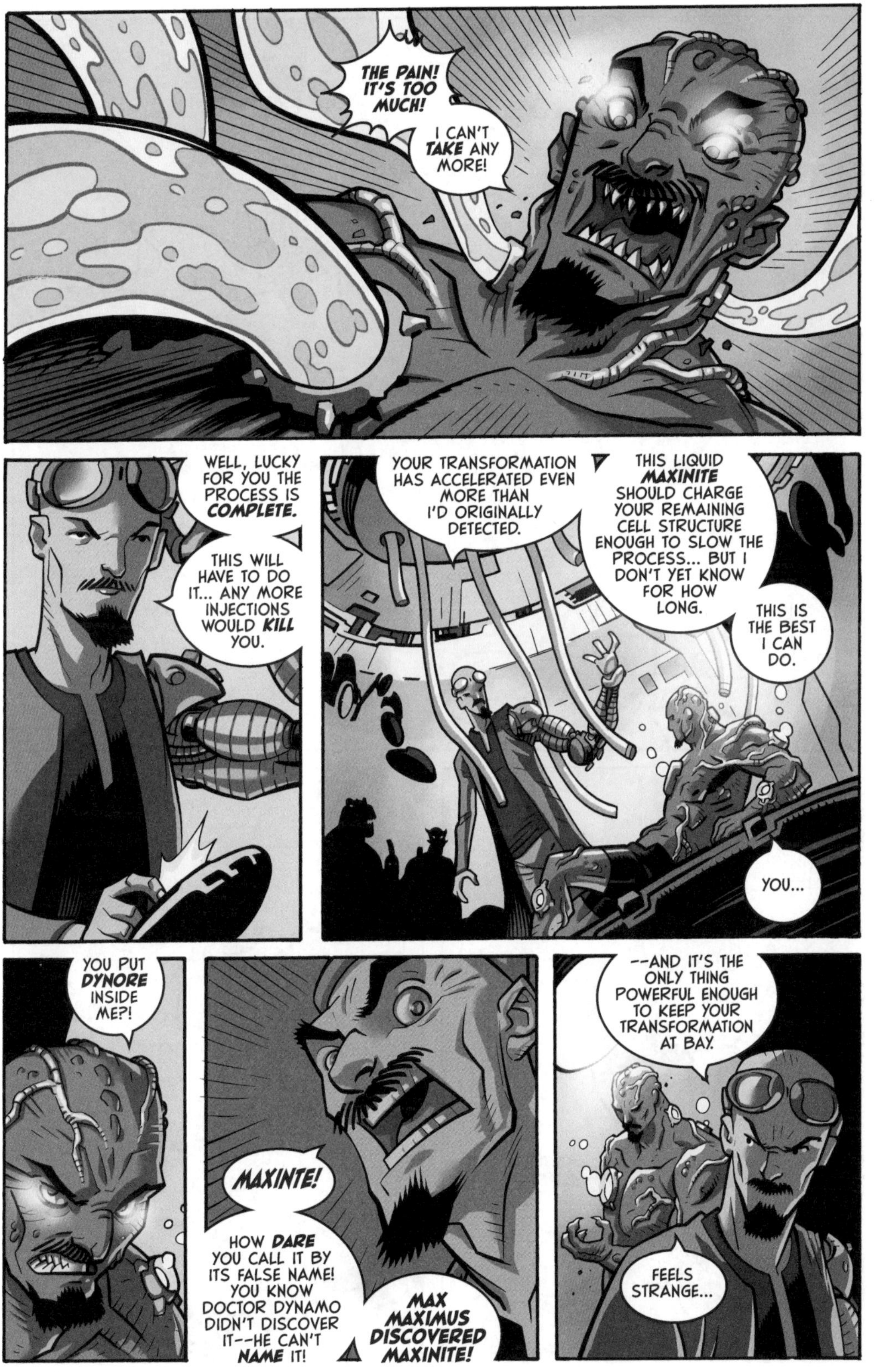
THE PAIN! IT'S TOO MUCH!
I CAN'T TAKE ANY MORE!
WELL, LUCKY FOR YOU THE PROCESS IS COMPLETE.
THIS WILL HAVE TO DO IT... ANY MORE INJECTIONS WOULD KILL YOU.
YOUR TRANSFORMATION HAS ACCELERATED EVEN MORE THAN I'D ORIGINALLY DETECTED.
THIS LIQUID MAXINITE SHOULD CHARGE YOUR REMAINING CELL STRUCTURE ENOUGH TO SLOW THE PROCESS... BUT I DON'T YET KNOW FOR HOW LONG.
THIS IS THE BEST I CAN DO.
YOU...
YOU PUT DYNORE INSIDE ME?!
MAXINTE!
HOW DARE YOU CALL IT BY ITS FALSE NAME! YOU KNOW DOCTOR DYNAMO DIDN'T DISCOVER IT--HE CAN'T NAME IT!
MAX MAXIMUS DISCOVERED MAXINITE!
--AND IT'S THE ONLY THING POWERFUL ENOUGH TO KEEP YOUR TRANSFORMATION AT BAY.
FEELS STRANGE...

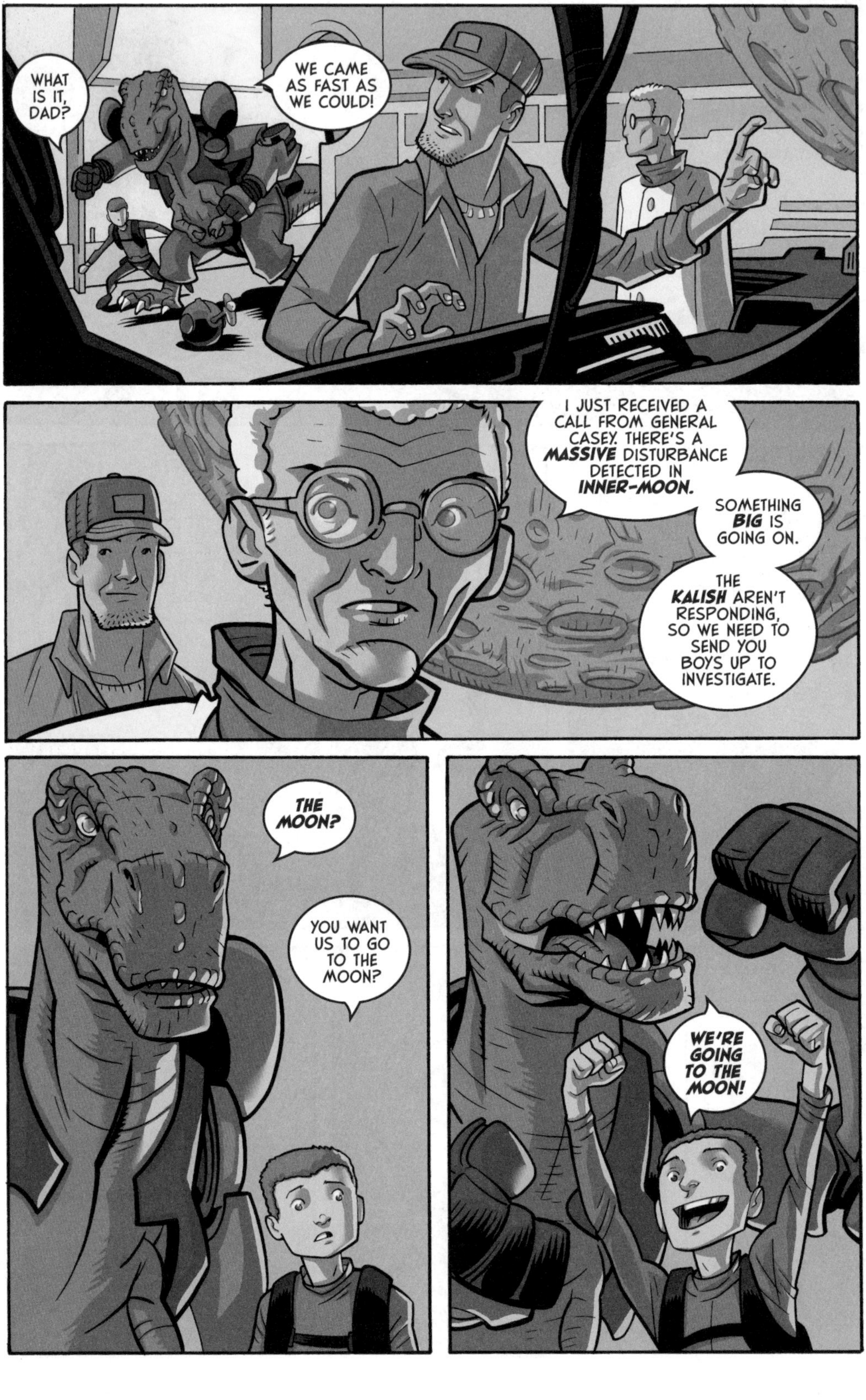
WHAT IS IT, DAD?
WE CAME AS FAST AS WE COULD!
I JUST RECEIVED A CALL FROM GENERAL CASEY. THERE'S A MASSIVE DISTURBANCE DETECTED IN INNER-MOON.
SOMETHING BIG IS GOING ON.
THE KALISH AREN'T RESPONDING, SO WE NEED TO SEND YOU BOYS UP TO INVESTIGATE.
THE MOON?
YOU WANT US TO GO TO THE MOON?
WE'RE GOING TO THE MOON!

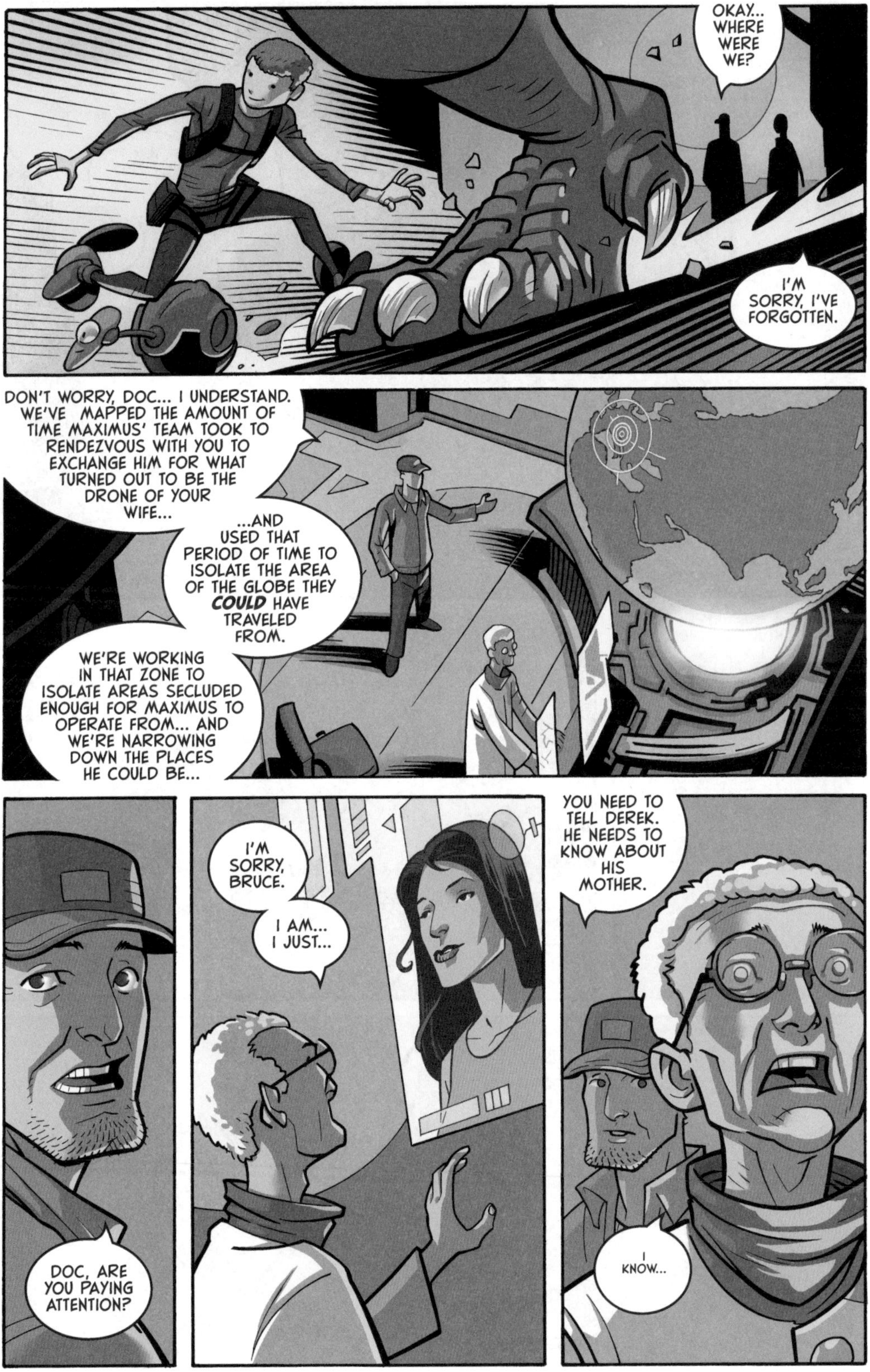
OKAY... WHERE WERE WE?
I'M SORRY, I'VE FORGOTTEN.
DON'T WORRY, DOC... I UNDERSTAND. WE'VE MAPPED THE AMOUNT OF TIME MAXIMUS' TEAM TOOK TO RENDEZVOUS WITH YOU TO EXCHANGE HIM FOR WHAT TURNED OUT TO BE THE DRONE OF YOUR WIFE...
...AND USED THAT PERIOD OF TIME TO ISOLATE THE AREA OF THE GLOBE THEY COULD HAVE TRAVELED FROM.
WE'RE WORKING IN THAT ZONE TO ISOLATE AREAS SECLUDED ENOUGH FOR MAXIMUS TO OPERATE FROM... AND WE'RE NARROWING DOWN THE PLACES HE COULD BE...
DOC, ARE YOU PAYING ATTENTION?
I'M SORRY, BRUCE.
I AM... I JUST...
YOU NEED TO TELL DEREK. HE NEEDS TO KNOW ABOUT HIS MOTHER.
I KNOW...

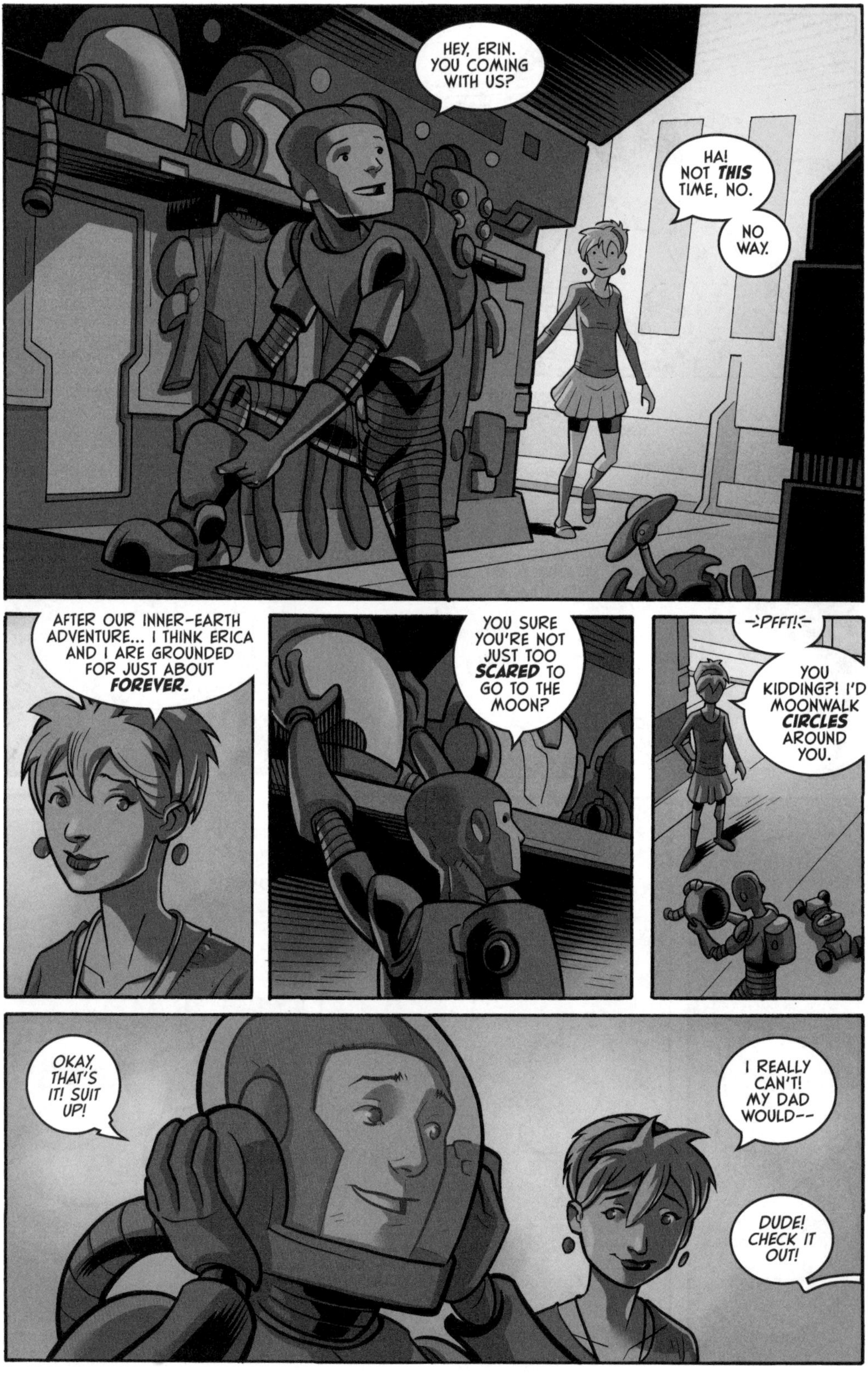
HEY, ERIN. YOU COMING WITH US?
HA! NOT THIS TIME, NO.
NO WAY.
AFTER OUR INNER-EARTH ADVENTURE... I THINK ERICA AND I ARE GROUNDED FOR JUST ABOUT FOREVER.
YOU SURE YOU'RE NOT JUST TOO SCARED TO GO TO THE MOON?
PFFT!
YOU KIDDING?! I'D MOONWALK CIRCLES AROUND YOU.
OKAY, THAT'S IT! SUIT UP!
I REALLY CAN'T! MY DAD WOULD--
DUDE! CHECK IT OUT!

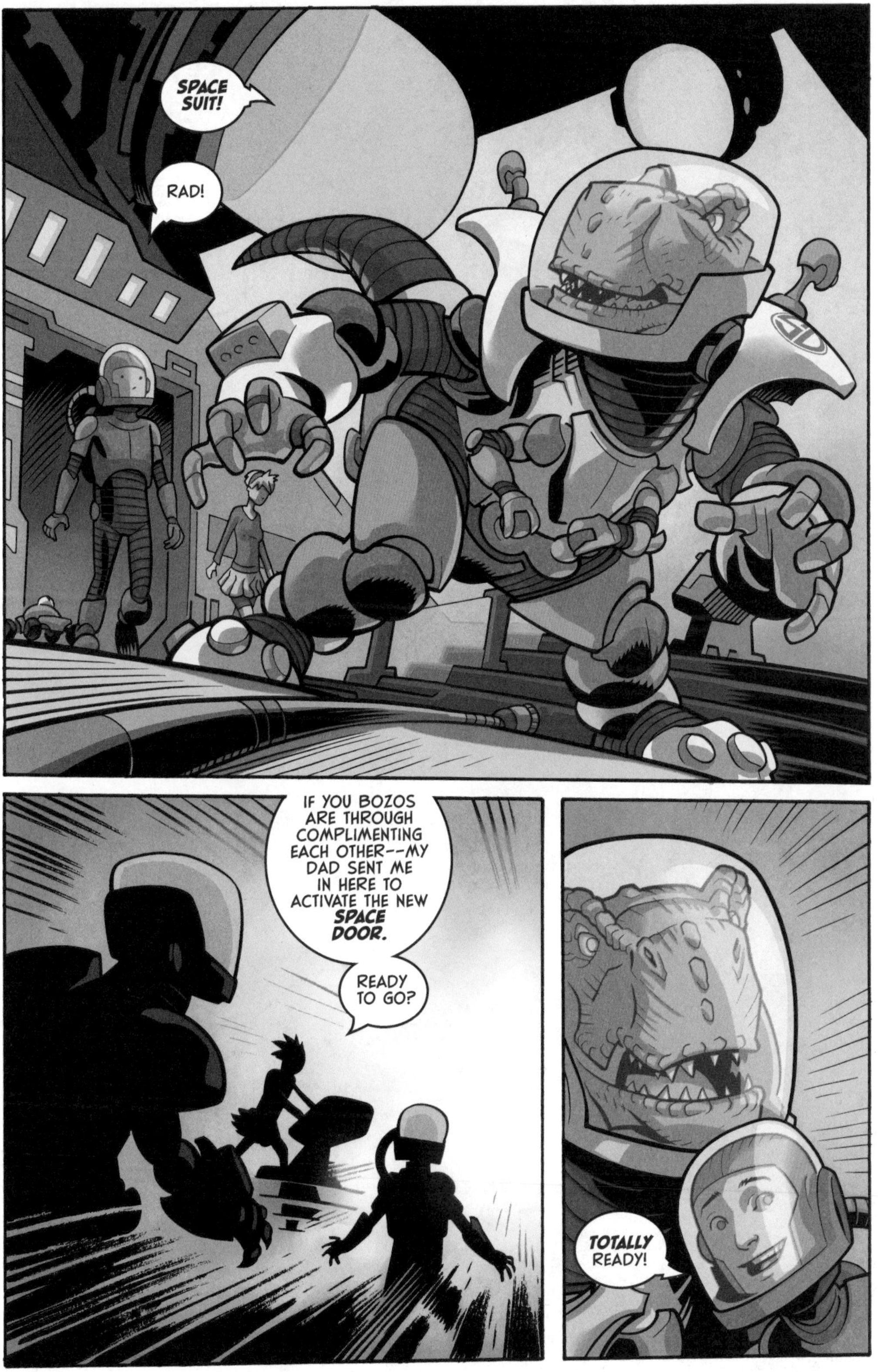
SPACE SUIT!
RAD!
IF YOU BOZOS ARE THROUGH COMPLIMENTING EACH OTHER--MY DAD SENT ME IN HERE TO ACTIVATE THE NEW SPACE DOOR.
READY TO GO?
TOTALLY READY!

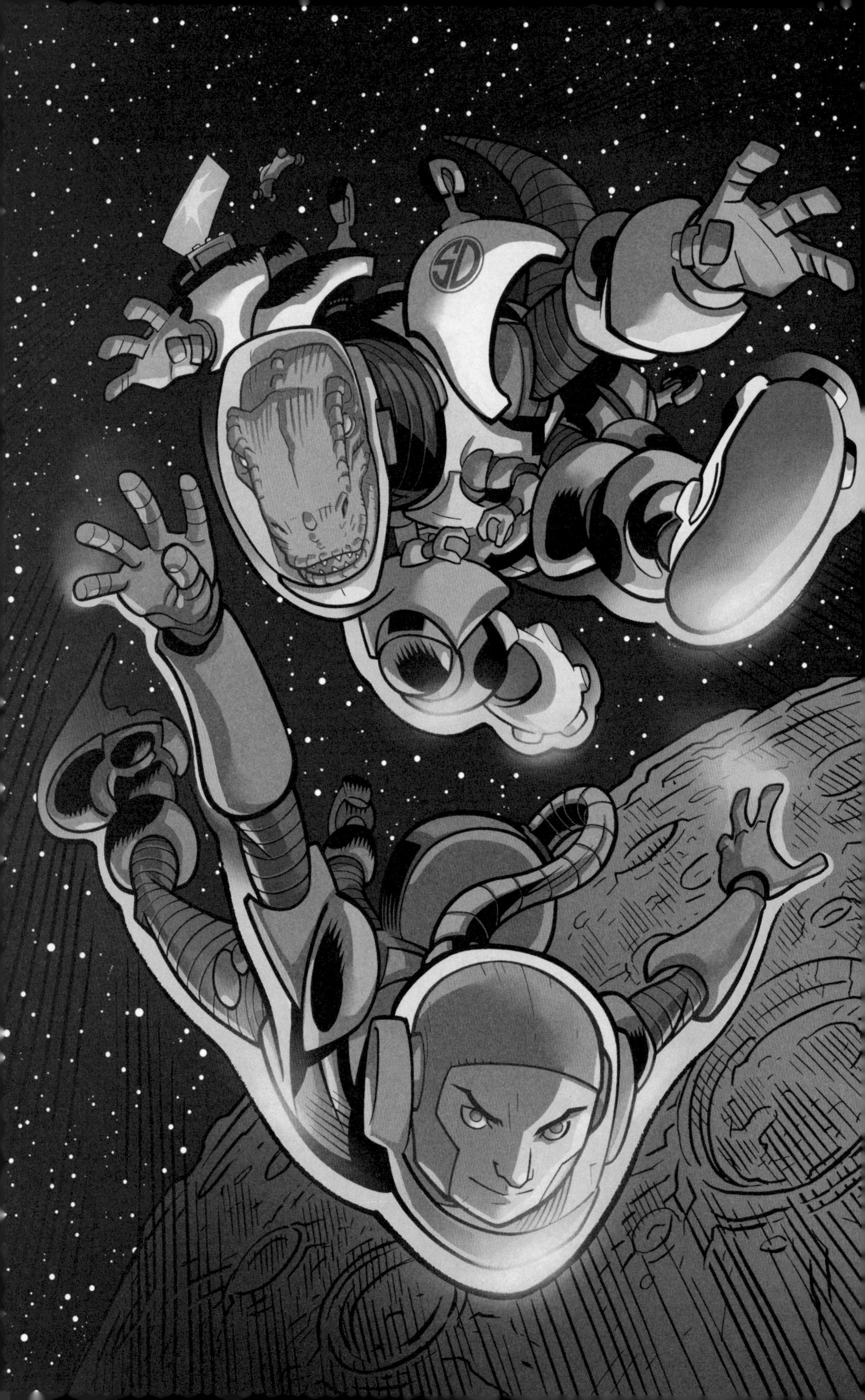

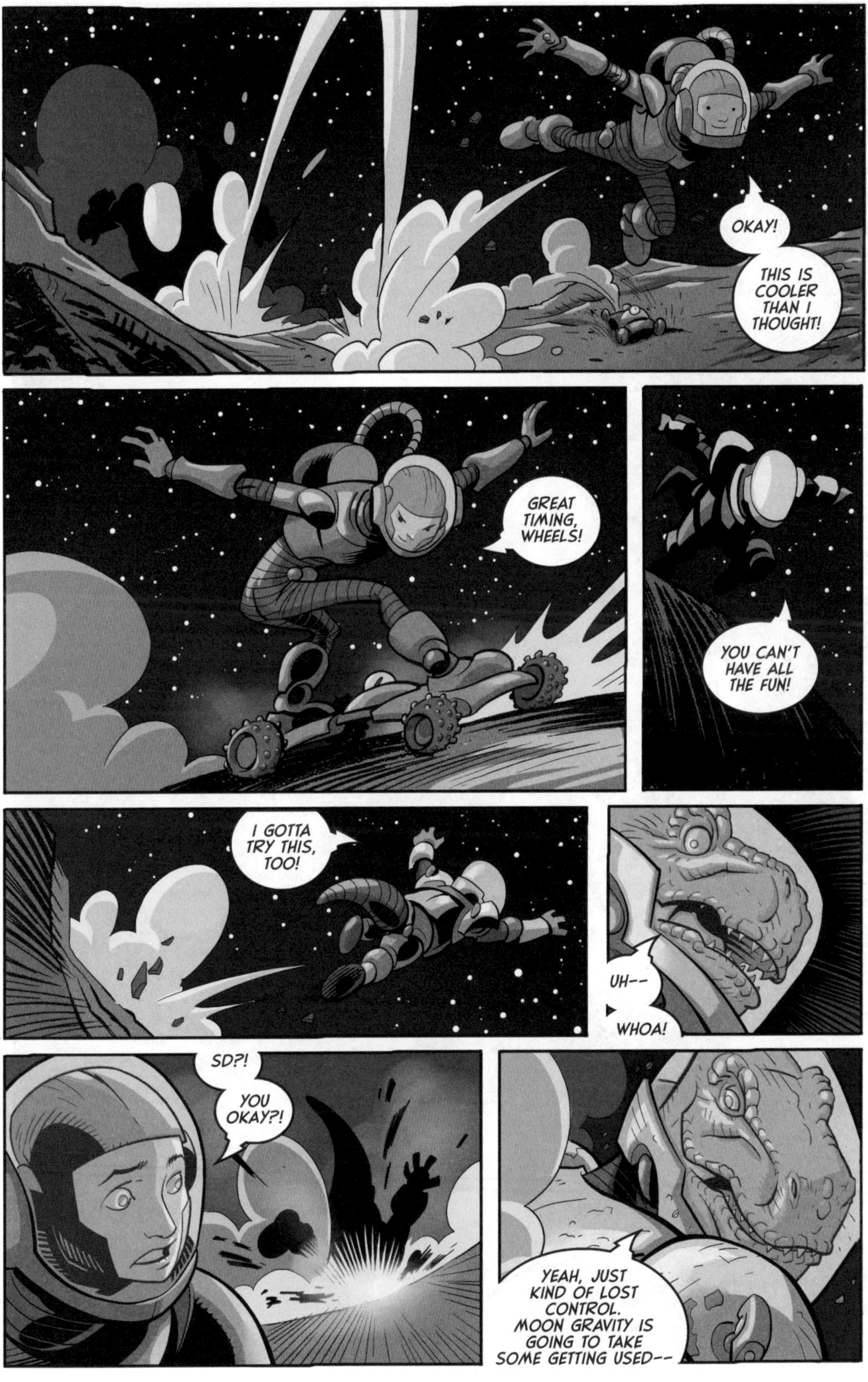
OKAY!
THIS IS COOLER THAN I THOUGHT!
GREAT TIMING, WHEELS!
YOU CAN'T HAVE ALL THE FUN!
I GOTTA TRY THIS, TOO!
UH--
WHOA!
SD?!
YOU OKAY?!
YEAH, JUST KIND OF LOST CONTROL. MOON GRAVITY IS GOING TO TAKE SOME GETTING USED--

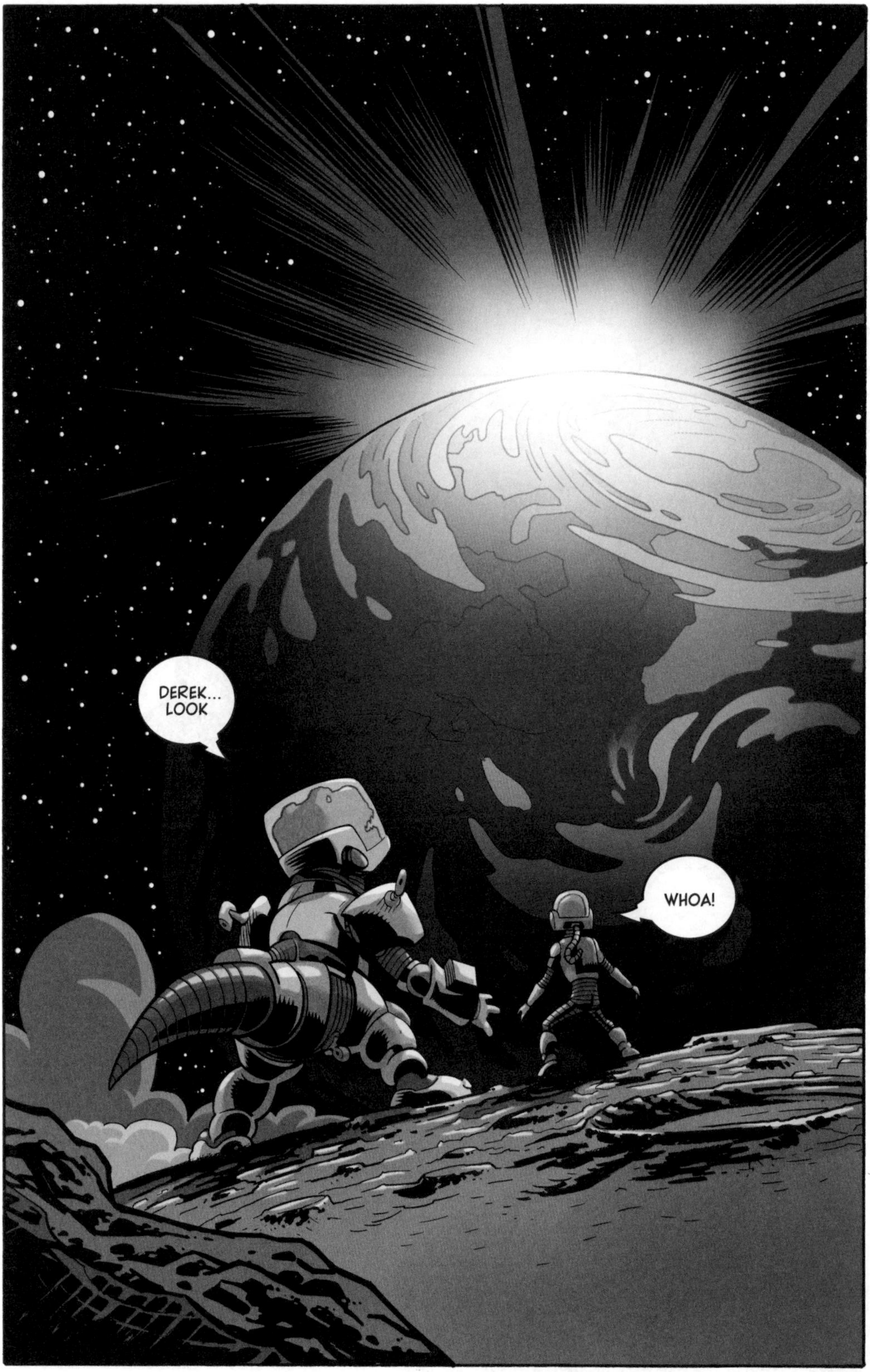
DEREK... LOOK
WHOA!

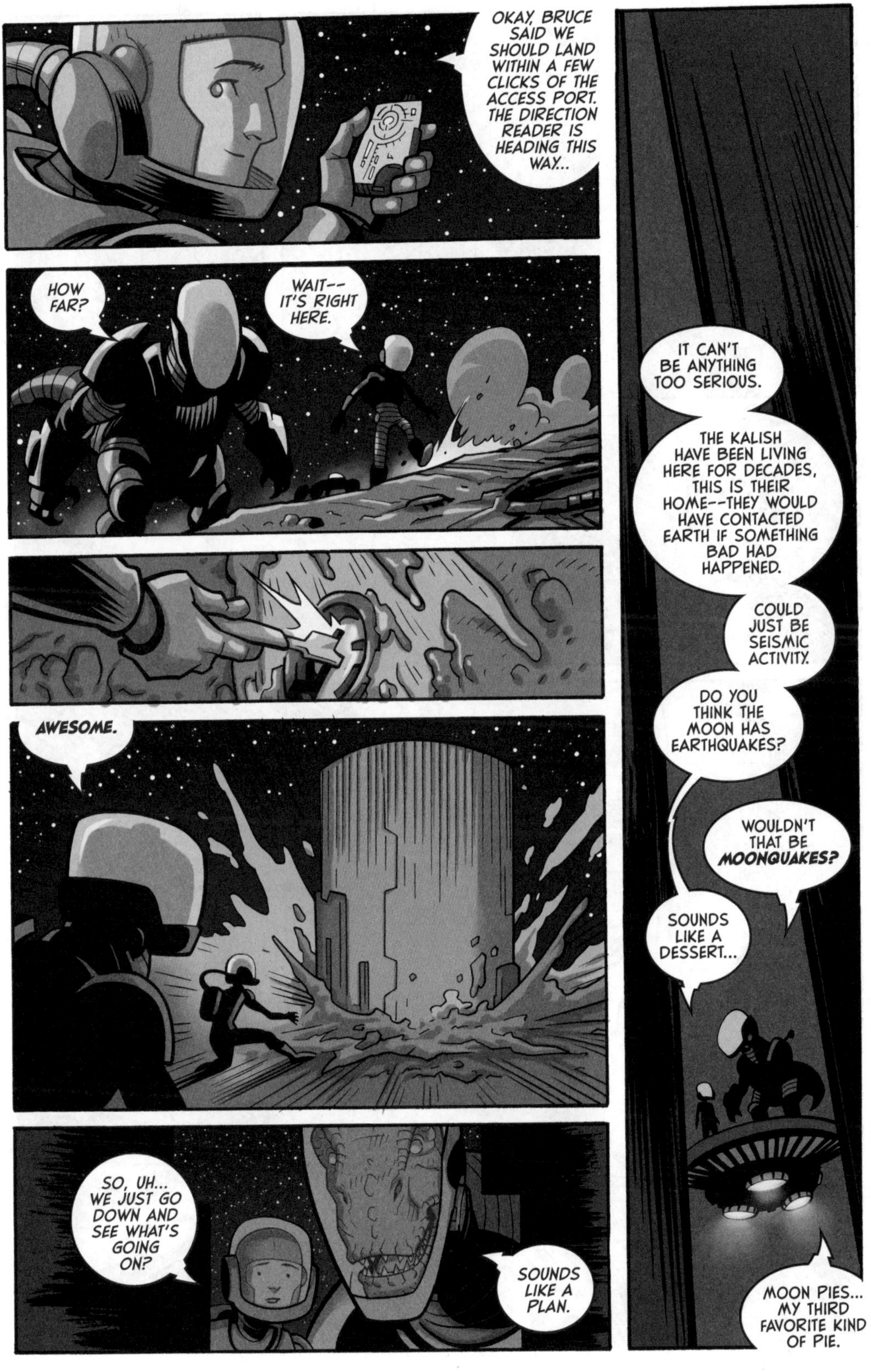

OKAY, BRUCE SAID WE SHOULD LAND WITHIN A FEW CLICKS OF THE ACCESS PORT. THE DIRECTION READER IS HEADING THIS WAY...
HOW FAR?
WAIT-- IT'S RIGHT HERE.
AWESOME.
SO, UH... WE JUST GO DOWN AND SEE WHAT'S GOING ON?
SOUNDS LIKE A PLAN.
IT CAN'T BE ANYTHING TOO SERIOUS.
THE KALISH HAVE BEEN LIVING HERE FOR DECADES, THIS IS THEIR HOME--THEY WOULD HAVE CONTACTED EARTH IF SOMETHING BAD HAD HAPPENED.
COULD JUST BE SEISMIC ACTIVITY.
DO YOU THINK THE MOON HAS EARTHQUAKES?
WOULDN'T THAT BE ***MOONQUAKES?***
SOUNDS LIKE A DESSERT...
MOON PIES... MY THIRD FAVORITE KIND OF PIE.

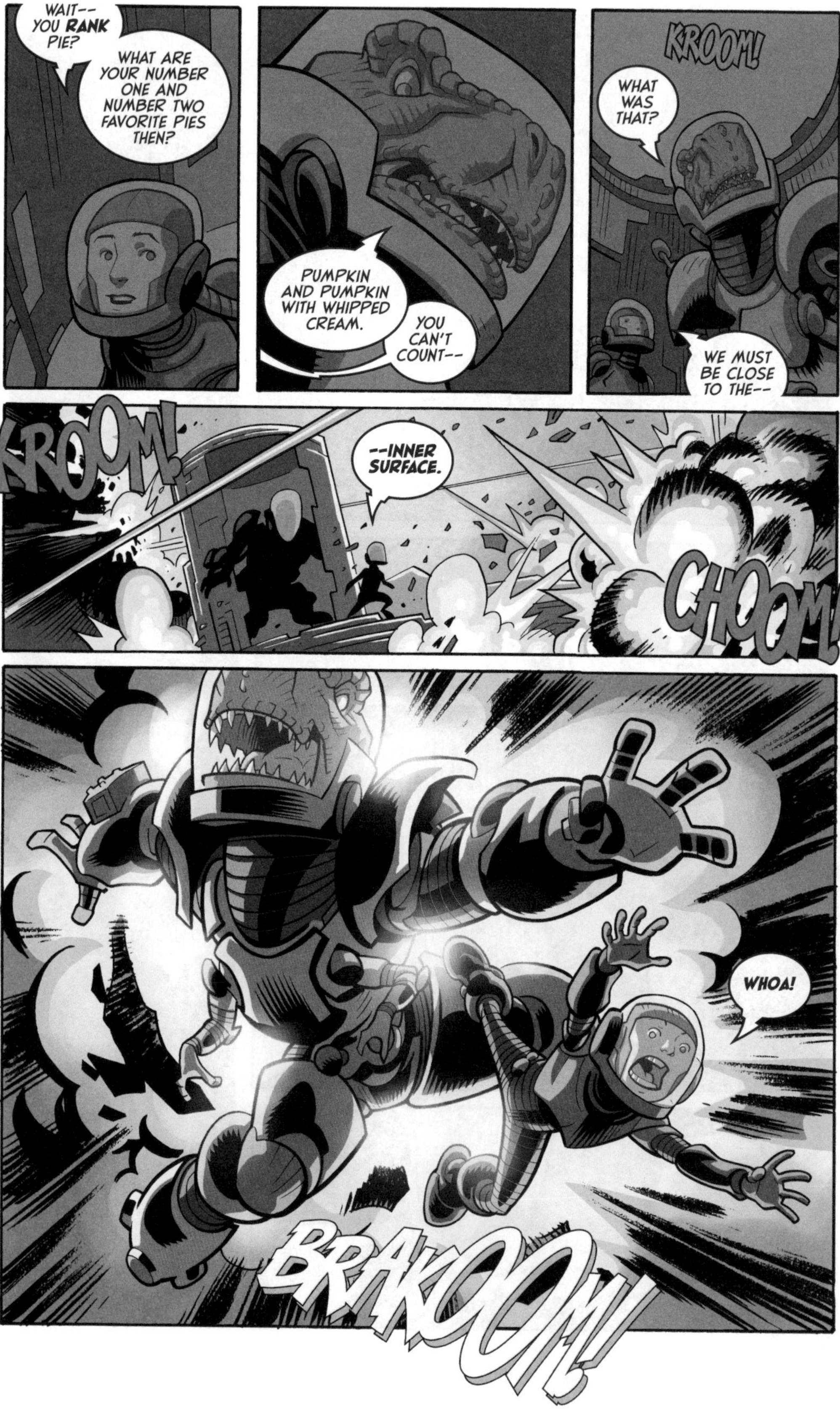
WAIT-- YOU **RANK** PIE?
WHAT ARE YOUR NUMBER ONE AND NUMBER TWO FAVORITE PIES THEN?
PUMPKIN AND PUMPKIN WITH WHIPPED CREAM.
YOU CAN'T COUNT--
KROOM!
WHAT WAS THAT?
WE MUST BE CLOSE TO THE--
KROOM!
--INNER SURFACE.
CHOOM!
WHOA!
BRAKOOM!

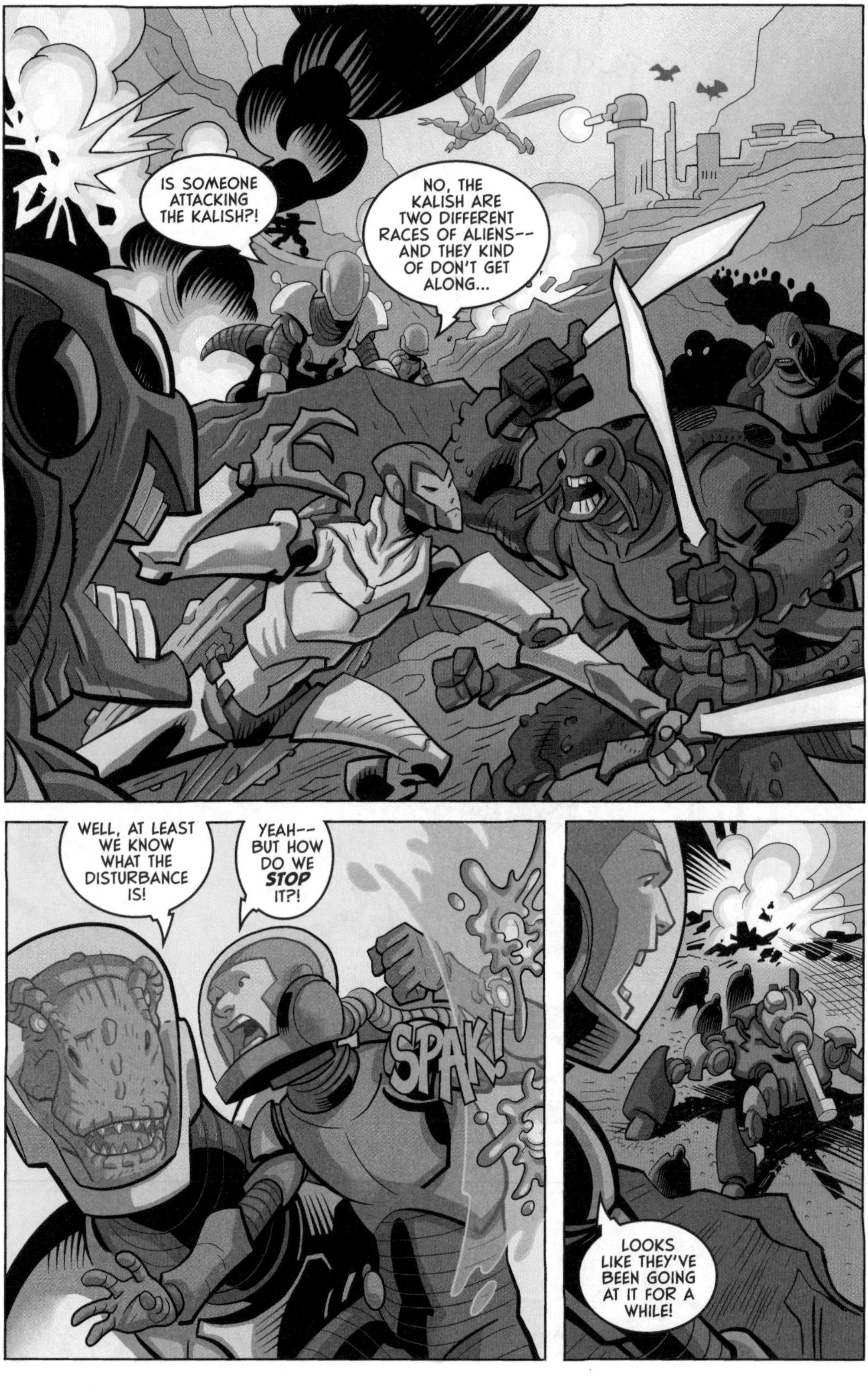
IS SOMEONE ATTACKING THE KALISH?!
NO, THE KALISH ARE TWO DIFFERENT RACES OF ALIENS-- AND THEY KIND OF DON'T GET ALONG...
WELL, AT LEAST WE KNOW WHAT THE DISTURBANCE IS!
YEAH-- BUT HOW DO WE *STOP* IT?!
SPAK!
LOOKS LIKE THEY'VE BEEN GOING AT IT FOR A WHILE!

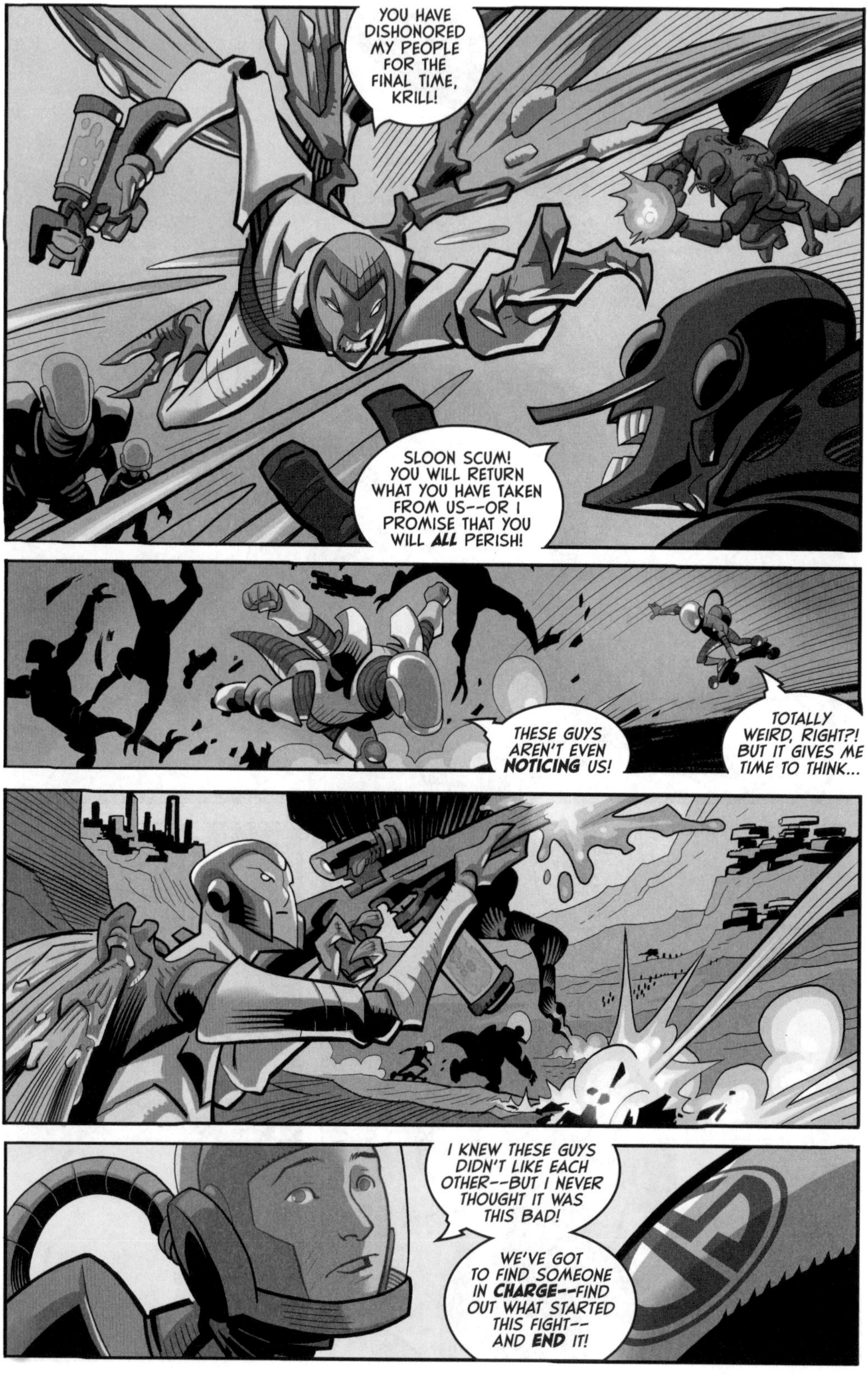
YOU HAVE DISHONORED MY PEOPLE FOR THE FINAL TIME, KRILL!
SLOON SCUM! YOU WILL RETURN WHAT YOU HAVE TAKEN FROM US--OR I PROMISE THAT YOU WILL **ALL** PERISH!
THESE GUYS AREN'T EVEN **NOTICING** US!
TOTALLY WEIRD, RIGHT?! BUT IT GIVES ME TIME TO THINK...
I KNEW THESE GUYS DIDN'T LIKE EACH OTHER--BUT I NEVER THOUGHT IT WAS THIS BAD!
WE'VE GOT TO FIND SOMEONE IN **CHARGE**--FIND OUT WHAT STARTED THIS FIGHT--AND **END** IT!

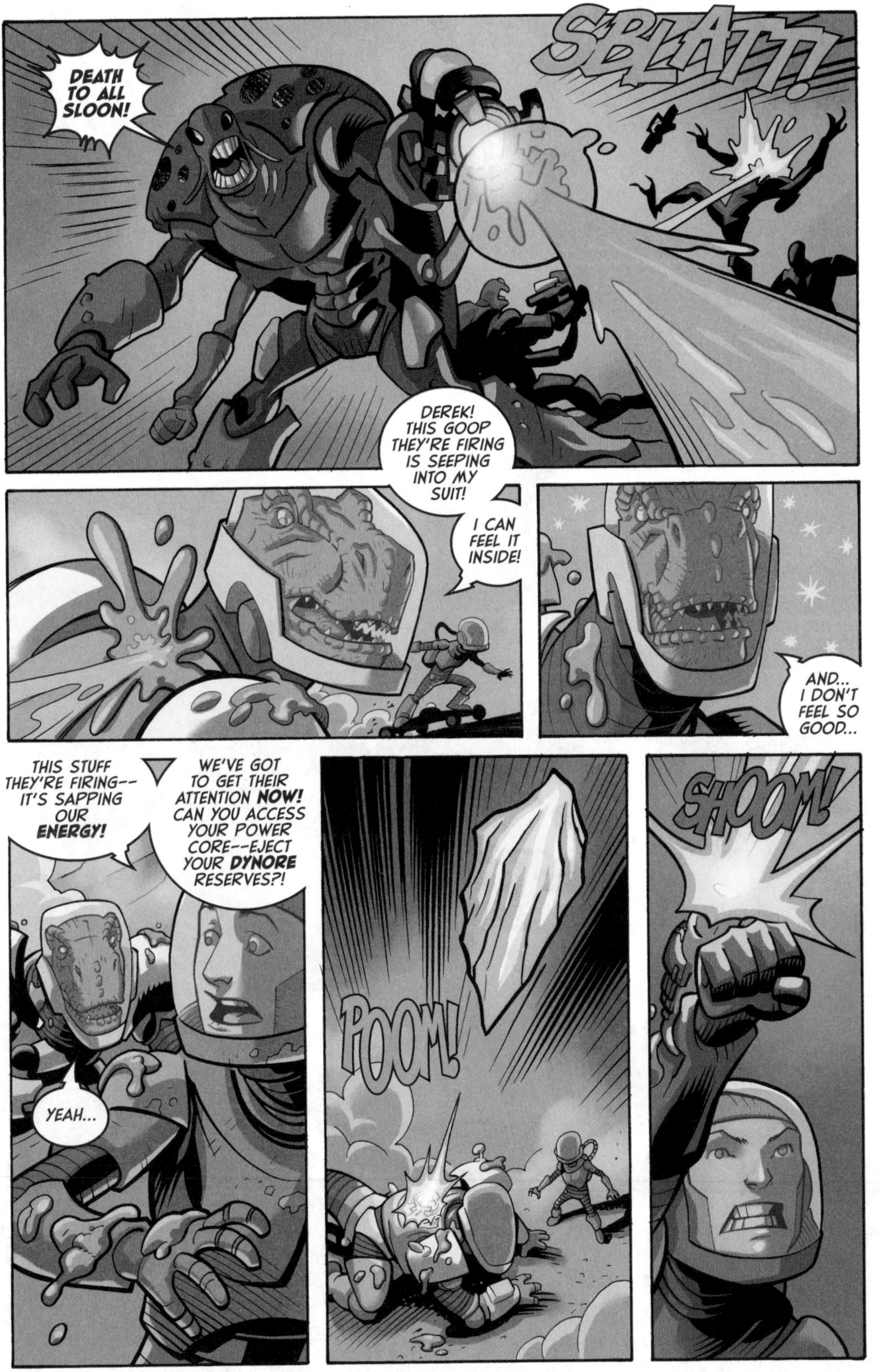
SBLATT!
DEATH TO ALL SLOON!
DEREK! THIS GOOP THEY'RE FIRING IS SEEPING INTO MY SUIT!
I CAN FEEL IT INSIDE!
AND... I DON'T FEEL SO GOOD...
THIS STUFF THEY'RE FIRING-- IT'S SAPPING OUR ENERGY!
WE'VE GOT TO GET THEIR ATTENTION NOW! CAN YOU ACCESS YOUR POWER CORE--EJECT YOUR DYNORE RESERVES?!
YEAH...
POOM!
SHOOM!

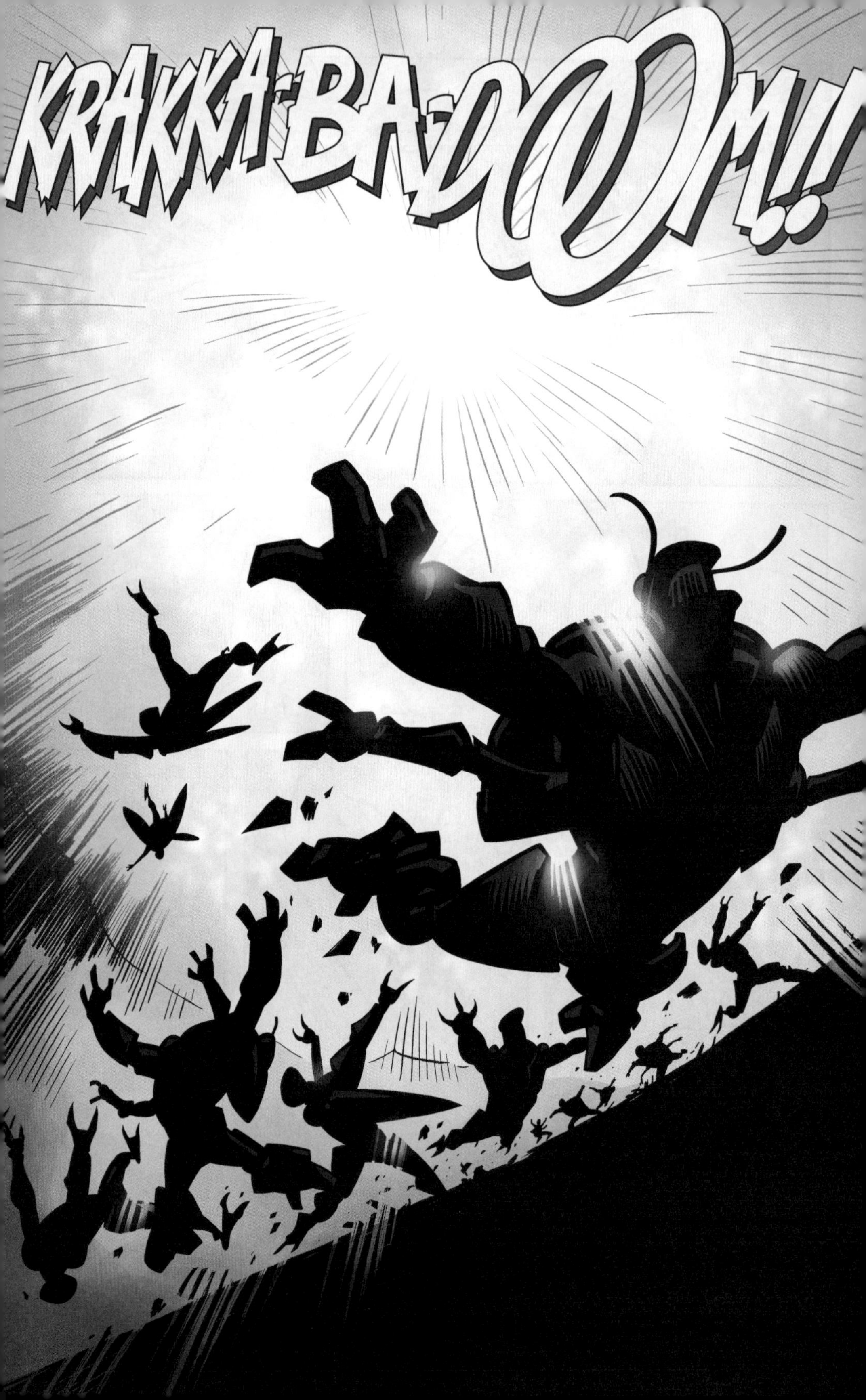
KRAKKA-BA-DOOOM!!

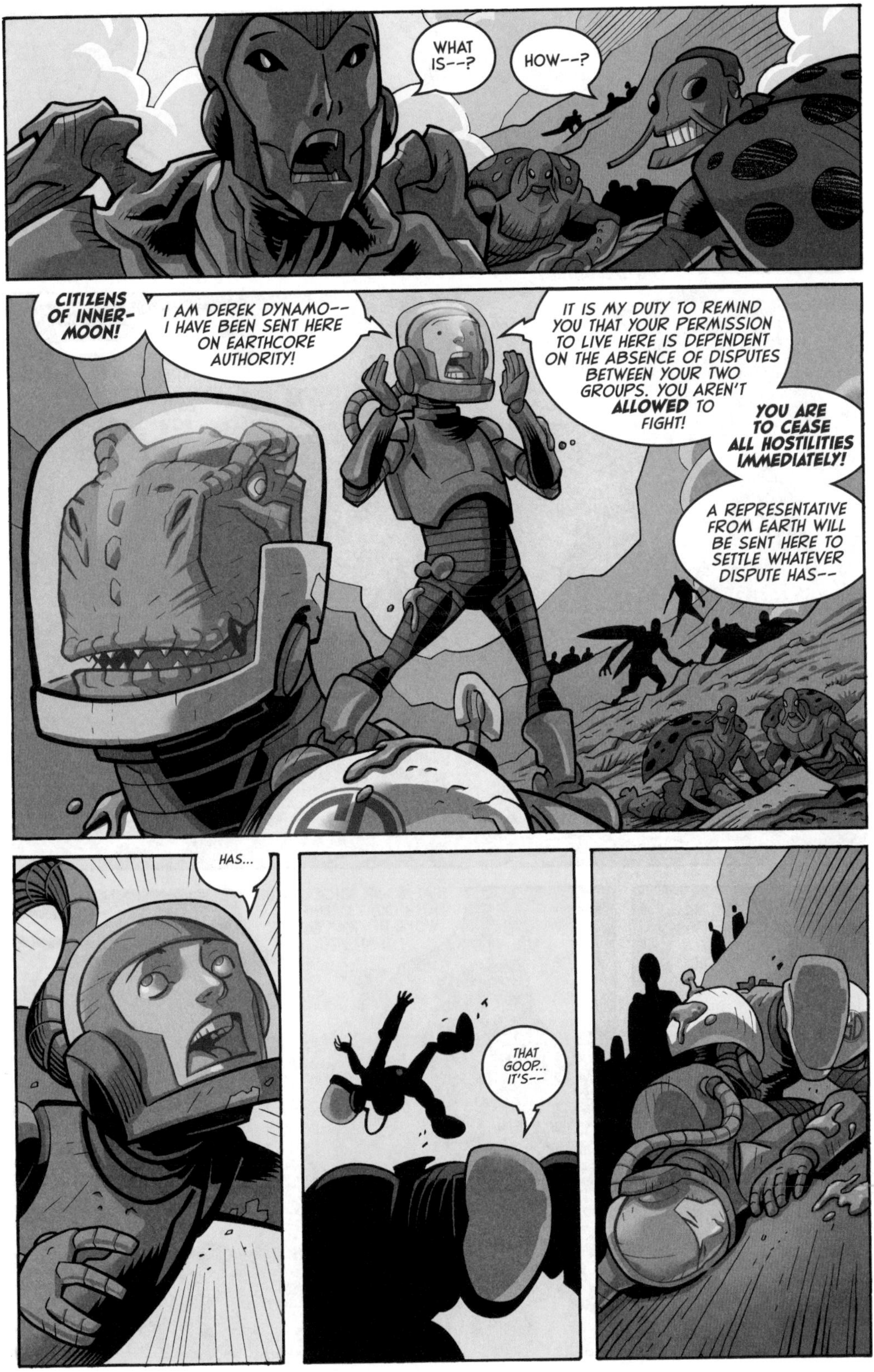
WHAT IS--?
HOW--?
CITIZENS OF INNER-MOON!
I AM DEREK DYNAMO-- I HAVE BEEN SENT HERE ON EARTHCORE AUTHORITY!
IT IS MY DUTY TO REMIND YOU THAT YOUR PERMISSION TO LIVE HERE IS DEPENDENT ON THE ABSENCE OF DISPUTES BETWEEN YOUR TWO GROUPS. YOU AREN'T **ALLOWED** TO FIGHT!
YOU ARE TO CEASE ALL HOSTILITIES IMMEDIATELY!
A REPRESENTATIVE FROM EARTH WILL BE SENT HERE TO SETTLE WHATEVER DISPUTE HAS--
HAS...
THAT GOOP... IT'S--

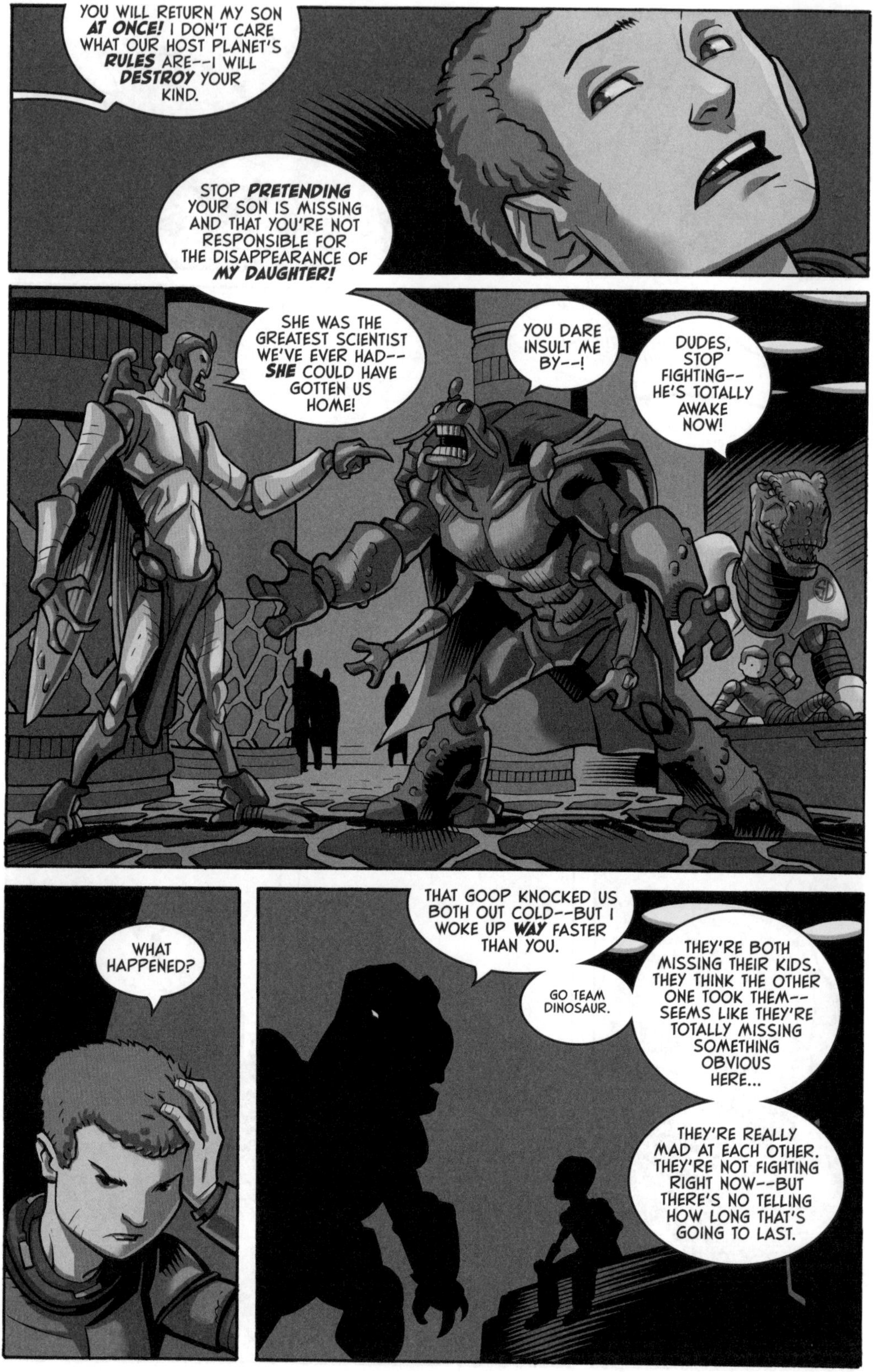
YOU WILL RETURN MY SON AT ONCE! I DON'T CARE WHAT OUR HOST PLANET'S RULES ARE--I WILL DESTROY YOUR KIND.
STOP PRETENDING YOUR SON IS MISSING AND THAT YOU'RE NOT RESPONSIBLE FOR THE DISAPPEARANCE OF MY DAUGHTER!
SHE WAS THE GREATEST SCIENTIST WE'VE EVER HAD-- SHE COULD HAVE GOTTEN US HOME!
YOU DARE INSULT ME BY--!
DUDES, STOP FIGHTING-- HE'S TOTALLY AWAKE NOW!
WHAT HAPPENED?
THAT GOOP KNOCKED US BOTH OUT COLD--BUT I WOKE UP WAY FASTER THAN YOU.
GO TEAM DINOSAUR.
THEY'RE BOTH MISSING THEIR KIDS. THEY THINK THE OTHER ONE TOOK THEM-- SEEMS LIKE THEY'RE TOTALLY MISSING SOMETHING OBVIOUS HERE...
THEY'RE REALLY MAD AT EACH OTHER. THEY'RE NOT FIGHTING RIGHT NOW--BUT THERE'S NO TELLING HOW LONG THAT'S GOING TO LAST.

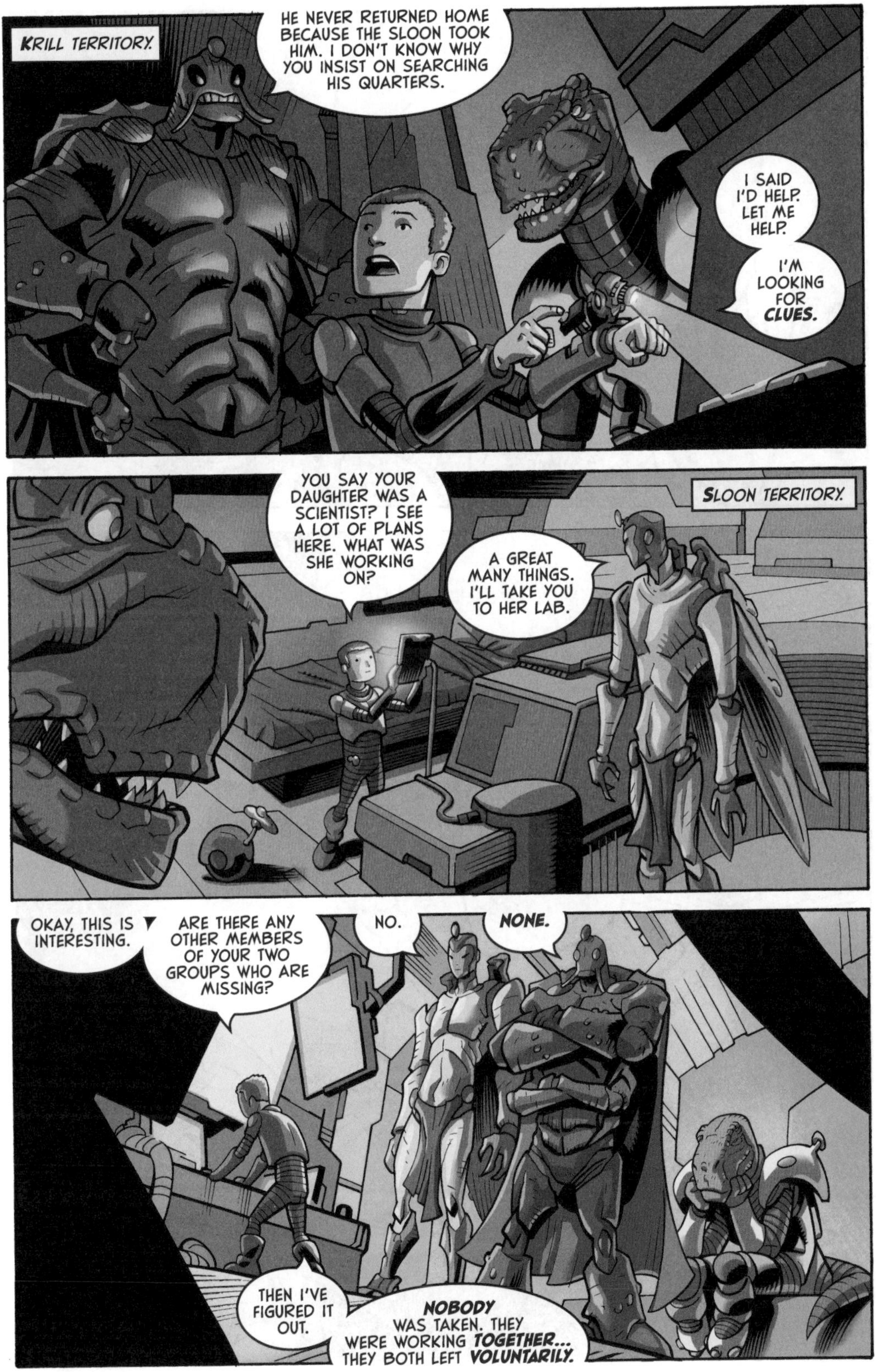
KRILL TERRITORY.
HE NEVER RETURNED HOME BECAUSE THE SLOON TOOK HIM. I DON'T KNOW WHY YOU INSIST ON SEARCHING HIS QUARTERS.
I SAID I'D HELP. LET ME HELP.
I'M LOOKING FOR **CLUES.**
SLOON TERRITORY.
YOU SAY YOUR DAUGHTER WAS A SCIENTIST? I SEE A LOT OF PLANS HERE. WHAT WAS SHE WORKING ON?
A GREAT MANY THINGS. I'LL TAKE YOU TO HER LAB.
OKAY, THIS IS INTERESTING.
ARE THERE ANY OTHER MEMBERS OF YOUR TWO GROUPS WHO ARE MISSING?
NO.
NONE.
THEN I'VE FIGURED IT OUT.
NOBODY WAS TAKEN. THEY WERE WORKING **TOGETHER...** THEY BOTH LEFT **VOLUNTARILY.**

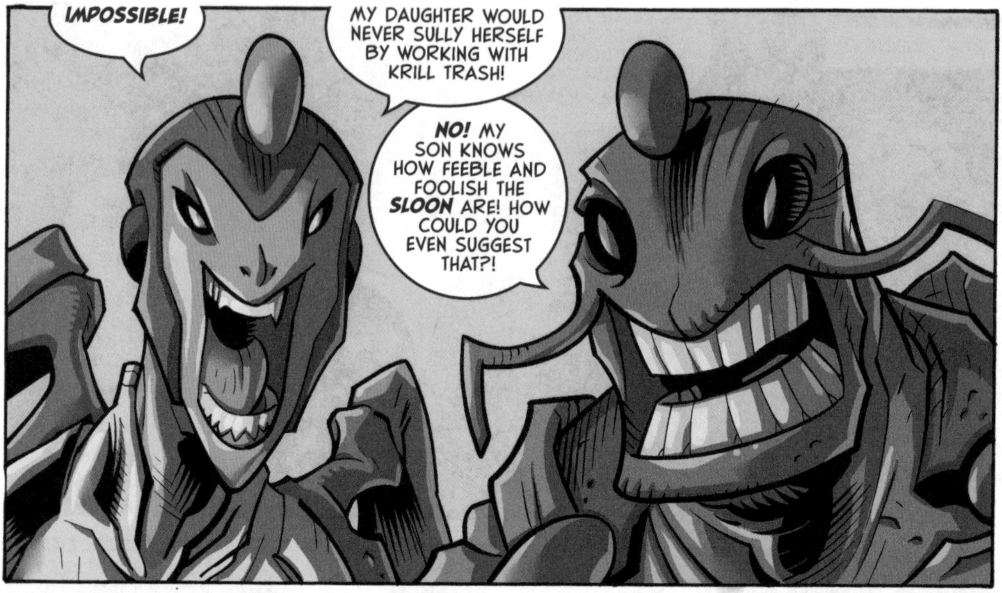
IMPOSSIBLE!
MY DAUGHTER WOULD NEVER SULLY HERSELF BY WORKING WITH KRILL TRASH!
NO! MY SON KNOWS HOW FEEBLE AND FOOLISH THE SLOON ARE! HOW COULD YOU EVEN SUGGEST THAT?!

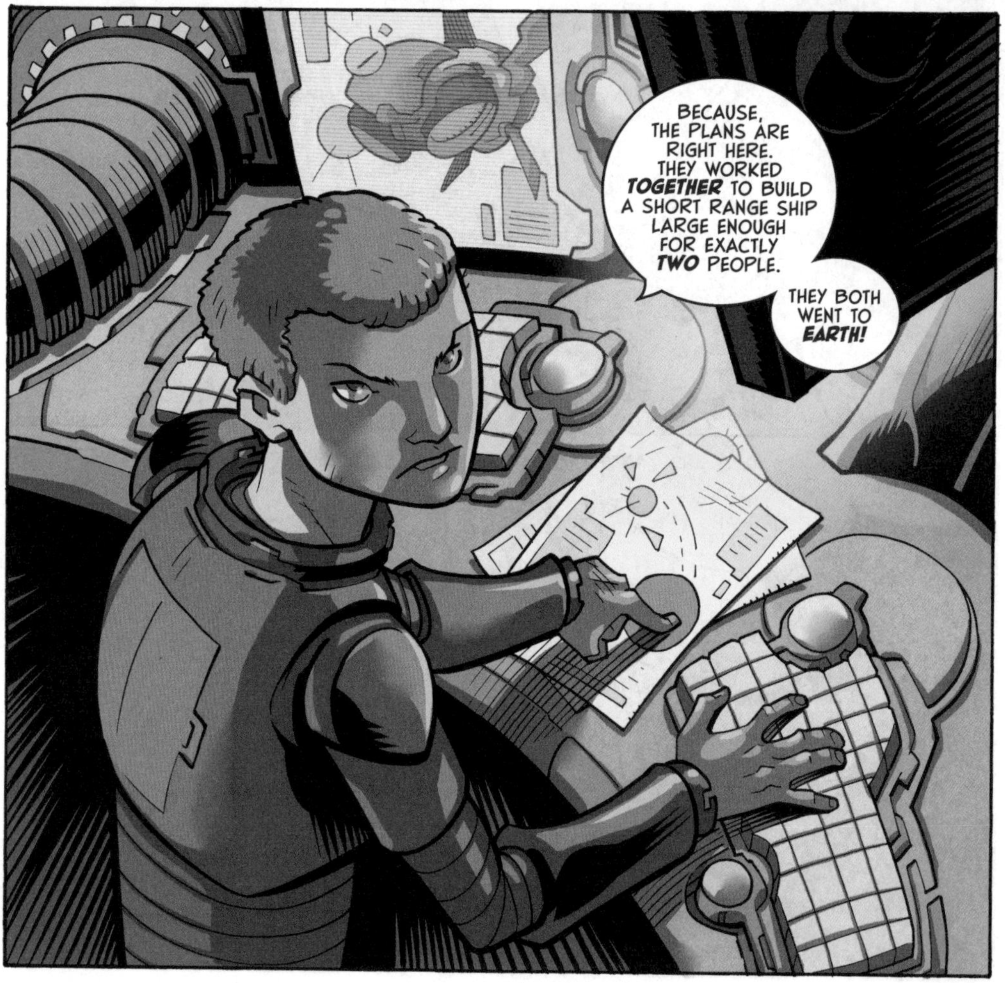
BECAUSE, THE PLANS ARE RIGHT HERE. THEY WORKED TOGETHER TO BUILD A SHORT RANGE SHIP LARGE ENOUGH FOR EXACTLY TWO PEOPLE.
THEY BOTH WENT TO EARTH!

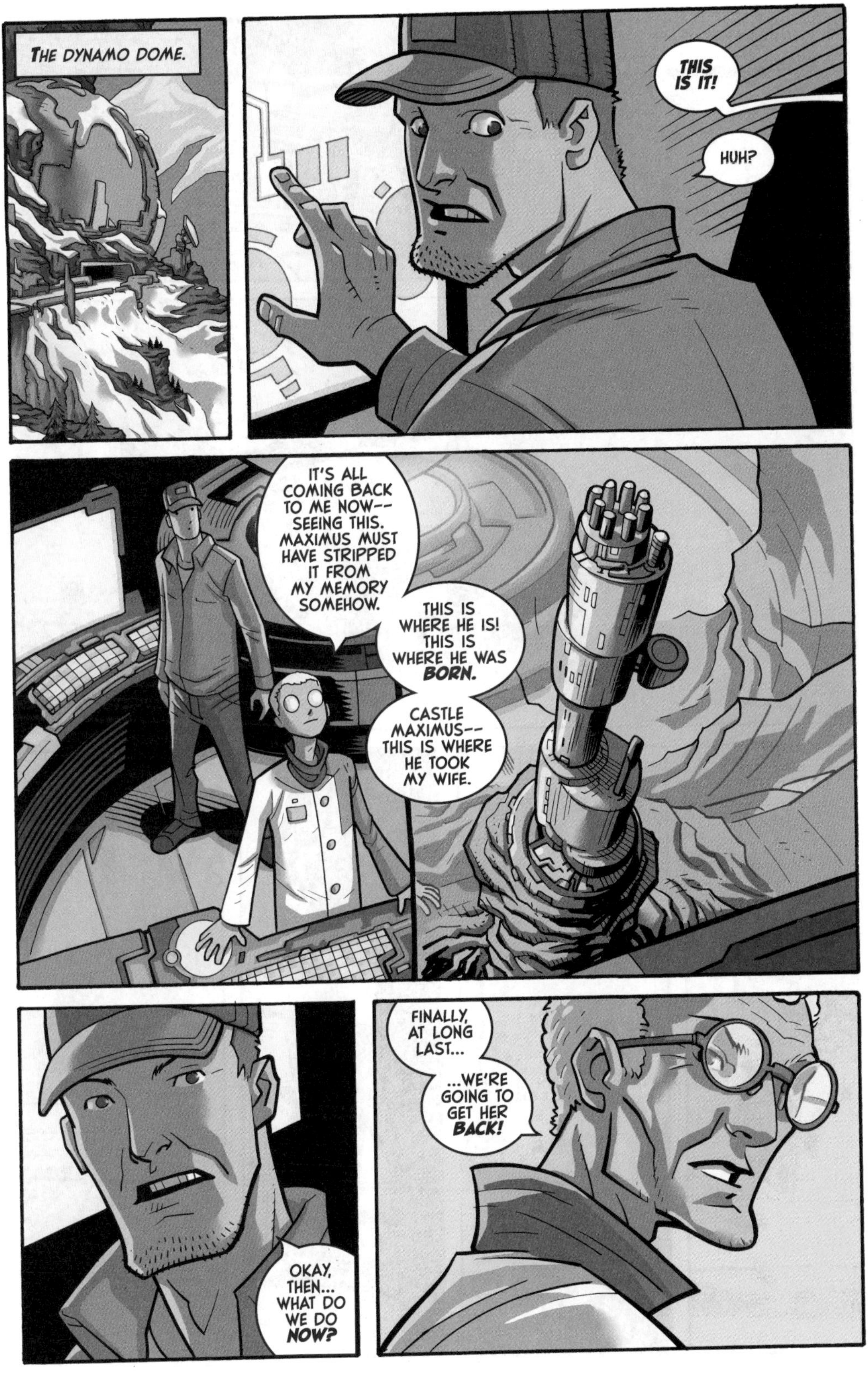
THE DYNAMO DOME.
THIS IS IT!
HUH?
IT'S ALL COMING BACK TO ME NOW-- SEEING THIS. MAXIMUS MUST HAVE STRIPPED IT FROM MY MEMORY SOMEHOW.
THIS IS WHERE HE IS! THIS IS WHERE HE WAS **BORN.**
CASTLE MAXIMUS-- THIS IS WHERE HE TOOK MY WIFE.
OKAY, THEN... WHAT DO WE DO **NOW?**
FINALLY, AT LONG LAST...
...WE'RE GOING TO GET HER **BACK!**

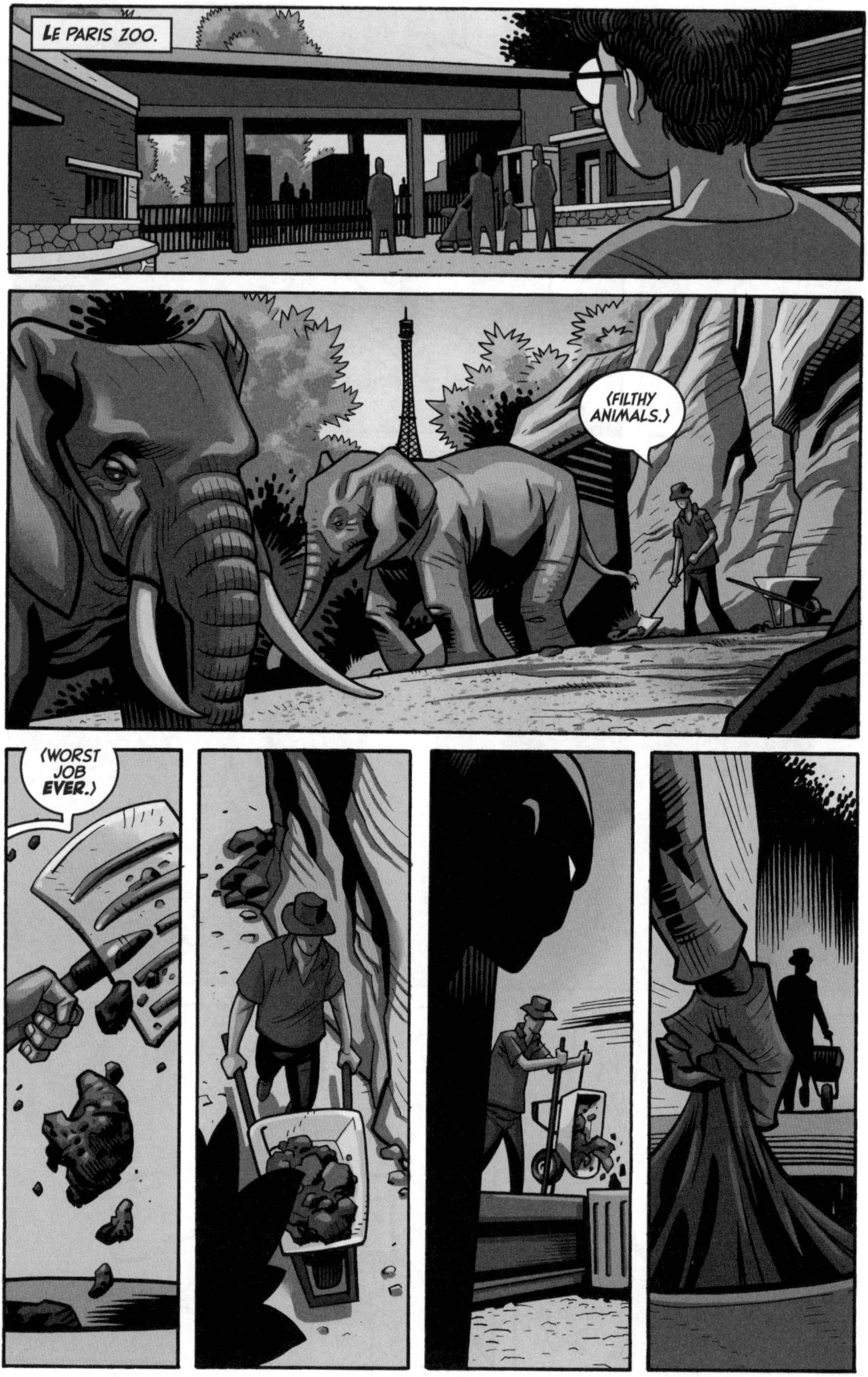
LE PARIS ZOO.
‹FILTHY ANIMALS.›
‹WORST JOB EVER.›

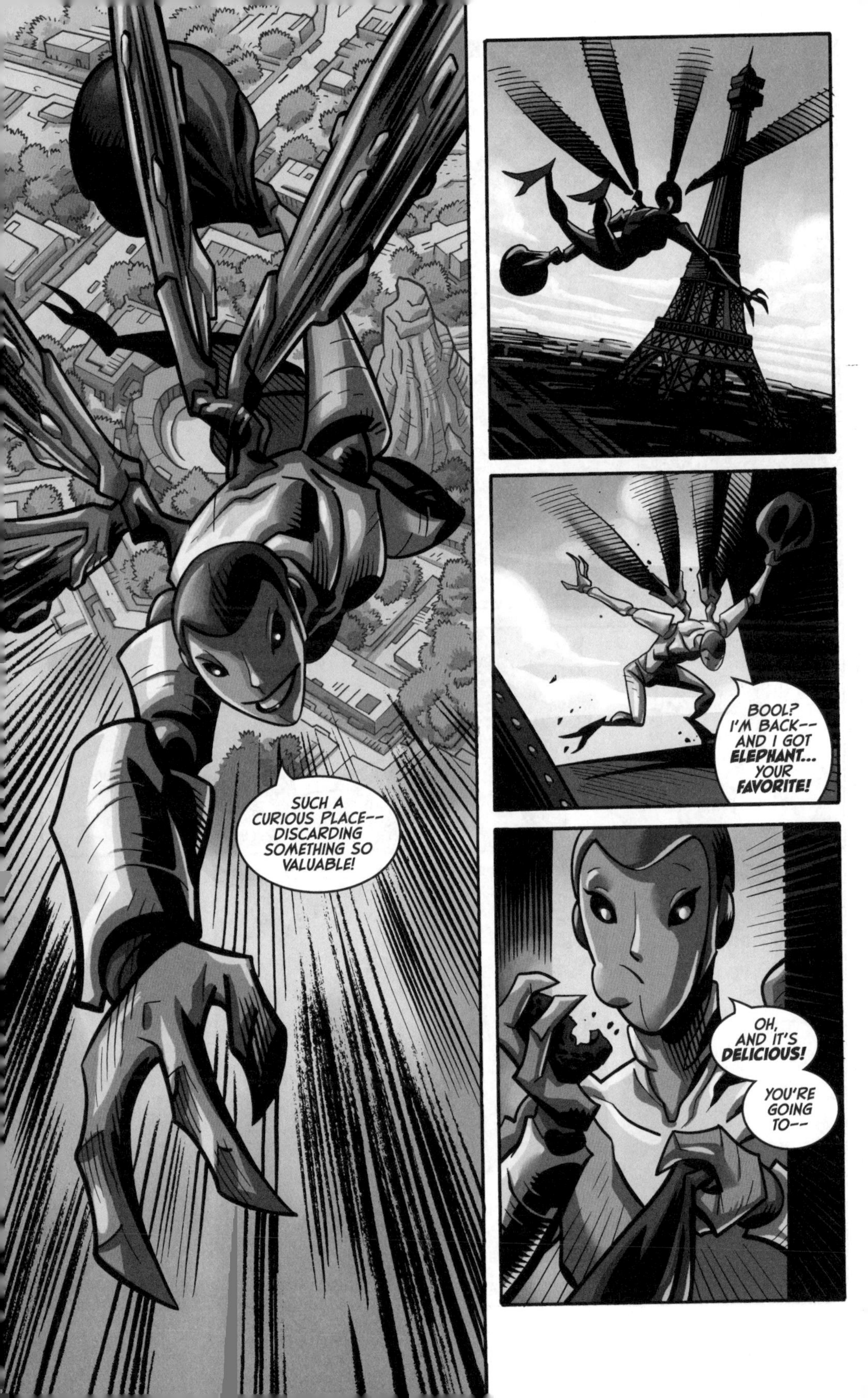
SUCH A CURIOUS PLACE-- DISCARDING SOMETHING SO VALUABLE!
BOOL? I'M BACK-- AND I GOT ELEPHANT... YOUR FAVORITE!
OH, AND IT'S DELICIOUS!
YOU'RE GOING TO--

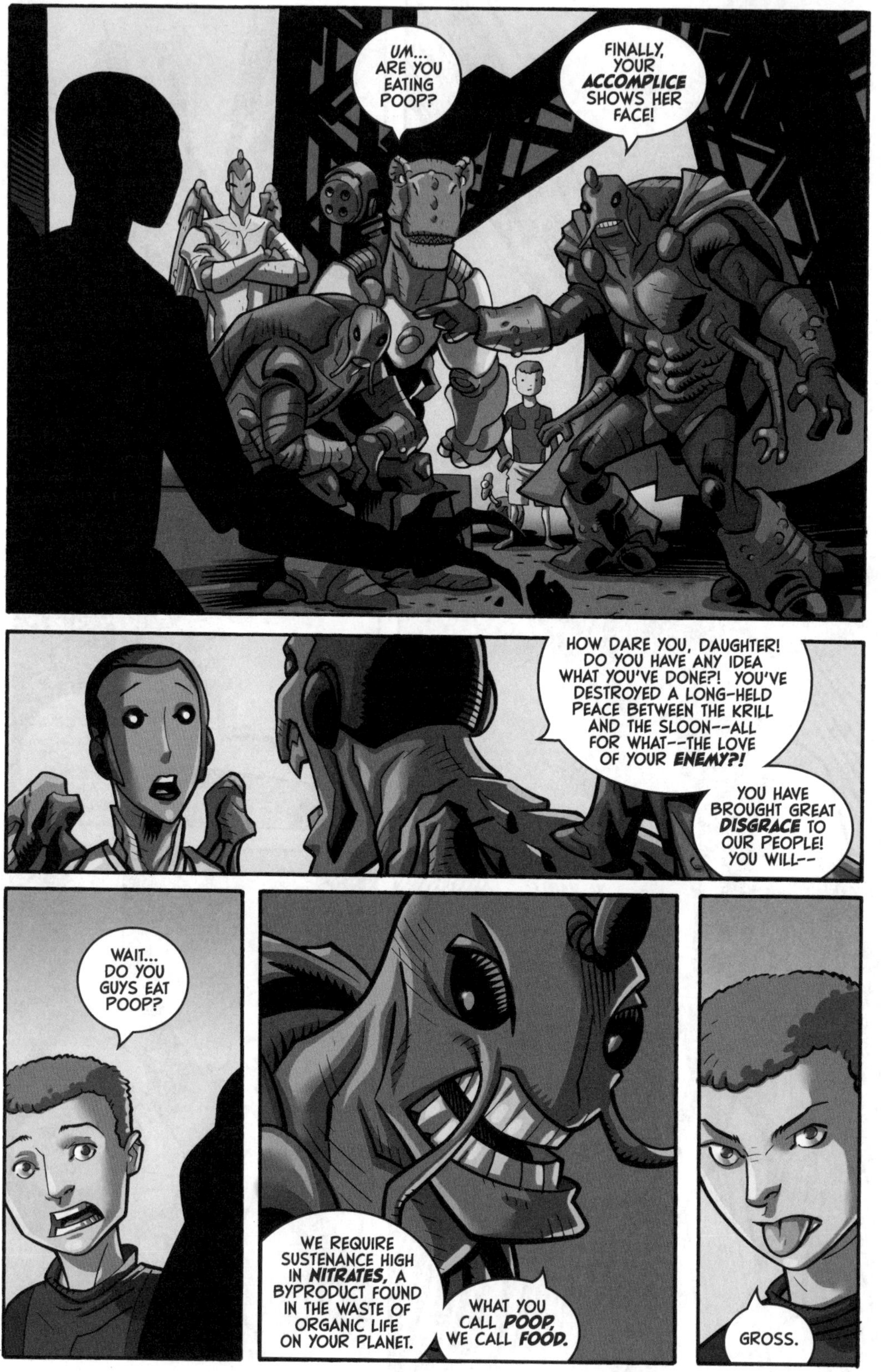
UM... ARE YOU EATING POOP?
FINALLY, YOUR ACCOMPLICE SHOWS HER FACE!
HOW DARE YOU, DAUGHTER! DO YOU HAVE ANY IDEA WHAT YOU'VE DONE?! YOU'VE DESTROYED A LONG-HELD PEACE BETWEEN THE KRILL AND THE SLOON--ALL FOR WHAT--THE LOVE OF YOUR ENEMY?!
YOU HAVE BROUGHT GREAT DISGRACE TO OUR PEOPLE! YOU WILL--
WAIT... DO YOU GUYS EAT POOP?
WE REQUIRE SUSTENANCE HIGH IN NITRATES, A BYPRODUCT FOUND IN THE WASTE OF ORGANIC LIFE ON YOUR PLANET.
WHAT YOU CALL POOP, WE CALL FOOD.
GROSS.

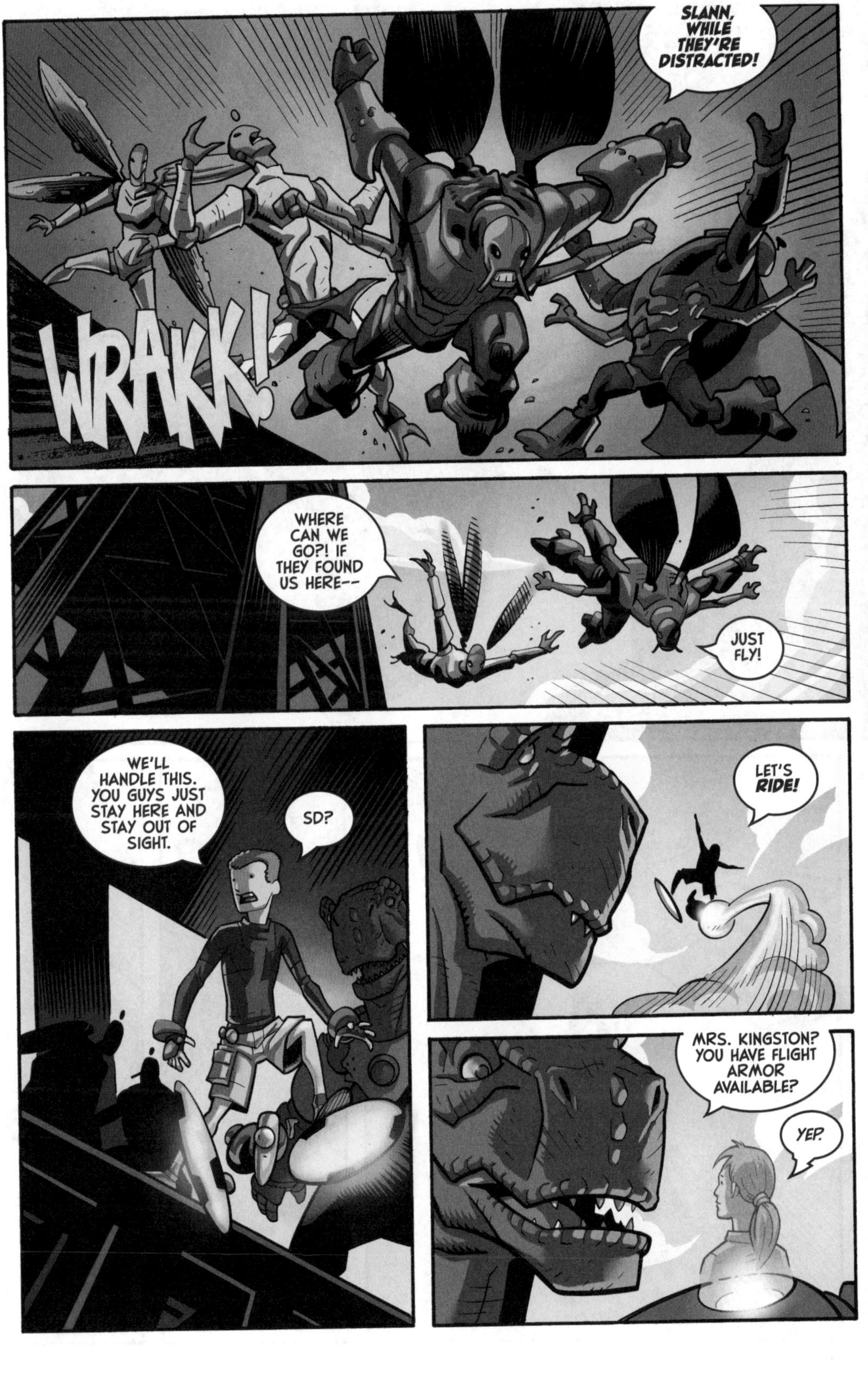
SLANN, WHILE THEY'RE DISTRACTED!
WRAKK!
WHERE CAN WE GO?! IF THEY FOUND US HERE--
JUST FLY!
WE'LL HANDLE THIS. YOU GUYS JUST STAY HERE AND STAY OUT OF SIGHT.
SD?
LET'S RIDE!
MRS. KINGSTON? YOU HAVE FLIGHT ARMOR AVAILABLE?
YEP.

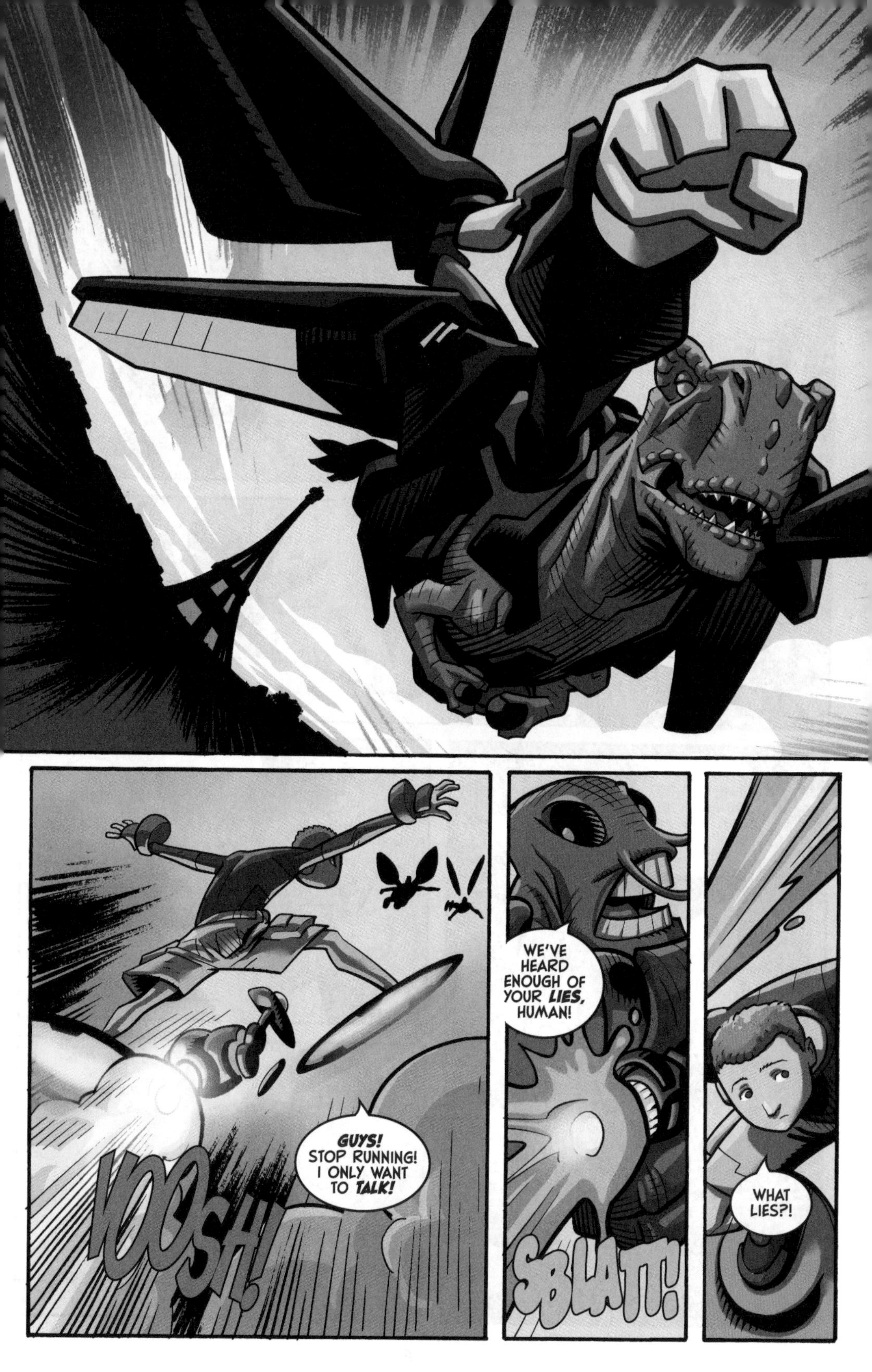
GUYS! STOP RUNNING! I ONLY WANT TO TALK!
VOOSH!
WE'VE HEARD ENOUGH OF YOUR LIES, HUMAN!
SBLATT!
WHAT LIES?!

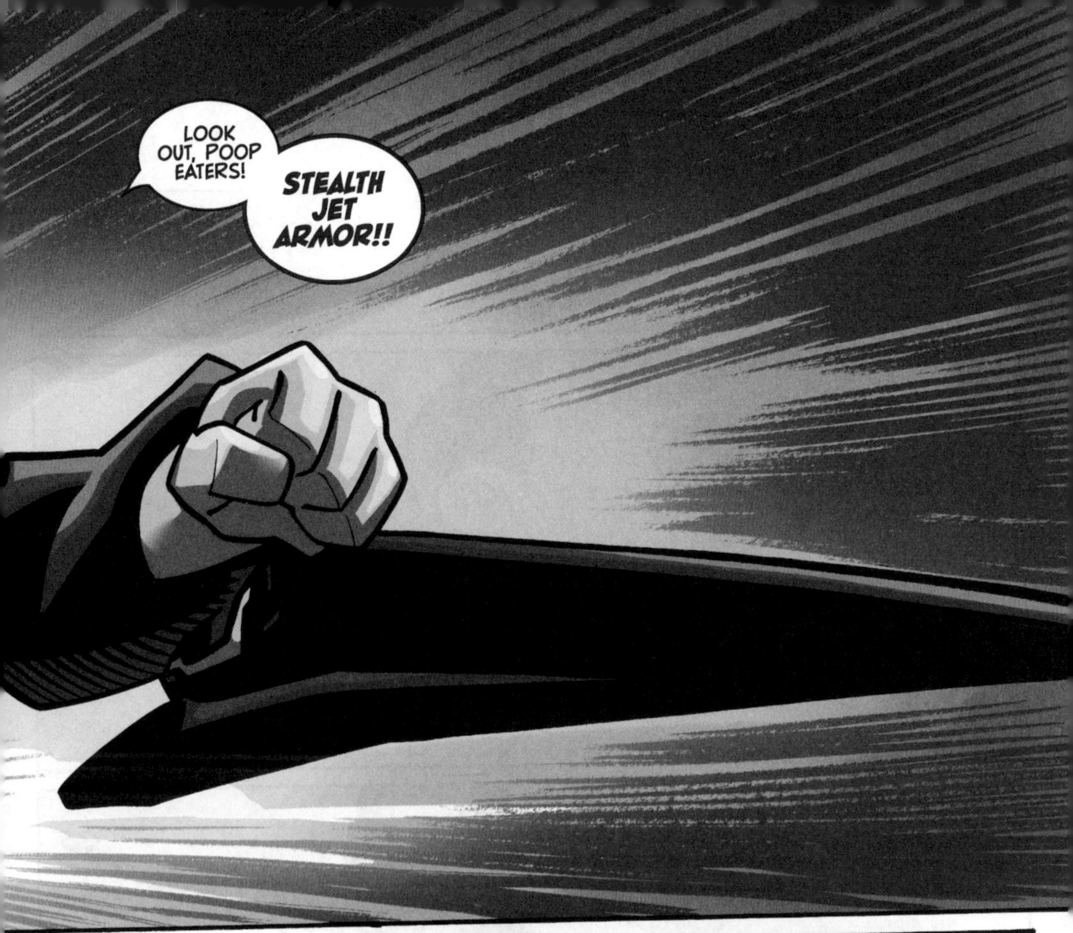
LOOK OUT, POOP EATERS!
STEALTH JET ARMOR!!

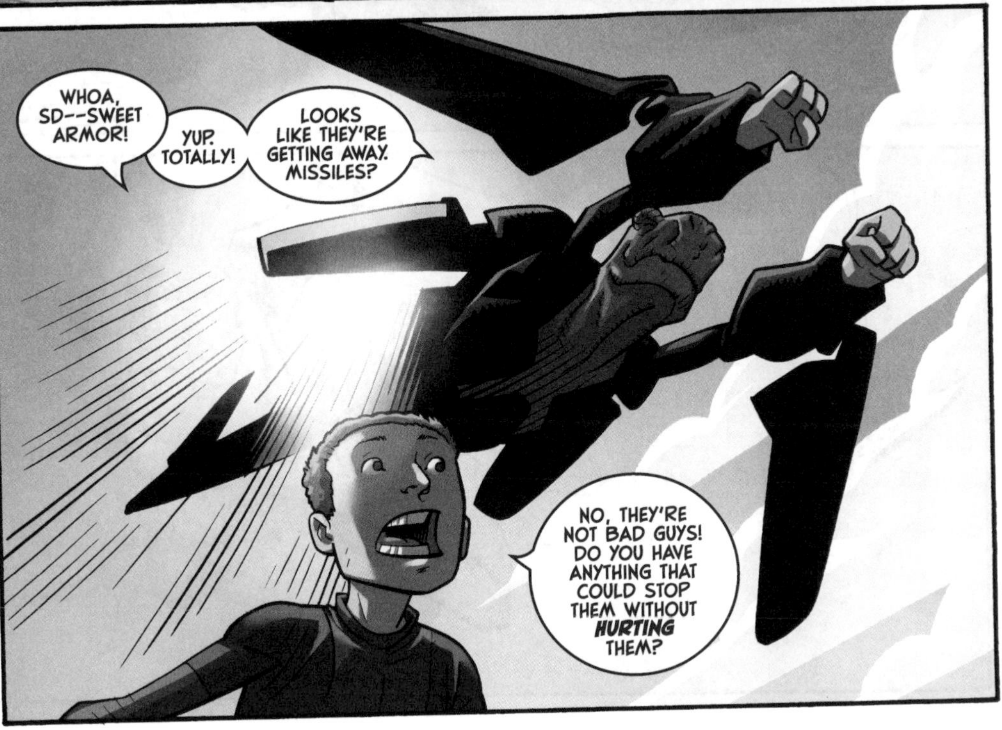
WHOA, SD--SWEET ARMOR!
YUP. TOTALLY!
LOOKS LIKE THEY'RE GETTING AWAY. MISSILES?
NO, THEY'RE NOT BAD GUYS! DO YOU HAVE ANYTHING THAT COULD STOP THEM WITHOUT HURTING THEM?

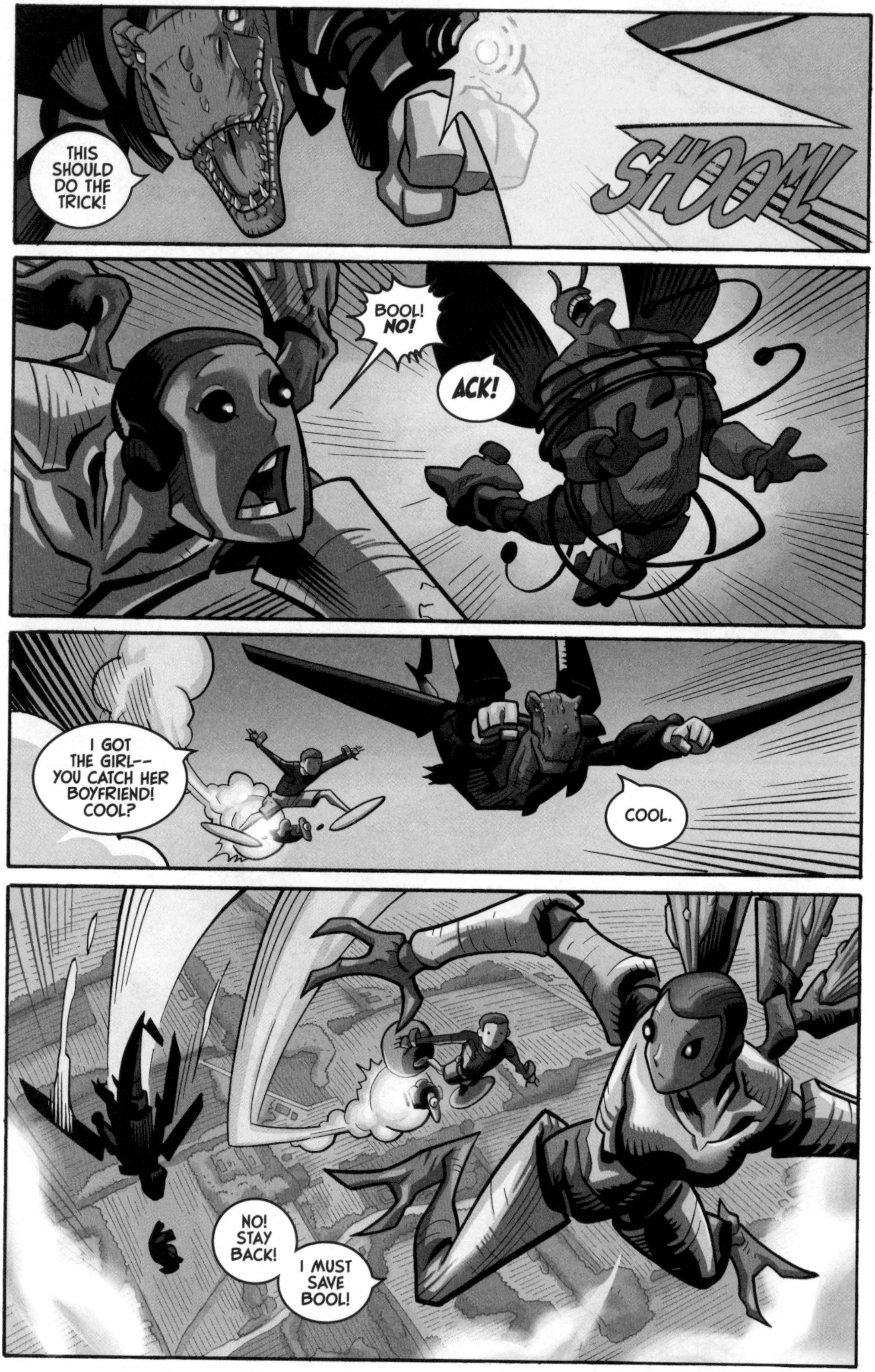
THIS SHOULD DO THE TRICK!
SHOOM!
BOOL! NO!
ACK!
I GOT THE GIRL-- YOU CATCH HER BOYFRIEND! COOL?
COOL.
NO! STAY BACK!
I MUST SAVE BOOL!

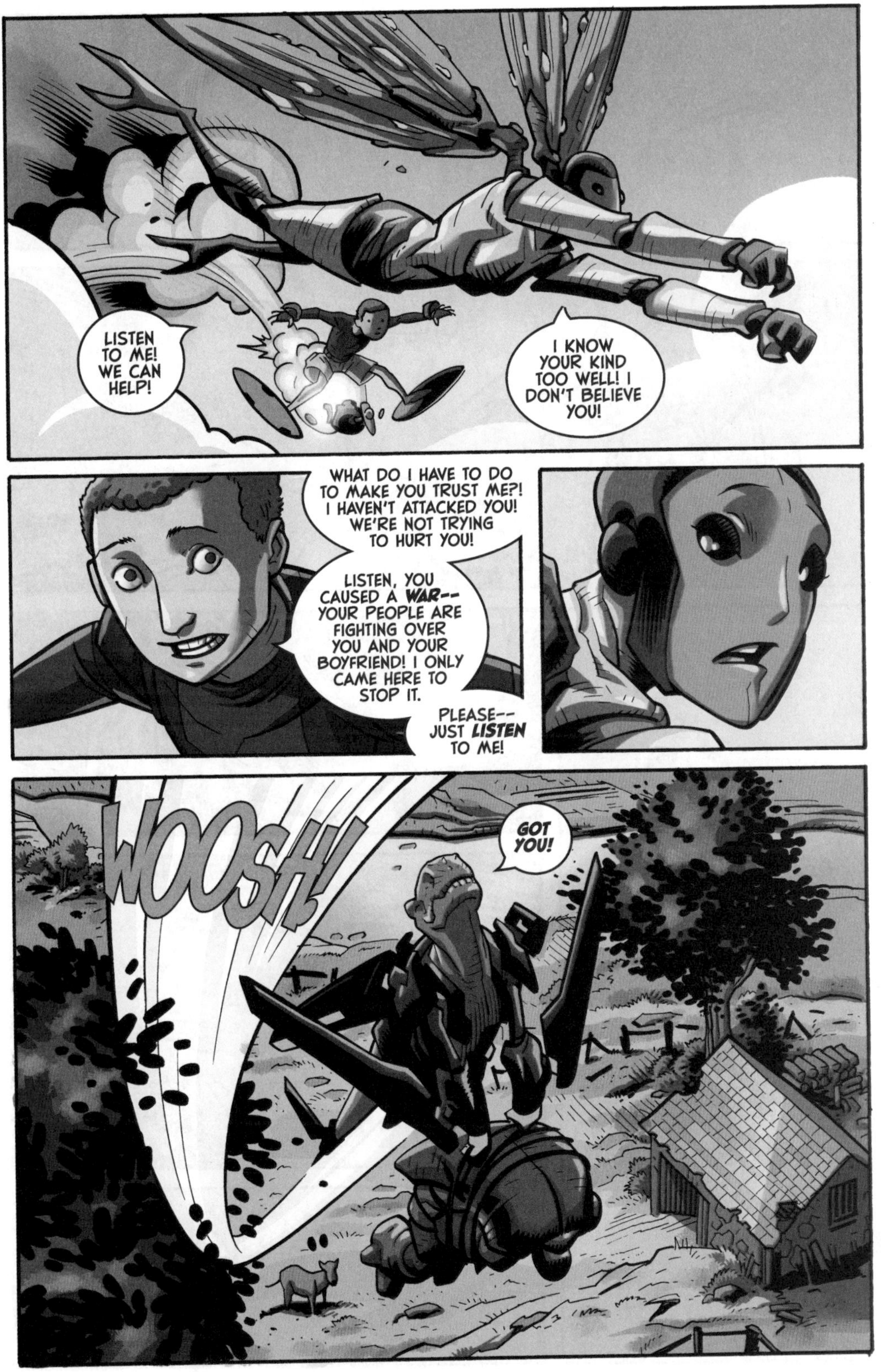
LISTEN TO ME! WE CAN HELP!
I KNOW YOUR KIND TOO WELL! I DON'T BELIEVE YOU!
WHAT DO I HAVE TO DO TO MAKE YOU TRUST ME?! I HAVEN'T ATTACKED YOU! WE'RE NOT TRYING TO HURT YOU!
LISTEN, YOU CAUSED A WAR-- YOUR PEOPLE ARE FIGHTING OVER YOU AND YOUR BOYFRIEND! I ONLY CAME HERE TO STOP IT.
PLEASE-- JUST LISTEN TO ME!
WOOSH!
GOT YOU!

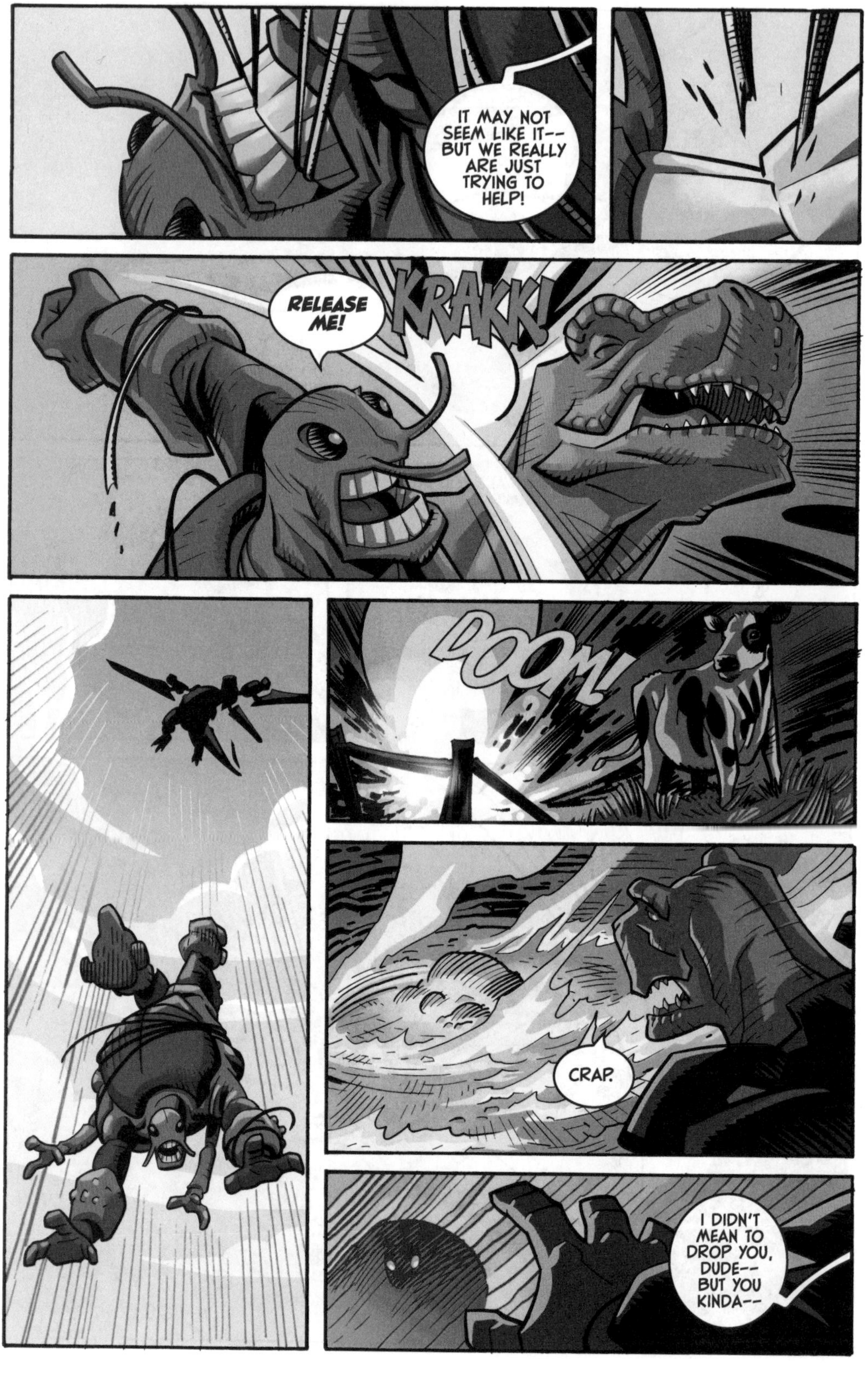
IT MAY NOT SEEM LIKE IT-- BUT WE REALLY ARE JUST TRYING TO HELP!
RELEASE ME!
KRAKK!
DOOM!
CRAP.
I DIDN'T MEAN TO DROP YOU, DUDE-- BUT YOU KINDA--

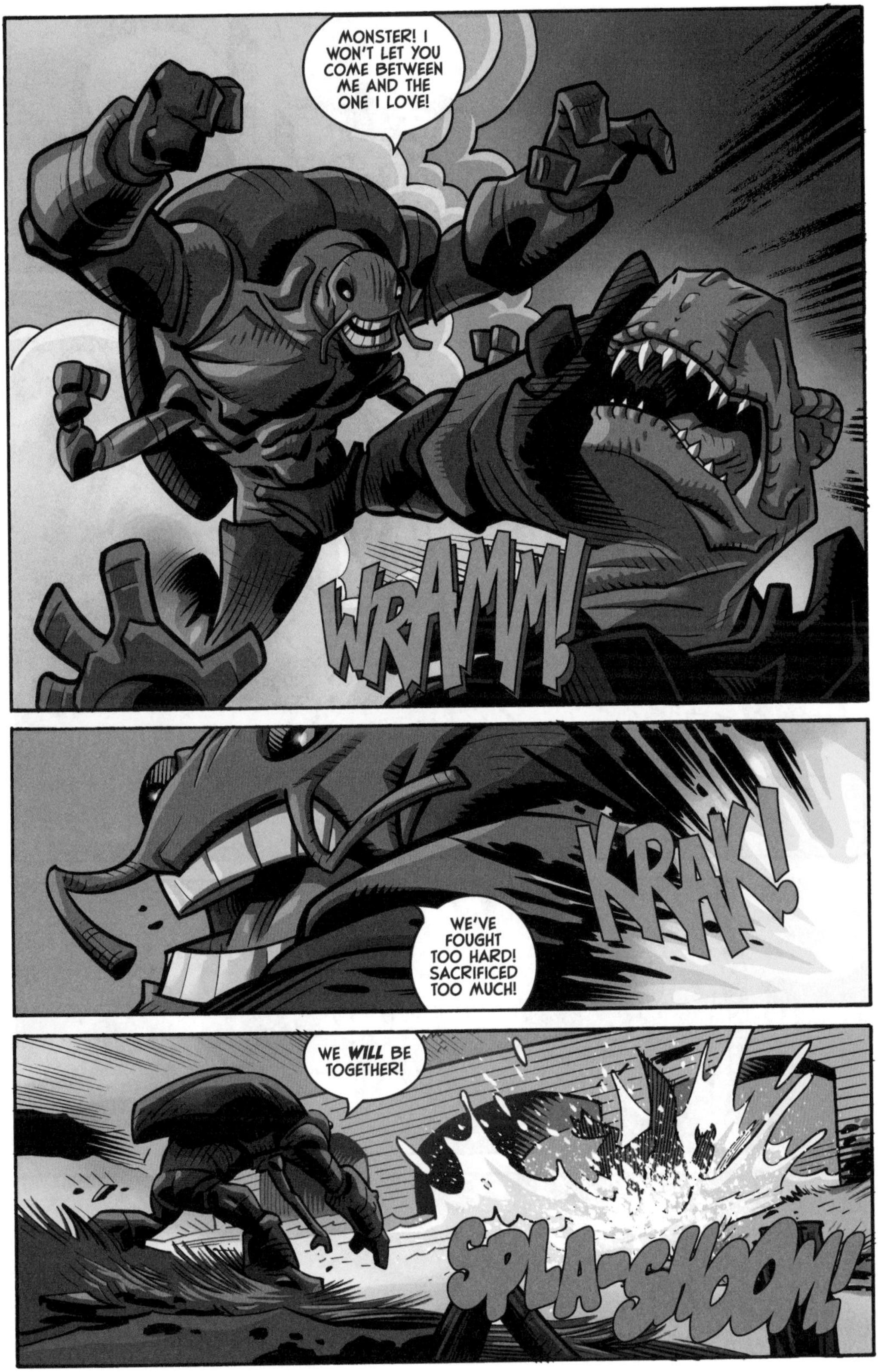
MONSTER! I WON'T LET YOU COME BETWEEN ME AND THE ONE I LOVE!
WRAMM!
KRAK!
WE'VE FOUGHT TOO HARD! SACRIFICED TOO MUCH!
WE **WILL** BE TOGETHER!
SPLA-SHOOM!

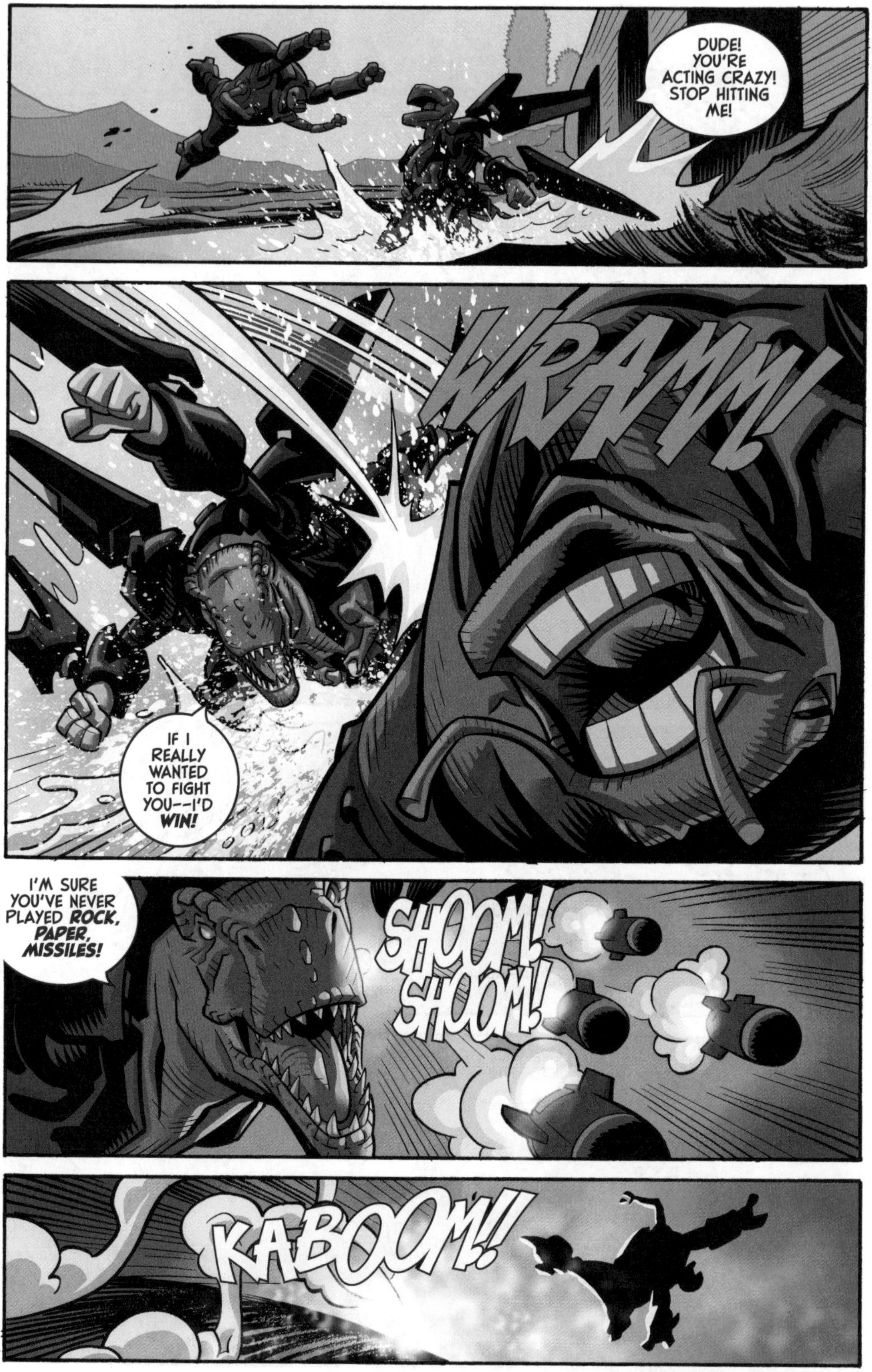
DUDE! YOU'RE ACTING CRAZY! STOP HITTING ME!
WRAMM!
IF I REALLY WANTED TO FIGHT YOU--I'D **WIN!**
I'M SURE YOU'VE NEVER PLAYED **ROCK, PAPER, MISSILES!**
SHOOM! SHOOM!
KABOOM!!

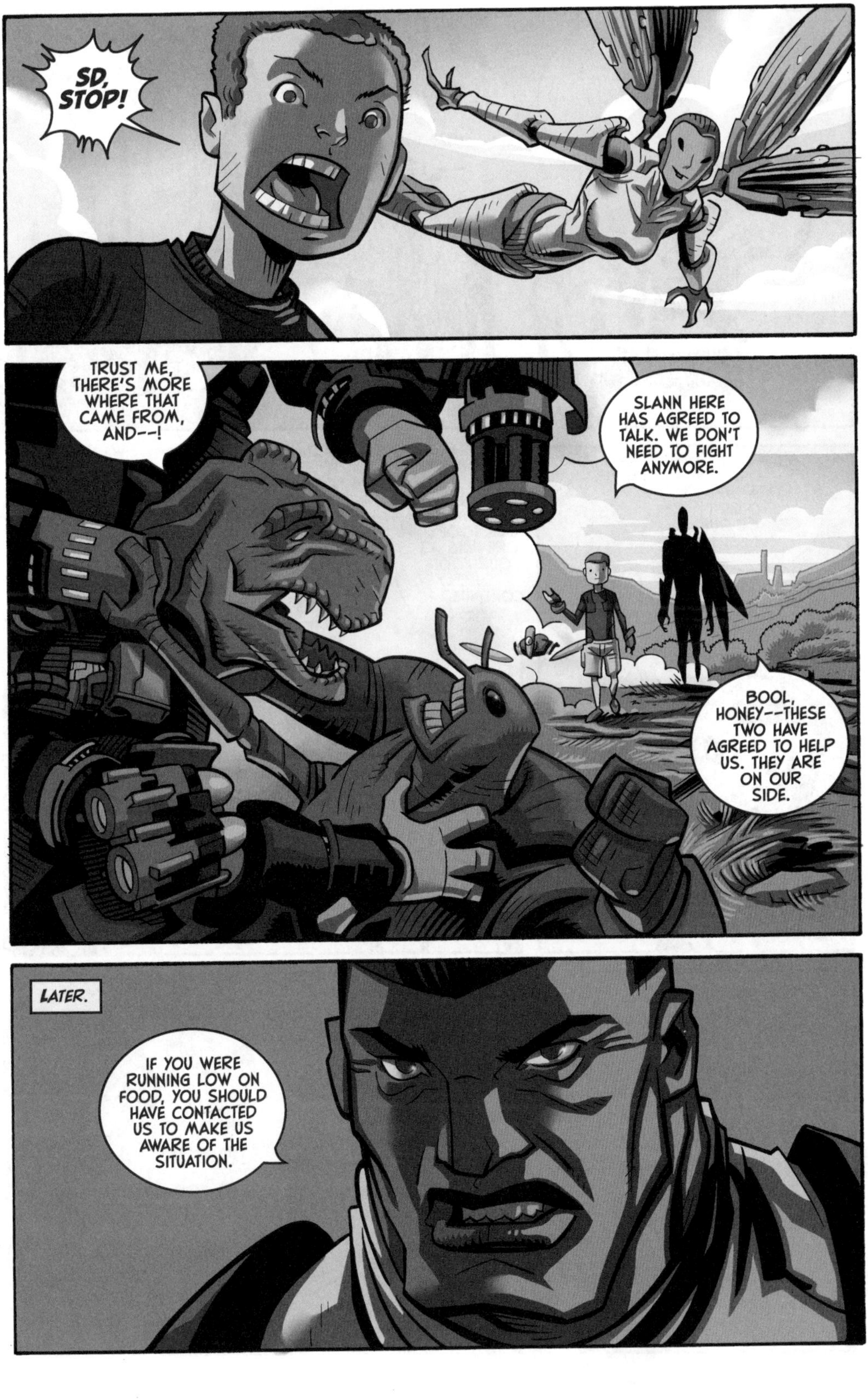
SD, STOP!
TRUST ME, THERE'S MORE WHERE THAT CAME FROM, AND--!
SLANN HERE HAS AGREED TO TALK. WE DON'T NEED TO FIGHT ANYMORE.
BOOL, HONEY--THESE TWO HAVE AGREED TO HELP US. THEY ARE ON OUR SIDE.
LATER.
IF YOU WERE RUNNING LOW ON FOOD, YOU SHOULD HAVE CONTACTED US TO MAKE US AWARE OF THE SITUATION.

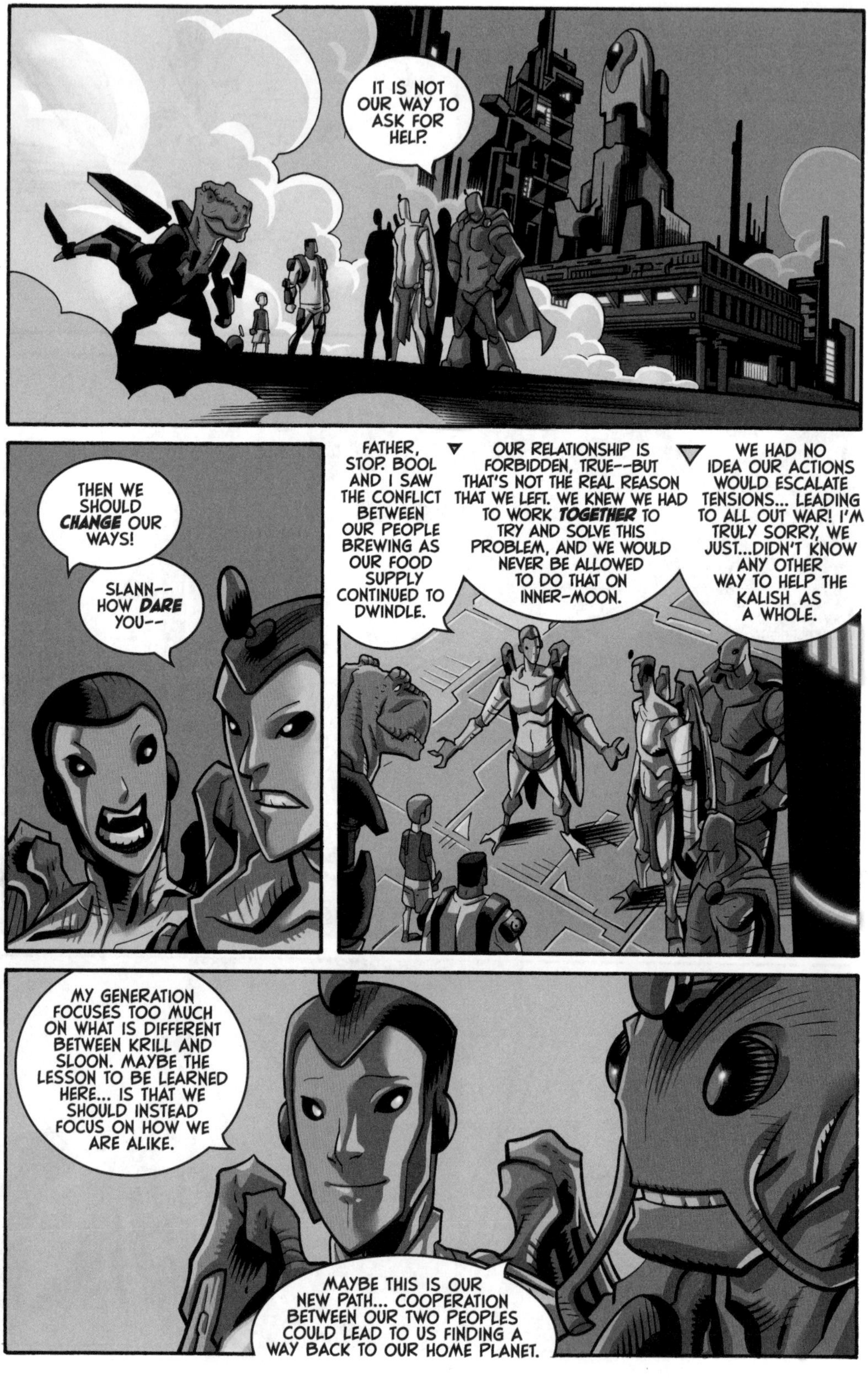
IT IS NOT OUR WAY TO ASK FOR HELP.
THEN WE SHOULD CHANGE OUR WAYS!
SLANN-- HOW DARE YOU--
FATHER, STOP. BOOL AND I SAW THE CONFLICT BETWEEN OUR PEOPLE BREWING AS OUR FOOD SUPPLY CONTINUED TO DWINDLE.
OUR RELATIONSHIP IS FORBIDDEN, TRUE--BUT THAT'S NOT THE REAL REASON THAT WE LEFT. WE KNEW WE HAD TO WORK TOGETHER TO TRY AND SOLVE THIS PROBLEM, AND WE WOULD NEVER BE ALLOWED TO DO THAT ON INNER-MOON.
WE HAD NO IDEA OUR ACTIONS WOULD ESCALATE TENSIONS... LEADING TO ALL OUT WAR! I'M TRULY SORRY, WE JUST...DIDN'T KNOW ANY OTHER WAY TO HELP THE KALISH AS A WHOLE.
MY GENERATION FOCUSES TOO MUCH ON WHAT IS DIFFERENT BETWEEN KRILL AND SLOON. MAYBE THE LESSON TO BE LEARNED HERE... IS THAT WE SHOULD INSTEAD FOCUS ON HOW WE ARE ALIKE.
MAYBE THIS IS OUR NEW PATH... COOPERATION BETWEEN OUR TWO PEOPLES COULD LEAD TO US FINDING A WAY BACK TO OUR HOME PLANET.

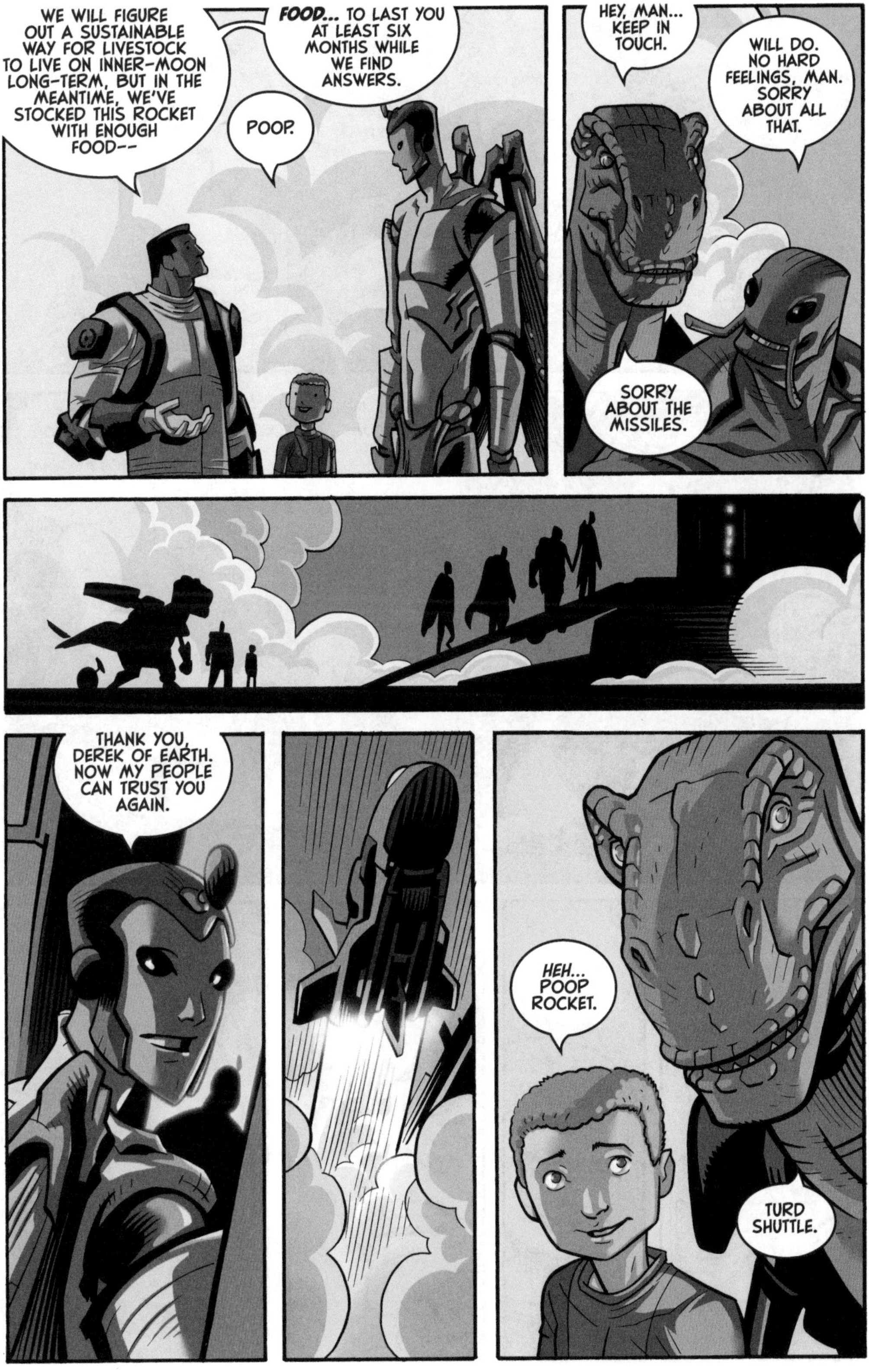
WE WILL FIGURE OUT A SUSTAINABLE WAY FOR LIVESTOCK TO LIVE ON INNER-MOON LONG-TERM, BUT IN THE MEANTIME, WE'VE STOCKED THIS ROCKET WITH ENOUGH FOOD--
POOP.
FOOD... TO LAST YOU AT LEAST SIX MONTHS WHILE WE FIND ANSWERS.
HEY, MAN... KEEP IN TOUCH.
WILL DO. NO HARD FEELINGS, MAN. SORRY ABOUT ALL THAT.
SORRY ABOUT THE MISSILES.
THANK YOU, DEREK OF EARTH. NOW MY PEOPLE CAN TRUST YOU AGAIN.
HEH... POOP ROCKET.
TURD SHUTTLE.

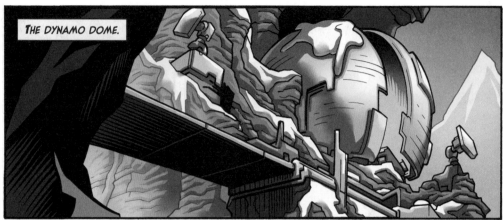

THE DYNAMO DOME.

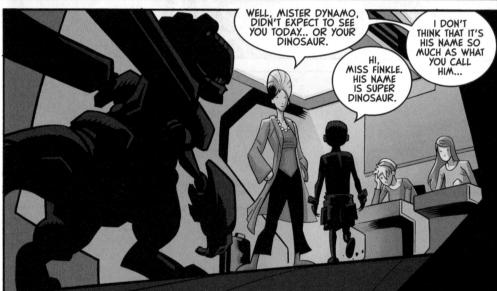

WELL, MISTER DYNAMO, DIDN'T EXPECT TO SEE YOU TODAY... OR YOUR DINOSAUR.

I DON'T THINK THAT IT'S HIS NAME SO MUCH AS WHAT YOU CALL HIM...

HI, MISS FINKLE. HIS NAME IS SUPER DINOSAUR.

MISSION OVER?

YEAH, IT WAS KIND OF AWESOME. WE--

GIRLS, PLEASE. FINISH YOUR TESTS.

MISTER DYNAMO, PLEASE SEE YOURSELF OUT.

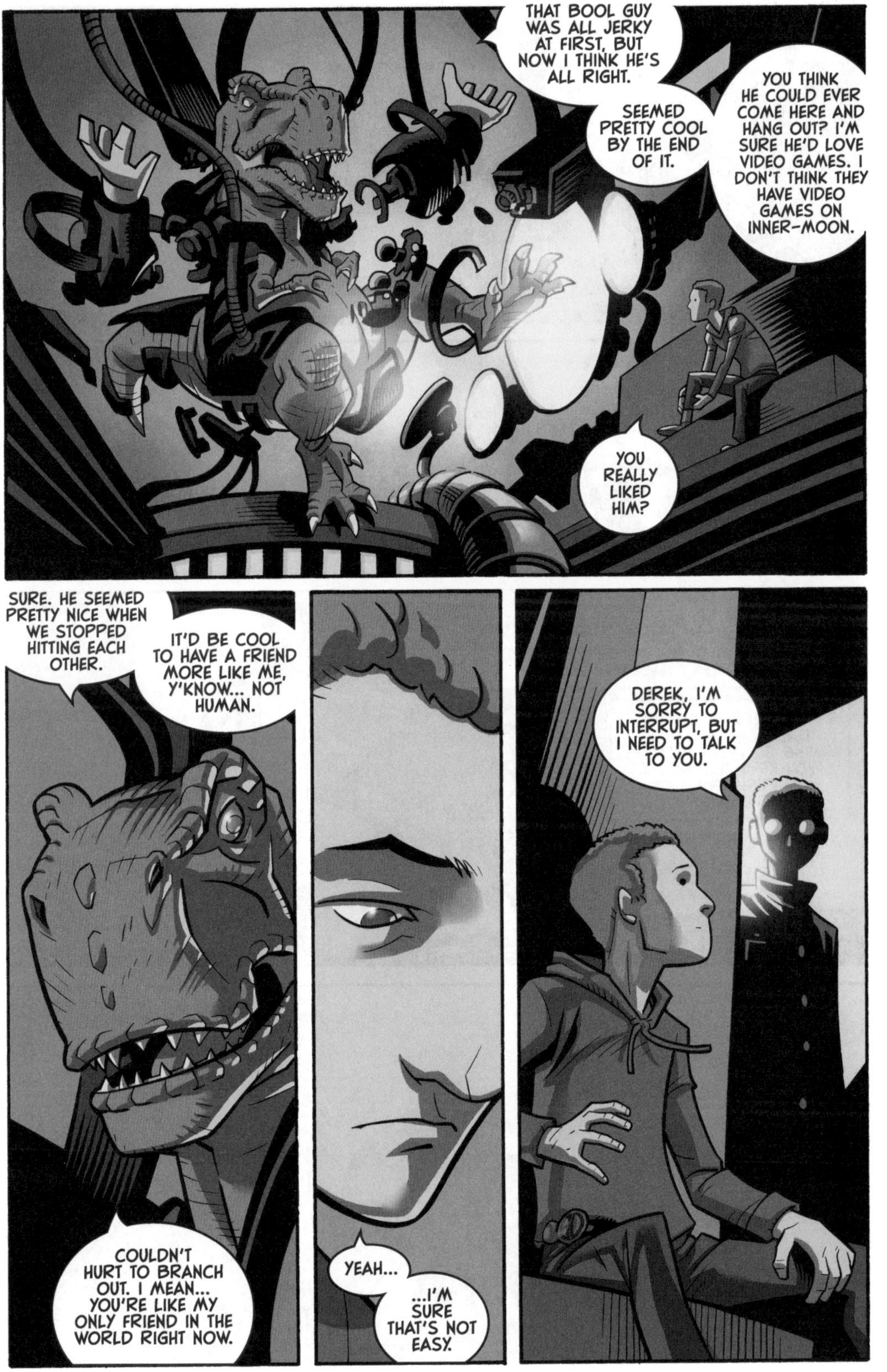
THAT BOOL GUY WAS ALL JERKY AT FIRST, BUT NOW I THINK HE'S ALL RIGHT.
SEEMED PRETTY COOL BY THE END OF IT.
YOU THINK HE COULD EVER COME HERE AND HANG OUT? I'M SURE HE'D LOVE VIDEO GAMES. I DON'T THINK THEY HAVE VIDEO GAMES ON INNER-MOON.
YOU REALLY LIKED HIM?
SURE. HE SEEMED PRETTY NICE WHEN WE STOPPED HITTING EACH OTHER.
IT'D BE COOL TO HAVE A FRIEND MORE LIKE ME, Y'KNOW... NOT HUMAN.
COULDN'T HURT TO BRANCH OUT. I MEAN... YOU'RE LIKE MY ONLY FRIEND IN THE WORLD RIGHT NOW.
YEAH...
...I'M SURE THAT'S NOT EASY.
DEREK, I'M SORRY TO INTERRUPT, BUT I NEED TO TALK TO YOU.

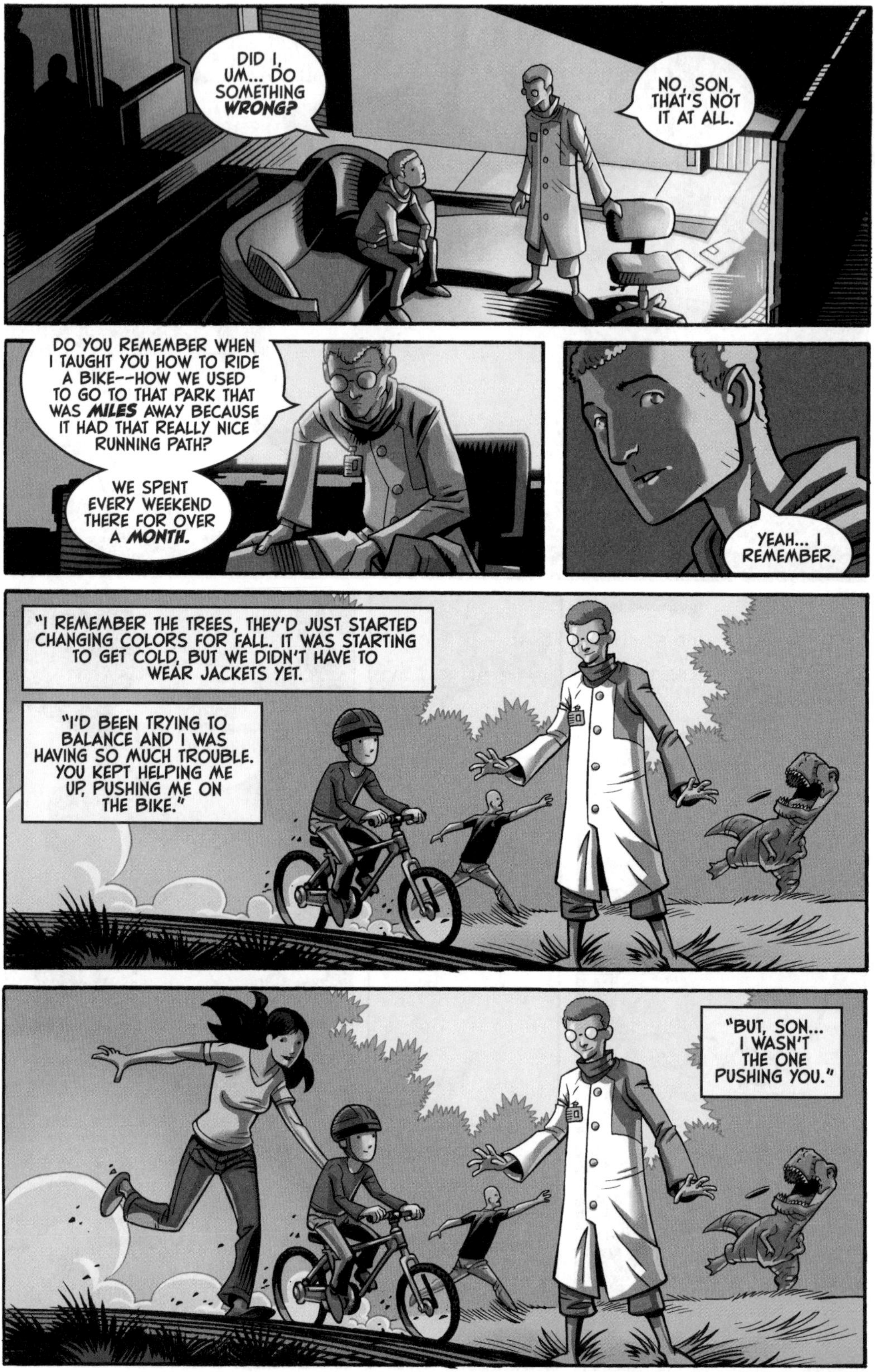
DID I, UM... DO SOMETHING WRONG?
NO, SON, THAT'S NOT IT AT ALL.
DO YOU REMEMBER WHEN I TAUGHT YOU HOW TO RIDE A BIKE--HOW WE USED TO GO TO THAT PARK THAT WAS MILES AWAY BECAUSE IT HAD THAT REALLY NICE RUNNING PATH?
WE SPENT EVERY WEEKEND THERE FOR OVER A MONTH.
YEAH... I REMEMBER.
"I REMEMBER THE TREES, THEY'D JUST STARTED CHANGING COLORS FOR FALL. IT WAS STARTING TO GET COLD, BUT WE DIDN'T HAVE TO WEAR JACKETS YET.
"I'D BEEN TRYING TO BALANCE AND I WAS HAVING SO MUCH TROUBLE. YOU KEPT HELPING ME UP, PUSHING ME ON THE BIKE."
"BUT, SON... I WASN'T THE ONE PUSHING YOU."

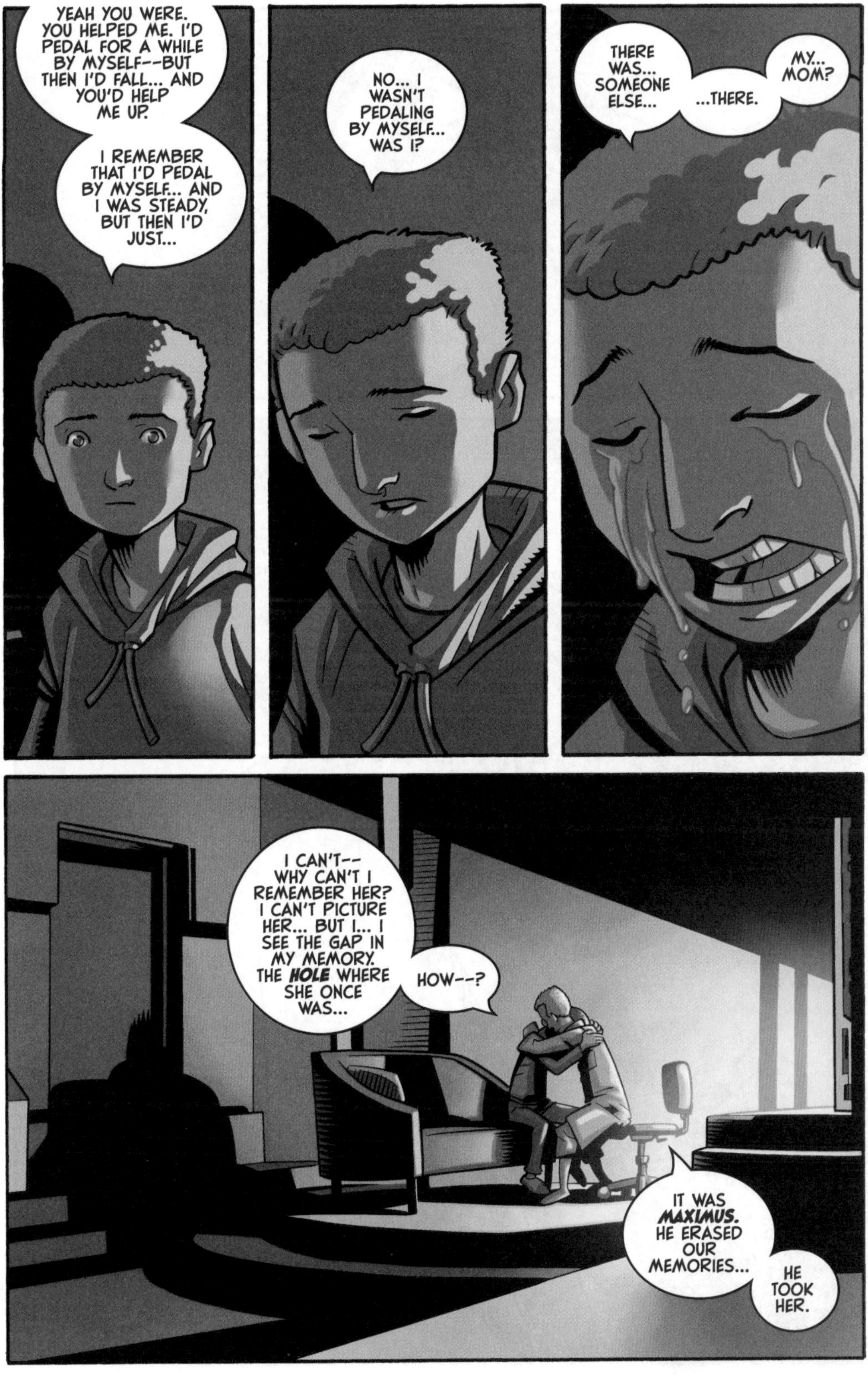
YEAH YOU WERE. YOU HELPED ME. I'D PEDAL FOR A WHILE BY MYSELF--BUT THEN I'D FALL... AND YOU'D HELP ME UP.
I REMEMBER THAT I'D PEDAL BY MYSELF... AND I WAS STEADY, BUT THEN I'D JUST...
NO... I WASN'T PEDALING BY MYSELF... WAS I?
THERE WAS... SOMEONE ELSE...
...THERE.
MY... MOM?
I CAN'T-- WHY CAN'T I REMEMBER HER? I CAN'T PICTURE HER... BUT I... I SEE THE GAP IN MY MEMORY. THE HOLE WHERE SHE ONCE WAS...
HOW--?
IT WAS MAXIMUS. HE ERASED OUR MEMORIES...
HE TOOK HER.

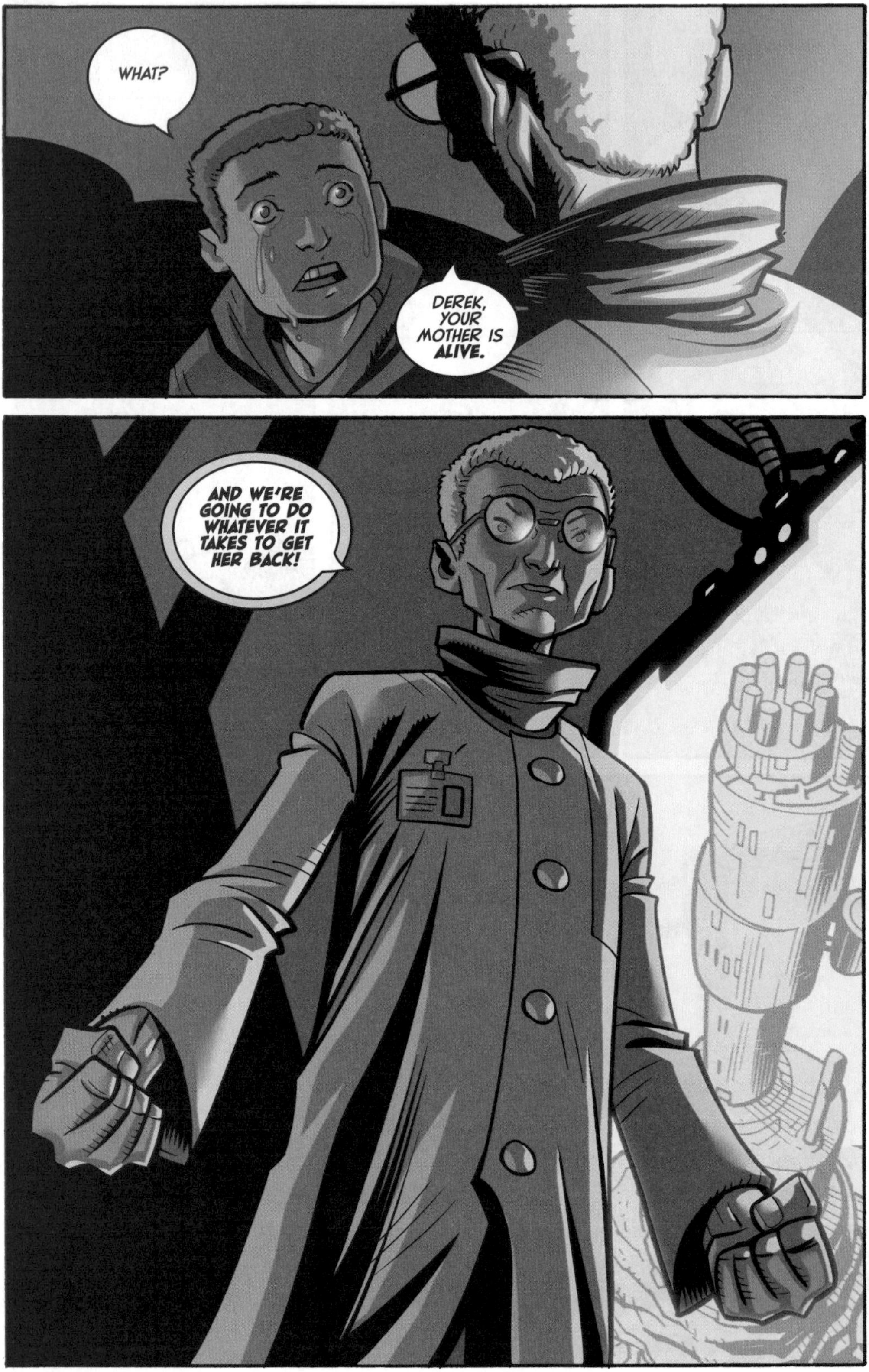
WHAT?
DEREK, YOUR MOTHER IS ALIVE.
AND WE'RE GOING TO DO WHATEVER IT TAKES TO GET HER BACK!

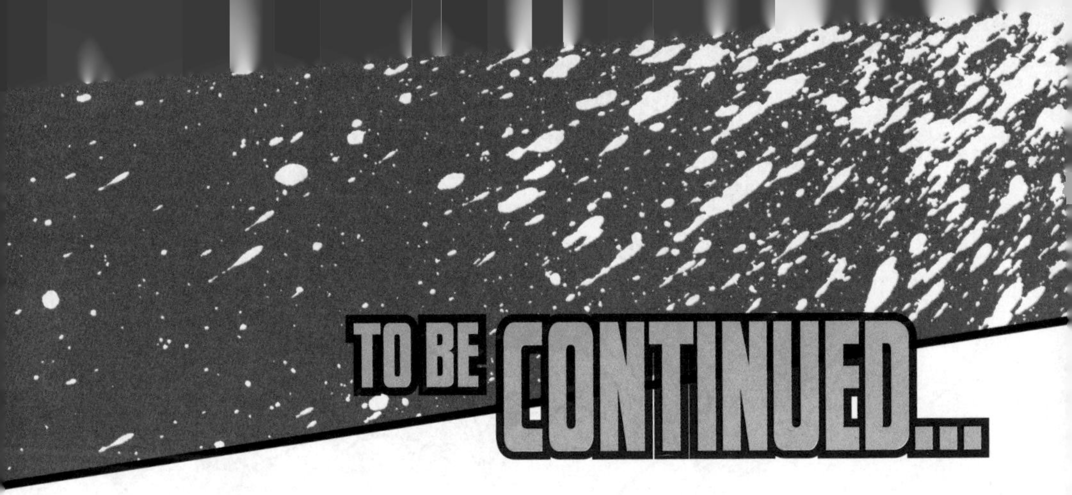
TO BE CONTINUED...

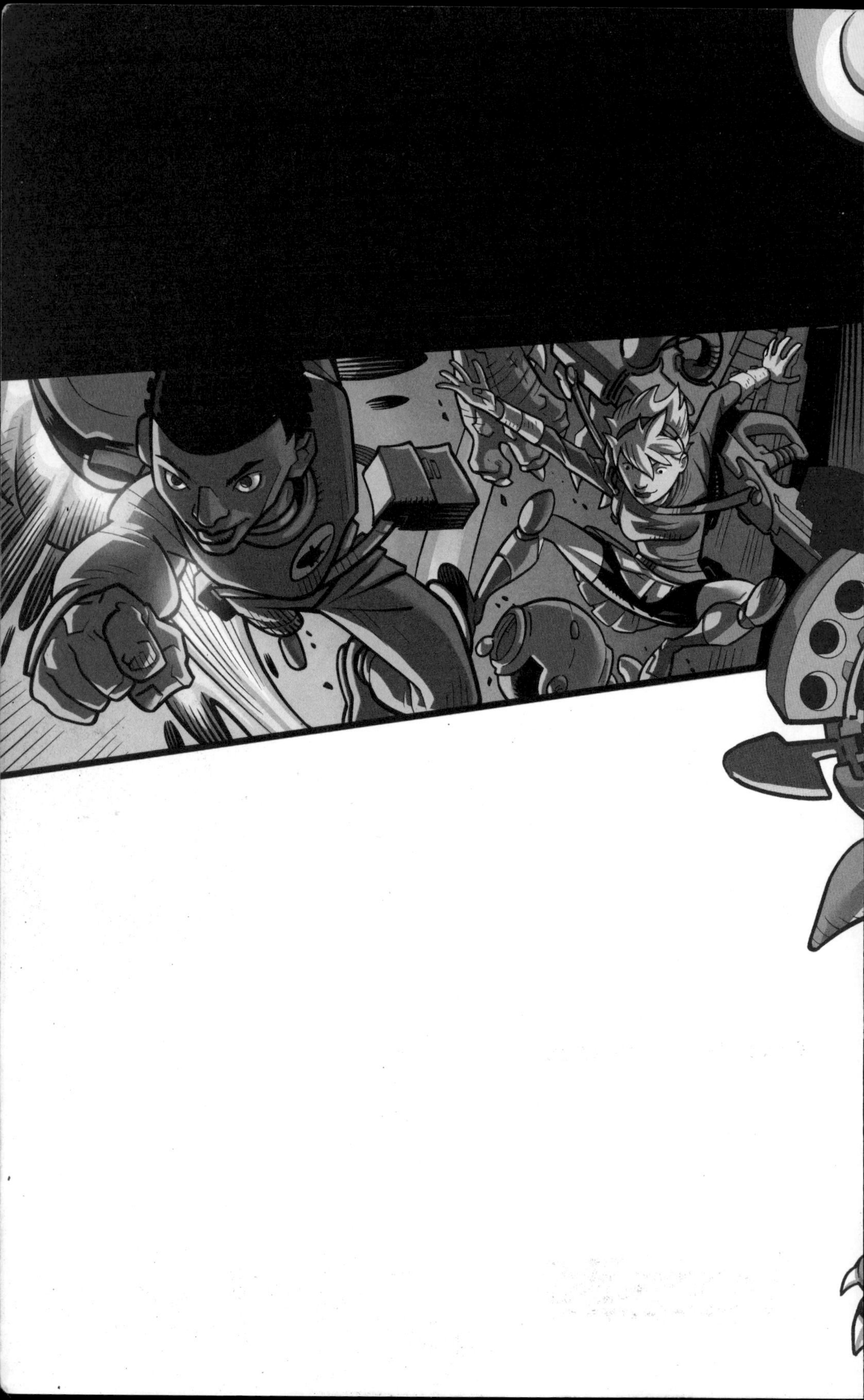